The Urbana Free Library

To renew: call **217-367-4057**
or go to **urbanafreelibrary.org**
and select **My Account**

FIRST WE WERE IV

Also by
A L E X A N D R A   S I R O W Y

The Creeping

The Telling

alexandra sirowy

FIRST
WE WERE
IV

SIMON & SCHUSTER BFYR

NEW YORK   LONDON   TORONTO   SYDNEY   NEW DELHI

SIMON & SCHUSTER BFYR

An imprint of Simon & Schuster Children's Publishing Division
1230 Avenue of the Americas, New York, New York 10020

For information about special discounts for bulk purchases, please contact Simon & Schuster Special Sales at 1-866-506-1949 or business@simonandschuster.com.
The Simon & Schuster Speakers Bureau can bring authors to your live event. For more information or to book an event, contact the Simon & Schuster Speakers Bureau at 1-866-248-3049 or visit our website at www.simonspeakers.com.
Jacket design by Lizzy Bromley
Interior design by Hilary Zarycky
The text for this book was set in Berling.
Manufactured in the United States of America
First Edition
2 4 6 8 10 9 7 5 3 1

Library of Congress Cataloging-in-Publication Data
Names: Sirowy, Alexandra, author.
Title: First we were IV / Alexandra Sirowy.
Other titles: First we were four
Description: First edition. | New York : Simon & Schuster Books for Young Readers, [2017] | Summary: Hoping to ensure their friendship will outlast high school, Izzie and her friends form a secret society devoted to mischief that rights wrongs and pays back debts, but it spirals out of control when the whole town wants to participate.
Identifiers: LCCN 2016044586| ISBN 9781481478427 (hardback) | ISBN 9781481478441 (ebook)
Subjects: | CYAC: Best friends—Fiction. | Friendship—Fiction. | Secret societies—Fiction. | High schools—Fiction. | Schools—Fiction. | Conduct of life—Fiction. | Mystery and detective stories. | BISAC: JUVENILE FICTION / Social Issues / Friendship. | JUVENILE FICTION / Legends, Myths, Fables / General. | JUVENILE FICTION / Mysteries & Detective Stories.
Classification: LCC PZ7.1.S57 Fir 2017 | DDC [Fic]—dc23
LC record available at https://lccn.loc.gov/2016044586

To Joe,
thanks for the universe.

FIRST WE WERE IV

1

By the time the police arrived, there were three of us left. Three originals. Three best friends. Architects of what was once a secret society.

The difference between leaders and initiates was evident. We designed it that way, dictated that initiates wore the white of sacrificial lambs and us bloody red. No confusion over who appeared to be in charge.

There was a chaotic minute under the star-choked sky. Volleying accusations and bodily threats. I tried to kick out of the arms of an officer because I still hadn't had my fill of revenge. Never would I. And you know, the dagger tipped in blood didn't exactly help our case for looking faultless.

They herded the initiates into a line, ordered them to keep their mouths shut. Still, those kids, those snakes, whispered stories and secrets in the way the dying confess, anticipating forgiveness. Good little boys and girls, eyes innocent saucers, except they'd terrorized a whole town.

Our dagger lay a little outside the ring of fire. There was

the truth serum, a few muddy, crimson sips they'd dredge up from the bottle to test. And the idol on a pile of rocks, her smile calling out from on top of her burial mound. No sense would be made of her origins.

Police circled the meteorite, probing the scene, coming up short in front of us three, searching faces for clues. Accident or murder.

They would ask the wrong questions later on, after the ambulance left without its sirens wailing, when the three architects and our six recruits were in the police station.

There was lots of hand-wringing and *Make me understand*. Parents arrived. Our initiates had been shaking their fists and snarling at authority just an hour before. The rebellion had drained out of them and they buckled with relief at the sight of their moms and dads. I didn't acknowledge mine. All the adults needed help understanding how the night happened.

"October happened because September did."

An officer warned me to stop being snarky.

"I'm not," I whispered, voice all cried out.

"Then answer," he demanded.

"Because August. Because July. Because June. I can keep going if you need me to."

That was the only answer they'd get from me. Afterward, I stopped talking. For a few weeks. I sat in my room, on the top of my desk, watching the Pacific battle the shore. I sketched the four of us. Together. Hardly needing to watch the progress of my pencil. There was something unnerving in our eyes when the pictures were done. A glimmer of foreshadow that I hadn't noticed was present before. Had it been? My best friends. The loves of my life. Strangers. Reeling. Ferocious.

I held my tongue and the lesson sunk in.

No matter how much you see, there are bottomless seas you don't.

What I am certain of is the heart of it.

First we were four.

Now we are three.

2

There is an ancient rock at the edge of Viv's apple orchard, where the foothills bubble up, brittle gold grasses encroaching on the sky. The rock's gray metallic face is smooth, except for pits and crevices on its north side. At the height and width of a house, it's unmovable. Its top is as flat as a stage.

Graham, Viv, and I were eight, sucking on watermelon Blow Pops, our scabbed knees under our chins, Graham's ankle in a cast, as we watched the scientists cut up from the road alongside the orchard in jeeps.

They were real-life versions of the scientists in khaki vests, baggy cargo pants, and hiking boots from the glossy pages of our *National Geographic* magazines. We crept around their tents and stole the wooden stakes used to cordon off the rock so Viv could play at stabbing Graham and me, the vampires, in our hearts. After a few days, a strawberry-blonde scientist with a face full of freckles caught Graham, who was surprisingly swift on crutches. She must have hoped that we'd quit vandalizing if we felt included, so she told us about the rock in the whispery tone adults use when they want to impress kids.

The rock was one of the largest meteoric fragments to hit North America. Someone dated it to have been there for at least 50,000 years, an age Freckles called recent in terms of meteorites. What baffled them was that there was no crater, no giant gash torn into the land from it shooting from space. The meteor appeared to have been placed there, gently set in the rambling foothills.

The rock itself wasn't even the significant part, not then.

The drawings were.

The three of us had discovered the drawings—actually, Graham broke his ankle and *then* we discovered them. Graham, Viv, and I had been stretched out on the rock. That was back when we'd pretend it was a desert island and water ran to the horizons. We liked to act as though we were stuck on top with no choice but to stay until the sky dimmed. It was one of those afternoons drowning in sun; I was biting an apple, making shapes in the red skin with my teeth. I showed Viv a butterfly as a tiny green worm poked through the alpine-white meat of the fruit.

"Eat it," Graham said.

"Worms can live inside your belly," Viv cried. "Don't do it."

Graham sprung to his feet. "If you eat it, I'll jump." He pointed to the undulating expanse of grass. It was twelve feet, at least.

"Will not," Viv countered, lips twitching with uncertainty.

"Will too. Just like when you thought I wouldn't climb to the barn roof, or that Izzie couldn't hold her breath for a minute underwater, or"—he began hopping in place—"that Izzie and I wouldn't race through the Ghost Tunnel and we did, we did, *we did*."

"On the count of three," I said.

"One, two . . ." Graham paused, glancing over his shoulder where he was poised at the edge of the rock. I held the apple, worm-side to my mouth. Graham and I met eyes before he gave an exhilarated whoop and yelled, "Three!" He shot into the air, his eyes on mine until he disappeared. Graham didn't believe in looking when he jumped.

The worm popped between my teeth as Graham shouted out in pain.

Viv and I found him clutching his knee to his chest, his lips grimacing, his eyes intent on a vague brownish-red design I would have mistaken for dirt smeared on the rock. Even back then, Graham noticed ancient and in-the-ground things.

The freckled scientist called it one of the oldest and most complete surviving figurative drawings done by ancient humans. The scene was of the space rock, surrounded by men and women kneeling. Above them, on the rock, there were four-legged animals of an unidentifiable species. Whatever they were, the animals either didn't exist anymore or couldn't be classified using the pictures. Some experts thought they could make out paws, others hooves; still more saw horns rather than ears. The geochemists and archeologists went digging.

They found eight birds of different species, their tiny

skeletons fully accounted for. Each was buried on its back, wings splayed open to the sky. Long stripes of linen fabric were wrapped from one wing tip to the other, mummifying the remains.

We were there, this time on lawn chairs we'd dragged up to the string and stakes demarcating the excavation. Sweat streaked Freckles's forehead as she blinked dirt away, her arm shaking as she uncovered the first bird in its burial shroud. The birds were buried at quarter segments around the rock, two in each grave. Eventually someone observed that their wings were oriented pointing north, south, east, and west. Each tiny bone of the skeletons was marked. Scratched in a series of designs. Tests were done in laboratories and bone-dating specialists decided that the birds hadn't been buried at the same time but at different points over hundreds of years.

Freckles and her team had plans for more excavating until Viv's parents were fed up and ordered everyone to clear out. Ina and Scott Marlo didn't want scientists mucking about their orchard during harvest. They wanted to make their own hard apple cider. The rock would just have to remain a mysterious space rock. Those four-legged animals would have to stay unidentified. The birds would be studied elsewhere, packed up and carried away.

For weeks it was all we talked about. At first it was the birds that captured my imagination. Birds had a little magic in them—they had wings and flew. Nightly at dinner I'd ask my parents about them. *Why were they buried? How did they die? Who buried them?* Nothing they said could appease my curiosity. I re-created the birds, wings spread, in my yogurt parfaits, on the beach, in pictures I snapped of Graham and Viv staged on the ground. Finally, when Dad found me doodling birds on his and mom's architectural plans, they intervened. Mom ordered me a ready-made rock collection to try to encourage an interest in geology, but it was the telescope Dad set up on the veranda that hooked me enough to move on from the birds.

Viv's parents furnished their backyard barn, wrapped a red ribbon around it, and gave it to Viv as a play fort, hoping to distract her from the meteorite. To draw our play in closer to home. But the mystery of the space rock kept us buzzing. How were there horned four-legged beasts that scientists didn't know about? Who were the people pictured on the rock? Were they predators or prey?

Graham and I filled his wagon with library books— fantasy and science fiction paperbacks from the library's rummage sale, archeology texts from its shelves, a few we stored under our beds about human sacrifice and ancient burial customs. We looked for answers in their pages. We pored over bad illustrations of Papua New Guinean cannibals. I made my mom print out every news article she could find about the comet probe Philae that had been launched a few years earlier and wouldn't land on its comet for six more.

We searched for answers. But the threads we followed led us farther from the space rock. The ploy of the barn worked. It was better than a fort. We grew preoccupied with other play. Our universe returned to revolving around what it had before the drawings were discovered: *us*.

From the time I was four years old, my universe had been steadily expanding.

I started as one.

First day of preschool: I remember the odor of crayons, the grainy cracker crumbs in my pockets digging under my nails, and how much I wanted to talk to the other kids, all sparkly in their first-day bests, but I kept chewing my tongue because I had nothing good to say.

Snack time rolled around and the teacher handed out sweets. I was cross-legged and bouncing over cookies. We sat in a misshapen circle, and I watched the boy across from me take a cookie out of a bigger boy's lap, smile at me with his mouth full of stolen chocolate chip cookies, chew, swallow, and then deny it emphatically when the victim tattled. Graham was halfway to the time-out corner when I piped up.

I had no idea that Graham was acting out because his dad had moved to Chicago. Graham was the most interesting kid in the circle and he was being sent away. I'm not proud of lying, although I'm also not sorry. Graham and I were awarded an extra cookie each; one for the *wrongly* accused and one for the *honest* witness. Our bond was instantaneous. I'd broken the rules for him; I'd saved him from the solitary horror of time-out.

I was one and then: Graham. We were two.

Viv came next. She lived down the street. I considered

the orchard behind her house an enchanted forest and she was the enigmatic creature who ruled it. I'd spot her rocking on the porch swing with her mom. Dad would stop the wagon or call for me to slow on my bike. He and Ina knew each other from growing up in Seven Hills. Mom didn't seem to know Ina, although eventually I realized there was another reason Mom ignored the Marlos. I couldn't ignore Viv. She was a sliver of a figure, imposing because of how decorated she was: swallowed by voiles, feathers fanning her hair, her mom's heels swimming on her feet, lipstick hearts on her cheeks. The brave survivor of a dress-up chest explosion.

First day of first grade, Viv wore a silk dress with a train that dragged behind her and carried a grown lady's handbag. Kids circled Viv, sang *little old woman* at her. The next day they made fun of the way she stuttered words beginning with S—a problem she went to speech therapy for. As that got stale, kids said she wasn't in speech but in resource, which was code for her having a learning disability. The whole thing spiraled when they called her retarded.

Graham and I found her crying at the sunlit reach of the tetherball courts. She was curled on her side, velvet cape sticking to her sweaty neck, cheek on the warm asphalt, mouth open as she sobbed.

Graham and I were in the middle of one long game of chicken. It was fun to see how deep we'd walk into the hills before turning and fleeing. How long we could stand the dark of Graham's creaky, musty attic before the ghosts scratched our arms. Other kids were boring. Our minds sparked. Our hands danced. But Viv wasn't boring. Like us, she was engaged in her own battle of will.

She kept wearing costumes and vintage women's apparel even though she was picked on. She didn't stop laughing in her raspy way even when kids imitated her meanly. The feathers and tassels were her armor.

Graham and I had been two. With Viv: three. We had a whole apple orchard as our kingdom. We didn't need to fit in with the others. Three was plenty.

The business with the rock when were eight was a hiccup; an anomaly that the external world became a part of our adventures. It was a temporary stretch of our universe. But the universe snapped back, shrank to accommodate only us.

Until Harry's family moved to Seven Hills when we were twelve.

Until the girl was found on the rock.

3

Graham was on his way with a watermelon to meet Viv and me at the meteorite. We had planned to hurl the melon from its top, for no reason other than wanting to throw what was sure to break. The summer months were spent fleeing boredom. Belly flopping from Viv's diving board until our fronts were slapped red. Daring one another to eat the least ripe and sourest apples off the trees. Camping on the rock with my telescope. Acting out plays that Viv wrote while on the meteorite. Sled races down the steepest sand dunes.

Viv and I were running late. We'd been lounging on the back lawn, weaving daisy chain crowns and admiring our new, brightly colored flats that her grandmother had sent us from where she lived in India. We lost track of time. "Seventh graders have the same lunch period as eighth and we'll get to eat right next to Luke McHale. We could sit in his circle. If he asks us. If he sees I have cupcakes to share," she said, breezy and hopeful. Viv was looking forward to the start of school in a few weeks.

I didn't have sunglasses on and I was weaving around the trees, squinting at the orchard set on fire by the silver tinsel that scared off birds. Halfway to the rock we heard the eerie, frantic squawks. We should have known by the way the smell punched us in the face that it would be bad. But there were often putrid scents in those hills covered with cow patties and snakeskins. I was preoccupied with Viv swearing Luke was the cutest boy in the eighth grade.

The apple tree nearest the rock was full of crows, their sleek coal bodies hunched in between the glittering holographic tape. They reminded me of this photo of baboons on the plateau of a hill in Ethiopia. Their broad, hairy backs were a wall blocking out whatever they surrounded. I just knew they probably did something awful—*violent*—once the photographer lowered his lens. It was what the photo didn't show that made me swallow twice. I had wondered if animals could be wicked or bored.

"Wait for Graham," Viv said, catching my wrist, trying to keep me next to her. She was wearing one of her long bohemian skirts and the gold, pink, and blue of her slippers poked out from its drape.

"Can't. I'm too curious," I told her, twirling her under my arm, slipping my hand from hers while her skirt caught air. I scaled my way up the rock's face. At the top, the stench was crawling up my nostrils, making my eyes swell with water. A stiff, hot wind in my face intensified it.

I blinked three times before I believed the body was there.

"What is it?" Viv called. I glanced down at her. The flower crown looked like snowflakes in her chestnut waves.

"Stay there and call Graham," I said. She cocked a hand on her popped hip. Waved her brand-new cell phone at me. All mock attitude. "Please, Vivy."

I didn't tell Viv to call 9-1-1. I was twelve. My brain didn't have a setting for an emergency too big for Graham. Not then. Not at first.

Viv called him. "You're late. Why walking? Couldn't you strap the melon to your scooter?" Pause. "Weirdness on the rock."

From the angle and the distance, I made out the body, tatter of clothing, naked skin. A big, shaggy vulture hunched over it. I inched closer. Long brown hair. Arms open.

My breath grew shallow.

A bruise as livid as her purple bra ran from her chest to the waistband of her buttoned jean shorts. A second bruise like a choker around her neck. A girl. On her back. And those arms, they were thrown open as if she were midflight. The girl's T-shirt had been slashed down her sternum, its halves peeled back to expose her bruised rib cage and tucked under her arms as if she had wings. There were rocks, too, at the bottom of the wings like feathers. They pinned the fabric in place.

Wings. Like those of the vulture worrying her belly-button into a larger hole with its beak. A cloud tapered across the sky with the look of a white fissure in the blue. The sky was cracking. It would fall soon.

The vulture looked reluctantly away from its meal, a patch of soft tissue hanging out of its hooked beak. There were holes in her thighs, too, just under the hem of her cut-offs. Channels cut into the muscles; the white gleam of bone.

She was dead. Not bleeding. Not moving. No blood that I could see on the rock.

"Oh my God," Viv whispered. I hadn't heard her crawl up. She stood with the back of a hand to her mouth, the other clutched her stomach. She lurched to the side and dry heaved.

I returned to the girl. Not a woman. Not old enough. But older than me. She wore a real bra, not a tiny one with padding like I did. Her breasts were like hills as she lay on her back. Death made her look caught, trapped. I wanted to swat the flies from her brown hair. Knock the rocks and her wings away. Help her up so she could run.

My stomach churned, tears stung, arms lost feeling at my sides. She was not so different from me and Viv. Except she had wings.

The vulture had swallowed by then and it cawed shrilly. Its head bowed for another bite. I rushed forward, shouting. It hobbled to the edge of the rock, faking indifference, but kept one gleaming eye my way.

I was directly over her. Gravel decorated one side of her face. Her knees were dirty and cut. The single white sneaker she wore was stained, the rubber sole partially detached and wilting from her foot.

"What happened to her?" Viv whispered.

"A nightmare," I said.

"Why is her shirt open like that?"

"Like wings," I said and then shook my head.

We called 9-1-1 before Graham hiked up, the watermelon braced on his shoulder. Then we called my house, where my dad answered, and he called Mom because she wasn't home. Viv's dad was away on business and we left her mom for last because she was in recovery after surgery to remove a tumor from her chest a few weeks earlier. Viv and I sat in the dirt, waiting for the grown-ups. Graham stood by the girl on the rock, keeping the vulture at bay.

The rest of that afternoon was superimposed horror on our familiar kingdom. Where we played and pretended and dreamed and dared. Viv had to wait inside with her mom for the police because Ina had buckled against an apple tree, too weak from surgery. Dad steadied Ina and walked them back through the orchard. I sat with Graham and the watermelon as the EMTs and firemen checked the girl. I knew she couldn't be saved. My legs stopped being legs. Graham kept muttering stuff like, *How could our rock be involved in this?* We'd just been there two Saturdays before. Sleeping bags. Flashlights. Liter of root beer over ice cream in Ina's giant lobster pot. The rock was just an extension of the orchard and the orchard an extension of our barn. Ours.

Police cruisers parked along the weed-dotted access road connecting the street with the orchard. A few neighbors hiked up to watch. A boy our age came the nearest and froze, a scarecrow in between trees. I watched him pull a notebook from his back pocket and take notes. Graham walked in his direction. My mom had arrived by then; Dad had returned from helping Ina.

My parents told me to pay attention to the plainclothes officer talking to me. He asked if I recognized the girl, and suddenly I wasn't sure. "Maybe," I said.

I closed my eyes and saw my face instead of hers. The officer asked if I could take another look. It was important. I wanted to give her a name. Help her. My parents and the officer crawled back up the rock with me.

She was a stranger. The wind became a dusty, battering force, snatching sheets of paper from a clipboard, skimming them across the dirt until they netted in the weeds. Graham was alone with the melon. The new boy and his notebook were gone.

As my parents guided me away, I turned to glimpse the girl's face between the officer's legs.

"She's like me," I said to my mom. A girl.

It was the officer who replied. "Nah, hon, nothing like you, just a runaway asking for it." He licked his thumb and brushed away a fleck of dirt on his otherwise shiny boots. "These girls leave their nothing towns and head west or south to Los Angeles and they end up hitchhiking on the interstate. Get into the wrong truck. Get hooked up with the wrong people. Drugs—" Mom's hands pressed over my ears. Too late.

When we were home Mom made chai and put my iPod on in my bedroom. Dad brought out an old nightlight that projected stars on the ceiling; its white constellations hardly registered in the summer evening light. A tear leaked from his eye when he kissed me on the forehead. After they left me, I sat in my desk chair at my window staring out at the gray ocean. *Nah, hon, she's nothing like you, just a runaway.* I couldn't get the officer's voice out of my head. She was a girl. Untied sneaker. Temporary tattoo of a heart on her ankle that had faded with washing. Ordinary. I was ordinary. How had she asked to be hurt?

She looked like one of the girls who were sometimes on the beach. Viv and I had seen them once or twice. Viv had radar for girls just above high school age. Free girls. Those who didn't live here. Dramatic lives full of shrieking and chasing one another around their circle and falling into the laps of boys with them. Viv tore a slit up her Free People dress after we watched them. Stretched the neckline so it hung off her shoulders. For a while she talked about hanging out with them, in the same dreamy tone she used when speaking about Luke McHale. She heard from a classmate, who heard from their older sister, who bought pot from a girl on the beach once, that there were teenagers who came to Seven Hills for its fabled beach and waves. Word had spread that you could camp at night in the Ghost Tunnel, officially the Golden Hills Tunnel, that there were plenty of orchards to steal fruit from, and that the police wouldn't bother you unless you drew too much attention.

I wondered then, in my room, after finding the girl's body, was she one of those surfing-by-day-and-camping-by-night-in-the-tunnel girls?

Neighbors gathered on the Marlos' front lawn the next day. Viv tried to eavesdrop from the porch swing. They shooed her away before she learned anything useful. But she could tell the adults had hunches.

That same day, a woman I recognized only from seeing her on parade floats visited us. Dad introduced her as Mayor Carver. Mom said they needed to have a grown-up talk with me. The woman started out nice. *So sorry you had such a scare.* Her tone grew accusatory as she warned me not to share details of the *incident* with anyone but my parents. *You don't want to scare people more than they already are, do you? I didn't think so. Then you shouldn't mention how she looked. No need to tell anyone about the T-shirt and the rocks and all that nonsense.* I didn't answer.

On the third day after, Viv, Graham, and I were in the barn. I was sprawled on the floor, back of my skull on the flat of a raised nailhead protruding from a plank. It hurt, but I was the kind of bored that makes you pick a scab, that used to make Graham and me dare each other to reach into a snake hole. Viv was tossing chocolate-covered raisins at the book in Graham's hands, and he was complaining that I'd given up on the true crime paperback we were three-quarters of the way through, each taking our turn with a chapter, when there was a knock on the slider. I sat up too fast. Amid the stars firing off, the strange boy with the notebook waved through the glass. There was a rush of relief, like I'd been raw and itchy waiting for him to show up already, and once he had I could be normal again.

Harry's family had moved into the ranch house up the street, the one the grown-ups called *the rental*. Harry's dad was trying to resuscitate its patchy lawn; his mom was giving the shutters a fresh coat of paint. Harry came searching through the apple orchard like we'd drawn him in as the sirens had three days before. It seemed close to magic to me. Really, Graham had hung out with Harry the day before and invited him to find us in the barn the next afternoon.

It was obvious that our threesome had been inadequate once he was with us. He plopped down on a beanbag chair and showed us his notebook, full of observations from the few days he'd lived in Seven Hills. He'd noticed things from when I found the dead girl that I hadn't. Like that an officer started taking pictures of Graham's watermelon in the dirt like it was a part of the investigation. And that a woman who had a dog wearing a sweater stood chatting with the police. Mayor Carver, Graham informed us. Harry was born to be a journalist.

Before I realized it, I admitted that I'd been dreaming about the dead girl. Graham admitted he'd been late with the watermelon because Stepdad Number Three refused to give him a ride; Graham hoped his mother would divorce him soon. Harry had a way of getting you to say what you were dying to, just by being a good listener.

Viv, gnawing on her nails, stayed quiet and eyed Harry. He tossed one of her chocolate-covered raisins into the air; her caution waned as one after another pinged off his teeth. He was terrible at catching them, but his eyes shone as he kept trying. He was nothing like the boys at school with their easily shattered egos, boys who lashed out if you laughed at them. Eventually Viv blurted, "You didn't see me at the rock when we found the girl because I had to go in the house and wait for the police with my mom. She has cancer. It means she gets tired really easily. But I was there."

Harry gave a solemn nod, seeming to understand that even in this awful thing, no one wanted to feel left out.

How didn't the three of us combust without Harry?

In the middle of all the intrigue, we became four.

Within the week, Viv's dad found tracks circling the ancient rock and leading through the orchard. They were slots made by something between a paw and a hoof. The plainclothes officer snapped pictures. He asked if we'd seen signs of the girl squatting in the barn or camping in the orchard. Did food disappear or sleeping bags vanish? Had we ever found the remains of candle wax on the rock? Bizarre symbols drawn on top? Which didn't make sense because in the next breath he told us she wasn't killed here in Seven Hills, but elsewhere, where a bad person hurt her and tried to get away with it by dumping her in our nice little town.

Regardless, I thought of her as Goldilocks.

Picture it. Charming seaside town. Seven golden foothills forming a wall around it. Past the threshold of sight and sound from any neighboring cities. More pastel beach cruisers than cars. Rooftop decks with barbecues and chairs facing the sea. A scatter of sand across sidewalks, blown in by the wind. And kids of the summer, barefoot, freckled, and sunburned.

In Seven Hills, windows and doors stayed open to catch the salt spray off the Pacific.

A body shows up. A girl. About nineteen. Blunt force trauma. Strangulation. No sign of sexual assault. At first the police hide that she was staged. And then a photo of the body is sent anonymously to the Seven Hills newspaper, and the whole town learns that she was killed and staged to have wings, on an ancient meteorite, its own history involving birds, buried in the identical position. The mysteries pile up. No one does a thing.

The police never talked to us about her again. School started. Viv and Graham had also received visits from the mayor, asking them not to scare our peers with what we saw, like Goldilocks had been a particularly grisly nightmare, better forgotten in the light of day.

From a classmate whose parent wasn't careful about being overheard, we gathered that Goldilocks remained a mystery. During the first week of classes he reported to a grave audience of middle schoolers in the cafeteria. The police believed one of two things had transpired: Either the runaway was dumped by someone who didn't live in Seven Hills or the whole killing had been committed by her band of runaway teens. They'd heard about the meteorite and traveled to worship an alien-devil on its altar. They were troubled youths—drinking, drugs, sex—and one of them ended up sacrificed on the rock. Our classmate reported his mother saying *Surprise, surprise. Girls like that always think it's a game until it isn't.*

Whichever explanation, the police said whoever committed the crime had moved on. Fled. Would never risk returning. Had never meant any harm to Seven Hills or its residents. *Nothing to fear. You're safe here.*

All those strange pieces were laid out, begging us to pick them up. We wouldn't until five years later, after the night of the slaughterhouse. When we did, rather than setting out to solve Goldilocks's killing, I'm ashamed to say our motivations were closer to this:

I wanted to play a game.

Boredom was always chasing us.

I dreaded saying good-bye.

Revenge seemed like a bright idea.

4

The slaughterhouse's silhouette was black and flat against the sky. It was the first Friday night of September, a little past ten, the heat stubborn, stuck like the backs of my thighs on the vinyl upholstery. Radio stations turned to static in Seven Hills, but even if they hadn't, Harry's speakers didn't work. The air conditioner blasted lukewarm air. We would have been more comfortable in my hatchback, or Graham's sedan, and especially in Viv's roomy SUV. But Harry was the only one of us who'd bought his car with money he earned; what kind of jerks would we have been to refuse riding in the spoils of all that hard work?

Harry's car dipped and jumped over the road's potholes. He drove so slowly that there wouldn't have been a breeze with the windows down, but plenty of mosquitoes. Viv periodically slapped her neck until, with an elongated sigh, she shook her hair out of its braid and hid under it.

"If one more bloodsucker bites me, I'm going to start biting back," she said. She didn't stutter on S words anymore, just overenunciated them in a way that made me think she was remembering having been teased.

"I'd like to see that," Graham said.

Viv twisted, snapped her jaw, and smiled. "I bet you would."

She flipped the front vents closed. "I think they're crawling through the air conditioner."

Harry made a noise like a snort and flicked it off.

We were ten miles outside of town, navigating a one-lane road through a ravine, headed to its only destination, the slaughterhouse. It was easy to forget this place existed. Who'd want to remember? A hundred or so seniors every September, that's who. And the four of us, along with our peers, as the timeworn tradition of Senior Class Slumber Fest dictated, were about to spend the night there. Basically we were planning to slumber it in hell.

Graham lifted his flask. His mother had arrived home the day before after a summer-long absence. His head touched the car ceiling each time we hit a bump and his strawberry-blond hair stood with static electricity. "This one's for Izzie. The only girl who's seen me naked and managed to resist jumping me."

I tucked my legs beneath me and took a nip of the spicy liquor. "I don't think you being six, scarfing too many cookies, puking on your pants, and needing to take a bath at my house counts as me seeing you naked." Viv laughed so suddenly she snorted. She covered her face. Her eyes smiled out between her fingers; there were tiny glow-in-the-dark skulls painted on her nails.

"How were you not scarred for life?" Harry asked.

Viv giggled. "Who says she's not?"

Harry mimed tipping a hat to her.

I threw my arm to my forehead. "It's only because I've seen hundreds of guys naked that I'm able to block out the trauma of Graham."

Graham pinched just above my kneecap, a spot that made me laugh abruptly and shove him away. "More like my naked glory ruined you for all others." He took the flask as he slouched back.

Viv winked at me and said, "I think Graham's teensy-tiny little baby weenie is why Izzie won't go farther than kissing."

"She's right," I whispered, hands over my heart, "I imagine it in place of the boy's face. It's why I can't stomach baby carrots."

Harry groaned. "Now I need a lobotomy."

Viv flipped the mirror down. "Baby carrots are an abomination of nature," she stated without a trace of humor curling her mouth's reflection.

Graham tapped his window. "Why are there no other cars on the road?"

"I told you, you made us late," Viv huffed. "Every senior is going to beat us and they'll take all the good spots." Our headlights illuminated long-abandoned farming equipment scattered in the barren landscape.

Harry drummed his palms on the steering wheel. "How do you know a good sleeping spot from a bad one in a slaughterhouse? Don't they all inherently suck?" He raked his hand through his brown hair, leaving the sides vertical banks. Viv laced her fingers watching him, trying to resist licking her palm and styling his hair. "And there will be at least three missing seniors other than us. The Animal Rights Club isn't coming," Harry directed to Viv, "out of protest."

"Fascist bullies." Her chin jutted out. Viv was club treasurer sophomore year. She'd had three rescue bunnies, her parents had trained assistance dogs, and she'd teared up during those animal rescue commercials with puppies behind bars. One unlucky day she was spotted in leather riding boots; Viv was shunned.

Graham perked up. "Did I tell you about that lecture in my Ethics and Activism course on how the slaughterhouse caught fire?" Graham loved to audit classes in his mom's department at the University of Santa Barbara.

"Some disgusting smoker dropped their cigarette and burned the place down," Viv replied absently, riffling through her purse. She craned around and held a chandelier earring to her earlobe, sending a whiff of honeysuckle perfume into the rear seat.

"Space empress chic," I declared. The pressure I felt when Viv asked for my opinion on accessories and clothes led to theatrical embellishments. Better to overdo it than disappoint.

Graham pitched forward for our attention, one finger raised. "But it wasn't an accident."

The car shuddered over a metal grate. "What happened?" Harry asked.

Graham settled forward, elbows on his knees, hands

tented under his chin. "Sixty years ago"—he got his eager-to-teach expression—"there weren't laws about the treatment of animals. None of this free-range, veggie-fed yoga meat. They would just pack the cows onto the killing floor, gas them, and butcher them."

Viv crawled up on her knees, propped her chin on the seatback, and glared. "If this is just meant to frighten me, I'm going to tell Jess Clarkson about your baby carrot."

I shook my head. "I don't get why guys—*why you*"—I nudged Graham's shoulder—"are interested in Jess. Her brain function is nil."

Graham cupped his hands at his pecs and raised a sly eyebrow. "Really? You can't think of two gigantic reasons why I'd be interested?"

I stuck two fingers in my throat and gagged.

Viv's eyes flicked down to her front before she crossed her arms there. "God, when did you become such a skeeze? You used to be my squishy Teddy Graham."

Harry tipped his head back, laughing. "He's always been a perv, Viv. Even when he was a chubby little dude who let you call him Teddy Graham and Graham Cracker, he used to talk about jerking it and—" His voice broke away as Graham lunged for him and the car swerved left. Graham tried to cover Harry's mouth. "And he used to brush up against—" Graham caught Harry's collar. Harry made a gurgling, hacking noise but righted the car.

Viv's earrings danced on their silver hooks as she half shrieked, half laughed. "Sit down, *Teddy Graham*."

I yanked his elbow and he slid back, all shamefaced grin. "Okay, okay." His hands went up in surrender. "I used to brush up against girls in line during the seventh grade. I wasn't a sexual predator. I was *twelve*. And I wouldn't do it now."

"No, now you just study on the bleachers by the pool whenever the girls' swim team is doing laps," I said. "Now you drool over Jess."

"You'll see, Pendleton." He leveled a finger at me. "That girl wants me. We're in the middle of a passionate courtship."

"Does she have a thing for seventeen-year-old boys who use words like *courtship*?" I asked.

"This is why girls think we're weird," Viv said. "We spend all our time with them." She motioned to the boys.

"I don't understand why you think our sophisticated loner status is such a plight, Vivian," Graham said.

"Don't lump me in with Graham's perviness," Harry told her.

Viv patted him on the shoulder and then said to Graham, "Harry's basically a monk compared to you." Graham snorted. "*He is*. We didn't even know he was going out with that shy little what's-her-name from work until he broke it off."

A stich formed between Viv's brows as she stared into the dark of the rear window. No one was certain where to go from there. Viv had been furious that Harry had developed a crush on a girl, taken her out twice, and kept it from us. Harry insisted it wasn't about having a secret. It didn't work out with her anyway, although he'd never said why.

"May I please get back to the story?" Graham asked, exasperated. "I'm not screwing with you guys. They gassed the cows, but the gas wasn't fatal. They were paralyzed by it and couldn't struggle when hoisted up on big hooks to be butchered." He dragged his finger across his neck. "They would bleed out, mooing."

At a swell in the road, we had an unobstructed view of the slaughterhouse. Windowless, anonymous, with the atmosphere of all creepy abandoned buildings. Cars were parked haphazardly around it. Our classmates were a shadowy mass at the entrance. My hands were shaking and I slipped one in Graham's. His fingers folded over mine.

He continued, "This one employee couldn't stand to see the cows suffer anymore. He planned to burn the place down, stop all the carnage. He thought that once the flames caught, the cows would stampede to freedom and the slaughterhouse would close. So he set the fire and the alarm sounded, but rather than open the gates for the cows to run, someone hit the gas button and all the cows were paralyzed." Graham paused. Viv's fingers on the headrest were dappled red and white. "They burned alive."

"Crap," Harry said.

Graham spoke, waving our joined hands. "But the fire was extinguished before it finished the cows off. They were burned. Thrashing and beating their skeleton heads on the ground."

"I'm going to vomit," Viv said, rolling the window open. We got a strong, hot whiff of ash and death. After sixty years, how did the place still reek of decaying flesh? "This is why I'm a vegetarian," she muttered, rolling the window back up.

We were quiet for a minute until Harry said, "Cheese-burgers smell much, *much* better."

I laughed through my nose, failing to hold it in. Viv said, "You're becoming as gross as Graham, Harry."

"Really," Graham said, "that's the big insult all of a sudden? You're as bad/vulgar/pervy/substitute-the-negative-adjective-of-your-choosing as Graham is?"

The car slowed as Harry searched for a parking spot. The smell was suffocating, all hot and heavy, inescapable. I bounced my heels in place and flapped the pages of a paperback I had pulled from my purse to give to Graham, but had forgotten about. I was snapping the cover open and closed when Graham pressed it shut.

Light from outside shone as a bar across his flinty irises. He wore wire-rimmed spectacles that would have appeared boring on a face less complicated than his. "There aren't actually bovine corpses left in there, Izzie," he told me softly.

"I know that."

"Do you?" He tapped my bouncing knee. I dug my heels into the car's floor.

"You have to read this one next." I tossed the paperback to him. He turned it over to the front cover.

"If I'm lifting the moratorium on dystopian, you're going to start reading detective novels again."

"We'll see." I sounded wrong, nervous. He cocked his head. Slumber Fest was not my scene any more than it was

Graham's. Or Harry's. We didn't go to our classmates' house parties or beach ditch days, half because we weren't invited and half because we had more fun in the barn. We could be ourselves there.

For some reason I wanted to convince Graham I wasn't as miserable as he suspected. "There'll be Jell-O shots—I've never had one. And it won't kill us to mingle with the kids we've gone to school with forever."

"Uh-uh," Harry said. "I'm here on official news blog business. Covering the story. No mingling."

"Slumber Fest is an adventure," I said emphatically.

"What I don't get is why Slumber Fest is at a slaughter-house," Harry said.

"Because that's the tradition. It's . . . it's an *institution*," Viv told him, her voice high and adamant.

He gave her a look like, *But why?*

"I don't think it's because our classmates like the idea of mass cow homicide," Graham said. "The slaughterhouse bit of Slumber Fest is irrelevant. The chills are the point. Chills and thrills are like a permission slip to do whatever or *whoever* you want." Graham crinkled the corners of his eyes at me.

"There are so many better places," Harry said. "Like down on the beach."

"Or the picnic spots on the hills," I said.

"Or the lighthouse in Berrington," he answered.

"Or the old pier's carousel house. Or Ghost Tunnel," I said.

"Oh, there'll be ghosts. The spirits of massacred cows will haunt all the meat eaters," Viv boomed, and cracked up.

I laughed too, though nervously. I wasn't all hyped up on adrenaline because of chills and thrills. It was our senior year. Soon we'd scatter. We wouldn't live on the same street. The four of us wouldn't go to the same college, and even if we were no farther than me at UCLA, Graham in Santa Barbara, Viv in San Francisco, and Harry who knows where because he needed financial aid, it wouldn't be the same. Siblings move but stay close because of blood and bossy parents. I wanted a force as strong for us. I wanted something gigantic to happen that would make geography irrelevant.

There was a sense of shared anticipation among our classmates at the slaughterhouse's entrance, like in class right before summer break. It made me jump a little, even though circles of conversation didn't open up as we squeezed in. The artsy alternative kids, poetry girls, and the Brass Bandits shared space. The lacrosse players, arms bracing coolers, had declared temporary peace with the soccer team, and they were knocking around and feinting punches.

Viv's arm tightened around mine. The year before, three senior girls had started the night single and ended up coupled. Viv didn't have a specific boy in mind—Luke McHale was a hundred crushes in the past. She wanted a tall, creative, anything-but-blond guy. The slaughterhouse was where she planned to make it happen.

Right then I followed Viv's narrowing eyes. Her last and most important criteria for a boy: They couldn't be tainted by her nemesis, Amanda Schultz. Amanda was flanked by her two best friends, the girls Graham called imminent sorority girls, Rachel Wyndamer and Jess Clarkson. To Graham, the title wasn't a judgment but a fact.

Viv's features pinched as she stared at Amanda and her plush pink beanie with rabbit ears. Viv nudged my side for me to look. "I think Amanda's stuffed animal hats begin as actual stuffed animals she steals from little kids."

"But she only steals them from kids with cancer," Graham chimed in, propping an elbow on my shoulder.

"No, not kids, *babies*," Harry said.

A trace of a smile warmed Viv's eyes.

"Or maybe she's a witch and they begin as real animals she captures and kills to stuff and turn into hats," I said.

Viv's heart-shaped face exuded light. "She's a rabid stuffed animal."

"With a PhD in psychological torture," Graham said, the interest thinning in his voice.

"Ironic that she used to give me tons of grief over how I dressed and now she wears decapitated toys on her head to cover up how pure evil she is," Viv said. I pulled her closer.

"We should pretend she doesn't exist. Just ignore her," Harry said.

Viv's smile soured and she whispered, "Except she's already erased me."

"No one can erase you," I said.

Graham shrugged. "She did literally erase Viv's name in last year's yearbook." She'd substituted "Nobody" for "Vivian

Marlo" under Viv's picture. Viv either wanted to end Amanda or be her. I wasn't sure then which she'd choose.

Word reached us soon that the fire department was inside, checking that the building wasn't going to cave in on us. Graham shook his head, feigning disgust. "How pedestrian."

"This is supposed to be death-defying," I said, stomping a foot.

"I'm going home if I'm not risking life and limb," Graham complained, garnering us dirty looks. Our classmates did not usually appreciate our brand of humor.

The bodies coiled tighter. My arm pressed into Harry's, but I angled away from the contact. I never took Harry's hand or jumped on his back like I did with Graham. You had to ground Graham like you would a live wire. Grab him before his stories got out of control. Except then you'd catch a little of his electricity and be that much more alive for it.

Harry wore a fixed and intent expression. Next to Amanda was Conner Welsh and his two closest friends, Trent and Campbell. Amanda, Conner, and their friends made up a little flock of despicable sheep. Our togetherness made us outcasts; their togetherness made them nasty tyrants. Most kids paid homage in order to be ignored by them. Viv and Harry weren't so lucky. Just then, Conner snatched a bottle from a paper bag in one of the Brass Bandits' hands. The trumpet player, Henry, whirled around and started to protest, saw it was Conner, and instead raised his hands in surrender.

Conner swigged, his boys jeering at Henry until he

disappeared into the crowd to get away. Laughing, Conner mimed slapping the butt of cheerleader standing in front of him, Trent thrusted his hips in her direction, and Campbell, usually the least offensive of them, belted out a burp that scaled a full octave.

"Science is wrong about Neanderthals going extinct," I said to Harry, jerking my chin at the boy band—Graham's name for them.

Harry's features shifted to neutral as he looked down his shoulder at me. "Cockroaches always find a way."

Just then, a graying, paunchy man—the fire chief—climbed on top of a car hood, raised a bullhorn, and shouted, "Everybody home! The building is not structurally sound." He continued yelling for us to disperse, until the objections drowned the bullhorn out. Putting up a fight didn't work because firefighters emptied out of the slaughterhouse and herded us to our cars.

"We've just witnessed the end of an empire, friends," Graham spoke from the corner of his mouth. There was a volley of shouts about moving the party to the beach or to Amanda's house. None of those invitations were extended to us.

We were in the car bumper-to-bumper with our classmates for several minutes before Viv spoke. "I've been looking forward to Slumber Fest my whole life," she said, the back of her hand placed morosely on her forehead.

Graham pushed his glasses up his nose. "You won't even eat beef. Sleeping in a slaughterhouse would have been hypocritical."

Her hair whipped back and forth and her glowing polish made comet tails in the dark. "Seniors bragged about it every fall. A couple years ago everyone played spin the bottle."

"Then we probably would have caught mono," Harry deadpanned. "Sleeping in a slaughterhouse doesn't beat eating pizza from Lunardi's and swimming."

Viv emitted a high-pitched noise of disbelief.

"I only wanted to do it because it reminded me of the adventures we used to have," I admitted. I gazed out the window.

My thought process went like this: sleeping in the slaughterhouse would have been a coup; it was unoriginal, though. This was the last year we'd spend in Seven Hills; we couldn't waste it on stale adventures; the fire chief saved us from a brief and stupid exploit.

I was struggling to make the final leap. I hugged my knees and relaxed while listening to the others talk. Their voices braided and became one long, golden note that felt comforting in my ears. It reminded me of Viv's fingertips, like butterfly wings on my skin as she did my eye makeup, and Graham jumping off the end of the diving board with me on his back, and Harry smuggling king-size candy bars into the movie theater.

The end of our lives together was racing toward us. Graduation stood on my chest. If I didn't do something, we would blow into one another's pasts, and these three brilliant, dazzling friends would be lost to me.

5

"Is she happy?" Viv asked. We shared the barn's blush-colored sofa, her legs on my lap. The tart, fermented cider had its fangs in my tongue. It washed away the taste of the deep-dish pizza we had devoured after the slaughterhouse.

The barn was as hot as the car had been, the baby hairs framing Viv's face curling with humidity. Graham paced, sending eddies through the air, his steps resonating up into the eaves of the loft where we stored our sleeping bags and camping tent. We almost always thought we didn't need the tent until the mornings we woke bitten by bugs. Viv, her forehead misshapen with lumps, would cross her heart with a manicured nail and swear never to go again. But she'd braved the mosquitoes for me four times that past summer.

"Who cares if she's happy?" Graham said with an abrupt turn. "She's my *mother*. This is my fifth stepfather. She leaves for two months and this is what she brings me?" He beat the air with a wooden figurine. "It's a doll."

Viv smothered a giggle in her palm.

"C'mon, man. Maybe the guy's decent?" Harry said.

Graham threw himself into a chair, its legs shrieking against the distressed white floorboards. Harry settled with his back against the sofa. He smelled metallic with sweat. *Everything* smelled of sweating skin. My limbs were noodles. I wanted to swim.

Graham drew my attention with a dragged-out sigh. "Actually," he said, knocking a fist on the souvenir, "it's not a doll." Thoughtfulness crept onto his face "It's an idol, one of worship. She used to send such interesting stuff, though. Unusual, exotic, *grisly* artifacts. Oh." His eyebrows leaped up. "Remember the flesh-eating beetle colony from East Borneo? Used to pick skeletons clean?"

Viv shuddered and combed her fingers through the tangles in her hair. "I remember that dead mouse you and Harry tried to use them on." She gave him a reproachful look. "Grotesque. Anyway, you're just pissy your mom didn't bring you along to China or Japan or wherever. *Poor Teddy Graham*, didn't get another stamp in his passport."

Graham looked up, surprised, and then smiled showing his teeth, eyes twinkling at being pegged. He was four and stealing cookies again. "Sure, I wish she'd brought me to Myanmar or that I'd at least met the old dude before she married him. He teaches at NYU. He won't even show his face until Thanksgiving."

"Then nothing's changed," I said. My eyes stuck to the idol. It was carved from pale yellow wood, smooth and glossy. Graham had stomped into the barn when he and Harry

arrived to pick us up for the slaughterhouse, tossed the figurine on the couch, and barked, "Don't ask." But it was all he
went on about after we returned. "Where'd she find it?" I
wondered.

Graham jumped up and knelt on the faded Turkish
rug, instantly cheerier that there was a story to be told. He
propped the doll so it was standing on my knees. The idol was
featherlight. Harry twisted for a look and Viv sat, one pointy
shoulder poking out of the netting of her swimsuit cover-up.
We huddled around the idol like it was special, as though
deep down we knew that stupid, nothing doll was a spark to
our kindling. I brushed a finger along the lines of its crescent
moon and the curve of its robe. A woman. Indeterminable
age. Hawkish features. A charge ran into my fingertip when I
touched her cheek and I snatched my hand back.

"My mother found it in the market of a village where
she was doing research." Graham's mom studied near-extinct
cultures all over the world. "The village is on the Irrawaddy
Delta. She's the idol of a cult that worships her. An *ancient*
cult. They make tea from a special plant they find in the jungle to have ritual visions."

"To get high?" Viv asked.

Graham's dimples deepened. "More of an altered state of
consciousness to communicate with *her*." He thumbed the
idol's head. "They make blood sacrifices, too."

Graham's whirling thoughts showed through his gun-
metal eyes, like waves through a spyglass. I smiled. "Is any of
that not bullshit?"

He smirked. "Could be. It's stuff I've read. All I know for sure is that my mom found her at a market and she has no idea where the idol originated from."

Viv stuck her tongue out at Graham. I didn't mind that he loved to slip lies in with the truth. The opposite. I was good at spotting them. I loved his stories. "She's a mystery," I said.

Viv stroked the idol's face. "She's pretty. Can I have her?" Graham tipped his head and handed it off. He forgot about the figurine as soon as it left his hands. I did too, for a while. Viv tossed it aside, wanting it a little less now that it was hers.

"Are we swimming or what?" Harry asked, heaving himself up with a grunt. He and Graham stood side by side, same tall height, one caramel and one pale sugar. I felt a tiny nibble of fear. I pulled my Polaroid camera out from under a throw cushion and snapped a photo. I fanned my face with the picture, waiting for their figures to appear. They were so beautiful. Next year, other girls would see it. College girls would appreciate Graham's sophisticated, brainy confidence. They'd flock toward Harry's thoughtful sincerity. They'd date the kind of girls who drink espresso, smoke hookahs, and backpack across Europe. How could I compete? Graham and Harry's memories of their childhood buddy Izzie would be replaced with shiny new ones of reaching up shirts in dorm rooms.

Viv was destined for a million boyfriends. She'd make friends who knew what to look for at vintage clothing shops and who knew what to say about new Broadway plays. In college, there'd be snapshots of roommates and Cancún spring breaks on her walls, rather than Polaroids taken by me. Would we all even visit Seven Hills at the same time once we were gone? Graham used to say that in a zombie apocalypse, this town was exactly the kind of remote that keeps you alive. They'd be done with this place.

I needed to find a way to seal us all together. For good. In more than a picture.

"I've been thinking about a way we can make this year special," I began, picking at the edge of a temporary tattoo I had on my thigh. A heart.

Graham turned to listen, halfway to the door leading out to Viv's mom's raised planter boxes.

"There's a senior prank on the principal after home-coming," Viv replied brightly. She thumbed the heart tattoo, identical to mine, on her wrist. I smoothed the edges of its twin. I wanted it to last. We'd bought them together on our last trip to the mall.

"We should do something just for us," I said. "Not a prank voted on by student gov. That's weak."

Viv said, "Senior prank night is legendary."

"It's not," I blurted. She stopped tracing her heart tattoo. "Vivy, we're not going to be reminiscing about driving a golf cart into the pool or putting a pig in the principal's office in forty years." I looked to Harry and Graham. "We'll laugh about it for a night and then poof, we'll forget. This year is all we have." The words were final. I sunk up to my shoulders in the sofa cushions.

There was a shuddering skeleton of thought in my head and all it needed was vital tissue so it could dance. A sharp bit was poking me in the kidney; I tugged out the wooden statue Viv had flung aside.

I turned it over in my hands. There were tiny starbursts engraved in the fabric of the woman's robe, her eyelids were closed, and her fingers were steepled. There was a quality to her that reminded me of those drawings we'd discovered on the ancient rock. The commonality: They made me think of invisible things. Of fear and love and belief. "I want us to have something that matters." I was uncertain. Grasping. "Not matters to the world, but to us. I don't want the world to know about it. And even if we haven't talked for ten years—"

"That will never happen, Izzie," Viv said fiercely. She stood.

"It will, Viv. It's what happens. But not if we had more."

"More?" she said with a scoff. "We are *best* friends. We are bonded. We spend every day together."

"But we won't see each other every day," I said. "Not even once a week after this year." I glanced at the idol—was she smiling? "What if we invented something? An event that was bigger than us. Something that would keep us together because we'd do things for it that no one else would know about."

"You mean sex things?" Graham asked. His brow cocked and there was pink in his cheeks. He'd unbuttoned his shirt for a swim.

I frowned at the divot in his square chin. "Secret things."

The words tickled my tongue like a serpent's hiss. Who didn't want secrets? "Remember how our dares made it feel like we had our own world?" *Where nothing could get to us*, I almost added.

Up on the rock, I learned that wasn't true.

Graham took his time answering. "Sure. When I wanted to escape from dinner with Stepdad Number Three, I switched my brain to thinking about beating you swimming to the sea lion rocks or down the dunes on cardboard."

Viv was nodding. She'd been the frequent observer of our challenges. Harry's eyes went back and forth between us. He'd missed our games. Most of our daring stopped with Goldilocks. "We should make up our own mischief rather than the unoriginal stunts the rest of our class is pulling," Harry said.

"Exactly," I said, bouncing in place, instantly giddy that Harry *got it*. "We do our own slaughterhouse Slumber Fest or we think of a better event."

"Better how?" Viv asked, her eyes still narrowed.

"Better meaning not purposeless," I explained.

"What's our purpose?" Viv said. She'd moved to stand between the boys, one hand on Graham's shoulder, swaying into him.

"What's the point of sleeping in the slaughterhouse?" I asked.

"To get a really gorgeous boyfriend," Viv said, nudging Graham's hip with hers.

Harry shook his head. "It's dangerous."

"People *think* it's dangerous," Graham replied.

"What's the point of pranking the principal?" I asked. "It isn't even pretend dangerous."

"The challenge," Harry answered.

Graham said, "Spitting in perceived authority's face."

"Breaking the rules," Viv sang.

"But Principal Harper is expecting a prank," Graham continued. "It's the only time students pay attention to him and teachers slap him on the back for being a good sport. He's got a hard-on for it."

"So let's prank everyone," I said. "Let's be half as brave as we were in preschool." I raised my eyebrows in challenge to Graham.

"I don't think we'll be able to steal every single cookie in Seven Hills," he said. "Or fake a chicken pox epidemic."

"Oh c'mon," Viv moaned. "It wasn't an epidemic. You just convinced your parents that you two had them so you could stay home, and I had to eat lunch alone for an entire week until your mosquito bites healed."

"We used simple syrup to attract them," Graham said to Harry.

"And Earth to Izzie, what about teachers and parents?" Viv went on. "If we do something big, we could get into trouble."

Harry toed at the rug with his sneaker. "Only if we get caught," he said softly. He opened his mouth to speak again, closed it, then said, "I think Seven Hills probably deserves a prank played on it."

"We're not breaking the law, Viv," Graham chewed on

the words. "Something that punks all of *them*, everybody who isn't us, but ultimately isn't without reason."

"And why stop at one prank?" I said. "We do a sequence. We start a group dedicated to clandestine activities. We'll have rituals." I waved the idol at them. The good ideas were falling from the sky. "Ones that we swear to repeat. We confess our secrets." It seemed a silly thing to say since what secrets could we have? "We form a secret society and it doesn't end with high school."

Graham said in his professorial tone, "Aren't secret societies mostly a bunch of rich white men huddled around a campfire, colluding to rule the world?"

I flicked my bangs from my eyes. "Who says they have to be? Lots of things started out as old white dudes because they made them that way. This is about our bond."

"You sound so touchy-feely. Can we make this more badass?" Graham said. "Like we're going to wreak havoc and undermine social order and end up anarchist heroes who get laid by Jess Clarkson?"

"She's all yours," Harry said.

"Okay." I nodded enthusiastically. "So our charter is as follows."

"Charter? How do you say that with a straight face?" Viv wondered.

"If we don't take it seriously, what's the point?" I asked.

"She's right," Harry cut in. "You guys talk about college and roomies and new cities. I'm getting the broke-as-a-joke version. Stuck going to community and living here until I transfer. If Izzie's charter is going to keep us seeing one another and talking, I'm serious about it."

Viv tugged at Harry's T-shirt sleeve. "Har, you are not a loser. Even if you live at home until you're forty."

Graham bobbed his head, the cynical smirk gone. "I'm in. I'll make our secret society as touchy-feely as Izzie and Harry want."

"Yes, yes, yes." I fanned the air with the idol, unable to sit still. "We have to swear allegiance."

"Before we know what we're swearing to do?" Graham said with a chuckle.

I sprang to my feet and held the souvenir to the rafters. "Swear on this, our most holy—"

"Not holy," Graham said. "Not if this is about social change, mischief, and subverting the hierarchy of old white dudes."

"Okay. Swear on"—I tapped the idol to my head—"swear to our irreligious idol of mischief, chicanery, rebellion, and eternal friendship that we're now the Order of"—I looked around the group—"Four? There are four of us. And we'll carry out clandestine rituals and pranks in the Order's name." And then I said this one last thing. "We swear that the Order doesn't end, *ever*, not until one of us dies and we aren't four anymore."

"Izzie Pendleton." Graham threw his arm over my shoulders. "You are a mad genius."

6

The airy fizz of morning gossip and the timbre of the espresso maker met us Monday at Cup of Jo. Viv and I claimed a space at the front window. Harry and Graham joined the sea of high school students waiting to order.

Viv swiped through the feed on her phone. "The whole school went to Amanda's after the slaughterhouse," she murmured, scrolling down the band of photos for me to see. Amanda and her friends caught midair doing cannonballs into the pool. A series of Conner and a bunch of guys with a floating beer bong. Half-lidded selfies under the sunset glow of hanging lanterns. Candid snaps of a sing-along, vodka and beer bottles used as mics.

"Why were we the only seniors not invited?" she asked, thumbing back to Amanda's profile where her pictures appeared professionally staged and shot.

I took the cell out of Viv's hand, closed the app, and tucked the phone into her purse. "Most of them probably weren't *officially* invited." I read Viv's emotions clear as if her skin were transparent. She knew what it felt like to be accepted and this wasn't it. At performing arts camp, the theater kids wrapped her up in their cast circles like big group hugs. She got used to being applauded and admired. Anyone would. It made the silence at home deafening.

As they found us, Graham was in the middle of telling Harry, "No way, it was loaded. Weird. Cryptic."

Harry passed around cronuts and said to Graham, "You're being paranoid. She was smiling a normal barista smile when you paid."

Graham lifted the first cup from its carrier and I saw that *Icky*, rather than *Izzie*, had been scrawled up the side. I winced taking it. He examined the next, a shadow passing behind his eyes. "Dr. Spectasaurus at your service," he said grimly. "I knew the barista was trying not to laugh at me."

Harry gave his cup with *Rags* written across it a long, protracted blink. "Sorry I called you paranoid."

Viv held hers, displaying its *Nobody* to us. She rose up on her tiptoes. "I didn't even see Conner here. How does he do it?" It wasn't the first time Conner's special nicknames had appeared on to-go cups.

"Pays off the barista," Graham suggested.

"Or threatens them," Viv muttered.

"But why?" I said. As far back as I could remember Amanda had it out for Viv, but my recollection of Conner in grade school wasn't so sinister. I remembered Conner letting me win at tetherball the day I returned to school after my grandfather's funeral; Conner being one of the only boys to give Valentines to every single kid, not just those who were his friends.

"Why does a scorpion sting?" Graham asked. "It's in his nature. Last week he left a flaming paper bag of dog crap on the band room's doorstep while the Brass Bandits were practicing. He's a pathological bully."

Viv's free hand riffled through her purse. "Usually this would bum me out, but today it seems pathetic that he went to the trouble." She freed a purple Sharpie, uncapped it, and scribbled on the cup. Then she traded hers for mine. The *Nobody* was blacked out, and *IV* was penned beside it. "Voila," she said, "no more Icky, Nobody, Dr. Spectasaurus, or Rags. We're the Order of IV." She continued on with the boys' coffees. "The Roman numeral is more badass, huh?" It was.

The simple, penned *IV* blunted Conner's insult. We ate our cronuts, our only care in the world getting equal parts raspberry filling and chocolate ganache with each bite. Those *IV*s were beacons reminding us we had a secret.

I carried our secret with me like a shield all day. When Conner rapped his knuckles hard on my desk as he passed in third period, just like he did almost every day, I didn't startle. When his best friend, Trent, who sat to my right, leaned over and chortled, "Hey, Icky, how was Cup of Jo?" I smiled and said, "Super." When I wanted to speak in class, I did, unafraid of Conner's or Trent's usual barks of "Icky."

We ate lunch on the rectangle of lawn between the band room and the auto shop. Other small groups ate there too, but like us, they were peripheral. Not outcasts per se, just gathered in the hinterlands where the lunch real estate wasn't as contested as the courtyard.

Viv had a smattering of plays around her, picking them up at random, reading a few pages and tossing them to the grass with a disappointed groan. She was looking for a perfect audition piece for the autumn performance.

A sketch pad was open on my lap, ready for me to tackle the first plein air assignment of my first-ever art class. Instead of capturing the shimmer of light playing on the trees, the tip of my pencil was working on Graham, shading in all the shadows in his wavy hair. I'd already finished Harry bent over a textbook. He often worked on homework at lunch because a few afternoons a week he had shifts pushing carts and bagging groceries at Hilltop Market. I wished for my Polaroid, which was funny because I never felt comfortable enough at school to bring it along. Photos taken on my cell weren't the same; they came out too forced and posed; they could be easily deleted.

Once I finished Graham, I planned to sketch Viv into the picture too. She was hard to get right; there was too much going on in her eyes and she was too pretty.

She looked up like she'd read my mind and craned to see the sketch pad. "You're getting really good."

I rotated the pad. "You were looking at it upside down."

"Still. It looks just like Graham and Har."

Harry closed his astronomy textbook. My cheeks were warm as I showed him. "I like it," he said.

Graham tore his eyes from his book. "Remind me why you're taking art this year?"

I frowned. "Because my transcript needs to be more well-rounded."

"Said your parents," he replied.

"Actually, it's a direct quote from the school counselor. My electives are always history and gov."

He held up one finger. "Those are your interests. They're academic. Art is . . ." He waved his hand airily.

"Fun—which is what electives are supposed to be," Viv said. She yanked on a fistful of grass and tossed it in Graham's direction.

He watched the green confetti fall on his pant legs. "It's not too late to drop art and transfer into Mrs. Fisher's genre seminar. This semester it's Society and the Mystery Novel."

I arranged my pencils in their case. "I'm going to stay in art."

"You used to be obsessed with mysteries," he said, growing more adamant.

"*Used to* being the operative phrase," Harry said.

Graham pointedly ignored Harry. "But I think you still are, Izzie. It's only because of the rock and what you—"

"Stop being bossy," Viv told him, slapping his hand out of the air. He frowned but swallowed the rest of what he wanted to say. Graham knew why I'd stopped liking books with detectives and mysteries and crimes five years earlier. Books like that asked *what if* and *how* and *why*. Those questions were too real after Goldilocks. Someone should have been asking them about her and no one was.

Viv lifted the hair from her neck and fanned herself. "It's as hot as July. Bring me one of those big mint chip ice cream sandwiches from work tonight, Har."

"You guys want them too?" Harry offered.

"Absolutely," I said. "Thanks."

"Yeah." Graham pulled a twenty from his pocket and handed it to Harry. "I love those."

"I've got them," Harry said. Graham watched the bill flutter in Harry's hand for a second before accepting it back. Graham probably would have tried insisting, but a silhouette cast a shadow on the grass.

"'Sup, Rags and Riches," Conner Welsh said.

The greeting managed to transport me back to middle school, the turning point in Conner's evolution as a bully. Amanda and Conner lining kids up against the fence for social sentencing. Amanda declared us Rags or Riches; Conner pelted us with balls either way. If Amanda thought your sneakers looked shabby that day, you could have a pony at home and she'd still proclaim you Rags. But Harry, whose family rented a house that Conner's parents owned, was consistently sentenced.

"Rags," Conner said, squatting beside Harry, "I got a problem. I've got this lunch tray and it's full of soggy beef nachos and tofu curry that smells like old man runs. Take a whiff." He raised the tray. Harry's expression went flat. "I hit too many balls at the range last night. My arm's trash." He crooked his neck and grimaced. "I think I might drop the tray, spill the nacho cheese on the walls, and the tofu shit on the floor. But fuck, Rags, if that happens, who'll clean it up?" His mock concern shifted to a sadistic smile. There was a thin scab on his bottom lip. Conner Welsh, always looking for an excuse to fight. "Oh wait, it's your dad's job to clean up my mess."

"Harry's father is the school groundskeeper," Graham said sternly.

"Janitor," Conner countered. "Or do they go by *custodian* now? All that PC shit. Can you help me out, brother?" I was sick knowing exactly what was coming. "If you take this tray off my hands, I won't have to drop it. Your dad with his gimp leg won't have to crawl onto his hands and knees to clean it up. Or should I say fuck it?"

Graham was up on his feet, reaching for the tray. "I've got it," he said. He'd done that once before; the tray ended up in his face, chili dog mashed on his shirt, one spectacle lens broken.

"No, Spectasaurus," Conner said, shaking his head with an impatient sigh. "Only Rags can help."

"Conner, there's a trash can right there," I said.

Viv had curled up, her knees to her chest, her vintage sunglasses hiding her eyes.

Harry took his time wrapping up the leftover half of his turkey sandwich in its aluminum foil. He placed it neatly on his paper lunch bag and pushed up from the ground. "I'll help you out, Con," he said, nobody home behind his eyes. "No worries." My eyes stung watching his long, bouncy gait to the trash can with Conner's soiled lunch tray. Harry took his time scraping off all the bits of food before placing the plastic neatly on the designated rack.

Conner watched Harry, barely reacting. "Good man," he told him as Harry rejoined us. "Thanks for your help." He nodded, a customer thanking staff who'd waited on him. "I can always count on you, Rags."

No one watched Conner go.

Viv sniffed loudly behind her sunglasses.

My nails bit into my palms.

Graham rested his elbows on his knees and after a heavy silence said, "I think it's time we invent our secret society."

7

Viv was on her knees, elbows on my hatchback's center console, chin cradled in her hand, fingers thrumming the corner of her mouth. "What kind of secrets could the boys have?" she asked. The rear car doors were ajar and a gentle fall breeze crept in. I nuzzled my chin into the chunky collar of my sweater.

"Video game addictions. Porn on their laptops," I mumbled through the cotton weave. Her nostrils flared.

It was the second Sunday since the slaughterhouse, and we'd been busy creating our secret society. We started where good students do: with research. Graham utilized the university library. Harry, Viv, and I scoured the Internet.

It wasn't hard to uncover articles about groups like the Bavarian Illuminati, Skull and Bones, Freemasons, and the Bohemian Club. Even some of the habits of the groups rumored to be the most secretive could be uncovered. For example, membership to the Seven Society at the University of Virginia was so secretive that members were only indicated when they died, with a wreath of black magnolias in the shape of a number seven on their graves.

Telling fact from fiction in the accounts wasn't necessary. Our search was for inspiration for our very own superclandestine group of pranksters. We didn't care if what inspired us was conjecture or reality.

As far as we could tell, secret societies had a few things in common. The first was secrecy. Those who belonged adhered to a code of silence. The members usually worked in secret to achieve a hidden agenda, anything from drunken debauchery to world domination. Most secret groups had rules about who got to boss who around, who made decisions, how membership and recruitment worked. And many of those groups had rituals and ceremonies that made them unique, terrifying, bizarre.

Our Order's structure would be democratic. There would be three rules: never tell, never lie, and always love each other and be friends. Our mission was mischief in Seven Hills.

The Order began as something out of my head, yes, but each of us gave it its shape.

Viv decided we needed a ceremonial holiday. Inspired by the crescent moon on the idol, she consulted a lunar calendar. It was fate: a blood moon in two Saturdays.

I added the secret-telling ritual. I knew almost everything about the others. I reasoned that learning more would make us even closer. I recalled the stories my mom had told about the midnight initiations of her girls' school. They crowded around the lake and sent little slips of paper with their most guarded secrets onto boats sailed across the water's glassy surface. They were lit on fire; the paper burned; the secrets were released into the night. Rather than send our secrets up into the universe, we'd trust them with one another. It would be declaring *I trust you three more than anyone*.

Graham and Harry liked reading about revolutions and they said we should call our pranks *rebellions*. And they were rebellions against everyone who wasn't us, so we did.

There, on that first night we were out as the Order of IV, under the cloak of darkness, I felt rebellious. The car rocked and the boys finally returned from scouting our school parking lot. Graham's head bobbed between Viv and me. A black beanie cut off his eyebrows.

"No cars in the lot. Good to go," he said.

We drove down the lane used for the campus security golf cart squad and circled to the auditorium. The cart port was the best place to conceal my hatchback while we snuck through the halls. The clock tower a few blocks away in the knoll chimed to twelve as we slipped from the car and kept to the shadows along the rectangular building.

We were two blocks from the ocean, and waves beating the shore sounded like a million distantly whispered secrets.

The secret-telling ritual had been easy. Inventing our first rebellion, not as much. Sedition wasn't boiling our blood— not then. When we tried to brainstorm, we drew blanks. Viv succumbed to giggles over our dumb silence. She rolled off her beanbag chair and landed unceremoniously in the tangle of her skirt, the fabric riding high on her tan thighs.

I pounded my fist into the couch and yelled that she was a flipping genius.

Viv had been written up at least ten times for what our all-male school administration called *indecent dress*. Seven Hills High's dress code only included policies for skirt length, heel height, and bra straps. It was sexist, but the code was also unevenly enforced. If you only got written up three out of ten times for letting your hot-pink bra straps show, the odds were in your favor. Don't be a killjoy, let it go, girls would grumble if you complained. What if protesting the rule led to a crackdown on platform wedges? Everyone kept their mouths shut. I was done with that.

The Order of IV made our voices louder.

The four of us stalked into the one hundreds hall, beyond the courtyard and its amphitheater. We'd start there and plaster our flyers every few lockers up the halls. Graham and Harry tailed Vice Principal Bedford during lunch on Thursday and Friday. It could have taken weeks to get the evidence we needed; instead it took one and a half lunch periods. Harry snapped a photo of Bedford, twelve-inch ruler in hand, leering after two girls passing him in the corridor. His eyes were trained on their butts; then Graham, in a feat of bravery I was sure he'd exaggerated, slid down the hall on his knees, got right behind Bedford, and took a picture as he measured one of the girl's sundresses.

I smacked the first flyer against a locker and Viv tore off a piece of tape with her teeth. She bared them and growled. I smothered a laugh, tasting latex dust from the gloves we

wore. No fingerprints. No security cameras. No staff scheduled at night since Harry's dad was jumped on campus a year
before.

"I cannot wait to see Vice Principal Pervert's face," Viv
declared. "*There are better things to measure. Stop ogling
your students,*" she read the caption. Each flyer was signed
IV. Four seasons, four directions, four chambers of a heart,
four elements, and four of us. Before we'd left for campus,
Viv gave us Sharpie tattoos of the symbol on our wrists,
a *IV*, the official sign of our membership. I felt that *IV*
tingling on my skin. Our secret order, its rebellion, was in
my blood.

The prank made me feel more exotic than I was used
to feeling. Our perfect universe had expanded from the
barn and the orchard to include our school, a place where
I mostly flew under the radar and focused on studying until
the moment the day's final bell rang and we could leave for
our real lives. As we used up all five hundred flyers, our magic
rubbed off in those halls and I was actually looking forward
to returning to class on Monday.

When we were finished, Graham pulled a can of spray
paint out of his pocket. The *click-click-click* as he shook it
traveled the corridor. The crickets chattered in response. His
arm cut a sharp line in the dark and we heard what sounded
like air escaping a balloon. I remembered him telling Viv that
we wouldn't be breaking the law. Funny—I was usually better at detecting his bullshit. He stepped back to admire his
masterpiece.

"Har's dad is going to have to scrub that off," Viv hissed.

Graham shook his head, but it was Harry who spoke. "They'll just paint over it. Easy fix."

As we dashed away, I turned and grinned at the *IV* like a bloody wound carved into the door Bedford and the other school admins would arrive to. No one would connect the graffiti to us, kids who never showed up to class hungover, never reeked of pot, and never got sent to the counselor's office. We were as good as invisible.

And I thought each of us wanted to remain unseen.

"Your sip." Graham passed me the bottle. There was a sea of tiny white candles in the barn, the flames turning the honey wooden planks of the walls to melted toffee. We sat in a circle on the floor with our backs north, south, east, and west. When Graham suggested the formation, I recognized it. The four sets of birds were buried around the rock this way.

We placed the idol at the center of our circle; she looked lit from within, soft, serene, an all-knowing fairy godmother. I took a nip of the booze, hissed like a cat at its fire, and passed it to Graham. He took a long sip, holding my eyes, and said, "What? I want to be in the right state of mind."

Viv's laugh was cut off by a hiccup. "Same, same," she said. "Liquid courage." She retreated to her place as Graham relinquished the bottle. "Who wants first?" she asked, perched on her folded legs. "Remember the rules? Never lie. Never tell. Always love each other." She leveled a slender finger around our knot. "As friends forever. We tell secrets, something no one knows."

Graham said, "What about chronicling it? We record ourselves talking about the rebellions or whatever else, and we'll cut the footage together at the end of this year." He was rolling up his sleeves, as if all this thinking was actual physical labor.

"Or save the recordings to a shared folder on our cells so all the videos are in the same place," Harry said, pausing from chewing on the side of his thumb.

Graham tipped his head. "But we have to agree: No one watches it until graduation."

A nod circulated. Viv placed a hand over her heart.

"In two Saturdays there's a blood moon and the Order has ceremonial rites," she said. There was a conviction behind those words, *ceremonial rites*. Her peasant blouse pooled at her waist and twin braids made a dark tiara on her head. "And everyone has to hold the idol when they're sharing. The Mistress of Rebellion and Secrets will burn your hands if you lie." Her eyes widened, showing their wild, glossy whites.

For a moment there was only the air winnowing through the gap of the sliding door.

"Now for scandalizing one another," Graham said in a deep, melodramatic voice. His legs were kicked out in relaxed confidence. He wasn't wearing glasses or squinting, so contacts. This wouldn't be weird for a normal person, but Graham always said he wasn't going to stick a finger in his eyeballs just so Conner would stop calling him Dr.

Spectasaurus. Graham raised a brow. "You want first, Pendleton?"

I gave an uncertain smile, reached for the Mistress of Rebellion and Secrets, and sat with her between my crossed legs. "Here goes," I said, and then I plunged in, scrunching my eyes closed. "I only got an A in Geometry because I programmed proofs into the calculator I used during tests. I cheated."

I opened one lid at a time. Harry's smile showed his square front teeth. Graham scowled and asked, "You're kidding, right?"

"No, it was going to ruin my GPA and I just could not remember—"

"No," Graham said, "I am saying that you have got to be kidding if you think that's the kind of secret that's going to make us closer."

Viv crawled forward to give me this incredulous glare, the flame of a candle illuming one side of her face. "Izzie, grow a pair of boobs and try again."

I took a breath, tightening my grip on the idol. An uglier secret waited behind this easy-to-share confession. Disfigured and deeply rooted. Saying the next words felt like scraping them free. "My parents fight." The idol's smile urged me on. "It's worse than it used to be. Not just yelling. Mom throws picture frames. Dad stomps on the glass. Mom screams she wants a divorce. They swear at each other, name call. I turn music on so no one outside will hear. Dad leaves, sometimes for the night. When he comes back they close themselves in their office, then they act like they have amnesia. Like I didn't sweep up the glass or hear what they said. They expect us to eat dinner. Be normal." Viv had crawled back over to be close. I continued in a guilty whisper, "I wish they *would* get a divorce. I'd rather have two houses than one filled with shouting."

Viv's hand fit into mine. Harry's warm eyes and Graham's troubled frown steadied me. Resigned, I'd listened to fights or tried to escape them by hiding in my closet or telling myself that grown-ups squabble like violent toddlers all the time. The fights, beyond my control, made me feel trapped and spinning.

"I didn't know they still freaked out on each other," Viv said. Graham's eyes went puzzled beyond her head. She squeezed my hand. "My turn." I gave her the idol and she crawled back to her spot. "Boys always talk about jerking off." She was gazing into the face of the idol, one corner of her mouth in dimple. "But girls do it too." She glanced up, sooty lashes framing her round, innocent eyes. "I figured out how to get off when I was thirteen."

My cheeks flamed. Viv's lips made a perfect O. She couldn't conceal that she was surprised at herself. Harry became engrossed in picking at his thumb's cuticle. Graham's mouth was ajar. He joked about it all the time. I rolled my eyes or ignored him. Viv talking about it made me feel stripped naked, and that made me disappointed, because why should I feel differently about Graham and Viv talking about the same topic?

Graham gave a shake to his head, snapped out of it, and said, "Good on you. Me now." He waved for the idol; Viv traded it for the bottle. Shadows were rushing through his eyes and he had color under the blond freckles of his cheeks. "I've been in love twice." He wore his smuggling-cookies smile. "Once with Viv and once with Izzie." He snatched the bottle back from Viv and took a long, dramatic drag, eyes ceilingward. Viv chewed her bottom lip, staring at the same unexceptional spot in the rafters.

How hadn't I noticed that it was a sauna until that moment? I pulled my sweater over my head and left my hair disheveled against my face.

"I'm not in love with either of you presently," Graham said. "Was that clear?" Our eyes met; his looked hurt.

I flashed a reassuring smile. "A hundred percent."

The silence stretched on until Harry saved us.

"My mom's parents haven't talked to her since she married my dad," he admitted.

"You visited them last summer," Viv said, reluctantly turning to knit her brows at Harry.

He hooked his arms around his knees and shrugged. "I know. For a long time they didn't have anything to do with us. Then they sent Simon and me letters and then cell phones so they could avoid calling the house. They'd invited us four years in a row. Last summer I was upset about my dad. I needed to get out of here."

Viv's head tilted a quarter revolution. "What did your mom do to make them so pissed?"

"Married my dad," Harry repeated. "He didn't go to college or know who his dad was. He wasn't a doctor and he doesn't golf."

I choked on a noise of surprise.

Harry continued, "My mom met my dad while she was in college, and"—his voice became quieter—"she got pregnant. My grandparents wanted to send her away somewhere to have the baby, where none of their friends would find out. Then she'd come home and go back to school like it never happened. But you know my mom. No one makes choices like that for her. She didn't want to have a baby yet, keep it or not. She loved my dad. She had an abortion and didn't stop dating him. They kicked her out." His expression was grave. "The actual secret I'm telling is that I like having grandparents, despite how they hurt my mom and pretend my dad doesn't exist. I felt special when my grandpa took me golfing." A cynical tick of his head. "I guess I'm more messed up than they are."

"No, you aren't," I said forcefully. "You're the kid. They're the grown-ups."

"I feel guilty anyway, like I'm betraying my dad and mom," Harry added.

"You're not," Graham said.

"I'll hate your grandparents for you," Viv promised.

Harry rubbed his palms together, inhaled deeply, and exhaled, appearing less rigid and tense for it, which was strange because before, I hadn't noticed he seemed that way. "I forgot to hold the idol," he said with a sideways smile, hair flopping with a turn of his head.

"The Mistress of Rebellion and Secrets forgives you," Viv said.

Graham stood springily, bottle swinging at his side. My cheeks were still burning, but it wasn't from shame or embarrassment. Graham extended a hand for Viv and pulled her up beside him.

"Gimme," Viv said, hand opening and closing for the bottle's neck. Graham held it just beyond her reach and grinned.

"Come and get it, Vivy," he said, sliding the door open and escaping into the night. She ran after him. Then I was up, light-headed, room orbiting. Harry and I turned at the same time and there was this recklessness between us, his eyes darkening, his mouth open like he was a second away from laughing. We leaped into the night and caught the white flutter of Viv's blouse disappearing between apple trees.

Graham was calling, "Over here. Over here, come and—" The wind stole the rest away, and Viv's breathless laughter was the far-off cry of an exotic bird.

"This way," Harry yelled, and we swerved right. We ran doubled over, weaving in and out of a line of trees. We shifted directions again. The branches were weighted low with nearly ripe apples that shone like little silver moons. Shouts and laughter were ripping up through my chest. The orchard felt as endless as it used to when we were little.

We heard two yells, one triumphant and the other frustrated. Harry and I sprinted for a hundred yards more, following the sounds. We shot out of the trees. I stopped short, digging into the dirt, sending a spray of soil at the rock ballooning up from Earth. The breath felt knocked from my lungs.

I hadn't been to the rock for a long time. Only for an afternoon or two since I found the girl. The trees seemed to push me closer, shouldering at my back. My knees locked. Harry's calloused hand closed around my elbow, his thumb hot on my inner arm. "Look," he whispered.

Two figures on top of the rock: one with his arms raised toward the immensity of the night sky and the other, hair whipping, hips swaying in figure eights, dancing with the wooden doll as an extension of her arms. Harry went soundlessly up, and after a beat, I followed. Tugged by that invisible string between us all.

The meteorite was glowing in the moonlight, a stage set ablaze like the shooting star it once was. It didn't look like a dangerous place. Not the sort I needed to avoid; Harry, Viv, and Graham exchanging knowing looks when I refused their suggestions to bonfire, sunbathe, or stargaze there. Perhaps it could be ours again.

Graham and Viv turned as we joined them. Viv floated to my side, her arm wrapping around my waist, the idol trapped between our torsos. We spun as a tornado of loose hair, fabric, and the honeyed scent of nearly ripe apples. The world turned to streaks of dark and light. Viv's laughter gave way to humming a moody little snippet from a song she'd learned for a musical about witches.

When we were too dizzy to keep on our feet, we joined the boys, lying on our backs, the four of our heads touching. There were no cracks between us then. We outshone the star-choked sky. We stared into space and didn't wonder what was there because we were the universe. All wormholes led to us.

Retrieved from the cellular phone of Isadora Anne Pendleton
Transcript and notes prepared by Badge #821891
Shared Media Folder Titled: IV, Mon., Sept. 16, 12:35 a.m.

Video start.

A quarter segment of I. Pendleton's face takes up the screen. She laughs nervously and moves the phone farther back to reveal lavender walls behind her. White bookshelves with white-framed photographs to her left. Purple quartz book-ends and rows of books organized by color—red, orange, yellow, white, blue, and green spines.

"How should I begin?" Her eyes go around the room until they land on the cell she holds unsteadily. "Graham said it was fair play that we go before Viv and Harry. The Order was my brainchild." Rolls her eyes. "And Graham thinks that all my good ideas are his. So here goes. Hi. Hey." She waves at the lens. "I'm Isadora Anne Pendleton—Izzie. I think that our secrets were the most important part of last night." She pauses. "I have a real whopper of a history with secrets. Dad keeps secrets from Mom." Her voice is low and she looks sharply to the right (likely to the door). "I've heard Mom tell Dad that she senses the gaps. She knows he isn't honest. But last night, we told secrets and wore them like those badges Viv and I used to collect when we were Brownies in the third grade. I earned almost every single one our troop could. And the secrets didn't only make us closer. They made us better, too. Does that make sense?"

Her mouth screws up as she thinks. "Graham looked older and more serious. He wasn't trying to impress us with bullshit or stories. Viv was more alive like how she gets when she has a lead part and is about to go on stage and every little movement is on purpose and graceful and her eyes spark. And Harry, he got carefree after he shared and I never even noticed that he wasn't to begin with. So anyway, secrets did that." Her eyes are downcast. She looks up after several seconds and smiles. "The end."

Video stop.

Retrieved from the cellular phone of Graham H. Averbach III
Transcript and notes prepared by Badge #82827
Shared Media Folder Titled: IV, Mon., Sept. 16, 1:02 a.m.

Video start.

G. Averbach appears with gold and emerald paisley wall-paper behind him. Shelves to his right and left are laden with books and antique trinkets. He nods at the camera. "I am not going to be sentimental—looking at you, Isadora—or perform this like it's an audition—Vivian—nor am I going to film this like it's some sort of news documentary—Harry. I don't think that Izzie can take all the credit for the Order. I have been saying for ages that we weren't being enterprising enough with our free time, and if it wasn't for all our competitions, I don't think Izzie would have the guts for the Order." He thumbs his chin. "Then again, neither would I.

"The definition of a secret society is a club or organization whose inner workings, rituals, beliefs, activities, history, and membership are concealed from nonmembers." Brief stop. "Way back in the sixth grade, right when Stepdad Number Two bailed, I got into researching the Bohemian Club." He massages his brow. "Maybe it was my wanting a father figure that made me curious about a bunch of old dudes. The Bohemian Club is basically a Masters of the Universe club, full of white, powerful, rich men." Disdain-ful smirk. "They meet in the redwoods north of San Francisco and spend weeks colluding to rule the world and, since most already do rule it, scheme about how to get even more power." His fingers tent and move for emphasis. "Their opening ceremony is called the Cremation of Care. It's part dramatic production, part occult ritual where they burn stuff at the foot of a gigantic owl statue that represented human sacrifice to the Phoenicians. The ceremony symbolizes the shedding of empathy."

He slides his desk chair closer, its wheels whistling. His face takes up the whole shot. "My point is: Secret societies delve into dark shit. They have iconographies, saints, insignias, druid rituals, pseudo-pagan practices, sacrifices, and ancient ceremonies. And since I don't believe in half-assing it, I am going to make sure that the Order of IV has it all."

He stares into the lens as he reaches toward the tripod or mount.

Video stop.

8

We arrived to our palm tree–dotted school parking lot the following morning. My legs juddered with nerves. I wanted to run for the halls to see if the flyers were still posted. "Everybody act normal," Graham said through his teeth.

The morning sun zapped the moisture from the air. Summer dogging fall, as if it wanted to last along with our fun. Viv clung to my arm. Harry kept veering off, craning to see I-didn't-know-what deeper into the parking lot.

Finally I followed his frown to Conner and his buddies around his red BMW. I grimaced. Poor Harry, there was no escaping Conner. Seven Hills radiated out from the town square, the knoll, with ten or twelve long residential streets that reached like palm fronds on either side. Some of them climbed into the hills, others bowed close to the ocean. Our street, Driftwood, was home to a lot of our classmates, including Conner.

Conner's engine announced itself whenever he drove by,

going way above the limit, to his family's driveway. Neighbors had complained. A petition circulated for speed bumps.
Conner's dad silenced the uproar with gift baskets of wine
and cheese. It wasn't like the speed bumps were ever going
to happen without Sebastian Welsh's permission anyway. He
was the biggest developer in Seven Hills and sat on the city
council.

Viv left sweaty handprints on my sleeves as she drifted
ahead to a crowd pressed against the bougainvillea that grew
around each bank of lockers. I tightened my hairband and
faked a yawn. This was Monday, casual as flip-flops. If I hadn't
been so good at being invisible, my darting eyes might have
given me away.

A few of our flyers had slipped from the walls and were
kicked up in eddies from hurried legs. Others were passed
down lines of students who released blasts of surprised laughter as they read. Kids ruminated over the details.

"Someone finally called out pervy Bedford."

"It's signed 'I-V,' like an IV drip?"

"Nah, that's the Roman numeral four."

"Who's IV?"

"My personal fucking hero."

"Let me see," Graham said easily to a redheaded freshman. The boy obliged and the four of us circled the flyer,
playing our part. I shuffled through the appropriate facial
expressions: curious, surprised, amused. Our eyes clicked on
one another's.

Graham said, "Someone's got a serious set of—"

"Boobs," I said automatically. He smiled.

"Have any teachers seen this?" Harry asked a group snapping a picture of the flyer. That's right, it would be all over social media, spit in a thousand different directions in milliseconds like one of those confetti party poppers or a bomb with shrapnel, depending on your perspective. How didn't we imagine that some classmate's German cousin would be liking our flyer on their feed within the hour?

One of the kids shrugged at Harry, another said, "Hells yes. The principal and Mrs. Wu were in another hall tearing them down and Ms. Hendricks showed up and got in their faces." Ms. Hendricks was the school's news blog adviser and Harry's favorite teacher. "And she was all, 'You better leave those up. It's news.'"

Twenty minutes into first period, Principal Harper made an announcement over the intercom. I was trying to keep up with Ms. Ives's lecture on the precolonial history of medicine in Africa when the two-note tone sounded. Principal Harper spoke too near his mic, so that the saliva netting the corners of his mouth was audible.

"Good morning, student body. Many of you will have noticed the outrageous accusations plastering our school halls this morning. There's no cause for concern. My administration is taking this act of vandalism very, *very* seriously and we fully expect to identify the perpetrator shortly." The heel of my clammy hand smeared the ink of my notes.

The next news came in third period. The two synthetic musical notes had me twisting around. Viv was four rows behind me, chewing on a lock of hair, seemingly unperturbed that we were probably about to fall from anonymity. Each breath left the invisible laces of a corset cinched tighter around my chest. I was not built for crime. Not then.

But the principal's tone had changed to contrite. Pending an official investigation, Vice Principal Bedford would be taking leave. If anyone wanted to speak to the guidance counselor about the very serious allegations leveled against Bedford, sign-ups were on the school's web portal. The corset released my ribs and I slumped in my chair, too full of relief during the rest of class to really grasp the enormity of the events we'd set in motion.

There was an outburst from Trent in the desk next to mine. "Who scissor-handed the red beast, bro?" he exclaimed loudly toward the end of the period. He was hunched over his cell and his checks reddened when he realized he'd spoken out loud. "Sorry, Mr. Novak," he mumbled, continuing to text. The red beast was what Conner called his car.

At lunch, it was all over school that the district's superintendent had seen the picture of the flyer trending on social media. Journalists began calling for comments. Sexual harassment of students by staff was a newsworthy allegation. The cheerleaders were practicing in the quad when the superintendent's car came to a screeching halt, and she made a beeline through a dance formation. Amid the details that came in waves, there was also talk that someone keyed *Asshole* on Conner's car. The cherry on top of a perfect day.

Reports reached us of Bedford leaving campus with a

cardboard box. Three female students accused Bedford of making harassing remarks and staring at them suggestively. Parents tied up the school's phone lines, and a local cable channel's morning show got a copy of the school dress code, their reporter asking the school secretary if she thought the dress code had created an environment of impunity for the sexual harassment of female students. She answered affirmatively. The parents whose daughters were pictured in the flyer arrived to take them home. Graham said they'd lawyer up, slam the district with lawsuits. Lawsuits, lawyers, reporters, parents, *consequences*.

It hit me, abrupt and as hard as the water smacks your cannonballing form. We had a say in the world. As us, we were invisible. As the Order of IV, we were powerful. This revelation was as intoxicating as hard apple cider. I wanted to keep having a say.

On the drive home from school I watched Viv peek under her bandage to stare at the shadow left by the penned *IV* on her wrist. She felt its power too.

We listened to one of my playlists at the cell phone's full volume. Harry punched the horn to the beat as we drove through our neighborhood. Viv chimed in using her high vibrato. Graham was bent over his cell, scrolling through a feed of our flyers tagged in photos. The tip of his tongue went between his teeth in the way it did when he was surprised.

I was struck with a thought: *If you know Graham so well, how did you miss him having crushes on you and Viv?* Not crushes. He'd confessed to having been *in love*. The difference between loving and being in love doesn't exist until you experience it, so I wasn't entirely sure what Graham's secret meant.

I waved good-bye with both arms as Harry reversed from my driveway. There was a kick in my step as I used the rear door to the kitchen. I ditched my bag next to the table and shouted, "Your favorite daughter's returned." My parents ran their architectural firm from home.

I picked through the Greek yogurts in the fridge drawer. I hummed to myself, blurting occasional lyrics of the hip-hop song we had been playing in Harry's car. I was too high off the rebellion to care that I was muddling the words. Usually Graham, Viv, and I headed to the barn after school, and then Harry joined us after his shift at Hilltop Market, but that day Graham had a class at USB, Harry was driving the hour to Paso Robles to a vinyl store, and Viv was practicing for our school's upcoming *Antigone* auditions. I'd gotten the topic of the first term paper in Post-Colonial History and I was excited to begin.

I elbowed the fridge door closed and was going for a spoon when susurrant voices reached the kitchen. They were muffled, gradually more audible as I deserted the yogurt on the counter and tiptoed into the hall. Ours was a big, old, creaking house with wood floors that whined and brass door hinges that sang escalating notes like those my cello used to make while I tuned it, before I quit in the fifth grade. I stepped long to avoid an especially squeaky floorboard and went halfway to my parents' office. Stopped.

" . . . you aren't hearing what I'm telling you . . ." Those words of my mother's came sharp like a dagger through the closed door.

"We can't continue having the same argument, Ellison. You're either in this or you aren't. I won't be cast as a villain for the rest of my life."

"And so the blame is on me. God forbid you take any responsibility. . . ."

I reversed. I should have made more noise in the kitchen; lead with a loud joke rather than a silly hello they must have missed.

I left the yogurt but took my backpack to my room and shut the door.

I crawled into my egg chair that hung from a ceiling beam. Its wicker frame was small, left over from when Mom had to boost me up. I opened my laptop to distract myself.

The paper for Post-Colonial History wasn't due for six weeks, yet there I was, defining my research goals the day the essay prompt was given. The window was open and the salty air rocked the chair gently. I gradually let go of the sinking sensation in my stomach. My eyes drifted from my laptop to the water on the horizon each time I completed a bullet point and my brain skipped from post-colonial medicine in Africa to the Order of IV.

Our blood moon ritual was in two Saturdays. Viv would create the ceremony. What would our next rebellion be? I wanted another plan. I wanted to flex the Order of IV's muscles. Show our school that IV existed, was powerful, and in the shadows. For the flyers not to be a fluke, there needed to be more.

Slumber Fest wormed into my head. The grown-ups had snapped their fingers and decided that Seven Hills High School's oldest tradition was canceled. I might have acknowledged that the issue was safety and not adults being tyrannical, but then raised voices from downstairs made it into my egg, reminding me of how at the mercy of adults I was. I pressed my right ear into the cushion. I was sick of listening to what adults had to say, to me, to one another, always with their opinions.

I clapped the laptop shut. I wouldn't listen helplessly. Not on the day we took down pervy Bedford and the school's dress code.

I set my egg chair swinging as I threw myself from it, opened by bedroom door, and screamed, "I can't do my homework with all of your shouting!"

The tight voices went dead. I sensed Mom and Dad a floor below me, listening. I slammed the door. Leaned against it. A long sigh of relief slipped out.

At last. There was my voice.

Viv called me when she was through practicing for her audition. I'd set aside my finished research plan an hour before. "Did you go with the Ophelia or Viola monologue?"

"Ophelia," Viv sighed dreamily. "She's so tragic, mad. I don't even care that she's the ultimate manic pixie dream

girl. Mr. Lancaster's dropping hints that the spring production will be *Hamlet*. I want him to see that I was born
to play Ophelia. Amanda will be all, *Ophelia was a blonde
and so am I*. I won't let her snake it from me. Hold on."
She yelled away from the phone. Listened for a beat of
silence. Then, "Ina wants to know if you're having a veggie
burger?"

"I'm going to give my parents heart attacks and eat here
tonight."

She shouted back to her mom and then to me, "Uh-oh. Is
it zombies versus unicorns over there?"

"No. Mom texted about making pesto earlier. She used
emojis. I have to reward the effort."

"Have they been fighting since you got home?" She
sounded unimpressed by my stalling.

"They've stopped."

"It's not like when they throw things and your dad
leaves?"

"No," I whispered.

She waited a few seconds. "I didn't think *we* had secrets."

I flipped on the battery-operated strand of fairy lights
inside my chair. They were white and bright in my eyes. "I
was embarrassed."

"You want to tell her, don't you? You want her to know
because then they will get a divorce." It wasn't phrased as a
question.

I flipped the lights off. "I never said that."

"You said you'd rather have two houses than one full of screaming."

"It's not what I meant."

"Because you get that you wouldn't just blow up your family. You'd blow up mine."

"Hold on. I'm going into the closet." I pressed between the sweaters. With the door closed behind me I had absolute privacy. "We made a promise. I will never tell my mom what we saw. I'll never tell my dad that we know."

I could hear her breathing deeply on the other line. Her face was probably going runny like it did when she tried not to cry. "I'm sorry," she whispered. "If you want to tell, I won't be a bitchface about it."

I shook my head into the dark. "Subject change, okay?"

"Okay."

"I was thinking about Slumber Fest."

"Why? Wait—oh my god." Her voice jumped high. "Are you thinking what I am?"

"That it doesn't need to be canceled?"

"Throwing it would make the Order a legend," she said. "But they put up a barbed wire fence blocking the road to the slaughterhouse."

"Forget the slaughterhouse," I said. "What about the old railway tunnel?"

"The Ghost Tunnel," she said with delicious exuberance. "Oh my god, oh my god, oh my god. What's the plan?"

A few minutes later she hung up for dinner. I sat on my

desk and drew my knees to my chest. I stared out at the beach visible over rooftops. I tried to resist it, but what I saw in Viv's garden six years before demanded to be remembered. Fully.

Viv and I hopping along the stones set into an ocean of clover. My legs kicking out, following their archipelago by memory around the corner of her house. The wink of the sun off the glass walls of the hothouse as it came into view. A figure inside. Her mom in the poppy-red turban she wore during treatment. Another head, taller than Ina. My dad stooped over her and then their mouths fitted together. I froze, one foot off the ground in a doomed jump. Viv's pinkie finger hooked mine. Tears sprung to her eyes.

How could we tell? Her mom had cancer. And then the cancer was in remission, a miracle for Viv. And maybe the kiss had been a mistake, and what if we told and her mom got sick again? *Who* would we tell? What if grown-ups kissed in private all the time?

Later we understood. We named it cheating. On TV, families broke apart because of it.

It wasn't fair to us to decide between the lives we had and whatever would come after our parents splintered. They'd break apart because of *what we saw*. That's how we thought about it. It was what *we saw*, not the wrong *they did*.

That was wearing off the older I got.

It was easier to imagine telling. But I believed that Mom sensed the space between her and Dad, and because I thought Mom knew Dad was up to something I convinced myself that it wasn't my job to be honest.

Awful things happened all the time and people didn't do anything about them. *Just the way the world is.* Grown-ups had affairs, deaths went uninvestigated, Goldilocks was killed, and mean-spirited kids called you names.

Except the Order of IV had started to right the wrongs in Seven Hills.

Retrieved from the cellular phone of Vivian Marlo
Transcript and notes prepared by Badge #82827
Shared Media Folder Titled: IV, Mon., Sept. 16 9:08 p.m.

Video start.

V. Marlo sits with her back to a mirror. In it, the reflection of a window and the Marlos' apple orchard.

"How do I look? Oh god, forget that. Blah, okay," She gives her head a shake. "In super-serious mode. I thought we'd get busted for the first rebellion. Laymen don't think of actors as artists—laymen losers. But I am an artist. I just thought of our rebellion as performance art. And hello, silver lining: If we got caught, my face would have been on at least the local news. Stars have been discovered from less than that. But we didn't get caught and the rebellion worked. It's all anyone is talking about. People are losing their shit over who IV is and what they'll do next. The girls all think IV is a really hot guy, tattooed and bad boyish with a conscience, and the guys all think it's a girl in a full-body leather suit like a Marvel superhero. Seriously, no one is even mentioning homecoming, which is in less than two weeks. I have stolen homecoming's thunder."

She waves her free hand at the lens. "I kind of wish everybody knew IV was us. That would shut Amanda and her hyenas up for good. Forever. It would knock the stuffed animal hat right off her head. No one would ever buy that Amanda Gasbags and Witches Schultz had forgotten my name again."

She looks past the lens. "She would never get to treat me like I'm not as good as her. Everybody would not just know my name, they'd be saying it."

She focuses anew on the lens. "G, I, H, don't freak if you cheat and watch before graduation—and FYI, you'd be cheating baby diarrhea receptacles—I know we can't tell anyone. Duh, it's a secret society." She smiles. "I can't wait until the Slumber Fest reboot. IV is literally going to rule the school."

Video stop.

Retrieved from the cellular phone of Harrison Rocha
Transcript and notes prepared by Badge #82827
Shared Media Folder Titled: IV, Mon., Sept. 16, 10:31 p.m.

Video start.
H. Rocha sits on the floor with his back to his bed. Posters of musicians cover the wall. The shadows of a ceiling fan whirl across his face.

"Holy crap." He uses an excited whisper. "We got Bedford tossed out of school. We were a silent and unseen hand flicking that creep away. Mind blown." His free hand mimics an explosion. "I've read about revolutionary leaders and how they started out. Usually just normal teenagers who don't clean their rooms and worry about asking who they like out until one day something happens, like boom. Reality gets right in their faces. And then they know it: The world is a dick."

He tugs at his hair absently. "I used to like history because reading it was like reading fairy tales, but way more jacked up, like video games on 'roids. Even though I was reading about this world, I pictured the places as alien, ruled by trolls with really small gonads, nothing to do with me or Seven Hills.

"I guess that's only half false if you consider the guys who actually call the shots and push the buttons that end up blowing kids to pieces."

He frowns. "After my dad's attack, I stood over him as he was sleeping in his hospital bed and he looked way smaller than the giant who lifted me onto to his shoulders or the one I thought could keep us safe from anything."

His eyes close. "And that's when I realized that no one was going to do shit about my dad's attack. Whoever hurt him was going to get away with it."

His eyes open. "But the Order of IV is an unseen hand."
Video stop.

9

D o you see anyone?" Viv whispered. "My false lashes
are screwing up my vision."

"Move your head," I said. "No, the other way." I
peered through the windshield. "Maybe I see a group of—"

"*Shhhh,*" Graham hissed behind the wheel as a figure
streaked by on the far side of the shrub concealing the car.
He flicked the visor mirror shut, cutting off its glow.

"If my lash ends up looking like a caterpillar hanging
from my eyelid, I'm holding you responsible," Viv said, a
death threat implicit.

Darkness fleeced the hillside outside the car. For the last
fifteen minutes we'd listened to the slam of doors. Harry put
his lips right at my ear. "I hear something new."

"Voices?"

"Uh-uh. Music," he whispered. I shuddered at the warmth
of his breath on my neck and then, embarrassed, held my
hand to my ear to listen in an exaggerated way.

Viv twisted around. "That makes at least twenty kids

and music. Enough waiting. I'm ready to find my future boy-friend." Our Slumber Fest reboot had rekindled her plans.

"Five more minutes," Graham insisted.

Viv's hand was on the door lever. "I am physically incapable of being patient for one more second."

Graham gave a defeated sigh. "I guess fifteen minutes is enough to avoid suspicion." But Viv was already out of the car.

The tunnel burrowed into the mountain a quarter mile up, the spot burned into the darkness by a lit haze. Cars filled the dirt turnoff; every few seconds a new set of headlights swung like light saber beams across our path. Pine needles crunched under our shoes as we began hiking.

We converged on a herd of our classmates at the rail-road tracks. Viv was a gymnast balancing on the rail in plat-form espadrilles. She carried a shopping bag full of whimsical party hats, mostly unicorn horns; glow-in-the-dark wands and bracelets; and temporary tattoos. I doubted the gameness of our classmates, but Viv assured me, in a haughty tone, that it was the kind of paraphernalia *she heard* was found at raves.

Harry and Graham carried two sleeping bags each. I hugged a big camping thermos full of spiked hot cocoa. Bottles of cider clanked in Graham's backpack.

Our classmates carried lumpy armfuls of similar supplies. Shouts, squeals, and laughs chipped away at the night, making the dark seem less dense. Kids chanted "Slumber Fest."

Four days earlier, the Order of IV had unanimously voted to revive Slumber Fest.

Though Graham and Harry hadn't been enthusiastic about the tradition in the first place, they jumped at the chance to show our school that IV could dethrone a vice principal and follow it up with a party. Slumber Fest was student gov's domain. But those kids didn't even try to relocate or reschedule it. It was time we usurped their power, said Graham. So the Order of IV had taken what it wanted.

Invites were low-tech. The message simple:

> Slumber Fest
> Friday
> 9 p.m.
> The Ghost Tunnel
> Spread the word and BYOB
> -IV

Invites were slipped into only ten lockers belonging to reliably chatty social butterflies of the senior class. The fewer invites circulating, the less likely one would fall into the wrong hands. They were delivered Friday morning, giving the recipients twelve hours to spread the word and show up. The Ghost Tunnel was ideal: outside of town, up an isolated road, soundproof. Out of sight. A spooky enough reputation to make the invited gape with happy nerves.

Equipped with a crowbar, three hammers, and one ax, we had pried the boards from both ends of the tunnel late Thursday night. We arrived earlier than our classmates to the party and set up the bonfires and candles. We waited in

Graham's car until we could join the party with everyone else. Invited by the mysterious IV.

Thirty or forty kids crowded the opening of the tunnel. They were hanging back, hesitant to move deeper, a ruckus horde around the first bonfire. As our group and others arrived, kids broke off, loping for the next fire, then the next. There was the shadowy outline of an abandoned passenger car, still on its rails. Then a wall of black, the unseen stretch of tunnel running half a mile.

The smell of fire, earth, and wet stone evoked the sense of being in a castle. The stir of cold on my legs was the wind rushing through its never-ending corridors. The murkiness beyond the fires' reach was a good place for ghosts to haunt. The *IV*s painted in red on the walls wavered in the firelight; bloody warnings to invading clans. This was IV's territory.

I pressed deeper. More kids arrived, pushing to get inside, joining the ballad of greetings and calls for drinks.

Voices from yards away jumped over to you, like stones skipping on water because of the tunnel's acoustics. These tricks were why kids called it the Ghost Tunnel.

The keg was overwhelmed by clamoring cups. I wondered who'd lugged the cumbersome thing up, because we'd left only a few twenty-four packs of beer Harry got from a guy who ran a register at Hilltop Market.

Maisy Horowitz and Anna Spalding stood in the middle of a Twister board, taking neon-colored shots from mini paper cups.

"Hi, Izzie, Graham, Har. Drunken Twister later?" Maisy called.

"Maybe," I answered.

Maisy and Anna pointedly ignored Viv; they'd learned that Viv wasn't interested in smiles and casual hangouts with them. In the fifth grade, I found a list of names in the silver jewelry box on Viv's dresser when I was trying on her earrings. Two days later I figured out what those names had in common: Viv never forgot the kids who teased her in grade school. And though the teasing by everyone other than Amanda's lot ended years ago, and Maisy and Anna were nice now, their names somewhere near the bottom of that list, Viv's loopy childhood cursive kept me from getting close to them.

If not for Viv, our small group of friends would have been larger. But without Viv, it also would have been boring, joyless. Mostly we were outcasts of our own making.

The crowd parted for a multiheaded beer bong jouncing through like a desert queen carried on her man-servants' shoulders.

A few boys, underclassmen infiltrators, had Super Soakers, crowing each time their bolt of water hit an unsuspecting mark, until that mark was the back of the soccer team captain's head. He darted after their retreating figures.

On the other side of what had spontaneously become the dance floor, the four male members of the Brass Bandits greeted Graham with salutes. Near them was a group I always thought of as the poetry girls. They sat with notebooks open on their crossed legs and were seemingly unaware of the gyrations to their immediate right.

It was just as I'd hoped. All the groups at school were here—kids who didn't always get invited to parties, like me.

Viv drew me backward with a "Psst. I can't stomach their slamming. Not tonight."

It took me a moment to understand. "They're not doing slam poetry—are they?" I peeked back at the girls with journals.

"They look so . . . angry," Viv said. "They're repelling guys."

"They look like witches reading spells," I said. The girls with their middle parts; black, gauzy clothes; careless hair; and lace-up boots were taking turns reading from their journals. Their tongues beat their mouths to get the words out.

"Witchy does not equal hot," Viv said.

"It might," I said.

"Maybe to someone like . . . like Henry." Her glare darted to the Brass Bandit's trumpet player. He was nice, funny, tall, his T-shirt wasn't tucked in, and his acne flare-up of middle school was old news. I didn't see what would be so awful about a date with Henry. Graham was in the middle of talking to him and he didn't waste time on anyone who wasn't interesting.

"Where do we start Mission: Boyfriend?" I rubbed my hands in comic anticipation.

She narrowed her eyes at me. "You don't sound up for being wing woman."

"I'm ready," I said. I tossed my hair and gave Viv my most alluring smile, even as a strand caught me in the eye. I blinked to dislodge it. "Who are we checking out? Soccer players? Lacrosse? Younger men—I saw a couple sophomores."

A muscle by her mouth twitched. "No offense, but I'll probably be better alone. Just like being onstage." She leaned in conspiratorially to whisper, "Keep Graham and Harry away so they don't vagina block me." She extended her pinkie. I took it with mine.

I was relieved to be off the hook. Viv made a beeline for the soccer player manning the keg. Whatever being Viv's wing woman required, I did not have it. I'd been dragged along on double dates and to college parties. I had a talent for finding the one guy in the room more eager to talk NPR than make out.

Our last double date hadn't panned out. Viv liked hers, a college freshman, the son of one of Ina's friends. But mine, his roommate, told me I swung my mini golf club like a girl, snickered, and patted my head. Viv had told them both, on the middle of the course, that she'd started her period and we needed to leave.

"Look at her on the hunt," Harry said. He grinned beside me. "You up for an adventure?"

"We're supposed to keep Graham away from Viv so she looks single."

Harry nodded toward Graham. "He's debating video game consoles with Henry."

"Graham doesn't play video games."

"That's never stopped him before," he said with a comic crinkle of his lips.

I laughed. "So you're saying he'll be distracted for an hour."

"At least."

I swept an arm in front of us. "Lead the way."

Harry took off for the tracks. "You balance on that rail and I'll take this one," he said.

His clunky Vans padded one after the other on the left rail; Harry was unexpectedly lithe. My ankles wobbled. After a shambling ten feet, I couldn't stay up anymore. "You win," I said.

"Here." Harry hopped down and placed my hand on his shoulder. This time, leaning on Harry, I stayed up. "You win," he said softly. The air cooled as we walked deeper. Out of the corner of my eye I watched Harry nod and smile hello to people. I would lose sight of his eyes in between the bonfires, and when they appeared again, on me, I'd look away. My fingertips noted the rises and dips of the shape of him. They couldn't help it. His shoulder was unexplored territory under my increasingly warm hand. The music faded and the sigh of the wind became a never-ending song, like the ocean.

I was squeezing Harry's shoulder and staring at the silver run disappearing under my shoes when he stopped abruptly. We'd reached the abandoned passenger car. Trent and Campbell were sitting, lackadaisically swinging their legs between its guardrails, passing a joint back and forth. I dropped off the rail and away from Harry.

"'Sup," Trent said.

I gave an unenthusiastic tip of my hand. Trent wasn't as horrible as Conner; that wasn't saying much. Campbell held the joint out to us.

"No thanks," I said.

Trent squinted. "You guys puss out on a suicide pact?" he asked, indicating the big rectangular bandage on my inner wrist. Despite five scrubbings and one application of nail polish remover, the *IV* Viv drew was still a shadow. Harry had a lime-green bandage in the identical spot.

I forgot to be intimated by a loudmouth like Trent.

"How'd you know? We got one wrist in and realized that if we were dead, we'd never get to see you again. Guess we owe you our lives." I could hardly breathe at my nerve. The tunnel, the passenger car, Slumber Fest, the fires burning at our backs, the night—it all belonged to us.

Trent held his fist up and pretended to pull a crank with his other hand as he slowly raised his middle finger.

"Don't be a dick, man," Campbell said, knocking Trent's shoulder. To us, "Chill party, huh? How crazy is the graffiti? All the *IV*s." His beanie cut off his eyebrows.

"The chillest," Harry responded, rocking back on his heels.

Campbell smiled amiably, undeterred. "Bonkers about Principal Harper's car. IV knows how to party."

"What about Harper's car?" I asked sharply.

"Oh man, you didn't hear? IV tagged his wagon. A black *IV* across his driver's-side door. People are saying it must have happened at lunch, but they don't really know."

"Harper's such a bitch," Trent muttered.

"You start Ms. Ives's research essay?" Campbell had moved on to asking me, but my eyes were intent on Harry's profile. I focused on his expression of stone, willing mine to be as withholding. A *IV* painted on the principal's car. Not painted by us. I didn't even need to ask. Graham, Viv, and Harry wouldn't be so reckless as to tag a car in the middle of the day.

"I'm writing it on medicine in Africa. You?" I heard myself say to Campbell as he smiled patiently.

"Law and justice." And then he said something else I didn't hear because Harry swallowed, the knot of his throat bobbing, and I felt a wild yip rising up from my belly. A nervous yip; a triumphant one; both. We'd inspired a copycat.

Trent exhaled, coughing out smoke in bursts. "C'mon, dude," he said to Campbell. "They're obviously here for the privacy." He jerked a thumb at the passenger car. "To bone."

Trent swung under the rail to the ground. "And here I thought you guys were into goats and shit." He scattered rocks as he stalked in the direction we'd come from. Ina had invited our entire fifth-grade class to a birthday party for Viv. Since then, Amanda had spread rumors about the barn and what the four of us might be getting up to inside of it.

Campbell went after Trent, pausing for a moment by us. "See you in class, Izzie. Bye, dude."

I wanted to crack a joke at Trent's expense, but Harry was uneasily reordering his hands—front pockets to back pockets to hanging at his sides. The boning comment hadn't bothered me, but Harry's obvious discomfort made feel wrong for it. Like I'd crossed a line.

"Want to head back?" I offered. "Go tell Graham and Viv about Harper's car?"

"Someone probably already told them." He scratched

the back of his head. "Unless you want to head back."

"Not really." I started up the metal risers to the car. "I hiked here once, right after Goldilocks but before the tunnel was closed up."

"Goldilocks?" he asked.

I tripped on a metal stair. I'd never called the dead girl Goldilocks aloud. "That's what I named the girl from the rock because that cop asked us if we'd noticed stolen food or—"

"Or signs she was camping or sleeping in the barn. Goldilocks," he said. "Makes sense."

I hesitated where the compartment door should have been, its old brass hinges dangling purposelessly. I spun to face Harry and gave a stiff bow. "Good afternoon, sir. Ticket, please."

Harry made a show of retrieving his imaginary ticket from his pocket, smoothing its wrinkles on his thigh, and handing it over. I held it up to catch the firelight. Pretended to examine it. "You forgot yours," he said, waving his pinched fingers, grinning. I laughed, falling out of character. He offered me his arm. My hand slid into the crook of his elbow.

The passenger car was dark, only a few candles balanced on the window frames and in the eaves of the luggage compartment. The red of the seats and the purple of the glass-littered carpet richened as my eyes adjusted. The candle flames beat at the air we'd carried in, making the whole car seem alive, like the passengers had just disembarked, their shadows still with us.

"I think Viv decorated in here to have somewhere to bring a guy," I said.

"Operation Boyfriend Hunt," he said with a comical twist. "It was nice of you to think of doing Slumber Fest for her."

I thumped the head of a seat to my right and imagined a plume of dust rising. "I didn't. I wanted Slumber Fest for myself."

His brows tugged together.

"The Order went from being a game to making us powerful," I explained. "You are powerful." A doubtful flare of his nostrils. "I'm powerful. We even inspired a copycat. Before, I thought of myself as weird Icky, one of those four loners, the plain one who actually laughs at teachers' jokes, too young to do anything about her parents' fighting. I wasn't powerful because power was tied to stuff you can see."

"Like money," Harry whispered.

"Yeah, or age, gender, race, looks. But now it's like power can be invisible too. A breeze you capture and aim to send people in any direction. The direction I wanted was Slumber Fest. Here." I waved a hand, noted that it was shaking. There was too much eye contact and spilling of guts. "I felt like a joke before the Bedford flyers."

"You've never been a joke," he said.

"Thanks, but you're not exactly impartial, friend." I half turned to show him a grateful smile anyway. "So how come you went along with the Slumber Fest reboot?"

He shrugged. "I don't have a big, complex reason. You wanted to. Viv wanted to. Graham was going on about usurping student gov's domain. It wasn't going to hurt anyone."

With a twist of my stomach, I was glad to be alone with

Harry. Harry, who wanted to make his friends happy. There was the delicate tinkle of breaking glass crunching under my sneakers. I brushed the litter from two of the seats and took the one by the window.

"Tell me about coming here after Goldilocks," he said.

I breathed in and out. It was about time I confessed. That it would be to Harry made the words neatly queue up in my head. "You remember the cop who came out to the meteorite?"

"Denton. He's the police chief now."

I nodded. "He wanted to know if I'd seen Goldilocks before, and I was so upset I didn't know. We went up on the rock again, to look. I said that the girl was like me because . . . because she was. Her purple bra looked like it matched one I'd been begging my mom for. She had a heart tattoo on her ankle—I loved doodling hearts. And Denton goes, *She's nothing like you, just a runaway asking for it.*"

A parenthesis formed between Harry's eyebrows.

"He was a police officer. Don't they always tell the truth? If he said it was the girl's fault, wasn't it?"

"Hell no," Harry said.

"He thought Goldilocks was a runaway. You remember how there'd be girls on the beach? Girls who weren't from here. And they looked like they'd been camping, partying outside. Viv said she heard that teenagers who came to surf or party on the beach camped up here. I thought maybe Goldilocks did. I had to wait a couple of days, but the first chance I got, I hiked here."

"It could have been dangerous," Harry said.

"Could have been. But she was on our rock, Har. Before Goldilocks, Viv and I used to take turns laying on the rock. Pretending to be Sleeping Beauty. Just a dumb game. Whoever wasn't Sleeping Beauty was the prince and the prince had to kiss his princess to wake her up. But sometimes we'd play dead, refuse to open our eyes." My cheeks burned hot. "Finding Goldilocks didn't feel random. After the scientists left and we understood that our rock was a meteorite from space, we were obsessed. Its mystery became a part of us. It was there in our choice of books. It shaped our adventures. We played on the rock a lot before, but it became our epicenter. Camping and stargazing. Leaving messages in chalk so that if aliens were looking down on us, they'd see we wanted to talk to them." I laughed self-consciously. "Goldilocks on our rock—it felt like a message. It was like the meteorite drew her in. Like we did. Like we tempted the universe into sending us an actual mystery. And none of the people who were supposed to help were doing anything."

His hand cupped my knee. "So you did something. What'd you find?"

"A few girls. Teenagers or a little older. At first they let me sit by the fire. Even offered me a puff on one of their cigarettes. Laughed because of how much I coughed. I brought up the dead girl—God, I tried to do it casually. But their expressions just slammed shut. The one with the cigarette came in here. I followed. Her eyes were red. High or crying." I looked across the aisle. There she was again, balled up in a seat, blond hair uncombed, dirty bare feet. "I asked if she knew Goldilocks. Described her."

"Did she?"

"Sort of. They were all camping here, surfing, but they didn't *know* her know her, other than sleeping in the tunnel for a couple weeks. Goldilocks left for the gas station by the freeway one night. If she wanted a snack it would have been the only place open late. Blondie never saw her come back. I got excited and said we should tell the police. I'd call them and they'd talk to her. She lunged and pinned me." I pointed to the wall. "It was a pocketknife or glass." I raised my sleeve to reveal a fine white line, three inches long, on my shoulder. "She said she knew where I lived. Bullshit, but I was gullible. She said I needed to shut up or she'd make it worse than a scratch on the shoulder."

The girl, she'd pounced like a wild animal, desperation curling her lips away from her yellowed teeth. The rattle of a growl in her throat as her blade seared my skin.

Once the afternoon in the tunnel tumbled free, it dug its elbow into my chest, stung the scar on my shoulder. My only cigarette burned my lungs.

"You were twelve. You were scared. It's okay that you didn't tell anyone," Harry said.

I'd run through the tunnel, grasping my shoulder. The girls had returned to the fire. I sprinted by like a kid escaping a monster's den.

"She was more scared than me," I said. "They all were. Of the cops. Of everyone, maybe. Just a bunch of girls with

nowhere to go that was their own. Not like us. Nice parents and the barn and one another. I was too stupid to even
ask Blondie if she knew the girl's real name." We sat without
talking for a time. I listened to Harry's steady breath; with
each one, I leaned a hair closer to him. "Harry? How do you
handle not knowing who hurt your dad?"

"I don't. Handle it, that is." He ran his hands over his
head, hooked them on the back of his neck, and sighed
heavily. "The police failed—didn't even try, like with Goldilocks. My dad walks with a cane and everyone acts like it
was a practical joke gone wrong. Bunch of kids on campus screwing around. Unintentional. It wasn't." Harry's dad
spent over a year in physical therapy, but the limp would be
permanent. I knew Harry thought about the attack often,
though he didn't let on.

I felt a dark mood crushing us both. I sprang out of the
seat. "C'mon, let's go find fun. Let's have our Slumber Fest."

"Sure." He stood and followed me out of the passenger
car, but the weight of what we both knew didn't lift. I was
suddenly wary of us sleeping in the tunnel. What did we
know about the people who could be drawn in by the smoke
and light of bonfires? Really, what did anyone know about
anyone? Because even though I was twelve when I learned
that Goldilocks had been camping in the tunnel, I wasn't
too young to understand its significance. The true weight of
that afternoon laid in the realization that she'd been walking around my hometown when she met her end. It was the
same sort of knowledge Harry had to live with, accepting

that someone had hurt his father, a someone who Harry likely bagged groceries for.

The police and the mayor were adamant that one of two scenarios had played out. I knew them both to be impossible. Goldilocks wasn't killed in another town. Over the hills. Some depressing place. Inland. She wasn't dumped on the rock because her killer was trying to leave her far from his home—*his* because, come on, I was a realist. And I sat with those girls. Took a puff off their cigarette. I didn't believe it was fear of getting caught for hurting Goldilocks that had Blondie trembling as she cut me. She wasn't a killer; just a cornered girl. Goldilocks wasn't the victim of some band of lost girls and their twisted games.

She was right here, on our side of the hills, surfing by day, soaking up the sun on our beach, camping by night in an abandoned tunnel, crowding around a bonfire. A girl out for adventure. She was exactly like me.

10

Not all secrets liberate the teller.

By sharing with Harry that afternoon in the Ghost Tunnel, I had excavated memories that had been buried. Freed, they hovered over me, just like Goldilocks's death had for weeks after finding her. They were storm clouds reminding me that life wasn't a grand game. Death was present. Possible.

The rock had taught us many things. Its first lesson was to ask questions; wonder about mysteries; look to the sky. Its second lesson, taught by Goldilocks, was that mysteries are not always magical, they're terrifying.

Graham, Viv, and I had planned to submit college applications early in the autumn, right after they became available. We even convinced Harry that he might as well apply to his dream schools, in case any of them offered the financial aid he needed. This gutless enthusiasm to be good little girls and boys getting into college early had since worn away for me. I wanted to go, still; I just couldn't focus on the task long enough to start my applications.

When, on the Sunday after Slumber Fest, the four of us sat on the floor of my bedroom, all supposedly busy on our personal statements, I searched for Goldilocks.

This habit of mine was old. Its roots grew around that secret afternoon spent in the Ghost Tunnel. It was also not the only habit to sprout from that day.

When I'd arrived home that afternoon from the tunnel, T-shirt stuck in my congealing blood, I sketched Goldilocks from memory. I gagged on the metallic stink in my mouth from running too hard, too far. My nose ran and dripped. The pressure built in my throat as I tried to catch my breath. Her face took form at the tip of my pencil.

At the time it was a compulsion. *Draw her. Look at her face. She was real.* For the few days between my visit to the tunnel and when the photo of the crime scene was finally published in the newspaper, those drawings had purpose. I compared her face with the others. They made my search possible.

My laptop became a window into the world of lost girls.

For months, almost a year, I clicked through the photos of missing girls in the privacy of my bedroom. The authorities in most places made it easy. Photos were uploaded into searchable databases immediately. Those cops wanted their cases solved.

It was a simple task: appraise one, tap for the next. Seventh grade sped by. Luke McHale never invited Viv to join his lunch circle of eighth graders. I thought a lot about Denton saying the girl was asking for it. The only person I'd identified with a connection to the girl had given me an ugly scar on my shoulder. Maybe Goldilocks was the same kind of girl? One who'd lose it and cut you?

I knew even as a stupid little kid that no girl, not even one who cuts you, deserves to be hurt, dead, given wings.

Nothing much happened to make me stop checking the missing person websites. A year passed. If anyone was looking for her, wouldn't they have posted a picture by then? I gave up.

But there, more than five years later, in my bedroom, I started sorting through gone girls again. I reverted to my old habit as Graham, Viv, and Harry typed their personal statements. Presumably. It's easier to imagine them having their own secret crusades more and more.

All that clicking filled me with the conviction that I needed to do something for Goldilocks. The Order of IV needed to. But what? It was too late to save her life.

In third period on the Wednesday after Slumber Fest, Mr. Novak was writing out the discussion topics on the whiteboard, disregarding the laptop and projection screen to eat up class time. I was restless and craned around to see what Viv was up to. She was midwave and gave an exasperated eye roll. She pointed at a note being passed from Jess to Campbell, who sat directly behind me.

Campbell continued chatting and facing Jess as he tossed the note in my direction. I caught it before it hit the floor. A text would have been too ordinary for Viv.

I started to open the note. I stopped, flipped it around, and saw the black, bold *IV* drawn on the outer flap. My hand clapped over it. Pointless. Anyone who passed it along might have noticed the symbol. Behind Jess was Conner, then Gabby in front of Viv. Any one of them might have noticed the *IV*.

I slowly peeled back the folds, checking that there were no more insignias. Paranoia or eyes on me needled my scalp. The note was a single line in Viv's cursive, a heart dotting the *I*.

We should perform Saturday's ritual naked.

My cheeks were hot as I crumpled the paper into a ball. Four kids between Viv and me. Four who might have seen the *IV* or lifted a flap and spied "ritual" or "naked." The Order of IV was a secret society; its members staying secret was the whole damn point.

It grew soggy in my hand as I waited for class to end.

Viv spun the dial of her locker; if she noticed that I wasn't opening mine or that I was frowning at her profile, she didn't let on. She peered into the pink-framed mirror on the interior door and dashed away the mascara in the corners of her eyes. Auditions for the fall performance were scheduled for lunch. Viv wore a white dress that looked like it had been magically enlarged from a doll's wardrobe, violet Mary Janes, and white thigh-high stockings. Dressed to be memorable. Silly, she thought she needed the clothes. Amanda had given up on jeering over Viv's clothing once it became apparent that there were more cutting insults;

in her wardrobe choices, Viv couldn't be made to feel self-conscious.

She was trading the books from her bag for those in her locker by the time I whispered, "Why did you put a *IV* on the outside of your note?"

Her gold eyeshadow caught the light as she shot me a conspirator's smile. "Official Order business."

Conner was ten or so lockers down. He was standing with Rachel Fogarty, one of Amanda's best friends. Her lips were moving in a constant stream, but he was swiping at his cell, not even pretending to listen.

I controlled my volume. "People could have seen the *IV* on the note. Someone could put it together."

"Calm down already," Viv said loudly. "No one pays attention to us, remember?" Her arms flung open. "No one knows what we've done."

A girl walked smack into Viv's arm and muttered "Excuse you" as she continued by.

Viv smiled bitterly. "We are invisible."

"We won't be if you clue people in to you-know-what."

"Why do all of you think it would suck so bad actually getting credit?"

I winced and her eyes went round. "I'm not serious, okay? C'mon, Izzie." She stomped her foot playfully. "Resist making a little thing into a major thing." She went back to switching out her textbooks.

I was tongue-tied for a time. "I read your note" is what I finally coughed up.

No response as she grabbed a tissue and soundlessly blew her nose.

"I don't think doing our ritual naked is a good idea."

She gave me a brief sideways look away from her reflection applying lip gloss. "Why? Are you worried the boys won't be able to control themselves once they see your C-cups?"

I took an instinctive step back. "I just don't want to be naked in front of them. I don't want to see Graham or Harry naked either."

Moodiness flashed across her face. "You're sure about that? Not even Harry?"

Over Viv's shoulder Conner glanced in our direction. Rachel was still prattling on. "What? No," I said, motioning for her to keep it down.

Her hands went up in surrender; I saw the *IV* black and bold on the inside of her wrist. It had been faded and light the day before, hadn't it? She touched my arm and said, "I'm not saying you're lying. Just . . . remember when you swore you thought Luke McHale was a D-bag, but you stared at him more than I did?"

"Harry and Luke McHale aren't anything alike," I said.

"Sometimes you're in denial about who you think is hot. Seeing Harry naked wouldn't make you puke. You can admit it to me." Her nails rapped against the metal face of her locker. "I'm only trying to make our ritual memory-worthy."

"It will be, because we're doing it together."

She tossed her hair off her shoulder and winked at me. "Then we'll do it in our underwear."

"Do what in our underwear?" I asked, but Viv was already weaving through our classmates as the warning bell sounded. Conner was gone from Rachel's locker. I couldn't say how much he overheard or when he'd left or even if either point mattered.

Viv auditioned for *Antigone* at lunch. Harry, Graham, and I were on our patch of lawn. I was reclined, arms crossed over my face. I'd been cold since Viv and my fight—was it a fight? The sun was warming away its effects. I had over-reacted to the note. Viv was nervous for her audition and snappy because she was disappointed she hadn't left Slumber Fest with a boyfriend. I should have wished her luck for the audition.

"Why are you giving us the silent treatment?" Graham asked, knocking my foot with his. I propped up on my elbows and blinked into a blizzard of afternoon light. Gradually the sky became a blue bowl and Harry's and Graham's features materialized. My eyes lingered on Harry for longer. I mean, objectively speaking, he was attractive.

Graham gave an exasperated flourish of his hands for my attention. "The ritual, the rebellions, the secrets—it isn't enough. There needs to be a history."

"We have history," Harry said, hardly looking up from his laptop—probably busy drafting an article for the news blog. "On the night Slumber Fest was canceled, Izzie leaped up and said 'Let's start a secret society.'"

"That's weak and unimaginative," Graham complained. "You're supposed to be the best writer among us."

"That's how it happened," I responded.

"Oh," Harry said, popping a grape into his mouth and storing it in his cheek like a hamster, "he wants a revisionist's history."

"All history is revisionist," Graham said contemptuously, "but what I have in mind is more of a fact-and-fiction sandwich. The pieces are here"—his hands circled the air—"right in front of us. We just need to put them together as the story of our history."

"Stories are meant to be told. We aren't telling anyone about the Order," I said, mouthing the last, sensitive word.

"Do you know the difference between a meteor, a meteorite, and a meteoroid?" Graham asked. I swiveled my head, not committing to a nod or a shake—I wasn't sure what I knew.

"Communism," I said, flapping my hand for Harry to give me a cluster of grapes. It had been our language for *share that* or *give me some* since we'd all gone through a Russia phase sophomore year. The month had involved faux fur hats and Russian plays for Viv, long Russian novels for me, vodka and rants for Graham, and ruminating over revolutions for Harry.

Harry closed the lid of his laptop and answered Graham. "A meteoroid is a small particle from an asteroid orbiting the sun. It becomes a meteor if you can spot its flash from Earth. A meteor that enters Earth's atmosphere and hits Earth's surface is a meteorite."

"Our rock is a meteorite," Graham said, nodding. "It made contact. It's here. Permanent. A meteor's light is beautiful but doesn't last. That's what our Order is now: a flash of light, a pretty miracle, sure, but one that ends unless we let it hit

Earth. Just slam right into us." He pounded a fist on the grass. "We have to give it a story so it has legs, so it can stomp. It needs a story and we need to believe in it."

Harry flicked a potato chip crumb from his sleeve, offered me the bag, and looked dubiously at Graham. "I didn't know USB had a major in poetic bullshit."

Graham tented his hands and touched them to his lips. "I want to fool us into believing. It was a rush pulling off Bedford, but it felt crazier up on the rock afterward. It felt like we were tapping into something cosmic but fundamental. I want more of that."

"Okay," I said. "Go ahead, then."

"Fool away," Harry chorused, but Graham's attention had diverted to a couple of passing figures.

"Did you guys see that?" His eyes popped from his head. "Jess Clarkson just walked by and—"

"I know, *you want to be balls deep in her*," I mimicked Graham's deep tone.

Harry laughed with his head back and his mouth open.

Graham cracked a smile. "No, you little pervert. We shared this *look*."

"Okay, now back to ritual altars and the kind of pretend we buy," Harry said.

"I'm serious. Jess and I shared a moment." He yanked a book out of his bag and hunched over it, muttering, "You skeptics are going to owe me an extra-large pizza once she asks me out."

I craned past Harry and Graham. Jess and Rachel were

taking a detour through the land of misfits. They usually ate by the flagpole with Amanda and the boy band.

Jess hung back as Rachel's messy bun disappeared into the central corridor. Our eyes met. I didn't smile, nor did I stick my tongue out like I would have at Amanda. Amanda's campaign against Viv was usually a one-woman show; Jess was too wrapped up in appearing blasé about the world to participate; Rachel was too eager to be considered popular to go after Viv with much gusto. But Jess was paying attention now, looking curious. I wasn't used to people appearing curious about us. I collapsed back to the grass and pretended to be asleep for the rest of lunch.

The uneasiness didn't vanish until we were in the barn that evening and Viv performed her monologue for us. Graham pretended to be reading a book through her recitation. His eyes kept skipping up from the pages of *Ritual Ecstasy* as Viv squirmed on the ground, clawed at her wrists, and yanked on the pink wig she was wearing. Harry was on his feet giving her a standing ovation at her last line, "Good night, sweet ladies, good night!"

"Bravo," Graham called, clapping a hand against the hardcover of his book.

I snapped a Polaroid and watched a shadow become Viv, frozen in curtsey, pink hair gleaming. I smiled from the likeness to the real thing still curtseying side to side.

The cushions gave as she nuzzled beside me with a dreamy sigh, her wig tickling my cheek. She twined her pinkie finger with mine. "I shouldn't have sent the note in class."

My finger tightened on hers. "I forgot to tell you good luck before your audition."

Then she was up on her feet commanding our attention again. She pulled the Mistress of Rebellion and Secrets down from her pedestal atop the cupboard where we kept a mish-mash of board games.

Viv tossed her pink wig away. It landed at the foot of a side table we'd found at a flea market in Los Angeles last summer. I'd loved it instantly. Its four legs were carved to look like those of a griffon. I didn't have the hundred bucks it cost, though, so Viv snuck back that afternoon and traded the earrings she was wearing, which her grandmother had given her. She showed up with the table at the car. Viv was like that, full of surprises and sacrifices.

She said, "I've choreographed the ultimate ceremony for the blood moon. It's going to be otherworldly."

"Actually, the phenomenon is entirely terrestrial," Graham said.

"He means that the full moon is going to be eclipsed by Earth's shadow and that's why the moon will appear to have a reddish hint," I translated.

She play-pouted. "Har, promise you're not going to get all science-y on me tomorrow night too."

Harry paused texting on his cell to say, "Never."

"What's up with the ceremony?" Graham asked Viv.

But her attention was lingering on Harry. "I won't say until Harry tells us who he's texting. Do you have *another* secret girlfriend?"

Harry's head snapped up, a lock of his hair doing a slow-motion lift from his forehead. My stomach did a flip. *He has another secret girlfriend.* "I'm texting with Simon," he answered. "My mom's having a ladies' night."

"Where's your dad?" Viv asked.

"He's home. But he can't walk or stand much. Simon ordered pizza and they're watching a show about robots." Harry's voice gave away nothing but his expression was weary.

"Oh," Viv said, dismayed. "I thought your dad was better. Physical therapy and all."

"It helps. It just takes time because the leg was—" Harry's voice cracked.

"It was broken in more than one place, many fractures," Graham continued for him. "There was nerve damage, too, and nerves don't heal as easily as bones. The pain went away and then got worse a few weeks ago, which could be because the nerves healed with scar tissue."

Harry's features had gone runny. I felt a rush of affection for Graham. For all his bullshit and storytelling, he was capable of being kind in ways so subtle you might not notice him saving you.

"He needs another surgery," Harry said.

A divot formed between Graham's brows. "More physical therapy after that, probably. The nerves will heal. He'll get better." He gave a decided nod, which Harry mirrored and looked a little less lost for it.

I wasn't like Graham. When I was overwhelmed, emotions swarming me, I didn't know what to say to make things better. I wanted to cry, and since that wouldn't help, I changed the subject. "Tell us about tomorrow night, Viv."

She whisked our attention away, expert at being a diversion. She waved the Mistress and said, "She's who we're celebrating tomorrow night. She inspired Izzie."

My heart beat gradually faster as I listened to Viv describe our blood moon ritual. There would be ceremonial costume, a fire, a chant, a dagger, a blood offering, and we'd end telling secrets. It had all the elements of a grand performance, and Viv the perfect director.

The more I considered it, the more I was certain that Graham was right. Rebellions alone weren't going to keep us close forever. We needed to let the meteorite enter our atmosphere, to hit us. I'm not saying that the four of us would forget that our idol came from Graham's mom or that our Order was made up. We just needed to suspend disbelief.

Did I think about it in precisely those terms at the time? Can't say.

I wanted to keep being more than Izzie. I wanted to extinguish the helplessness returning inside of me the more I thought of Goldilocks. I wanted my voice to count. I wanted to believe in what was bigger than me, which is not such a terrible thing, except when others are hurt by what you invent. We were together, tripping with words and laughter, giddy to play mad scientists to our monster.

This is how I didn't notice the beginning of the end.

11

We formed a circle on the rock, the four of us and the Mistress of Rebellion and Secrets. At the center, in the spot Goldilocks had rested, we built up a pyre of sticks. The full moon was a single white eye peering down, unblinking.

It was past eleven, a few minutes before the eclipse. We were mostly trading uncertain glances. Everyone showed too much eye white and apple-red cheeks. We knew the way to begin; we'd outlined the steps, but none of us, especially paralyzed with awkwardness over what was to come, was exactly certain how to set the thing in motion.

Viv had detailed the Order's ceremonial rites after she had performed her monologue the previous night. Maybe Ophelia's madness hadn't released Viv, because her descriptions had come in swollen gushes. She wound her fingers in the hem of her white dress, her brown irises overtaken by coal-black pupils. The boys nodded their heads, mesmerized. Of course they were; boys are always for, as Viv put it, *a ritual disrobing*.

We came dressed in white, including the underthings we planned to strip to. Graham clutched an emerald bottle of absinthe, a green fairy with hair like Medusa's snakes on the label.

"It's the real stuff, straight out of Amsterdam from when my mom smoked pot and complained about capitalism while she pretended she wasn't a bougie undergrad from Boston," Graham informed us. "It'll alter our states of consciousness." A dangerous grin revealed his eagerness. "It'll fuck us up."

At the present moment he was knocking the bottle against his side, looking furtively at Harry, who held an actual dagger—a bronze-handled antique from Graham's trip to Jordan. Harry's bottom lip was between his teeth and the dagger looked about to clatter to the rock. Even Viv was a statue.

I glanced to the moon. The sky was leeching into it; Earth's shadow beginning to encroach. Someone needed to begin or the eclipse would end before we were done.

I shook my hands out at my sides and picked up the lighter fluid and the box of matches. I squirted the liquid over the sticks. The harsh odor stung my eyes. I discarded the bottle. I met Viv, Graham, and Harry's stares, and with a solemn nod struck the match and tossed it into the sticks. The fire caught and spread, flames unspooling at the sky with the look of bolts of glittery fabric.

The four of us made an involuntary "Whoa."

Everything moved. The flames and their shadows ran over the surface of the rock, giving the illusion that we were wading in running water. The tops of the apple trees feathered to one side, the wind playing with the orchard and Viv's hair, which looked like a lion's mane. "And now we shed our secrets and lies with our clothes," Viv said in a velvety voice.

From afar we were four white smudges as we undressed. My hands shook as I pulled my sweater above my head and my ankles from my shorts. The night air smacked my skin.

Graham took the first sip of absinthe and passed it to Viv. Her laugh was cut off by a hiccup. Harry coughed, his eyes pinkening as they blinked at the burn. I was folded in a thick fur coat after the bottle's third round. The rock was buzzing under my feet, tapping out a message.

"The stars are on fire," Viv said, gaping at the sky.

The shadow slid over the last sliver of moon. The black apple turned strawberry. I stared. I opened my mouth to swallow it. Instead I howled. Silly and shrill, then wolfish. The others joined in. I stopped to catch my breath as the howling gave way to the chant we'd memorized the night before.

> Blood runs north, east, south, west.
> Rebellions burn summer, winter, fall, spring.
> Secrets bind north, east, south, west.

Each repetition came faster until the words were lobbed from our mouths, breaking apart as they hit the rock. The shine of the red moon gave Viv a halo. Fire danced on Graham's lenses. My eyes slid to Harry, from crescent mouth to chest, to flat stomach to wrinkled white boxers. He watched me watch him. I smiled. He smiled.

Viv came forward. Harry placed the dagger in her open hand. She held its glinting tip to the moon. "The Order of IV offers a blood sacrifice to the Mistress."

Vaguely I thought *too late*, though Goldilocks's blood hadn't seeped onto the rock. She was posed, a dead ornament, left to the elements with vicious indifference.

Viv pierced the flames with the dagger. We'd agreed to prick our fingers, so when Viv dragged the tip along her palm, I gasped. She cut a diagonal line.

"Blood for the Mistress's blood moon," Viv said with feral delight. She bent and left a smear of blood on the rock.

She passed the knife to Graham, who stuck the blade into the flames. He let out a sharp exhalation when it broke skin and left a smaller black smear by his feet. "For the Mistress."

Harry went next. Trickles of sweat or absinthe—the bottle was being passed again—slid between my breasts. I held my breath as Harry brought the dagger to his palm. His head was cocked to the side, his thin, long nose casting a shadow on his cheek as the dagger moved. "For the Mistress," he murmured.

My knees went springy as I accepted the knife. It required more pressure than I anticipated. I tried to blink away the tears as I knelt and wiped the blood on the rock, tiny particles of stone and dirt digging into the wound, bringing on a new wave of tears. "For the Mistress."

The green bottle traveled. There was blood on the glass

and I was light-headed with relief that the cutting was over. Graham took the final gulp and hurled the bottle out into the darkness. I never heard it break.

Viv was motionless except for her fingers swirling at her sides, like she was stirring the heat rippling off the fire. She'd worn a white lace bra transparent enough to hint at nipple.

She was the first to start pirouetting. It was stupid and dangerous to be drunk and dizzy between a bonfire and a drop. But we were bigger than four kids who could be injured. We were eddying, swirling human pinwheels.

I twirled and the fire zigzagged. Our laughs funneled into the sky. We switched off gravity to float for a time. Eventually someone caught me by the arm. I came to a stop against a chest harder than my own. Graham had removed his glasses and from that angle I saw he'd smeared blood on the underside of his chin. I unsteadily tried to wipe it away.

"Time to offer our secrets to the Mistress," Graham's voice rumbled from his chest to my ear. Viv and Harry were holding hands and leaning away from each other, spinning and giggling. We had agreed to share secrets after each rebellion. But Slumber Fest's secret had been postponed to be shared under the blood moon. Another offering.

I sat in front of Graham, his bent legs my recliner. Viv was poised and glowing. Harry was on his back, arms crossed and supporting his head. I imagined he was counting the stars. He said to no one in particular, "The twinkly bits are just distractions from seeing what else is up there." No, not counting the stars. Harry was trying to decipher the dark.

Graham said, "Me first."

My head was going haywire. Viv was laughing for no apparent reason, and each laugh was an invisible finger drawing hearts on my arms. Graham's knees were hot on my shoulder blades. I shifted and the hooks of my bra bit into my spine and his knee. My bra was touching Graham. I wondered if he wanted to reach up and unhook it. Sometimes you imagine things you don't even want.

"Tell us all your secrets," Viv said in a placeless accent.

Harry did a slow clap. "Man up," he shouted. He and Viv giggled.

"You're all yammed off too much absinthe," Graham said. "You all know that I'm a kid of divorce," he continued drily. "My dad doesn't call or e-mail or text. He's never sent me a birthday card, not even a shitty free e-card. So I, uh, well . . ." I couldn't see it but was dead certain he was smiling mischievously. "Last November sixteenth he wasn't going to get away with it again. I looked up his address online. You guys know that website Busy Bunny? The one you post small jobs that you're willing to pay people to do? There's a website that's similar but for minorly illegal stuff. I hired someone to take a dump on my father's porch"—a beat—"every day for the week of my seventeenth birthday."

"Evil genius," I said as Viv cried, "That's the most disgustingest, grossest—ugh, I freaking heart you."

"Seven hot, steaming dumps are too good for him," Harry said. He was trying to sit cross-legged but wasn't flexible enough. "I can't outdo that. Let me think. Ummmm."

He twiddled his fingers on his chin. "Okay. Here's my most embarrassing moment that *almost* no one knows about and will instantly be forgotten by you guys. I can't believe I'm gonna tell you this." He shook his head at himself. "Remember that really lifelike fairy statue my mom has in our backyard? The *topless* fairy my mom called *whimsically erotic* when she brought it home?"

"Oh yeah," Viv said. "I used to stare at her boobs wishing mine would grow as big."

"You're not the only one," Graham deadpanned.

"Hey." Viv flung her hand in Graham's direction.

"Let me finish. Your chest *did* get as hefty as Harry's mother's topless fairy statue."

"You did not just call a part of me hefty."

"Let Harry finish," I shouted.

"Thank you." Harry bowed his head. "I was twelve, yeah? And there were boobs in my yard. My mom caught me touching them and touching—fill in the blank."

"Twelve-year-old Harry was jerking it while fondling a garden gnome," Graham stated.

"She was a garden fairy." Harry covered his face.

I squealed.

"Same difference," Graham said.

"This would make the best comedic monologue ever." Viv sighed.

"Viv," Harry said sternly.

"It would. Me now." She straightened the lace on one of her bra cups and rested a finger on her bottom lip. Her face saddened. "I've never been kissed," she said. "By a boy, I mean, because Izzie and I used to play this Sleeping Beauty game."

"Shit," Graham said.

Harry crawled over to pat her on the shoulder.

I stared. Viv kissed a guy named Dylan during our only year at sleepaway camp together. She called him the Labrador because of the bouncy way he followed her around. Her second kiss, and first official boyfriend, was at drama camp the next summer. There were games of spin the bottle after that. Rushed makeouts in the woods behind the cabins.

"Seventeen and never been kissed," she said. She looked apart from us, as though she had stepped onstage. I swallowed. Why was Viv lying? Maybe in a way she never had been kissed? She'd never gone out with anyone at school. She felt underappreciated outside of her theater life. Not by me. Or perhaps my first instinct, that the three of us had become the audience, was correct. It didn't matter to me in the moment.

"My turn," I announced. I wanted to boost Viv up closer to the moon, convince her she mattered. "My secret is that I love Viv more than I love anyone."

Viv shimmied her feet in the air and exclaimed, "No fair. I could have said that about yooooooou."

Graham's legs pulled away from my spine; I caught myself before falling. His features were neutral, the smear of blood a slash under his square chin.

Viv was asking Harry how many girls he'd kissed and I wanted to listen in, but Graham wouldn't release his hand when I tried to pry it from his lap. He was angry, and as far as I could gather, it was with me.

Then those dimples divoted his cheeks and I thought him a second away from tickling me or bursting out some ridiculous comment about the history of kissing.

"Hey, Vivy. You want to be kissed?"

Viv and Harry turned in unison; two puzzled faces. I was waiting for Graham to add, "Got you" or "So kiss Izzie again."

Instead Graham was up, offering Viv a hand. They were standing chest to chest before I knew it. Harry raised his dark eyebrows at me. I shook my head. Graham was holding Viv's bare waist. His fingers were resting where her lower back connected to her butt. *Graham was touching Viv's butt.* I let a hysterical giggle rip free.

Viv tilted her chin, parted her lips, and her eyelashes fluttered shut. *An expert kisser.* That's all I saw because Graham's giant head closed in on her delicate face.

I closed my eyes and held my head. "I think I'm hallucinating. Viv . . ." She had had more kisses than Graham. At drama camp, during those all-night games of spin the bottle and truth or dare, Viv had probably kissed more girls than Graham ever had. The two of them were kissing.

I dropped my hands. The bonfire gobbled up the last sticks. I was sweating but cold. I wormed closer to the fire. Still cold. My stomach contracted for food. The kiss ended. I can't say who pulled away first because I was staring at Harry, whose expression was bewildered. Pleasantly, though. Not the twisted-up puzzlement I felt on my face.

Viv's fingers fitted with mine. I was skidding forward in time. A few seconds here and there. The apple trees swayed overhead. When did we clamber off the rock? Viv's lips were red and bitten and I wondered if it was because of Graham.

Viv and I were dancing and then we were pinkie swearing. So serious about a topic that gave way to laughter. We were holding each other tight enough that it should have hurt. Our cheeks pressed together. Viv whispered, "Top secret . . . always wanted to kiss him." I nodded solemnly like I shared the same secret desire of wanting to kiss Graham, when I already had kissed him, three years earlier, and never dreamed of repeating it. But no—it wasn't the time to tell Viv about that kiss.

One of the boys took up howling again. The other was on the rock dousing the fire. The eclipse had ended. The moon was white and watchful once more.

Too late. It had missed everything.

12

Our bodies blasted through the orchard. I careened off course. Viv caught my arm. Then we were at the pool, midflight, loose cannonballs smacking the deep end. Messy, explosive splashes.

I surfaced and shouted, a spray of water from my mouth, "Ina and Scott will hear."

Viv's rivaling yell, "They're in Santa Barbara."

"I knew that." My words turned to bubbles underwater.

Harry had gone inside in search of food. Graham was heavy-lidded watching us splash from the diving board.

"When I have my first starring credit and I buy my McMansion, I'm going to have a pool with a lazy river and rapids," Viv said breezily.

I crawled up the deep end's ladder and drew in a pool recliner with my toe.

"Don't crack your head open," Graham called as I tee-tered above the cement before sliding onto the inflatable. I stuck my tongue out at him.

"And I'm going to have a squad of hot pool boys that service my lazy river." She paused to giggle into her hand. "And I'll have one of those cabana poolside tiki bars. And you guys know I've always wanted a giant trampoline."

"A giant trampoline?" Graham said. "That's not dreaming big, Vivy. You'll need one of those skydiving simulation rooms if you ever want me to come visit and kiss you again."

"You're making me lose my appetite," Harry said on the deck, a plate of hot dogs in one hand and barbecue tongs in the other.

"Tofu?" Viv asked. She was also on a pool inflatable, her favorite, in the shape of a unicorn, her head resting against the back of its head, its horn appearing to rise up from her crown. She had one thin wrist in the water, gently circling.

"Yes, your majesty, the phony meat will be grilled to a char just the way you like it," Harry said.

We ate like that, chlorine-puckered fingers stuffing food into our mouths, stomachs cramped with giant bites. We found room for ice cream afterward.

The newly full moon lowered. Graham had gone to the barn for sleeping bags but hadn't returned. Viv fell asleep in a deck chair, snoring lightly in intervals. Harry and I treaded water.

The pool lights were sunken midday suns. Harry floated in their glow. I'd noticed his boxers were see-through when wet twenty minutes earlier as he backflipped from the diving board. My chest was flushed and my eyes practically ached from not peeking again.

"Are you weirded out that I'm a lawn gnome–fondling deviant?" he asked, brushing one of the inflatables away as it floated slowly and steadily at him.

"I always suspected you had a seedy underbelly."

He paddled in a tight circle. My legs were tired and I let myself slip under before kicking up. When I paid attention again, Harry was closer. "I can't get what Denton said about Goldilocks out of my head. He didn't even try, did he?" Harry said.

I shook my head. "No. She wasn't worth investigating. To him."

"My mom started talking about it after my dad was attacked. Stuff like, 'Look what they get away with in Seven Hills.'"

"They?"

He shook the hair from his eyes. "Guys, I guess. Rich ones, since this is Seven Hills."

"All that Rags and Riches crap—Amanda and Conner are worthless. You know that, right?"

The grim line of his mouth softened. "I know you're smart, Izzie. I know I'm going to miss hearing what you think after you move for college."

I flicked water his way. "We're going to text every day."

"Shake on it?" He extended a hand. I took it. Two shakes and our joined hands sunk under the water. I had to let go to keep treading, otherwise I would have held on longer.

I glanced over to Viv, pale and motionless. Something in the way she was positioned on the lounger brought me back to Goldilocks. The way she looked when I found her. An abrupt ache filled me. "I can't get how Goldilocks was posed out of my head. Arms and T-shirt and rocks forming wings. Just like the birds the scientists dug up. Wings and birds and girls, they're always here," I said, tapping my forehead. "That was the point, huh? On Goldilocks's walk from the tunnel to the gas station, she encountered the guy who killed her. He hit her with his car. Accidentally or on purpose. Finished her with his hands. Definitely on purpose. Then he needed to get rid of her. He thought fast. Settled on the creepy rock, mystery surrounding it. Put her there. Gave her wings. Made it look convincing. Mysterious. Connected to the weirdo rock. Confused people. Made it look like the farthest thing from what it really was."

"What was it?"

"A plain old murder. Violent. Guy killing girl. It's usually guys."

"No ritual murder?" Harry asked.

"Probably not. He hit her with a car—that doesn't say ritual. There's never been anything else to suggest someone's obsessed with the rock. But so what if the killer was inspired a little by it? Doesn't change anything. Goldilocks is dead. Killed here. Killed by someone in Seven Hills."

"After my dad was attacked, I got nightmares," Harry said. "Always the same. I'm walking through the rear hall at school, like he was. I see the shadows on the bleachers by the soccer field and the red butts of cigarettes in the dark, and I go over, like he did. But then I hear a girl's voice. In the dream it's

Goldilocks. I run up to the bleachers, but she's disappeared and these faceless guys kick me bloody on the ground like they did my dad."

I was silent, searching for a way to phrase what I wanted to without worsening Harry's pain. "When we were talking about playing pranks on Seven Hills, you said the city deserves it. You were angry," I said.

"I *am* angry. Don't I look it?" In a moment of lightness, he growled. His jaw sharpened and his brows slanted inward. "What if my dad had taken a hit to the head? What if the guys hadn't stopped when they did? The district said it must have been teenagers from another high school on our campus to party. My dad interrupted. Why would kids from Lovett or Arcadia drive forty-five minutes to drink on our soccer field?"

My fists were clenched under the water. "Who do you think it was?"

Harry stared intently at me, then shook his head. "Maybe some older college kids home for Friday night? But I believe they're from here, just like the guy who hurt the girl. No one wants to look too hard because they don't want to believe their neighbors or neighbors' kids could be that messed up."

The wind swooped down on us and I shivered at its invisible force. Its timing set us on a doomed course—how many people can say that about the wind? It made me think of the Order, our very own invisible force. Our power. How we could wield it. "We're not just four dorks having pizza-eating contests anymore," I said. "We're the Order of IV. We cut down Bedford. We can find who jumped your dad."

He blinked at me for a time, trying to work it out. "My parents want to move on. It would upset my dad if I did stuff to bring it up."

I chewed my bottom lip. "Goldilocks, then," I said. "We can make the police investigate her death."

"How?"

"New evidence they can't ignore."

He raised a dubious eyebrow. "They ignored a dead body."

"It'll be loud and in their faces. And we'll keep doing it—whatever it is—until they start looking for who hurt her."

I waited as he blinked at me, something flickering in his eyes. "What?"

"You." He gave the side of his thumb a nibble. "I wish the others would let you talk more."

I didn't shrink from the compliment; didn't really take it as a compliment, actually. "I don't need anyone to let me talk. If there's something I want to say, I say it."

"But Graham and Viv are loud and you're a good listener."

"You listen."

We were silent except for the water slapping the porous walls of the pool. I swam for the ladder and hung there. Harry paddled and hooked his elbows so we were side-by-side.

I released one hand from the ladder and faced him. I was aware of every little drip of water needling his neck. I wanted to kiss them from his skin. A flicker of nerves in my chest. Yes, Viv had been right. At least about this. I noticed Graham and Viv, but I observed Harry in a different way. I wanted *unfriendly* things from him. I pictured sliding down the wall until our fronts met, wrapping my legs around his waist. Pressing. Whatever usually prevented these thoughts from rising to the surface had been undone by the absinthe. My hand moved from the ladder to the wall.

"I don't know how to dance," he admitted out of the blue. "I love music. I can't move to it, though." He shook his head, frustrated. "I can move to it, I have legs and arms, but I do this dying fish thing. Ugly. Humiliation for all." Harry didn't usually ramble. I became more aware of his expression rather than his body below the water. "Remember when you and Viv had dance parties? Even the way you walk is dance-y." He gave me a sideways look. "Not in a bad way. It's good. I'm a hundred percent sure that you are a much better dancer than I am, is what I'm trying to get out." He laughed quick and nervous. "Do you want to go to homecoming with me?"

Yes, I thought. The answer caught in my throat. How long had I fought thinking of Harry differently? And what would happen if I admitted to myself, beyond this drunken night, that I wanted us to be more than friends? What would happen to the four of us? Then again, I had watched Viv and Graham kiss not too long before and nothing had changed. I hoped.

"Yes," I said.

"Yeah?" His smile shone. "Even though my dance moves will do your rep unrepairable damage?"

"Even if the whole school laughs and points," I said. He

ducked under the water, sending up a surge of bubbles. I glided away from the wall, floating on my back, grinning up at the night sky.

I had my first ever homecoming date and I was glad the moon had witnessed Harry asking me.

Retrieved from the cellular phone of Harrison Rocha
Transcript and notes prepared by Badge #821891
Shared Media Folder Titled: IV, Sun., Sept. 29, 11:06 a.m.

Video start.
H. Rocha sits at his desk, one hand bracing his forehead.

"I'm breaking the rules—the implied rules, since no one said outright we couldn't vent about other stuff on here. If I don't talk about it, I'm going to explode.

"Yesterday, before the moon ceremony, I was with Simon. My mom has a patch of wildflowers in the front yard. She was as excited as Simon is over ice cream when she planted the seeds. She drinks her coffee standing over them. She refuses to pick them. What's the point of flowers you don't pick? She loves them, I guess. Simon loves the butterflies that come. Used to come." He sniffs and exhales.

"I have to watch Simon out front with his net. Once he trailed a beetle and didn't look up until he was six houses down. Yesterday Simon was catching butterflies and then all of a sudden he sprints to the porch and says, 'I wanna go inside.' I told him to go back for the net he dropped by the flowers. He wouldn't. When I did, Conner's car rolled up at our house." A bitter laugh. "His house.

"He gets out, and you know the way he acts like the whole world belongs under his shoes? He stomps into my mom's flowers. The asshat is just trudging on the flowers she loves. I said, 'What the hell are you doing?' He goes, 'Reminding you whose house this is.' I said, 'It belongs to your parents, not you.' Then he's all, 'You know someone fucked up the red beast last Sunday night?' But I can see over his shoulder that the car's already been repainted. And then he goes, 'If I find out it was you, Rags, I'm gonna do more than fuck up your mom's garden.' Then he kicks the flowers a couple times—if I hadn't been so pissed, I would have laughed at how dumb he looked. He got back in the car and drove away. My mom's wildflowers were all broken and bent." He rubs at the creases on his forehead.

"I made Simon promise not to tell it was Conner. Last time he egged the house and Dad called Mr. Welsh, they got into a shouting match. I listened from the kitchen phone. Mr. Welsh said that maybe he didn't need renters anymore, if they were going to give him headaches."

His drags his hands over his face.

"My mom loves this house."

Video stop.

Retrieved from the cellular phone of Vivian Marlo
Transcript and notes prepared by Badge #821891
Shared Media Folder Titled: IV, Sun., Sept. 29, 1:45 p.m.

Video start.

V. Marlo tucks her hair neatly behind her ears. Her face takes up the picture. "This morning Izzie and Har said they wanted us to help the dead girl." A long pause. "I couldn't sleep after we found her. I imagined stuff about her. I named her." She begins to whisper. "Abigail—Abby for short. And I'd play games, like what's Abby's favorite fro-yo flavor? What nail polish does Abby like? What does Abby want to be when she's older?"

Her eyes water. "I'm glad we're going to try to help Abby. But it'll be impossible to convince the police to figure out who hurt her. My parents think I was too young to understand why no one acted like Abby dying was a big deal."

She moodily shakes her head. "On the drive to the Lessing Summer Theater Academy, we go to a big rest stop for truckers with all these fast food counters and a weird gift shop that sells shot glasses and cleaning supplies. Depressing. It's mostly fat old men and a few families. Except there's usually a group of girls hanging around the bathrooms. Their clothes are faded and small. They look grimy, like they don't have parents at home to take care of them. My dad pretends he doesn't see them, but Mom looks sad. Once I saw her give them cash. Abby was like them." She brushes a fallen tear from her cheek. "No parents. Alone. Dropout. Runaway.

Not from here. They figured that meant she was into drugs or she did stuff for money. That's why the police didn't have to find out what happened to her. That's why none of the grown-ups cared much. She was alone and that cop Denton thought she was garbage." She grimaces. "It's going to be a bitch to convince a man like that he was wrong."

Video stop.

13

"A re you high?" Viv asked. The car air was complicated with gym sneakers, a swimsuit stale with saltwater, and Viv's perfume. The sounds of the packed school parking lot jumped in through the open moonroof of Viv's car. It was Monday, two days after the blood moon. Her expression was curious. "You have the same look that Jack Robertson has in first period from eating edibles for breakfast."

I made a face. "He eats them every morning?"

"Probably thinks it makes him so badass. What's up with you?"

I picked at the silver polish on my nails. "I slept crappy."

I'd been an idiot. Harry and me in the pool. Under the lowering moon. Alcohol in our bloodstreams. Everything asleep around us. I'd been swept away. In the morning, worry snagged me like a splinter on a sweater. Our secret society had three rules: Never lie, never tell, and always love each other. It was the final rule that Viv amended when she recited it the first night the Order gathered in the barn. She said, *always love each other, as friends forever*. Was it my imagination that she emphasized *friends* as though to say love each other as *only* friends; that her eyes skittered from me to Harry; that it was on her mind when she accused me of wanting to see Harry naked? Was Viv worried that Harry and I would ruin what the four of us had? Would Graham? I wasn't worried. The four of us were unbreakable. Mysteries, a meteorite, bullies, a murder, and an attack had only made us stronger.

Viv unzipped her makeup bag. "Look up," she said, smoothing concealer under my eyes. "Close them." She brushed shadow on my lids. A blunt pencil ran steadily from the inner corner to its outer. "Now this." She handed me mascara. "Presto. You look like you got ten hours."

We zigzagged between parked cars. Viv's cinnamon hair was in a braid, slung over her shoulder, threaded with a long white feather. Crystals dotted the ends of her wing-tipped eyeliner. She was a work of art. I linked my arm with hers.

I resolved to tell her by lunchtime about Harry and me. She did not deserve to be lied to. Neither did Graham, but I was counting on Harry to tell him.

We approached the campus's front courtyard and flagpole. Viv shielded her mouth, saying, "Amanda's dressed like a stuffed animal again." Amanda's crew—Jess Clarkson, Rachel Fogarty, Conner's boy band—was sprawled in a bohemian circle on the cement around the flagpole. Their legs, backpacks, water bottles, and lunches all in identical red-and-black shopping bags from a fancy yoga apparel shop were landmines in the middle of the busy courtyard. Conner and Trent stripped the backpack from a passing freshman, launched it back and forth, knocking kids out of the way to clear their path. Campbell was watching them with a sort of surprised confusion, which made me think he was dismayed in his choice of friends.

Usually when the four of us drove to school separately, we met up in our lunch spot before the bell. That morning Graham had texted from the line at Cup of Jo. My chai latte would be waiting for me. We approached our turn. Viv changed her mind. Most people would avoid their sworn enemy. Viv refused to hide from Amanda.

"I look too good today not to rub it in her face," Viv said. I tightened my arm around hers. Viv held her head high, a steely concentration hardening her eyes as she guided me in the direction of the flagpole.

Out of the corner of my eye I saw Amanda and Jess sitting back to back. When we were five or so feet from Amanda, Viv stopped. She stretched her arms above her head, arched her back, and gave a loud yawn. She smiled impishly at me and flipped the braid off her shoulder. She was a bull's-eye tempting an arrow. Amanda's eyes were glued to Viv's profile.

I braced myself for the insult she'd toss at Viv. Sometimes I was collateral damage.

Unexpectedly it was Rachel who spoke. "Rags and Bitches," Rachel called with a condescending wave.

"Rags isn't there, dumbass," Amanda snipped.

"I know, just the bit— "

There was a threat in Amanda's eyes. Rachel became absorbed in the rings stacked on her fingers. Amanda shook her head and continued talking to Jess. "Like I was saying, he was definitely at least nineteen and . . ."

Viv had started off again, her hand tugging me with her. It didn't make sense, Amanda shutting her own friend up, sacrificing the opportunity to cut Viv down. Amanda's eyes were locked onto us as she continued her story about the at least nineteen-year-old. Jess hazarded a heavy-lidded glance our way.

Conner stepped up on the bench to openly stare over the heads of our classmates. I couldn't classify their expressions. Not sour or cruel. Bored. Hungry, maybe. I faced front. Viv hummed the theme song to the *Twilight Zone*.

I chalked it up to a case of the Mondays or a new, insidious method of torture courtesy of Amanda. Subtler than sticking lipsticked sanitary pads to Viv's backpack freshman year.

The day continued down an unusual spiral.

My phone vibrated from my backpack during first period. I checked its screen when Mrs. Ives wasn't paying attention.

Sup, Iz. It was from a number not saved in my contacts.

Who is this? I texted back.

I watched those three little dots appear and disappear and reappear as I waited.

Finally, one name. Conner.

I flicked the volume button from vibrate to silent and stowed the phone. I stared at the blank page of my notebook, felt a stitch between my eyebrows form, felt it turn into a headache. The period ended and I checked to see if Viv had texted for a summit at our lockers.

A new message from Conner lit up my screen.

Heard your friends had blowout Saturday. My invite get lost?

I left the classroom, shoving my cell deep into my backpack and jamming the books on top. The pink bandage that I'd worn on my palm since Saturday night flashed up at me. The Order of IV was private. Us dancing around in our underwear, drunk, cutting our hands with a dagger, smearing blood on the rock, Graham and Viv kissing, it was all intimate and Conner referring to it as a party—knowing anything about it—made me feel exposed. Skinless.

I kept imagining the vantage point someone on the street would have had looking up at the rock. No clear view of the meteorite. But the flashing police lights in the orchard had drawn Harry in years earlier. A flickering bonfire might have been just as conspicuous.

I wanted to be in third period with Viv, to show her the texts and for her to roll her eyes dismissively. But when I got there, she was in her seat, playing with the tail end of her braid, talking to Jess, who was perched on Viv's desk like they were long-lost best friends. Most casual thing in the world.

I ducked into my desk. Hid my bandaged hand between my knees.

Conner entered the classroom just then. His attention snapped right to me. He hammered his knuckles on my desk. "Hey, Iz. Waiting for your reply."

Iz. Not Icky. Not Ickadora. Not Rags and Riches or Rags and Bitches or Gasbags and Witches or any of the variations his friends came up with. "Don't hold your breath," I muttered, averting my eyes. He snickered as he threw himself into his seat.

"Why'd you ignore me before class?" Viv asked as we headed for our lockers after the bell released us. I led her by the wrist into the restroom. A girl was at the sink, close up to the mirror, inspecting the pores on her nose. I closed us into the handicapped stall. Viv was wearing her poppy-red sunglasses.

"Why was Jess talking to you?" I said, barely audible.

She shrugged a shoulder nonchalantly and tilted her head to the ceiling as if basking in the sun. "She wanted a crumb of my attention." She dropped her chin. "Is that so hard to believe?"

"Um, yeah."

She lifted the glasses. "Campbell Avers was over Lorin Yu's house Saturday night." Lorin lived across our street from Viv. "Campbell ducked into the orchard to smoke. Walked a little too deep and saw the light. He thought we were having a bonfire and that a bonfire meant beer. He was stoned so most of what he saw he's hazy on."

I pressed a thumb between my eyes. "I'm having an aneurysm. What did he see?"

"Us. Stripping. He watched until he saw me waving the knife."

My hand went to my throat. "Oh my god."

"Deep breath."

"He saw us taking off our clothes," I whispered. "He saw you with the dagger. What if someone connects that with—" I held four fingers up, not daring to say it. She slid her glasses back on. "Why are you smiling?"

"Dramatics become you, my darling. Maybe it's the lighting in here." She gazed up at the window near the ceiling. "Maybe I need to take bathroom selfies."

I grimaced, feeling sheepish. "Maybe I'm being a little paranoid."

She flicked her braid behind her shoulder. "Listen. Campbell told Trent, and Trent told Conner, and Conner told Amanda, who told Jess and Rachel. Campbell thought he saw more than just four of us. They think we had some epic naked bonfire. That's all. Let them feel excluded for once. Jess was just juicing me for info."

"But you didn't tell her anything."

"No way. Screw Amanda and her suckface friends."

I chewed on the end of my ponytail and nodded. "They think we had a party. Okay. No crisis. They'll get distracted by lunchtime and be done with us like that." I snapped my fingers.

"Exactly," Viv echoed my sentiment. She squeezed my shoulders. "Now I've really got to pee."

We were gathered in the barn that evening. I was trying to finish my homework fast, which wasn't easy since the beginning of the school year grace period with a lighter workload was over.

Harry sat beside me at the round table. Graham and Viv were talking on the couch. Their airy, hard-to-grasp sentences kept zipping past my ears. I strained to put together what they were discussing. The Order? Conner? Amanda?

"You guys are giving me FOMO," I said.

Graham and Viv's heads pulled apart, and Graham blinked at me through his spectacles. "Say again?"

"FOMO," Harry replied. "Fear of missing out."

Graham snorted. "Is that what the kids are saying these days?"

"What are you guys whispering about?" I asked, not in a humoring mood.

Viv and Graham exchanged a meaningful look.

Viv set her hands primly in her lap and said, "We're comparing what we know about the girl."

I shoved my calculus text away a second after Harry closed his book. We relocated opposite the sofa. Graham rubbed his chin where he'd been allowing a few strawberry-blond hairs to sprout. "The unknowns outnumber the knowns," he said. "None of us know who killed the girl, or who dumped her on the rock, or who left her T-shirt on the rocks to look like wings. We don't know if the perpetrator was one individual or if there were multiple perpetrators involved. There's no physical evidence left over. The case is five years ice cold. There's likely no solving it. But we do know who's to blame for that."

"Denton," Viv said.

"Yes. He was the lead officer on the case," Graham

continued. "When someone dies and it's obviously foul play, there should be an investigation."

"It's like everybody agreed to make it go away," Viv said. "And then a few years later, the same thing happened with Harry's dad's attack."

Harry stopped chewing the side of his thumbnail. "But it's the girl I want us to help, not my dad."

Graham looked reluctant to accept this. "You're sure?"

"Yeah." Harry bobbed his head adamantly. "Dredging it up would scare Simon and make my mom sad again."

Nah, hon, she's nothing like you, just a runaway asking for it. I sat on my hands. On the morning after the blood moon ritual, when Harry and I had shared that we wanted to help Goldilocks, I told Viv and Graham about what Denton said. I described searching for evidence of Goldilocks in the Ghost Tunnel. I admitted the truth about the scar on my shoulder— that it wasn't a souvenir from my grandmother's near-feral cat. Viv had run her shaking finger over its ridge.

Graham removed his glasses and cleaned them on his shirt as he slowly shook his head. "Everything the cops and city hall said was an excuse not to investigate."

Viv piped up. "First the cops said she wasn't offed in Seven Hills, just dumped here."

"The police didn't even tell anyone about how the girl was staged until the newspaper received a photo taken of the crime scene and they had no choice but to comment on it," Harry interjected.

I hunched forward, intent.

"Indeed," Graham said, his fingers fussing with his shirt-sleeves. "The newspaper said they suspected that the picture had been taken by a first responder on the scene, and that whoever had taken the photo released it once it was clear that the police weren't being forthcoming with the town." I could remember the EMTs and firemen and -women who arrived to check on Goldilocks. Yes, if anyone would have been outraged and shocked by the police's apathy, it would have been a rescue worker. "The cops told everyone it was just a body dump, and then once word of the photograph and the bizarre paw prints spread, they changed their tune and floated an additional theory. She was a part of some wannabe Satanic cult of teenagers that came to Seven Hills to hump and drink on our rock. Their fun turned deadly and one of their own ended up dead before they fled town. A theory that completely disregards the fact that the girl had a massive bruise on her torso, likely from a car hitting her before she was strangled. But the police were probably aware of that fissure in their story. If you ask me, that impact bruise is the damning evidence. There was no one person or someones obsessed with the occult or our meteorite. The whole crime was spur of the moment. Not ritual at all."

"Whatever theory the cops tried to sell," Viv said, "they were adamant that Goldilocks either didn't die here or the killers weren't from here. No reason to look further. They said there were no leads so they couldn't pursue him or them. The mayor made a speech. Remember? She was all 'Life in Seven Hills is precious and outsiders can't wait to ruin it.'"

"I remember her saying, 'We have to stick together.' She kept repeating it. 'If we stick together, there's nothing to fear,'" Graham mocked her robust voice.

"She came to talk to the three of us the day after we found the body," Viv said. "The sneaky witch wanted us to keep quiet about the girl's shirt being cut open. How she had wings. She didn't want us to ruin their little cover-up. Maybe she thought if people knew about the wings, they'd be more frightened and doubt that it was an accidental and isolated killing. If it had something to do with the rock and the killer was in Seven Hills, couldn't it happen again? They couldn't let people panic thinking that."

I winced remembering her visit. Why hadn't Mom and Dad sent the mayor away? They should have told me, *Talk about it. You're not alone.* Instead I heard, *Keep it to yourself. Don't spread rumors.* In the weeks after, their fights grew more intense. Dad spent more nights at hotels. And when they weren't fighting they sat on opposing sides of their drafting table in the office, working on architectural plans in silence.

Harry said, "It was right before Carver's reelection. My mom volunteered to work on her campaign to meet people."

"A murder investigation would have been bad luck for her," I said. I avoided Mayor Carver when I saw her around town with her constant companion, a bougie golden Labradoodle that wore argyle sweaters during the winter months, but I hadn't aligned her with Denton in my head until now.

"Yeah, especially if the police were investigating Mayor Carver's neighbors," Harry said. Mayor Carver lived only a couple blocks away. "With no clues, the cops probably would have had to go door-to-door asking for alibis and info," Harry further reasoned. "It would have been our neighborhood they canvassed."

"Parents would have freaked if they thought there was a murderer still on the loose," Viv said, feigning a shudder.

"That's why the police and city hall were so adamant that the perp didn't live here. That whoever killed Goldilocks had moved on once the crime was committed, all to keep people calm," Graham said, fist hitting his palm.

Harry was nodding. "Tourists wouldn't care that our beach is nice or our restaurants are bomb if there was a widely publicized murder investigation."

"Maybe people would have stopped moving here," Viv said. "Like those families who moved into the new development Conner's dad built a few years ago."

"Mayor Carver, Denton, Sebastian Welsh, people who have shops and restaurants," I said, "all had reasons to want a murder investigation shut down."

"To never start at all," Harry said.

We hadn't uncovered a deeply buried secret, and yet, because we'd never talked about why the girl's murder had gone uninvestigated, our realization became the fifth member of our group. We were quiet thinking about what it screamed.

I was a big reason we didn't usually talk about Goldilocks. I had shut down twelve-year-old Graham when he tried to convince me to solve the case ourselves. When he had complained that I had stopped reading mysteries with him. His curiosity was a reminder of my own.

"Our next rebellion should be aimed at PC Denton and Mayor Carver," Graham said. Aimed like you aim a weapon. "We exposed Bedford. Now we'll expose Denton and Carver."

"Revenge," Viv sang, and clapped her hands.

"More like takedowns," Graham told her.

"Can't we give them a new lead to follow?" Harry said. "Like you tell them about going up to the tunnel, Izzie."

Graham blustered, "Izzie's story is too easy to dismantle. No offense, Izzie, but you were twelve and you'd just found a dead body. Who'd listen? Everything you know was told to you by a bum who attacked you."

I narrowed my eyes at him. "She wasn't a bum."

He implored with his hands. "Bum. Runaway. Weird girl who travels around squatting in tunnels—it's hearsay and unreliable. A girl with a blade? The cops might even blame her." He held a finger in the air. "There are over two hundred thousand unsolved homicides in the United States, and I read that only one in twenty cold cases result in an arrest, and only one in one hundred in a conviction. Shit odds. The Order can't make it solvable. But we can make Carver and Denton pay for not solving it when they had a shot."

"Uh, hello, revenge," Viv said, waving both hands.

"How do we make Carver and Denton pay?" Harry asked.

"First we have to make them think about Goldilocks," I said.

"We can't off another girl to jog their memory," Viv said.

"No. But we can copy another aspect of the crime," Graham pointed out.

She earmuffed her hands to her ears. "I don't even want to know what gruesomeness you're suggesting. Not tonight. Let's just celebrate that we're getting revenge."

Harry raised his water bottle to the ceiling. "To taking down Carver and Denton."

Viv twiddled her fingers evilly together. "Revenge is ours—hers."

"To the all-powerful Order of IV," Graham exclaimed.

I leaped up to grab the Mistress of Rebellion and Secrets and held her high. "To rebellions and secrets and revenge and justice and cutting down all the villains in Seven Hills."

We were four knights marching into battle against evil. It wasn't quite justice or revenge we were after, but their unnamed stepsister. I crowned us brave.

14

It was the day after Conner had texted me the first time, and Jess chatted up Viv. We were on our usual square of grass for lunch. I brooded over the text chain I had going with Conner. Four more messages had arrived today, all of them follow-ups to the "Heard your friends had blowout on Saturday. My invite get lost?" of the day before.

Amirite you forgot to send my invite?

Okay. Don't beg. You're forgiven.

If I'm invited to the next blowout.

Gotta be naked though.

Harry was restless, chewing a bite of sandwich with lazy agitation. "Conner used to have his buddies hold me on the ball wall so he could hammer balls at me," he said. "If I fought, he'd threaten to tell his dad I kicked his ass. He said if his dad thought I was beating on him, he'd kick my family out and we'd be homeless."

My hand went to my mouth. "Oh, Har."

Graham tilted his head in a dubious manner and said,

"Not homeless. Your family would have found another home."

"My point is why would that dick expect an invite to our party?" Harry said. "Why did he slap me on the back last period and ask me what's up?"

"I think technically it's a naked party with Izzie he's interested in," Graham said. I hurled my unopened bag of pretzels at his head. He laughed as they collided with his chin.

"Conner gets invited to every party," Viv said with a shrug.

"That, right there, that's the attitude that creates the environment of impunity that spawns teenage tyrants like Amanda and Conner," Graham said.

"You think you drooling over Jess sends the message that what's hot is kindness?" I said.

"What's hot is red lipstick," Graham said, slyly grinning at Viv, who was reapplying gloss in her cell screen. Viv blew him a kiss. He turned to regard me steadily. "If you give less than a flying fuck about what Conner thinks of you, why don't you tell him to shut up next time he texts you about nakedness and parties?"

I held up my cell. The screen was dark and it would have been more significant a gesture if the text that I sent in reply to Conner's fifth message was displayed. It had been my only response.

"I think her *unsubscribe* was badass," Harry said.

Graham munched on my pretzels. Harry offered me half of his cookie. I took a bite—snickerdoodle. Viv's watchful silence made the cookie go dry. I coughed into my hand. I still hadn't told her about homecoming. I was increasingly nauseated at the prospect.

Viv said, "Amanda and Conner have treated us like underlings for ages. I don't see that finally having something they want is such a fail."

"Neither do I," Graham said. With his mouth full of pretzels, he added, "Can we talk about Denton and Carver rather than these mediocre excuses for villains now?"

I shushed him.

As if Graham had conjured them, there was Jess and Amanda. They ambled at an unhurried pace, lunch circles going quiet under their slow shadows. Just out for a stroll. But I knew they were headed to us. They dropped their backpacks upside down on the grass and sat next to us, royalty a head above the rest.

"Hi, Fantastic Four," Amanda said with exaggerated friendliness. She was wearing a unicorn hoodie, its horn shimmery and wilting to one side. I tried sending Graham a mental message to call it a limp dick to send her scurrying away.

Viv lounged back on one elbow and lazily shielded the sun with her hand. "Hey, yourselves," she said after a feigned yawn.

"What were you guys talking about?" Amanda asked.

"Nothing," Harry said, as close to a snap as I'd ever heard from him. He put his headphones on.

"You looked pretty into nothing," Amanda countered. Too late, he was bobbing his head to music.

She gave a nervous titter and looked out over the groups eating on the grass. "I get why you guys lunch here. It's all picnic-y."

Jess took her lollipop from its place in her cheek. "Super chill."

"Anyways." Amanda's attention went to Viv. "I felt weird telling Jess to ask you about your bonfire rather than just asking myself. I thought, *Vivian and I are so past all that middle school drama*."

Graham let out a bark of laughter. "Middle school? Seriously? I overheard you saying we have orgies with barnyard animals last week."

"Hmmm," said Amanda with a note of disbelief. "I mean, if *someone* said that, they probably don't really believe you have actual sex with animals." Her eyes lingered over Graham in a way that suggested he was the exception. Her icy blue stare returned to Viv. "My cousin is in college and she has a fake ID and people are always mistaking us for twins. I borrow her ID to buy kegs. All the time. I brought the keg last week, you know, to Slumber Fest. Anyway, I could get one for your next party. If you want people to have fun."

Viv's expression stayed remote. "Maybe. I'll try to remember," she said. I wondered at how she was hiding her satisfaction; she had finally gotten what she wanted: Amanda, sitting beside her, wanting her approval and an invitation. Normal things to want. Despite this, I frowned.

"Okay. Amazing. And congrats on getting cast as

Antigone." She waited for Viv to congratulate her back; we knew from Viv that Amanda had been cast as Antigone's sister, Ismene. "Later," Amanda finally said, popping up and needing to take a backstep to catch her balance. Viv's indifference had caught her off guard.

They were about to leave when Jess, wielding the lollipop, said, "Oh, hey. I asked the others and we have two free spots in our limo." She was looking at Viv and then her eyes cut to Graham and her smile became a touch less lifeless. "You should bring Viv to homecoming. You guys can ride with us."

Graham balked at her, then at his palms, and finally at me. School dances were an amalgamation of many of the things Graham loathed about high school—social hierarchies, popular music, adult supervision, our classmates, and the school gym.

"Want to, Teddy Graham?" Viv asked. Still, his eyes were glued to mine. I nodded infinitesimally. No wasn't an option. Not when a no meant humiliation for Viv.

"Fun," Graham said flatly. Harry groaned, though he'd been pretending not to listen.

"Text you," Jess said, and Viv gave a blasé shrug.

I wrapped up the rest of my chicken sandwich. I'd lost my appetite. What had just happened? First Conner's texts. Second Amanda and Jess being civil, friendly, to Viv. Third Viv acting distant but civil in return.

Viv's fingernails combed through the waves of her hair. Their bases were painted black. Gold Roman numeral fours stood out as the topcoat.

My attention cut to Graham, the light shadow of *IV* on the inside of his wrist, so light it appeared to be a projection.

We'd decorated ourselves with clues. I hadn't been paying close enough attention.

Others had. They suspected something was up.

I wanted to blurt it out to Viv. *Those girls only invited you because they suspect we're responsible for the flyers and Slumber Fest. Because they're curious if you'll let the truth slip.* My hands twitched to shake her shoulders. *Don't you see?* She had to.

They were manipulative. Amanda was cold. Cruel. Calculating.

"You've got that under control?" Graham asked. "I'm not going to a school dance unless it's for a damn good reason."

Viv slid her poppy sunglasses on. "There's a reason."

He gave a nod, satisfied.

I wasn't. "What's the reason?"

She ignored me, picking flecks of grass from her bare legs.

I rephrased. "We're talking about Amanda, empress of high school torture and her I'm-so-chill best friend, Jess, a girl who's allergic to acting like she cares about anything. Why would you want to share a limo with them?"

Her black lenses landed on me. "We took down Bedford. We're about to take down Carver and Denton. Amanda's only in drama to snake roles from me. She erased my name from the yearbook. She shouted that I had a chronic yeast infection in front all the eighth-grade boys." Her voice shook with rage. "I need to get close enough to hurt her back. I want us to take her down."

I crawled over, wrapped my arm around her, pressed my cheek to her wet cheek.

"I vote Viv can use the Order to get revenge on Amanda," Graham said. "I'm even willing to subject myself to a school dance for the cause."

The headphones had migrated to Harry's neck and he watched shadows play on the grass between his feet. "Viv has a right to stand up for herself," he said.

"Amanda suspects us. She has to." I tried to appeal to Viv. "Playing with her could get us caught."

"Any of our rebellions could," Graham said to me. To Viv he asked, "Will you get caught?"

Viv swiped at the tears I couldn't see under her glasses. "No," she whispered.

Mutiny. This was our Order—*my Order*. If we were discovered, how would we get revenge for Goldilocks? Pulling something with Amanda could ruin our chances. I stopped that train of thought. I was not in charge of the Order. We had agreed to be democratic, and even if I didn't like the outcome, I had to accept it. Nothing mattered more than Viv's feelings. I'd taken risks before to stop Amanda.

Viv had started to leaf through the *Antigone* script propped on her knees. By her soft, insistent sighs, I knew she felt as unresolved by our disagreement as I did.

My arm touched hers. "Hey," I said. "Obviously I'm in. I want to help."

She looked sideways at me. "Mean it?"

I offered my pinkie finger. Hers hooked mine. "Pinkie swear."

Viv could handle herself. Her name was erased from the yearbook, yet Viv never went crying to the school counselor. Viv might have ended the ridicule. But in Viv's experience, tides turned.

The adorned and stuttering Viv was ridiculed by Amanda starting in the first grade. As Graham and I were playing our game of chicken, Viv was engaged in a similar, though less friendly, battle. It began like all great wars do. One side had something the other wanted. Viv's life was flush with dazzling things. Ballerina pins made out of rubies, horse-back riding lessons, exotic trips to visit family abroad, and a mother who was the kind of beautiful that made little kids murmur *Princess*. I have always believed that from the beginning, Amanda was jealous of Viv.

Amanda teased other kids too, for offenses like wearing rainbow shoelaces she judged to be babyish. Those kids probably burned the offending items. Not stubborn Viv. She continued to dress as she pleased—loudly. Sending a message to Amanda: *You can't control me.*

So the war raged throughout grade school and Viv began striking back.

Amanda hijacked Viv's binder and scrawled *retard* on the front. Viv snuck into the classroom coat closet with a handful of live earthworms for Amanda's pockets.

Amanda disappeared Viv's book report as it traveled to the front of class. Viv set free the class guinea pig the week before Amanda's long-awaited homestay with Old Smoky.

Amanda egged Viv's house. Viv brought our class peanut

butter cupcakes, knowing Amanda was allergic to peanuts.

Amanda made a meme of Viv, illustrated pee trickling down her leg. Instead of retaliating, Viv bided her time.

Then, middle school. Amanda wasn't herself when we started the sixth grade. She appeared sallow and wore bandages on her thumbs. And hats. She was never without a beanie. That year, when Graham and I faked the chicken pox, Viv got her mom to write a note excusing her from PE. Amanda was permanently excused. Viv and Amanda sat idly on the sidelines.

They bonded over snap-in highlights, French manicures, and musicals. Viv opened up about her mom's cancer. Amanda confided in Viv about her anxiety disorder. Amanda peeled the cuticles back from her thumbnails. She gnawed at them until the pink skin bled. Then she began to lose her hair. Under all those hats, Amanda's scalp was patchy. Viv had played the role of friendly confidant perfectly. No more biding her time. Viv ripped Amanda's beanie from her head in the bustling school quad.

Kids aren't reliably cruel, though. There were those who snapped pictures. Who leaped away shrieking to suggest Amanda was contagious. There were more who wore beanies in solidarity. Who brought Amanda candy or said hey or smiled because inside they were nervous wrecks too.

Amanda's hair regrew. The friendly feelings Amanda had for Viv that lone week in the sixth grade never did.

No one tattled on any of Amanda's offenses because we'd

seen Viv hunker down, take it, her threshold elastic, until the perfect moment to strike. It was the game Viv wanted to play.

I should have known her offensive was coming; that it was only a matter of time until she saw the Order of IV as the weapon to end their war.

15

After school I dropped my bag in the farthest row of seats from the stage. Mr. Lancaster the drama teacher was making a few final remarks. I kicked my sneakers on the seat back in front of me and dove into the reading for Post-Colonial History as I waited for Viv.

I didn't notice Graham slump beside me until a rush of air hit my ear from him blowing in it.

"Ah, tickles," I said.

"Where's Viv?"

I dropped my feet and lifted to see the stage. Deserted.

"What the?"

"Did you fall asleep?"

"No, it's been like two minutes," I said, reaching for my cell. "Twenty."

"Sometimes she goes out the back," he said.

"She must not have seen me." I frowned faintly at how pathetic I sounded.

"Harry got called off from work. He's waiting in the car."

Graham scooped up my bag before I got to it.

I texted Viv while walking to Graham's car. Harry sat on the trunk, headphones on, mouthing the words until he saw us approach.

"You guys just missed her," he called. "Viv said to tell you she's going to the mall with Jess. Dance dress shopping."

I stopped walking. I held up my cell. Why hadn't Viv texted me? Invited me? I could play a role in her revenge scheme.

Graham clapped a hand on my shoulder. "Don't take it personally."

I brushed his hand off. "Easy for you to say. You're going to homecoming with her, riding in the limo. You probably won't want to be my friend once Jess recruits you for her axis of jadedness." My frown wavered. Graham grinned goofily. Harry bent laughing. What I'd said was that absurd. Graham would never ditch me; neither would Vivy—not for real.

The three of us stopped at Cup of Jo for supplies before heading to the barn. Without Viv present, the barn remained our territory.

The boys sprawled on the rug with laptops and note-books between them. I was hungry after my chai latte and the barn's fridge was empty except for mustard, a can of whipped cream, and cider.

I tapped on the French doors of the main house's kitchen. Before Ina's diagnosis, she had worked as a pediatrician at the big hospital over the hill. Recently she'd started to see patients at the tiny clinic in Seven Hills, her schedule unpredictable.

I hadn't seen her car in the driveway. Scott would be at his office downtown. I let myself in.

I had a wheat cracker in my mouth when I spotted the brown jacket on the dining chair. Soft brown canvas, brass buttons, a collar you could pop up or fold down. Water resistant. A hidden pocket in the lining. A gift to my dad on his last birthday. From me. I stopped chewing.

The floorboards on the level above whined.

I flew out of the house, forgot to lock the door behind me, probably didn't close the fridge. I slipped on the pool deck wet from a sprinkler's runoff, the box of crackers dropping and skidding short of the deep end. A jolt in my elbows as I caught myself.

I collected the crackers. My eyes watered. I paused under the trellis covered in dainty white blooms and ignored a fat black bumblebee streaking close to my ear.

The math was plain. If Dad was at Viv's, and Viv and Scott weren't home, Dad was with Ina. Alone. Upstairs. An affair. That word teemed with melodrama. I kicked the trellis, dislodging a shower of white snowflakes.

I was picking the flowers from my hair as I rejoined the boys.

Desperate to stop thinking about Dad and Ina, I started talking about the teachers I planned to request recommendations from and how I wished I'd done more extracurriculars other than my lone season of track and field freshman year and that one meeting of the Steampunk Fashion Club Viv dragged me to. "But I hate staying at school after class.

I want to go home. Read. Be here. Do homework."

"Izzie?" Graham said.

I looked up from the blameless pillow I'd been squeezing to death.

"I have a confession."

He and Harry had been passing the can of whipped cream back and forth, and Graham had a tiny dollop on his top lip.

"I'm the one who left the picture of Jane Doe—your Goldilocks—for the newspaper."

I sagged into the foot of the sofa. "What?" I said, as Harry murmured, "How?"

Graham took a deep breath, gave a little nod, and plunged in with a practiced shine to his performance. "I was on the rock alone for a while as we waited for the grown-ups to arrive. I kept the vulture away. I got caught up. This sounds deranged, I realize. But kids get excited by macabre stuff. Finding Jane Doe was huge. I wanted a souvenir. You wait for something that big and insane. Like one of our mystery or adventure books. It happened to us twice. The rock and the girl. But then a couple days passed and still no word about the T-shirt and rock wings from anyone. Mom said the authorities didn't want to make the crime seem sensational. They didn't want people thinking a killer was on the loose looking to sacrifice girls. Mom knew better than to believe that." The sincerity in his eyes shifted to smugness. "She knew that if it had been a ritual killing, it would have been more authentic, actual feathers or birds, not a hasty copycat using what was there and easy. She thought

Goldilocks wouldn't have been the first victim or the last."

Graham stared at his hands as he continued, "I was ashamed over the picture on my phone. Horrified I'd taken it. I thought maybe I could use it for good? I slipped it under the newspaper's door. Once I was acting, it was hard to stop. I had the idea to leave the prints in the dirt around the rock." I coughed deliberately to cover up my gasp. "Like the animals in the cave drawings had come to life and circled it. Make it look even more sensational. Draw more attention. I thought it would frighten the cops into investigating. I never imagined they'd weave a story about a few kids and a séance or something getting out of control."

His eyes were as round as his spectacle lenses. How could I judge Graham for keeping a secret about Goldilocks when I'd also kept one? Graham had been trying to manipulate the police into paying her death more attention. Trying to make the town pay attention. I also understood what it was like to be caught up in a mystery. If I'd really wanted nothing to do with Goldilocks, I wouldn't have looked for her face online. Wouldn't have hiked up to the tunnel.

The police hadn't searched the orchard the day we found Goldilocks and so they assumed the prints had been there, along with her body. Her death and the animal prints were linked by proximity. In the cops' two scenarios, Goldilocks's wings were either her killer's effort to make his ordinary crime seem ritualistic or just part of the pageantry created by teen runaways acting out a sacrificial ceremony inspired by the rock. The police pointed to the paw prints as another related effort, fitting into either scenario.

Graham unfolded a piece of paper he pulled from his pocket.

"This is a scale drawing of the model I made," he said.

I studied the pencil rendering. I knew what it was to keep a secret like this alone. How the guilt blinkered you from seeing anything else but your mistake. I met Graham's eager, hopeful eyes. "You were a little kid," I said. "The cops had made up their minds not to investigate way before the tracks."

I handed it to Harry, who silently chewed his thumbnail.

"How did you make the model?" I asked. That's when I noticed Graham's mischievous smirk. "You still have it, don't you?"

Graham raised his hands. "If I did, we could use it to recreate the paw prints. But the tracks would have to go some-where that lots of people would see this time." He rubbed his stomach, leaving his shirt rucked up. "I'm starving." Harry handed him the whipped cream, and Graham nozzled a pile of it into his open mouth.

It was one thing knowing where we wanted our second rebellion to end up, another figuring out how to get there. "Ideas for where the tracks should go?" I directed to Harry.

"I'll brainstorm," Graham said. "You two figure out how to get enough blood."

I balked. "Why do we need blood?"

"The tracks can't just be left in dirt." He looked cocky at the unilateral decision. I began to wish I hadn't told him he was forgiven so easily.

. . .

Harry and I walked home in the rose glow of dusk. A cold mist rolled off the ocean and I hugged my arms close. Another few minutes and the fog would overtake us.

Harry lagged a half step behind. There was the faint burr of music from his headphones at his neck. "When you went for food," he said, "I told Graham we're going to homecoming."

As friends, I added in my head. I let up on my pace a little. "Did he ask if I bribed you?"

"That's what I expected, only the opposite, me bribing you to be my date. He said, 'Score, we both have dates.'"

I tripped. "He said that?"

"He's going with Viv. And there was that *whatever* with the kiss. He can't complain."

"Or tell us that high school dances are beneath us."

"Or lecture us on the history of homecomings."

"His lectures have reached soliloquy level."

"Viv gives monologues. Graham soliloquies. Shocker— everybody thinks we're mutants." He laughed lightly.

I swung around to face Harry. He halted so abruptly his backpack slipped off his shoulder. "Oops, sorry," I said. I started to bend to retrieve it, but Harry beat me to it. "All this sudden interest in Viv and us, Amanda has to suspect we're IV. What if she tells someone?"

He hooked the backpack onto his shoulder. "She'd probably have ratted us out already."

I let out a doubtful huff and listened to Harry's jean cuffs shuffle against the cement the rest of the way home.

In my front yard, I said, "It's make-your-own-pizza night. You want to stay?"

"I wish. I told my dad I'd help with dinner."

"Tell Simon I saw that barn owl again," I said, starting up the path. "Maybe he can help me build one of those owl houses to put on the roof."

"Izzie," he called. I spun and waited. "You were upset when you got back with the crackers. When you want to tell me why, I want to hear."

I smiled and jogged to the front door.

I hardly had an appetite for pizza. Mom and I used to be creative with topping combos. We'd pair purple potatoes with fresh mozzarella and truffle oil. With goat cheese we added yellow squash and thinly sliced heirloom pumpkins. Not that night. Mom's laughter sounded forced. Dad's smile was a decoy. And I intentionally left his personal pizza in the oven until his crust charred black.

Retrieved from the cellular phone of Isadora Anne Pendleton
Transcript and notes prepared by Badge #821891
Shared Media Folder Titled: IV, Wed., Oct. 2, 2:04 a.m.

Video start.

I. Pendleton's face is lit by bars of white light, shadows between them. "I can't sleep," she whispers. "I can't stop thinking about how we're going to get revenge on Carver and Denton for Goldilocks. How the Order—my crazy idea—is making it possible." She shakes her head wordlessly.

"Four. It's just a stupid number. There is an infinite amount of them. Numbers that could crush the universe with their size. How come one so tiny is so important?" She rolls onto her back, the camera held above her face and the bed. "Four seasons. Four forces of nature. Four directions. Even hearts have four chambers.

"While I was blocking Dad out at dinner, I tried to remember the four forces of nature from physics. I looked at my notes from class once I came up to my room."

Izzie holds a notebook to capture the scant light coming through the blinds. "So one-year-younger Izzie wrote: 'The four forces of nature are the four fundamental interactions of our universe. Gravitational, strong nuclear, weak nuclear, and electromagnetic. They can't be reduced down to smaller reactions.'"

"They're ground zero. Rules of the natural world. What I didn't write down but I remember is that the forces have different strengths, like gravity is surprisingly weak—except when physicists mess with the forces at really high energy levels and the forces get more and more similar. That makes scientists wonder if they aren't really manifestations of the same force." She drops the notebook to the bed.

"Graham, Harry, Viv, and I are like that. I believe we come from the same place—and no, Graham, I don't mean vaginas or sperm or whatever preciously you comment you'll make when you watch this someday. I mean we have our very own force that created the four of us for one another and that under pressure, when it matters, we're really all the same." She blows a kiss to the lens. "Of course there are four of us." **Video stop.**

16

We called our next rebellion the blood rebellion. Graham—glitter of mischief in his eyes, dare in his voice—suggested drawing our own blood to use. I wiped my clammy hands on my jean shorts and reminded him that there were police and DNA to consider. Briefly we cased the biology lab at USB. The plan, accessing their sterile stores with Graham's mom's faculty key card, was abandoned when Viv spied the camouflaged campus security cameras.

We settled on a butcher shop. During my grandmother's yearly visits, she'd buy a pint of blood for a traditional stew recipe from her *old country*.

In preparation for the blood rebellion, Graham took midnight walks past our targets. We schemed to hit them the Thursday night before homecoming dance.

Nearly a week had passed since the blood moon ceremony, two since we'd spurred our classmates up the mountain to the tunnel. I craved the net of invincibility that descended over us after a rebellion's show of nerve; the fire that raged in our chests as we bent others to our will; the strange stare of my reflection that said I was not the kid I once was.

I developed new habits, little ways to prove to myself that I was as special and powerful as I yearned to be. I tagged *IV* in Sharpie on the bathroom stalls. I escalated, carving *IV* into the window frames of my bedroom, the barn, the school library. I scrawled our insignia on the spines of library books and on the faces of lockers when the halls were empty of students.

Daily I drained the sugar bowl into the garbage disposal, and my dad, the lone coffee drinker in the house, glanced perplexed around the kitchen. I swiped his newspaper from the front porch; poured water into his sheepskin slippers; was a ghost stopping the dishwasher's cycle after he hit start. Each act as a vandal and saboteur whet my appetite for the next. Nothing counted unless it outdid the last in risk and destruction. At last I took his credit card and ordered three dozen red roses to be sent to Ina Marlo at her clinic, the note signed from my father. The doctors and nurses would talk; those were the kind of rumors that spread, weren't they?

These tiny mutinies were not mine uniquely.

The *IV* tagged on Harper's car by a copycat was not an isolated incident. I liked to think my classmates found my carvings and graffiti and became further inspired. Why not? Defacing the school and its symbols of authority was fun. I counted ten red *IV*s scribbled on locker faces in one day alone. In the girls' restroom, *IV* was written on the mirrors in pink lipstick and black mascara.

Then there were my friends.

Graham parked in the staff lot at school; he graduated to leaving his car idling in the red zone in front of Cup of Jo; shredding the parking ticket waiting under his wiper, its pieces ghosting in the street once we'd sped away. He stayed in the barn long after the rest of us left for home; the air stale with pot and cider the following day.

Viv arrived to lunch with Sun Tzu's *The Art of War* and pored through its pages. She was grave-faced when questioned about her revenge machinations; her black fingernails tented as she murmured, "I swear to tell you soon." Her makeup escalated: the line of her eyes hell black; her lips bloodred; a black triangle of birdcage veil in her updo, as though she was preparing for a funeral. She spent more time protectively hunched over her phone, tucking it into the folds of her skirt or caftan when someone scooted near.

Harry pilfered cans of red spray paint from work. His five-finger discount was pragmatic, necessary for our blood rebellion. But when he pulled the first two cans from his vest, I gave a theatric and sincere gasp.

I may have indulged in other plans to nudge Dad and Ina's affair into my mother's purview. My father getting caught—even if the evidence was fabricated, the crime was not—was better than me telling my mother about the affair. Better for me.

But then came the Thursday before homecoming and the night of our blood rebellion. All of my restless energy could once again be channeled into the Order.

Directly after school, Harry and I drove to the butcher shop in Berrington, an hour south. We paid cash—as anonymous as we knew how to be.

Harry and I tore out of the shop, each holding a white plastic vat of blood. The metallic scent swelled in my mouth and nose until I tasted it. The heavy liquid sloshed inside the buckets, slapping the top, a red glaze leaking out to streak my fingers. I gagged halfway to the car. Harry held his vat far away from his torso, his whole body weighted forward with its anchor, a look on his face of comic determination.

After we strapped each vat in with a rear seat belt, I was laughing hard, a stitch in my side, elbows on the car roof. We stood there, smiling across at each other, winded. The magic of a new rebellion was zinging through me and bringing out golden prisms in Harry's eyes.

We trudged into the dark at midnight, about the time Goldilocks left the Ghost Tunnel for chips and, unwittingly, to die. Ours was a coffee-colored night, murky with fog. Difficult to see more than fifteen feet ahead of us. The flashlights were unreliable, the fog bending the light.

Three of us in black. One of us in white. Rangy and stretched shadows overlapping in the beams of light. If you caught us from the corner of your eye, we looked like villagers marching a virgin off to be sacrificed. Except Viv carried a water bottle filled with blood, a can of stolen red spray paint, a second skin of leather gloves, and a mask. All of us did.

Seven Hills's long, crescent lanes ran parallel to one another, on either side of the knoll. Backyards didn't touch.

Instead, green belts with trails separated them. A dirt path in the belts connected the orchard with parklike open space two streets removed from our targets.

Insects were out in full force. I felt a winged critter land on my shoulder and flicked it away, its ping off my nail loud. The air fizzed and dampened as we sloped downhill, closer to downtown and the ocean. Our shoes were cushioned by the dirt that became fine and sandy.

We reached the first canal of black, glittering asphalt and paused at the edge of a tall fence to peer around its corner. I listened. Nothing. One by one we flitted across the street to rejoin the jungle of brittle grasses. A few yards into this new ribbon of green space a scamper of rocks had us swinging around. The light caught in the obsidian eyes of a cat. It raked its calico body along a fallen eucalyptus branch.

"Shoo," Graham whispered.

It meowed.

Viv kicked the tip of the branch, sending its silver leaves juddering like diamond fish scales. The cat shot into the fog.

We crossed one more street and came up behind the pastel rainbow of Seven Hills's oldest homes. Victorians that had been built by the founders, way back when isolated towns were like fiefdoms, their founders royalty. Normal families lived in most of them now, all except for two the town kept, for the mayor and the police chief.

Harry and I followed a thin reach of yellow grass in between neighboring houses to Landmark Lane. Viv and Graham continued on the belt until the Carvers', three houses

FIRST WE WERE IV • 181

down. Where the sidewalk began, I disguised myself. The black plumes fringing Harry's mask twitched in the breeze. His belonged to Viv's grandfather, the silver vines, delicate and diverting as veins, were hand-painted in Venice. Mine was thick with dust from Viv's attic, but it also smelled of her grandmother's leather trunk, a trace of the Chanel No. 5 she taught us to dab behind our ears, and the sourness of old wine.

The fog boxed us in. Nothing beyond the luminance of lampposts, each diminished from the last. I inched to the center of the street, turning slowly, straining to see through its layers for witnesses.

In both directions the gables of second stories ran like mountains peeking through the fog. I licked the salty mist from my lips.

Harry pointed to me, to himself, to Denton's driveway flanking the left side of his house. I inhaled the ocean air, held it in, and nodded. Low to the ground, careful where my shoes landed, I tiptoed. We skirted the police cruiser parked by the garage. Near the bottom of the flagstone staircase I withdrew the gray cast from my hoodie. It was dense and pliable like a rubber stamp.

The stream of blood from the water bottle wetted the pads. I coated the paw and stamped the prints in the pattern of an animal hunting in the yard. Coated the paw again. From the lawn to the flagstone stairs to the white planks of the porch, it stalked. Meanwhile, Harry painted the porch in blood. The nozzle of his water bottle skated the white banister. Red trickled down the white pickets in a charnel candy cane stripe.

Never had I smelled that much blood. My knuckles were weak at the scent; stomach roiled; nose twitched. It was not completely unpleasant. Closer to the moist potting soil of the vegetable garden than the chemical emergency room.

The animal pawed at the sunshine-yellow front door. I bared my teeth, unable to resist falling into the character of a beast. Blood smeared in determined streaks. Harry was working on the windows by then, squirting the blood in zigzags that ran to cover the panes.

I leaped down the front steps, crouched on the narrow path that meandered to the sidewalk. The animal left a trail down it. It cut onto the grass and took up its bloody mission by the mailbox. I made it rain, transfixed at the path each scarlet drop cut, wanting to dance to the pitter-patter on the cement. Harry doused the windshield of a white sedan parked on the street and the animal joined him, leaving its tracks on the car's hood.

Harry and I paused to take stock of what we'd done, of each other. He was rounded over, his elbows bent like the bowing front legs of a prowling beast, his hair locked into place by a blackening splash, and a bloody pendant at his throat. My chest heaved. I straightened up from my animal hunch. Had to consciously will myself to smile like a girl and not a dog baring its teeth.

We'd dressed Denton's porch in death. Painted in blood like it was finger paint. My chest rose and fell faster at the rush. A manic giggle escaped. My fingers played with their slippery coat of blood.

The mechanics of the plan had seemed tidy and remote. A series of supplies to be gathered. A night to show up. A message to send. My chest tightened with hope that Denton would get that message. *Her blood is on your hands.*

The ambush of blood our plan created was art. A forsaken, animal art. Like revenge. Like hunting prey. And now that we'd painted in blood, was there anything taboo or forbidden?

Graham and Viv met us in the waist-high grasses behind Denton's. Viv spun as we approached. Giant black pupils latching onto us, yet no recognition registered in them. Her white dress, slick and glistening with red, clung to her chest. A thumbprint of blood had dried on the corner of her mouth and both knees were capped in red like she'd been crawling. Graham's sleeves dripped on the dirt. The tip of his mask's long-hooked nose was black and wet.

None of us spoke. In hindsight, how bizarre not to compare notes or to check that all went according to plan. My tongue pushed against the back of my teeth as we jogged. I drew loud, openmouth breaths. Pants. Words didn't exist. We were wolves, bounding, the scent of blood on us driving the insects louder.

Not until we reached the Orchard did Izzie click on. I was shivering—how long had I been cold? Viv had disappeared from my side—when?

I cut off from the boys and sprinted in the direction I sensed her in. I burst upon our street. There was no more fog, only houses watching with their gaping black eyes. *I know what you did* stares. I went to retreat for the orchard. But there she was, materialized in the distance, down the street. I let my mask sag at the base of my skull, the ribbon taut on my throat as I ran. Viv was covered in blood. We both were. Anyone peering from between their curtains would call the police. I laughed, because would they? Would the neighbors who didn't give a shit about dead Goldilocks worry for us?

I closed in on her as she stood from the sidewalk and stared, spellbound by something on the roof. I checked behind me for Graham and Harry. If they noticed we were gone, they hadn't caught up with us.

"Viv," I attempted whispering, her name coming out a formless sigh.

I crept up on her like she was an animal that would startle. Or strike. She didn't react as I took her limp hand. "What?" I murmured.

"Mr. Kirkpatrick's house," she said, and I winced at the clarity and scrape of all those consonants.

"So?"

"He hoses off the sidewalk every morning. I always see him."

I could picture it. Mr. Kirkpatrick, hose in hand, wearing gardening gloves and clogs, power spraying the sidewalk. I'd seen it often enough.

"There was blood on it the day before we found her. He washed it off."

I closed my eyes and opened them like you do after a sneeze. Tingling. Dizzy. The whole night scene changed, though I couldn't say how. Words were easy then. "That's the morning after Goldilocks left the Ghost Tunnel for the gas station. Blood on the sidewalk that coincides with her time of death." I glared at the dark recesses of Mr. Kirkpatrick's house. No curtains or drapes. A sleeping, middle-aged man lying unconscious somewhere inside.

"He found blood and Mr. OCD freaked that it soiled his pristine sidewalk," she said, and then spat angrily at the ground.

My hands fisted around the plastic bottle, acutely aware of the lightness of the remaining blood. "It's not enough." Perhaps I meant the blood I had left or her spitting or both. I poured the blood onto Mr. Kirkpatrick's mailbox. The water bottle gave a last, wet gasp aimed at his living-room window. "Not fucking enough," I muttered.

"What are you doing?"

Graham and Harry were in the street.

"What the hell?" Graham whisper-shouted. Harry's hands were frantically waving; the spirit of the night still mystifying him.

One last look up at the dark, unshuttered windows of the second story and I said, "C'mon," to Viv.

She yanked her hand away.

"No," she said, eyes panicked. "There's worse."

"Worse what?"

"They heard her, Izzie. They heard the girl crying and they ignored her."

"Who are *they*, Vivian?"

17

Viv wrung her hands free of blood as she stood before us in the barn. It stained her wrists and forearms like a rash. The mask's ribbon at my throat rubbed the skin raw. I let it abrade the softness there. I focused on the manageable burn. It was easier waiting for Viv to explain with a distraction. *They. They heard her crying.* Goldilocks made noise. I had often wondered what kind. A tiny moan caught in her throat because she didn't see it coming. A harsh scream full of despair and understanding.

That people were asleep in their beds as it happened, and that one or more of them might have heard her noise, stirred, gotten up to investigate, never occurred to me. There'd be a 9-1-1 call. A witness account. A search party. Efforts made to find who was hurt. Goldilocks wouldn't have waited on the rock for me.

"There's stuff I've never told. I should have said it earlier. I—I didn't want to think about it," Viv whispered, knitting her fingers in the dirty, torn hem of her skirt. "I wasn't allowed to leave the house the day after. I tried to guilt my dad into bringing me to Izzie's by playing dead on the porch swing. I fell asleep. There were all these neighbors on our lawn when I woke up. Mrs. Holloway, Mr. and Mrs. Yu, Mr. Swinton, a couple more. They talked about two nights before the girl was found."

I shook my head impatiently. "We already know. You tried to eavesdrop and they caught you and left."

"If you couldn't eavesdrop, how do you know *when* they were talking about?" Harry asked. I dropped the empty bottle I'd been clutching and it rolled away from my feet.

Viv's fingers froze in the tatter of hem. "Because I lied." She took a beleaguered breath. "They didn't see me. I heard most of it. Confusing. Like, they couldn't agree on details. Mr. Swinton said it was two in the morning but the Yus thought more like midnight when—when—"

"When what, Vivian?" I jumped at the stern grown-up voice that came out of Graham.

"When they heard it. Mr. Yu said first there were squealing tires." Each word was shot from her mouth, over enunciated, like she learned to do in speech therapy for when she was nervous. "Mrs. Yu told him to take his hearing aid out and go back to sleep. Not to wake Lorin. Mr. Swinton said it wasn't squealing tires but a crash, like kids knocking over recycling bins on the curb. He heard a girl's voice. Mrs. Holloway only heard the animal."

"The animal," I murmured.

Viv kept going. "She said it was closer to three when the animal started moaning."

"Moaning." My voice shook.

"It moaned for a long time. Mr. Swinton thought it was a girl and that she was drunk and crying for no reason."

"For no reason," Harry whispered, rubbing at his eyes.

"Because girls just go around crying in the middle of the night all the time," I said, hands fisted.

"Did anyone go outside to see?" Harry asked.

Viv shook her head and said into her hands that now covered her face, "Mrs. Holloway turned on music to block it out and Mr. Swinton went back to sleep. This isn't the worst part."

Harry made a choking noise of disbelief.

"The Yus found a shoe in their front yard the next morning. A white sneaker. They threw it away." Goldilocks's shoe with its wilted sole flashed in my memory. Its mate had been missing. "And Mr. Kirkpatrick told them about the blood on the sidewalk. Grumbled about how it must have been road-kill and how there was too much wildlife in the hills. He called the cops. Told them they needed to get animal control on it."

There was a knob in my throat keeping me from breathing.

"He told the police the placement of the blood was weird for roadkill. It started in the shoulder and then just disappeared after a few feet on the sidewalk. Did the animal drag itself and then just fly away?"

"When?" I asked.

"He called them after he sprayed it down with water."

"The day before we found her," I said. "Denton got called out for her body and the day before a neighbor told the cops there was blood on the sidewalk. Yet they still tried saying she was killed in another town."

"Kirkpatrick told the cops about the blood. What about the other neighbors? What about the Yus and the shoe? The noises and all that?" Harry asked.

"No." Delayed, Viv shook her head. "Even after they knew about the blood on the sidewalk and the shoe, none of them told."

Graham pointed at Viv. "Not you either."

"My dad was there." Her eyes dilated. "He didn't tell. How could I? I was a little girl."

Graham's chin tilted high as he regarded her disapprovingly. "Twelve-year-olds can speak. Act. I slipped a photo to the newspaper. I did what I thought was right. Izzie went to the tunnel by herself. You knew how to dial a phone, right? You could have taken your bike to the police station. Walked."

"My dad knew," she said again, pleadingly. "I thought he'd get in trouble for not telling."

Graham's head descended to the table where he sat, and his voice came muffled and weary. "Someone got away with murder, first hitting the girl with a car, then strangling her. Why would there be consequences for not volunteering information?"

"It's easy to be logical now. But not everybody thinks like a scientist at twelve." She stared at the blood splatter on her hem. "I'm not the only one who made a mistake. You left the paw prints. Izzie got stabbed at the tunnel."

"You're right," I whispered. "Everyone but Harry kept secrets about Goldilocks."

"We were kids, you know," Viv went on. "Scared. Mixed up. What about the grown-ups? They ignored a girl crying for help or crying because she was dying. They threw and washed away evidence. They could have saved her."

There was stunned silence. The dark night through the glass slider beckoned me. I wanted to wade into the night, become a predator as invisible as the wind slipping through our neighbors' flower beds. Through their keyholes. Invade their houses. *Our neighbors*, people who baked special Halloween treats for the block's kids, were horrible. Selfish. The kind of indifference that pulls a pillow over its head to sleep through cries for help. I looked to the idol's face up on her perch. Her smile was bitter. I yearned to grab all the blood we had left over in the fridge. I'd hit the entire length of Driftwood Street—all forty or fifty houses. I'd paint them red.

"This is why the cops let it go," I said. Understanding fired in my brain like a limb coming awake after falling asleep. "The blood was in the road. They knew about it. A body was found. She had a bruise, from here to here." I ran a finger from my neck to the waistline of my jeans. "Even without knowing about the loud bang or the animal moaning or the girl crying, it sounds like a car hit her first. Connect the dots. It was someone who lived on our street. Had to be. Driftwood doesn't get through traffic, and after Conner's house there's his dad's last development that's just sitting there, no one living there yet." I swallowed. "Someone who lives here did it. Hit her with their car. Strangled her."

"Maybe Denton didn't want to look for who killed her because he was afraid it was someone he knew," Harry said.

I was up and pacing. "We've got to do something."

"We are," Graham said. "We will." A dangerous flicker in his eyes.

"Come sit," Viv said, patting the sofa beside her.

I pulled the end of my ponytail. "Can't. I just . . . I can't."

"We'll think bigger," Graham said. "Spare no one."

I stopped short and held his stare. "Yes. Promise."

"I swear it."

"Me too," Viv said.

"They'll deserve it," Harry said, meeting my gaze.

I was walking again, around the sofa. "It isn't enough to say it." I kicked at the edge of the carpet when it caught my sneaker.

"Please, Izzie. You're making me dizzy. There's too much blood in here." Viv pinched her nose.

"There needs to be blood." I pounded a fist in my hand. I smiled. That was it. "There needs to be more blood to show we're serious."

"To who?" Viv whispered, but her gaze cut to our idol.

I wanted to feel the night's mark. For it to leave a scar. Writing *IV* in Sharpie on our wrists wasn't enough. Sharpie was kid stuff and the Order was not. Ten years before, Graham and I gave ourselves tattoos with a safety pin and an inkwell. The outcome was identical freckles on the pads of our right thumbs.

"We're going to need a pin and your mom's inkwell," I told Viv.

No one questioned me. I lay on the rug when it was time.

"Remember when I pierced our ears?" Viv asked, kneeling at my stomach, wearing Harry's sweatshirt like a dress since she'd shed her ruined clothing.

"Hold still," Graham ordered with the authority of a physician.

Viv placed one hand on my waist and the other to hold my shirt up, revealing the side of my rib cage and the little *IV* in Sharpie she'd drawn as a guide. Graham sterilized the pin in the flame of a lighter. The pin lowered into the well of black ink. I closed my eyes.

The heat spread. Harry's fingers gently rested in my hair; Viv's nose brushed mine; Graham's free hand pressed steadily to the small of my back. I stared down Harry's black T-shirt with the slogan *Free Tibet*, what looked like a bloody checkmark streaked across the *F*.

I wiped away the excess ink and blood with an alcohol-soaked cotton ball as Viv declared, "Me now." Harry pulled his T-shirt up wordlessly once Viv's was done.

Graham handed me the pin after finishing Harry.

I stare at my tattoo in the mirror a lot now. In the future, some of us will need to explain their origin. I imagine the reasons we'll give for having a *IV* messily branded on our torsos. Will we tell the truth? Or will we gloss over the tattoos like we do all the other scars we share?

Retrieved from the cellular phone of Graham Haverbach III
Transcript and notes prepared by Badge #821891
Shared Media Folder Titled: IV, Fri., Oct. 11, 6:09 a.m.

Video start.
G. Averbach sips from a ceramic mug that reads *Professor*. "Consciousness is that we perceive the world around us and ourselves." His tone is pedantic. "First-person subjective experience of the world is the best definition I've come across. Most scientists think consciousness comes from the cerebral cortex in our brains, but it's mostly a mystery why and how humans have it. Altering your consciousness means changing your perception of the world and yourself in relation to it.

"Shit. Izzie, I can see you rolling your eyes while watching this. So here's your stinking point. I believe that last night my consciousness was altered.

"There are all sorts of rituals where ancient civilizations used trancelike states in order to feel closer to invisible elements and gods. There was rhythmic dancing, visionary plants, fasting, drumming, and consumption of serpent poison. And no, I wasn't dipping into the absinthe or snake venom last night.

"I became a beast. I'm not sure what conditions allowed me to feel . . . so detached from myself. There was blood everywhere. The wind and the waves hitting the shore sounded like music. Viv was a wraith in white, flitting up the mayor's lawn, then gradually, covering herself in blood.

"And Viv . . . you've never looked more beautiful." He drags a hand through his hair. "I don't mean this to be offensive, but I was incapable of not staring at your butt as you crawled around like an animal on the ground, blood up to your elbows. You were this close"—he pinches the air—"to getting kissed on the mayor's front lawn." He leans closer to the camera. "Graham went away. I wasn't him. The concerns and thought processes that make me *me* flew from my mind. I forgot that I was a person, not a mystery predator from the hills. It was like wearing a new skin for the night. And for the first time since maybe I was born, I stopped thinking. Utterly euphoric."

Video stop.

18

How must Denton's and Carver's houses looked to that first neighbor who went for her newspaper on the lawn or to the guy trudging to his driveway, intending to go for bagels?

Sleep in their eyes. The shock of a red paw print on the sidewalk. They blinked to behold their cozy world painted in blood. Petals of it blossoming into wild flower shapes on the sidewalk, mailboxes having wept blood overnight.

Perhaps a shout roused Denton from bed, his police ears picking it up before his wife, asleep in bed with him. Did he grab his gun and dash through his front door? Did Carver let her Labradoodle free in his ridiculous outfit for a morning tinkle? Was the dog lapping at dried blood by the time she followed him?

However it began, there were sirens when I woke. *Sirens* because when confronted with blood painting two of their neighbors' porches—windows, driveways, cars, and mailboxes—they called 9-1-1. Those same citizens who barely batted an eye at a victim remaining a Jane Doe and her killer going unpursued.

A student news blogger from school anticipated the need for pictures and drove over once she heard about it, snapping and posting photos to the blog of the gruesomely striking red paw prints. Other kids reposted the pictures on social media. Our unwitting accomplices, spreading the blood. They proliferated in the same way the snapshots of the spray painted *IV*s at Slumber Fest and the Bedford rebellion did. Bloody paw prints and red porches and scabby mailboxes turned out to be sharable too.

I scrolled through the hashtags as I waited for Graham to arrive. Even the photos snapped of Denton's house were jarring, strange in the daylight. I stared at each for a long time, catching myself wondering who doused the welcome mat with blood or the white blooms of the hydrangea? I did. I was the gutsy, angry girl who had. My mom called through the screen door for me to have a nice day, sweetheart. Couldn't she see the rebellion on me? The change? I was not her pliable, simpering little girl anymore.

I was watching a short video of Carver's house as I heard Graham's car turn into my driveway. Ornamenting Carver's front yard was a pretty stone fountain, three-tiered like a wedding cake, stone birds drinking up the water. There wasn't a spot of blood on the birds. But the water ran red, bubbled from tier to tier. I turned up the volume, caught the happily sinister gurgle of the fountain. The little stone birds drinking up the bloodied water.

"Have you seen them?" Graham said as soon as I slid into the front seat.

Harry said, "Look," and passed me his cell. He was a few pictures past me on the feed I'd been scrolling through. He'd expanded the comments left by users. I recognized a lot of the usernames as belonging to our classmates. Lots of WTFs. Lots of exaggerating. Harry tapped one in particular. "He's a junior." His comment claimed that a bloody X had been left on his door.

"Where does he live?" I said.

"Not at Carver's or Denton's," Harry answered.

Graham waved impatiently. "Show her the other one."

"Here," Harry said.

Another comment, this one alleging that a bloody noose had been left on her doormat.

"She goes to school with us too," Graham said.

"Unbelievable," I was saying as the car stopped for Viv. "They're making stuff up just to have something to add."

"Drive down Landmark," Viv demanded, leaping into the backseat, the top half of her face pixelated by her black bird-cage veil.

The usually sleepy residential street was clogged with traffic. Cars slowed to a halt with the morbid curiosity that makes motorists gape at ambulance lights. Middle school kids on bikes rode back and forth between the two bloody scenes. An officer stationed on Denton's lawn was gesturing for a few high school kids to keep walking. Their cells were angled at his reddening face as they snickered and moved toward Carver's.

"They're not cleaning it up?" Viv said.

I flattened my forehead against the glass. "Not until they're sure it's not an actual crime scene. Like with human blood."

We drove past Carver's at a crawl. "The fountain was brilliant," I said.

"Thank you." Viv bowed her head. "Can you see the sundial?"

I got up on my knees, could barely make out the central dial on Carver's lawn before Graham turned right, off Landmark Lane.

"I told you I'd find a dramatic place for IV to autograph its work," Viv said with hubris.

In class it was the pictures of *IV* written in blood and spray paint on the sundial, on the welcome mats, on the wood siding, that stirred up whispers and had my classmates hanging into the aisles to gawk at one another's phones. IV was at it again. Hitting the police chief's and mayor's houses. Badass. Flipping the finger at authority.

"That is some dark shit," Trent told me during third period, thumbing his screen. "I bet they'll hit homecoming too."

"How do you know it's more than one person?" Campbell asked from behind me.

Trent gave him a pitying glance. "No way does one dude pull this off."

"It could be a girl," I said, thumbing through my notebook, pretending I hadn't been committing to memory every last comment.

Trent spared me a pitying glance. "Maybe, but I bet the mastermind's a dude."

I scowled. "Why?"

"Girls lack the balls to think of hitting a cop's house."

"But it was all bloody," Campbell said, so eagerly his desk screeched forward. "Girls are comfortable with blood, bro. Trust me, I've got sisters."

I smiled down at my notes.

The whispers continued, evidence of our power. I floated a head taller in the school halls. Blood-warm satisfaction made me buoyant each time my T-shirt snagged the raw edge of the fresh tattoo. I was dangerous. The Order's invisible hand was tightening its grip on Seven Hills's throat. Merciless, we would paint the whole town in animal blood.

The four of us ate lunch in the courtyard because Viv wanted us to be in the middle of the action. At the center of the courtyard was a small outdoor amphitheater. Seven or eight cement bleachers rose up in a half-moon shape, the flagpole on the flat expanse of cement used as the stage. The drama department performed their spring shows there, right where Amanda and her crew always ate lunch. By the way Viv glared at their presence, I imagined she felt like an ousted queen, an enemy force permanently occupying her territory.

We sat up on the top row of cement bleachers. I didn't usually like the noise that came with hanging around the courtyard, but that day the buzz was about IV.

Amanda, Jess, and Rachel spied us and, led by Amanda, flocked over.

"Insane that IV struck again, huh?" Amanda said, standing on the riser below us.

Rachel tossed her ponytail from her shoulder and said, "Hope you guys have an alibi."

Amanda gave her a cutting look. "God, you banshee—keep your voice down."

Rachel retreated down a step like a kicked puppy. "I'm just teasing," she said. "God," she added, crossing her arms and turning away from us. As far as I could tell, Rachel was a watered-down version of an Amanda-Jess love child. Too aware of where she put her hands to act as cool as Jess thought she was; too eager to be heard to boss people around.

Graham said casually, "We all sat around, shooting the shit, talking about climate change last night."

"I bet you did." Jess gave a clipped laugh. Something stirred behind those usually bored eyes as she watched him. Her tongue went to her front teeth, like she was waiting for him to quip back, silently begging him to play, even. Graham had magnetism, but rarely did anyone outside of our circle notice. Usually our peers gave fake laughs at Graham's shameless wit before shuffling away. Their loss.

Graham became absorbed in removing the butcher paper from his deli sandwich. "Yeah," he said absently. "Meteorologists say this is going to be an El Niño year. I don't buy it. They said the same thing last year and the one before."

Jess's nostrils flared. "They're probably in the pocket of the rain boot lobby," she said. I laughed. Graham didn't glance up.

Harry had deserted his sandwich on its plastic wrap to listen to his headphones, eyes closed. He was waiting for the girls to leave.

Jess bent for a red licorice whip from our shared package. She twisted, offering Graham a view down her top. He looked. If he hadn't, I might have leaned over to check his pulse.

"I get it," Amanda said. "Playing coy. Okay. I'll let the charade go on a bit more. No one knows anything about anything over here. Bye—for now." A cross between a threat and a so long. She returned to the flagpole flanked by Jess and Rachel.

Lunch slipped by, my last opportunity to tell Viv about my date with Harry, before the homecoming parade. Rather than bloat larger, the urgency of the confession shriveled. Viv knew Harry and I would be at the dance. She probably figured we'd drive together. What did the tiny detail of it being an official date matter when the stakes around us were so much higher?

By the last period of the day, Harry's article for the school news blog had posted. It wasn't something he'd discussed with us. And I was glad it came from only his brain. He contextualized the pictures taken that morning. He wrote of the paw prints and compared them to the paw prints found five years before on the Marlo property, in the days after a still-unsolved murder occurred. He recapped the facts from Jane Doe's murder, for readers who needed a refresher. People would have likely remembered the paw prints from years before themselves, but Harry's blog made it impossible for people to pretend they didn't. Harry made it impossible for Seven Hills to ignore their deeper meaning. The town could interpret it however it wanted to—as a threat, a promise, a taste of what was to come, or a punishment.

The city of Seven Hills's official news blog even included a link to Harry's coverage in their own. They posted updates throughout the afternoon. The police identified the blood as belonging to an animal. Mayor Carver issued a statement assuring the town that the perpetrators would be found and prosecuted, and that despite rumors, there was no evidence of the incident being anything other than an isolated one of vandalism, targeting herself and the police chief.

> These things, as tasteless as they are, happen in the
> safest of communities. The vandals want to foster
> unrest and confusion by targeting community
> leaders. We won't allow them to win.

Denton issued no comment. I wondered if that was because we'd succeeded in unnerving him. As crappy an officer as I thought he was, he was still police. Wouldn't the connection to Jane Doe strike him as a personal attack? He knew what he'd done wrong, and just in case he'd forgotten, there was a little blood-stamped reminder all over his front yard.

That evening, Harry, Graham, Viv, and I watched the homecoming parade from the knoll, the square of park that was the center of downtown. Dressed for summer, a breeze the only proof of fall, our hands colliding in a party-size bag of candy. The sidewalk around the route was packed. We'd conquered a bit of grass near the sno-cone booth, making the streams of people divert, stealing bits and pieces of their conversations as they squeezed by.

Two men, one with a toddler on his shoulders dripping sno-cone slush in his hair, paused by us. "There were other reports," the man said, trying to wrangle the soppy cardboard from his little girl's hands. "Someone found a bloody rope," he finished.

His partner wiped at the dye between her eyes with a napkin, the little girl crying and squirming in response. "A teenager *claimed* he did on the Internet."

"Doesn't mean he wasn't telling the truth. What about that old codger with the prize vegetables on Driftwood? He a troubled youth lying for attention?"

That was the first we'd heard about Kirkpatrick. His house had appeared spotless when we drove by in the morning, and I had wondered if standing on his lawn had been a dream.

"But the mayor didn't mention any of that," he continued, wiping the little girl's sticky hands. "No deviating from her isolated vandalism line—oh look, there's a better spot." He led the way. "And don't tell me . . ." Their voices faded into the noise of the crowd.

I turned from watching them go. "Interesting," I said as I saw that the others had been listening to them also.

Graham nodded. "Indeed. Who knew that our classmates' desperation to seem relevant would be reliable enough to help our cause?"

"I did," Harry said, a flick of his eyebrow.

"Me too," Viv piped up. "First the copycat hitting Harper's car. Now kids lying online—all so they can feel in on it."

"Smells like team spirit," Graham intoned.

"For someone who hates school spirit, you sure do wear school colors a lot," Viv said of Graham's navy jacket and white polo.

"Accidentally," Graham said, sulking playfully. "I'd never deign to be so establishment on purpose."

Viv had ribbons of white and blue threaded in her twin French braids, silver glitter making blades of her cheekbones, and a black vintage cheerleader's cape on her shoulders. "How about you practice keeping your very bossy opinions to yourself for tomorrow night, 'kay?" Viv said, offering Graham a toothy grin.

Graham tugged one of her braids. "Are you saying I shouldn't be myself?"

Viv pulled it free. "Bull's-eye."

Graham's hands dove into her cape, tickling her sides. Viv's laughter came out in high peals. I looked away. They'd been cozier. More playful shoving, hand-holding, and whispering. While planning the blood rebellion, Graham had wanted to walk the route we'd use from Driftwood to Landmark at night. He'd texted Viv to come along rather than me.

Graham used to measure his words and actions carefully. His first secret, that he'd once been in love with Viv and me, was exactly equal. When had he stopped—the kiss? The homecoming date? Another moment I'd missed?

Really, way down in the selfish pit of my stomach, a spot I believe everyone has, I knew the attention he used to give was not equal. I got more.

Graham patted his stomach. "I need a churro. Har?"

"I could eat four," Harry said. "You?" I smiled and shook my head. "Viv?"

"I'm gonna get a sno-cone later," she said.

The boys went in search of the sweets. I pulled free a handful of candy from the bag and was picking through them when Viv spoke. "You want to hear something that's bananas?" I popped a mini-size chocolate bar into my mouth and struggled to keep it shut while chewing and nodding. "My best friend hasn't told me she has a homecoming date."

The half-macerated chocolate lodged in my throat. I swallowed hard; my eyes watered. "Did Graham tell you?" My voice was pitted.

A static burst came from the speakers set up around the knoll. We both startled. Patriotic-sounding music, all brass and drums, boomed. "Yeah." She yanked the bag of candy from me. "But I almost figured it out myself."

"I wanted to tell you first thing, but I psyched myself out." She rooted through the candy. "The four of us promised—love each other always *as friends forever*."

Her eyes stayed downcast. "You're breaking the promise?"

"No."

"You're going as friends?"

"I mean, no, it's a date. I don't know."

She made a small grunt.

Nothing else could be said because Graham was there again, hands clapped on Viv's shoulders, shaking her gently. "The line for churros reaches Mesopotamia," he complained. "Churros are the only reason I come to this."

"He wanted to give up because there were five people before us," Harry said, offering me his cup. "Frozen lemonade?"

There was a small shift in Viv's pretty face; it made her look ill. "I can't breathe," she said. "I need a sno-cone." She latched on to Graham's wrist and dragged him toward the booth.

Harry rocked on his heels. "What's up with her?"

The percussion instruments reached crescendo and for a few moments their battering was all I heard. "I think the floats started!" I shouted, rising up on tiptoes, trying to see.

"Graham told her we're going to the dance together, huh?" Harry said right into my ear. "Viv wasn't talking about it. I guessed she didn't know."

I searched for something in the crowd to make my creeping nausea stop. "I was crappy keeping it from her."

"Maybe." He was fiddling with the lemonade's straw. "But she was intense making us swear to love each other as friends forever. And the dance, it sort of changes stuff." He glanced up tentatively. "If you want it to." I couldn't look away from the warmth of his brown eyes. There was no more guilt tying my stomach in knots, no fear about breaking our promise. I let my smile answer him. Yes. I wanted. There was only the rush of Harry smiling back at me.

We watched the commotion of a police officer chasing boys on skateboards zigzagging along the cordoned-off street. I squinted at one of the boys. Did I see a white *IV* on his black backpack or was it another symbol, transmuted by distance? I went to ask Harry if he could make it out, but a glistening blue dome of ice appeared in my face. "Sno-cone for the snow queen," Viv said with forced generosity. "Here." The blue ice touched the tip of my nose.

I took it from her as it lurched at me again. "Thanks."

Viv slurped her cherry-red cone through the straw. I hated blue sno-cones. What naturally occurring fruit was blue? And Viv knew this, knew all my loves and hates. I stabbed the straw through the cone's outer shell of ice as the floats advanced like glaciers. I could think of worse punishments.

Our school mascot, a blue-eyed tiger, loped by and showered us with a toss of plastic-wrapped hard candy. Loud pops thundered sporadically—Principal Harper at the helm of his float armed with a T-shirt cannon, firing cheaply made apparel at dangerously close proximities. The boys and girls of the soccer and lacrosse teams waved from advancing floats.

Harry and I cheered for one in the shape of a pirate ship carrying the Brass Bandits and the school orchestra. Graham watched the parade with the bewildered look of an anthropologist observing an alien civilization.

I shouted across Harry and Viv to Graham, "Don't pretend you don't love this!"

"His veins run blue and white," Harry teased.

"What?" Graham pointed to his ear, smirking. "I can't hear you."

"He's going to try out to be Waldo the Tiger," I told Harry.

"He's planning to off the current Waldo the Tiger so there's an opening," Harry said.

Graham shook his head, but his eyes laughed.

Harry's hand brushed mine. The mascot made another pass on foot. Harry's arm went up to shield the two of us from the candy shrapnel. I turned into him. For a second our faces came close. The flicker of his lips was all I saw. Then his arm dropped as a curtain while the final float, homecoming royalty with their glitter cannon, came into my periphery. A storm of bright bits of paper winnowed around us. Flecks of color spiraled, changing from summer petals to fall leaves.

Our hands brushed again. He had confetti in his hair and I brushed off a speck of glitter from my nose.

"I'm starving," Graham complained. "Let's get a pizza before swimming."

"It's too cold for the pool," Viv said, holding the opening of her cape closed, chattering her teeth. I was warm in my T-shirt and shorts. "Besides, we've been invited to a house party."

Viv handed me her cell, a group text chain with Jess and Rachel on the screen. Jess's parents were away for the night and friends were headed over to *pregame homecoming*. Viv squeezed in between me and Harry, slung her arm over my shoulders. "I know you'd rather eat pizza and swim, but please? It's majorly important we go." My tongue was still puckering from the awful blue sno-cone. Viv was chewing her bottom lip.

I wanted her to forgive me. "I don't mind if everyone else wants to go."

"Why is it important?" Harry asked.

"To hear what they're saying about you know what," she answered robotically. I wasn't sure she was telling the truth.

"You're not actually considering going, Iz?" Graham asked. He was disbelieving, finger fused to the bridge of his glasses. "Do I really have to lobby for pizza eating—extra cheese, fennel sausage, *arugula*—versus standing in someone's kitchen, inhaling Conner's beer burps and watching girls suck face for his attention?"

Viv rolled her eyes at me and said, without swiveling to face him, "You're not into girl-on-girl action?"

Graham crossed his arms at his chest. "No. That's not every guy's fantasy."

"Isn't Jess your fantasy? She wants to know if you're coming," Viv said, swinging around. "I swear. Seeeee." She scrolled up in the text chain and presented the cell to Graham with a flourish of fingers.

He blanched reading it, ran a hand through his hair, and said, "Maybe it would be a travesty to graduate without having the authentic experience of a house party?"

His eyes settled on me. I knew he must be remembering the house party freshman year. It was right before Thanksgiving; Viv and Harry had both been out of town with their parents. Graham and I already had our authentic experience.

Once was enough. We never even relived it by talking about it.

"And if it would help your whole revenge scheme, who am I to say no?" Graham added.

I shoved my hands into my shorts pockets and tried to muster enthusiasm. "All right. We're all in."

None of us asked Harry what he thought. I realize now that I often mistook Harry being easygoing and mature for not having opinions. He had plenty. He wasn't like Graham, Viv, and me, projectile vomiting words like Earth's revolutions would grind to a halt if it didn't hear what we thought.

We turned up at Jess's front porch with a glut of other kids. Viv was snatched by Jess. "Conner's gonna burp the names of models," she told Viv, like *Hurry, you're about to witness history.* Everyone crammed in the kitchen that quickly began to stink of beer and stomach bile. Harry and I wedged deeper and deeper into the corner by the microwave as kids kept squishing by and stepping on my toes. I abandoned my beer and hopped up to sit on the counter.

From that height I had a view of Viv by the fridge, waving a lollipop like a royal scepter, laughing throatily. She was a quick study.

"What's with Jess and freaking lollipops?" I muttered. Graham was between Viv and Jess. Despite how into Jess he claimed to be, he was watching the ceiling fan spin rather than talk to her.

"What do you think she's planning?" Harry asked, elbow on the counter alongside me.

I knew he meant Viv's grand plot against Amanda. I grunted indistinctly.

"Why don't you ask?" he said.

I bit my lip watching Viv's expression alternate between aloof and manically entertained. "Have you noticed Viv trades stuff in for brighter, shinier stuff really fast? Like she never uses the same nail polish color twice because there's always a better color waiting. In theater, there's always a new role headed her way. It's easy to stay in love with it, I think." I slid down from the counter. I didn't want to watch her anymore. "I'm afraid to ask her what she's planning because I'm afraid something more exciting than revenge on Amanda has finally come along. I would understand if she wanted to make peace." I grimaced. "Accept it, at least."

"Not me. Where's the fun in fitting in?"

Viv's laugh sliced through the room's chatter.

"You think she'll be ready to quit tonight's experiment after that beer?" Harry asked.

"I love experiments," Conner declared, shouldering through the kids behind Harry, a cigarette dangling from his mouth; his already short polo sleeves rolled up to accentuate his biceps. "Who is our experiment fucking with?"

"Don't worry about it," Harry said, sending him an annoyed backward glance.

Conner gave a contemptuous crinkle of his brow. "I never worry, bro. But I am a nosy dick and I keep hearing stuff about you guys." He jabbed the cigarette in my direction. "You gotta let me in on your secret."

I batted away the smoke, twisted to retrieve my beer, and pretended to take a sip of the warm brew. Harry was newly absorbed in cracking his knuckles.

"I hear you like running around naked where they found that dead bitch when we were kids." He paused. "Yeah," he continued smugly, as if Harry or I had made some noise of admission, "I know all about your secret orgies."

I watched the beer swirl in my cup. My hand shook with the desire to throw it in Conner's face.

"Whoa, classy," Harry said. "You always talk about victims like that?"

Conner's grin grew mean. "When they're trash, yeah." He tapped the cigarette, ash falling to the hardwood floor. His attention latched onto me. "What about you, Izzie? I think you're probably the kinkiest. You like scissoring under the full moon?"

"I don't think you understand the fundamentals of that term," I said.

He turned to give me side-eye. "You know. One in every school. Carries her diary in her backpack. Doesn't do makeup 'cause it's sexist and shit. But get a few beers in her and she's stripping."

I gave him the glare equivalent of a middle finger.

"You're right, man, you are a dick," Harry said. "And we don't care if you wonder about us, just do it someplace else." He cut Conner out of our little corner with his back.

"Fuck," Conner said. "I'm trying to be a nice guy. We want to know what you're into. Everyone does after last night. People have eyes is all I'm saying, bro."

Harry's neck became red, the tendons pronounced.

"What happened to you, Conner?" I asked.

"Huh?" he grunted, running a hand through his yellow hair.

"You didn't used to be mean. Do you remember third grade when I came back to school after my grandpa died and I played you at tetherball? Big game. Our whole class watched. You usually crushed *everyone* at tetherball. But you let me win. So what happened to you?"

He recoiled—or maybe I imaged he did. "Shut up already, freak," he said, shoving past kids to get away from us.

Harry let out a loud, shaky exhale.

"Who cares what he thinks or says?" I told him. He nodded but the voltage in his eyes worried me, like he might go after Conner any second.

"Hey, listen." I tapped my ear.

The hip-hop song playing transitioned into something jazzy and old-timey remixed with hip-hop. Harry's frown eased. And then Conner was forgotten and we were talking about music—Harry's record collection, how he was saving up for a portable record player, how I missed the record player I'd had when I was younger, and the last concert I'd gone to with Viv in Los Angeles the summer before.

After music, Harry and I played a game where we picked someone out of the crowd and pretended to read their thoughts. I closed my eyes during a laughing fit and opened them to realize that most of the kids had left.

"C'mere," Viv slurred from her post at the fridge. She was between Jess and Rachel. Amanda sat on the kitchen island, drilling the cabinets with her stacked heels. Graham was taking a hit off a joint, standing by the open patio door with the boy band. Reluctantly Harry and I migrated over to Viv.

"Amanda wants to know what we do in the barn," Viv said clear enough that I doubted the initial slur in her voice. Her eyes twinkled. Sharp. Focused.

"Hang out and study," I said. I took a backward step. They were all staring at me.

"C'mon," Amanda whined, her heels hitting the cabinet with a vicious drive. "Study?"

Viv's eyelash extensions brushed her cheeks as she shrugged coyly. "Sometimes we do homework in there, when we're not bonfiring and—" She bit her bottom lip. "Oops, I forgot I can't say. I'm such a lightweight." And there it was: a juicy morsel she'd let slip to entice the others.

"C'mon, tell us," Rachel said, swaying a bit on her feet.

"Please," Jess said.

"It'll go in the vault," Amanda promised, raising her right hand to make a pledge.

Graham took a sip from a flask I'd never seen him with. "What do you think we do? Theories?"

I widened my eyes at him.

"You'll say if we guess right?" Jess asked.

Graham shrugged, handing the flask to Campbell.

Jess leaned forward conspiratorially. "I think you're pagans who worship anything with an evil eye, sacrifice four animals every full moon, read tarot cards, and don't believe in monogamy."

Was the emphasis she placed on *four* animals every full moon a coincidence? She was still leaning over, breasts bubbling up, tongue flicking her front teeth. Graham's eyes dimmed. "Creative," he said flatly. Why wasn't he picking up on her flirting with him?

"Oh, me now," Amanda exclaimed, childishly clapping her hands. "I think you're playing a high-stakes game of truth and dare. With dares like you shoot apples off of one another's heads with arrows and punk people who piss you off."

"And sex," Trent said, laughing, his bloodshot eyes running from me to Viv. "Campbell saw you butt naked."

"I never said naked," Campbell said, returning the flask to Graham's waiting hand.

Amanda twirled her cardigan's top button as she studied us. "Are you having sex parties?"

Conner coughed midinhale of his cigarette.

I feigned a yawn. "I'm tired. Can we please go?"

"Oh my god, I was kidding about sex parties," Amanda's hands flapped. "But listen." She smoothed her hair in a self-satisfied way. "I'm not dumb and you four aren't as smart as you think. It's obvious you're into something crazy and this year is basic as fuck, so we want in."

"You want in," Graham repeated a little bug-eyed.

"Yeah." She yawned with disinterest, but her wheedling tone betrayed her. "Whatever bonfire, streaking, truth or dare, prank pulling, punking shenanigans you guys are about, we want in."

"You can't have in because there's nothing for you to be in," I said. I turned to Graham, who'd driven us. "Home, please."

"What were you and Harry doing in Berrington yesterday?" There was a sweet snare to Amanda's voice.

I spun around. "Are you following us?"

"Please." She swatted the air. "Rachel's cousin does nails in downtown Berrington and she does Rachel's for free before every dance."

"I saw you," Rachel said. It rang of childish accusation.

I smirked. "You see us all the time."

"Why'd you buy so much meat at the butcher shop?"

"It's not your business, but my parents are having a barbecue," Harry lied smoothly.

"But you were carrying these huge containers and running," Rachel insisted.

"Big conspiracy. My parents like to grill," Harry said, and then to Viv and Graham, "If you guys aren't ready, Izzie and I will walk."

"Maybe," Amanda spoke over him, "if you let us in, we'd be better at not asking questions about what you guys bought at a butcher shop the same day there was a prank pulled with animal blood. Maybe then we'd be better about not spreading our *theories* around. Think on it."

A bolt of anger shot through me. I left before it came out as a yell or threat or curse. Even when we had the upper hand, Amanda somehow laid claim to it anyway. Amanda and I didn't have a history like she had with Viv. I didn't seek out ways to spar with her in the way Viv did. Save once.

Seven Hills High School's production of *The Breakfast Club* sophomore year. Amanda had the role of Viv's understudy. Opening night, Amanda, Jess, and Rachel sat in the front row, and as Viv recited her lines, Amanda hissed like a snake. *Sssssssss*. I watched the slow spread of red hives up Viv's neck. It took me until intermission until I understood that Amanda was reminding Viv of the years she stuttered on words that began with the letter *S*.

I followed Amanda to the restroom during intermission. Surprised her in the corridor by the theater's coat closet, yanked her in.

"What in the hell?" she cried.

I pinned her against the wall, elbow pressed to her neck, imitating the way the girl with the blade held me in the train car. "I promise that if you don't shut up during this performance, I will rip your wicked tongue from your mouth so you can't make *S* sounds ever again, snake." The burst of violence, the threat, had me trembling as I held her. She smiled like she'd won something. Adrenaline made me light-headed. Amanda leaned into my elbow and spoke in a raspy whisper, "If you don't let me go, I'll stand up in the middle of the second act and tell your bestie her thighs look like an elephant's."

I could smell the watermelon hard candy tucked in her cheek. It nauseated me. The closeness. I dropped my arms. "That's what I thought," she said as she knocked by me.

But she didn't make a peep during the second half.

"They want in," Graham said in the backseat of the car. "Who do you think Amanda meant?"

"Everyone who was there," Viv said. "Amanda, Jess, Rachel, Conner, Trent, and Campbell. The six of them."

"Do you realize what a coup this is?" Graham slapped the driver's seat back.

"Hey." I swiped blindly at his hand.

"Sorry," he muttered aside. "We haven't even tried to recruit them and they're begging to join."

"There's nothing for them to join," I said, steering onto our street. I slowed at Mr. Kirkpatrick's house and glared up at it. "The Order of IV is ours. That's the point. It would be different if we had more members."

"Absolutely it would have to change." Graham's voice already heavy with thought. "Think, Izzie. Everything we'd be capable of with recruits."

"Stop calling them recruits." My protest was halfhearted. *Recruits like in an army.* I was caught between fear that Amanda would ruin the Order for us and cravings for amping up our next rebellion.

"Imagine," he whispered, "if we had six foot soldiers to do our bidding."

Harry palmed his eyes beside me. "Do our bidding?"

"To help with the rebellions," Graham said.

Thoughts were streaking through my head at speeds that whistled, their colors running, mixing, forming new ideas. "If we want new members, why add kids who treat us like crap?"

"Because they'll have to grovel at our feet," Graham said.

"We'll give them orders," Viv whispered, like she was watching Amanda grovel already.

Harry stared out the window. "All of them would have to listen to us?" His tone sounded funny; I couldn't put my finger on how.

"Every single one would have to do what we wanted," Graham answered.

"Because they want in," Viv added.

"Doesn't everyone always want in?" Graham said, like it was the simplest lesson in the world.

Maybe it was.

The Order was always about belonging. Us. Together. Forever. Was it so unforeseeable that its allure would crook its finger and beckon to others? So unimaginable that other kids would be hungry for an idol, a bonfire, the moon, and secrets?

19

I stayed in my room Saturday morning, planted on my desk, watching the Pacific. Each wave rushed in darker, something ominous gathering. I snapped Polaroids, placing their unformed vignettes in single file across my desk. When I finally studied their captured moments, it was clear. The sea knew what we were planning.

Our third rebellion had been aimed at Carver and Denton. Intended to frighten and unnerve them. Pictures circulated. People gossiped. That boy lied about the bloody noose and the girl about the X marking her door. The mayor was forced to respond to the whole town in her statement. My own parents locked our windows, which were usually thrown open to the breeze. All that blood gnawed a little at the myth of the utopian Seven Hills.

The fourth rebellion would have a wider scope. We would aim revenge not just at Carver and Denton, but at those we knew hadn't helped Goldilocks. Maybe there were more whose indifference cost Goldilocks her life, or at least justice. Our next rebellion wouldn't target them all directly, but I hoped they'd get the message of our scattershot. *You are not safe.*

But we were small in number, and though our group was a universe to me, there was a limit to what we could do.

The Order had *one* invisible hand. With Amanda and the others, we would have many. All invisible. Omnipresent. Vengeful gods capable of endless aftershocks.

When Harry arrived Saturday evening to take me to homecoming, Mom and Dad had their cell phones out, Dad being sneaky about snapping shots and Mom instructing us to pose. I set my jaw and withstood the happy parent routine. Thus far, there was no evidence that the flowers delivered to Ina had caused the flourish of town gossip I'd expected.

"You look beautiful," Harry told me in the car.

I smiled at him. "You do too." I hadn't seen Harry in a suit since eighth-grade graduation. I remembered him looking like a coat hanger in his jacket. Since then, Harry had done a lot of broadening.

"This used to be my dad's." Harry pinched the fabric of his jacket cuff.

"It's perfect."

"Green is my favorite color," he said of my sleeveless dress.

The fabric was thin and delicate, pooling around my strappy sandals. "It's silk, I think."

"I like silk."

He opened the moonroof. It was a balmy night, moisture

in the air making my wavy hair wavier. I rested my head back and looked starward. "It's really clear. The stars are so bright."

Harry glanced up from the road. "When I was way younger, I was obsessed with astronomy."

"Did you ever have those glow-in-the-dark constellation stickers when you were little?"

"They covered my bedroom ceiling. You?"

"My closet. I used to tear all the clothes off the hangers to stare at them from the floor. Sometimes I'd make Graham or Viv sit and I'd talk like we were at the planetarium."

"That sounds—"

"Like I was a huge dork."

His eyes cut to me. "Like something I would have done. Are they still there?"

"No way. After we discovered the meteorite, we were all really into space. The possibility. And then it occurred to me how scary endless possibility is. Like, isn't there enough possibility on Earth where a zillion crazy-awful things can happen?"

"Or a zillion wonderful things. To me that's what's cool about space," Harry said. I watched his profile. His hair was combed to the side, and his shirt collar brushed just below the knot of his throat. I swallowed. "Anything could be up there. I used to imagine other planets and I'd make really long lists with the characteristics of their solar systems and how the lifeforms in them evolved. And for my favorite worlds I drew comics. Not good ones. Not like your drawings."

"What were the comics about?"

"Uh . . ." Out of force of habit, he pawed at phantom hair on his forehead. "One was about a family of aliens and another one was an alien war over resources. A lot of them had revolutions and heroes and battles with lasers. But my all-time favorite was about an alien boy sitting in his room drawing comics and imagining me, on Earth. It was like I had this interstellar friendship and no matter what happened, I had this friend out there, like a reflection, the same and different."

The tops of palm trees moved across the rectangle in the car roof. Between their fronds the stars burned brighter as Harry spoke.

"Do you still think he exists?"

"Who?"

"The teenager living on another planet, wondering if you exist. Taking a girl to his civilization's version of homecoming."

He shook his head. "What? No way. I was younger than Simon. He still thinks a fairy leaves him cash for baby teeth." He shook his head again. "Kids are crazy-stupid."

"Liar. You totally believe." I laughed and pointed to his deepening right dimple. "You're trying too hard to convince me."

He raised a hand in surrender. I wanted to pluck it from the air, to kiss his palm. "I'm not a liar. Not exactly. Maybe a boy like me is up there. I just don't buy that he's thinking about me. Why would he bother?"

"That's sad."

"Or realistic."

"Do you still have the comics?"

"My mom keeps my baby teeth in her jewelry box."

"So obviously," I said.

"Definitely."

It would have been motion-picture perfect if that year's homecoming theme had been the cosmos. A night of twirling past Venus and Mars. But our journey into the gymnasium remained a terrestrial one, to France. A fifteen-foot cardboard replica of the Eiffel Tower was midcourt, and teachers manning the macaron and sparkling lemonade tables wore red berets and horizontally striped shirts. Our classmates were in quiet clusters around the room. The night was early and sober.

Viv and I usually went stag to dances. Graham couldn't be persuaded and Harry got a subsequent pass. I felt short an appendage without her; her smile hopeful at the night, the way her eyes reflected the lights and decorations like she was trying to soak it all up, and the contact high of her enthusiasm would send me twirling onto the dance floor.

I fidgeted with my dress without much purpose other than looking the part of girl-with-date-at-a-formal. Easily said and awkwardly done. I had a blister forming on my heel, my forehead was starched with hairspray, I was sweating through my deodorant, and I had just noticed that only the nails on my right hand were painted. Harry tugged at his tie like it was constricting. Suddenly I wished he'd lose the suit jacket.

"Look," I said, fluttering my fingers.

"Nail polish on one hand. Cool," he said.

I patted my stiff updo and fluttered my lashes. "I'm very fashionable, you know." I dropped my hands. "You want to take your tie off, huh?"

"Uh, no. I mean"—his expression seized up—"I want to look how I'm supposed to, for you." He stuck his chest out, wincing slightly when his collar bit into his neck.

I reached over and worked at the tie's knot. "I want you to look like you." He smiled and shoved the tie into his pocket. "Good-bye torture devices for my feet," I said, kicking my shoes under a skirted table.

We were Harry and Izzie again.

Halfway across the dance floor a familiar laugh came from under the glittery planetary mass of a disco ball. Viv was a 1950s screen vixen; a glimmering figure in a silver gown.

Graham came striding up—classic black tux, cuff links winking at us, a shadow in the cleft of his chin, and enough bob-and-weave to his torso that I knew he'd been drinking. "You two have to liberate me from this nightmare of the American dream," he said loudly.

I waved at the cardboard Eiffel Tower and smiled cheekily. "You mean Parisian."

"You know what I mean," he grumbled.

Harry knocked his shoulder companionably into Graham's. "That bad?"

"The corsages are making my allergies flare up." Graham pointed to his watering eyes. "The limo is a white stretch Hummer, it was stocked with bottles of cinnamon whiskey and buckets of fried chicken, Viv's laugh has reached

DEFCON cackle, and I'm considering slitting my wrists in the bathroom so I don't have to go to her afterparty."

My throat tightened. "Whose party?" But I already suspected, didn't I? Inviting the others to our territory was the next logical step in recruiting them. A step that Viv wanted to take. The barn, the orchard, the rock—they were our fortresses. Where better to entertain the enemy? See if we could manipulate them into being our foot soldiers?

Graham pinched the bridge of his nose. No spectacles. "I buried the lede," he said. "Viv invited *them* to the barn, after the dance. They're going to drink our cider and invade our headquarters."

"They're going to ask us more about the Order," I whispered.

"Absolutely," Graham said. "Amanda has a one-track mind. She's already brought up you guys at the butcher four times. It's like she's trying to see inside my brain." A feigned shudder. "They're afraid they're missing out. Viv wants to let them in."

"So do you," Harry said.

Graham held his stare, unblinking. "Indeed, for slightly different reasons, I presume. It needs to be unanimous—on account of democracy."

"Izzie," Viv yipped. She plowed into me, arms pitched around my neck, her wet, breezy breath in my ear. "I'm in love with your dress. Where are your shoes?"

She swung away, one hand fastened onto my arm, trying to twirl me. "Whoa," I said, resisting her momentum. "Do you need water?"

"The limo was so fun, Izzie. We sang to music and snapped pictures and they're all following and tagging me." Like a tick, she was checking over her shoulder, making certain Amanda's group hadn't dropped out of orbit.

"Come stand with us. Jess was all, *When are your friends showing?* and I said you were coming, and now you're here." She squealed at the predictable order of events.

Concern was a slash to my chest. Was this bleary-eyed girl just a mask Viv the war queen was wearing as she plotted revenge? The invitation to the barn was strategic, wasn't it?

I was a husk on the sidelines of Amanda's court. Maybe Amanda's many air-kisses had dulled Viv's loathing? Or the way she repeated whatever pearls made her laugh, her reenactments so drab she was basically a vampire sucking the funny out of jokes?

Rachel returned from the restroom, and by the self-congratulatory smile in between sips of her flask, I could tell she had gossip she was dying to share.

She waited until Amanda drifted back from a group of lesser friends. Rachel announced, "I know something I bet none of you do." There were blotches darkening on her pale chest. She yanked up her strapless gown to cover up a sliver of bra showing.

Amanda's face flickered with impatience. "What, Rachel?"

"Patton Garvey was in the bathroom a second ago, and she was talking about how her boyfriend and some of his friends tore down all the curfew signs from the beach trails last night."

Our crescent beach was at the heart of Seven Hills, a few blocks west of the knoll. Five or six trails leading into the dunes began in the beach parking lot. Each was marked by a metal sign on wooden stilts with the sunset curfew posted.

"Why bother?" Campbell asked. "The cops hardly ever enforce the curfew."

"And even without the signs, the curfew would still stand," Graham added.

Rachel grinned. "It was like, a symbol."

Jess was nodding. "A symbolic gesture of giving the finger to authority."

"Exactly," Rachel said. "They even signed the asphalt where the signs had been."

"Dumbasses," Amanda said.

Rachel shook her head. "Not with their names, A. With *IV*."

Jess's head snapped to Graham, who stood beside her. I felt eyes studying my reaction. First a *IV* had been spray painted on Principal Harper's car by a copycat. Second I'd found the symbols on bathroom mirrors and lockers at school. Third there was a tale about a few of our class-mates pulling down curfew signs and leaving *IV*s in their place.

My hand curled into a fist at my side. Patton's boyfriend—I couldn't remember his name, only that he had red hair and freckles—had no right invoking IV for his pathetic excuse of a stunt. As Graham said, the curfew was still in effect, so the kids hadn't accomplished anything.

Rachel said to Viv's neutral expression, "You should be flattered. It's like fan art."

It was more than fan art. IV had inspired some kids to rebel against the authority they chafed under. My fist gradually loosened. This was power. We'd moved kids to action.

Across from me, with no inflection in her voice, Jess said, "I'd die for your dress."

"To wear at your funeral?" Graham said.

"Touché," Jess replied with a slight bow of her head.

Graham was all dressed up and standing next to the girl of his dreams. He yawned.

"I love this song." Viv's hands were moving to the music. "Teddy Graham—dance with me." Graham adjusted his bow tie and pretended not to have heard.

"Will you dance with me, Vivy?" Harry asked. My heart swelled watching Harry take Viv under the disco ball.

Graham closed the gap between us with an off-kilter stride. "Your date and mine are dancing." His bushy brows quirked up like it was the most preposterous thing. "I guess we better dance so people don't assume we're scorned." Amanda looked about a second away from marching over to us.

"Don't step on my toes," I said, walking onto the court. When we were out of their earshot, I said, "Those kids left IV on the asphalt where the signs had been."

"I didn't foresee us inspiring a revolution."

I flicked his pocket square at my eye level and held on to

his shoulders. He was like Viv, comfortable with the pomp of dressing up. "Revolution?"

"Give it time," he said with a haughty cock of his head. "I've been thinking about what increased recruitment for the Order would mean for its structure. Concentric circles. One inner core made up of us and—"

"And an outer circle made up of everybody else," I finished. "We'd get to keep the Order the way we want by adding an outside layer with different rules."

"Minions for your majesty," Graham said. "Or rather than concentric circles, the Order could have autonomous cells. They're harder to break up. That's how a lot of insurgencies and terrorists operate." I frowned. "It's a simple, ruthless fact," he continued, gravely serious. "We give the cells their marching orders and they're clueless about what the other cells are doing, so they don't get the big picture until after the rebellion." My attention had drifted to Harry and Viv. "Are you worried she's going to tell him she's never been kissed so he'll kiss her?"

I made a funny face at him. "No, freakazoid. I was thinking how nice Harry was to dance with her and what a mean bean you were not to." I pinched his plump earlobe.

"Ouch," he said without meaning it. "Maybe I was going to dance with her?"

I gave him an are-you-shitting-me look.

"Okay, mind reader, what am I thinking now?"

Without glasses his eyes had too much glitter. They suggested what I didn't want to think about. "Stop it."

"You want me to stop thinking?"

"Stop being a troublemaker."

He made a comically sinister face and said, darkly, "It's the night. The flask. Them wanting in. I'm power mad."

"Jess looks really pretty. You should ask her to dance."

"Ha," he huffed.

"She'll say yes," I said, peering beyond him. "She keeps looking over here. She's interested."

He snorted. "Don't hold your breath."

"Come on. Ask her to dance. You aren't the *worst* dancer."

He kept his eyes turned away. "Thanks for the self-esteem boost, but I'm talking Jess and me, the whole love story, not going to happen."

"W—"

He hushed me sharply and made steady eye contact. "Sorry—really. Just don't, okay? Not now."

I lifted one arm off his shoulder and pushed a corner of his frowning mouth up with a finger. He grinned big and fake. "You've liked Jess all of high school," I whispered. "Go. For. It."

Graham's complicated face looked stricken while he was at a loss for words. At last, his cheeks dimpled. "Haven't you ever ordered mint chip ice cream just to realize what you actually wanted was strawberry? There's no improving upon strawberry ice cream. I could have strawberry every day until I die."

"Are you actually comparing a girl to a flavor of ice cream?"

"What? I'd be salted caramel. Wait, that's your favorite,

isn't it?" He grinned without it touching his eyes and held me a little closer. "Are you having fun? With Harry. He's my best friend, other than you. You're my favorite."

I chuckled, pretending I thought he was joking

Graham's bluster drained from his face. He was watching me too carefully. Waiting. I wanted to say it back to him. To make his smile warm with sincerity. Out of the four of us, we were most alike, and loving him felt most like loving myself. Some hunch kept me from saying it, though. Some tiny rodent inside my head clawed its message: I wouldn't mean it as he had.

Graham didn't want to dance with Viv. He refused to ask Jess to dance. Graham was dancing with me. He'd returned to paying me more attention. That selfish pit in my stomach tingled.

"You are my favorite," he said, his eyes growing large and wounded, "but on our rock you told Viv that you loved her more than anyone, ever."

"I was trying to cheer her up," I said.

"You tried cheering up your friend by telling her how much more you liked her than your other two best friends, in front of them?"

"Guys?" Harry said, likely not for the first time. He'd been standing there, I don't know how long.

"That's messed up," I said to Graham.

"You are."

Harry brushed my arm. "Don't fight. You want to try the macarons?" Graham's hands still cupped my waist. They dropped away. Their heat lingered in the fabric of my dress.

I couldn't taste the chocolate of the first cookie. The second, vanilla and lavender, was sweeter. By the raspberry I was happily accepting sparkling lemonade in a plastic champagne flute from Harry.

We didn't rejoin Graham and Viv. We danced and talked, and it never felt like wrestling for control. There was no sharp edge to Harry. No scrape to him. No hidden meaning to what he told me.

I laughed and he laughed and we talked about space again—and music and Simon and where we'd go first if we were backpacking across Europe, and how we should make a plan to travel the summer after our first year of college—and by the time we walked to his car, our hands were hot because they'd been clasped for so long. I was smiling, blissed out, strappy sandals hooked on my finger, unembarrassed that my dress had a lemonade stain.

It was simple, sweet, and smooth with Harry, like the summer breeze that had blown him through the orchard to the barn in search of us five years before. I decided that he'd come not in search of us but in search of me. And for a little while, I forgot how the summer breeze that brought Harry had also stirred Goldilocks's hair.

20

Harry and I took a roundabout way to our neighborhood. The car was parked on the street and we walked through the orchard, stalling. Harry carried me on his back, a closeness that gave me goose bumps down my front so that I didn't need to put my shoes back on.

I liked the way he smelled, of grown-up aftershave but also of crayons because Harry had been helping Simon with an art project before leaving for the dance.

Harry was slightly winded, the echo of his breath in my ear even after I'd slid down his spine. "You sure you wouldn't rather get pizza and eat on the beach?" he asked.

I looked up the path, beyond the trellis. The barn, usually diffused with warm light, our real home and clubhouse, had lights and music blaring.

"This place is ours," I said. "How can we not be here for a party? How can we not be here when you-know-what comes up?"

He inclined his head, understanding.

We hovered over the glass slider's threshold. The barn looked under attack. Our sleeping bags and blankets had been booted out of the loft. They were on the wood floor in a confusion of color, faux fur, and nylon sheen. Amanda, Rachel, and Viv had arranged themselves on the piles. The effect reminded me of a photograph of Victorian explorers camping with Bedouins in the Arabian Desert, but with a lot more tan thigh and cleavage revealed. The girls were midgiggle attack, but Viv's eyes were open now. Sobered. Darting.

Conner stood on our couch, wing tips gouging into the satin, his smile bored, one hand strangling a bottle of cider by the neck while he shouted at Trent, who was raiding our fridge.

Graham sat at the edge of our table, ankle propped on his knee, spinning our ceremonial dagger beside him. Campbell and Jess were listening with upturned faces like they were kids at story time.

Our idol considered our potential recruits from her throne on the antique armoire. Hands palmed, eyes closed, a wolf's smile. The stars on her cloak darkened, coming into focus, until I saw them as a harbinger. Harry and I were preoccupied with space as kids. Our meteorite came from the stars. Goldilocks was placed at its altar. The day we discovered her, Harry found us. Me. What were the odds that Graham's mother picked up an idol in the Mekong Delta covered in stars? Without the Mistress, would the Order have occurred to me? Without the Order, would we have ever put together what we knew about Goldilocks? The idol smiled like it had been her plan all along. Mistress of Rebellion, Secrets, and Dead Girls.

That smile said, *Let the others join us. Let me have them. Let us fill the streets with blood.*

I took a step into the barn with an understanding that faded as I tried to seize it, grow it. This was not random but a cosmic weave.

"Last chance for pizza."

I started a little, pulled back to the present.

"We can't leave Viv and Graham to the wolves," I said, mimicking the idol's smile.

Really, we were the wolves. Neither Graham or Viv appeared swept away in the tide of attention. Viv's eyes were probing.

Graham was in the middle of a story. "The Ancients believed in ritual madness. Not madness like you're mentally ill but madness as in losing your mind as a release into the universe, and"—he waved hello without pausing—"you're consumed by the rush of it."

"What's that?" Conner called out from where he'd sat on the couch. His finger indicated the idol.

Graham and I met eyes. *Yes, let's make them our initiates.* We were dressed for homecoming, but I felt costumed for the stage.

"Nothing," Graham said too harshly. "Who wants another

drink?" Exactly the right amount of forced cheer and nervous bumbling as he offered around a bottle of cider.

"Amanda?" Conner called. "Hey." He snapped for her. She turned from the girls, begrudgingly. Our Mistress was staged on a leather-bound book, her pedestal, and white pillar candles surrounded her. I imagined Viv scheming: invite over a bunch of kids suspicious that you're up to something, ply them with cider, and wait for someone to notice the mysterious statue on an altar.

Amanda's eyes landed on the idol. She wobbled to her feet, yanking down her short hemline from riding up as she went. Her hands closed on the bottom shelf for a steadying moment.

"Don't touch her," Viv said. The barn went quiet.

"No one who isn't a *member* is supposed to touch her," Harry explained. Hands in his pockets, he strolled over to the armoire, worshipfully gazing up at the idol. "It could be dangerous." Graham hissed for him to be silent when it was too late to actually shush him.

Viv wrung her hands. "Maybe we should just tell them. Izzie?" Her stage voice flooded the rafters, perfectly inflected with anxiety. "Amanda's already half guessed."

That's how it was decided. No talk. No vote. The four of us working in symphony, invisible threads lengthening from our brains, linking to conspire. We would win the Order its foot soldiers and appease Amanda's lot into silence.

I shook my head hard, faking alarm. "Vivy, you know there's a process. The initiation. It's against the rules just to tell."

"The rules are there for our safety—your safety," Graham said, pointing to Jess. Her lips parted. "It would be too risky otherwise." He plucked one of his suspenders over and over, pretending to rack his brain. "You'd all have to swear to follow the rules too. You'd have to prove"—a brief pause—"no. Forget it. Dangerous idea. The initiation would be too much for you guys."

"Way too much," I muttered, grabbing the dagger off the table and indiscreetly slipping it on top of the armoire with the idol. I fought a smirk turning around to face them.

It was possible they'd call bullshit. Amanda, fellow actress, would recognize theater.

"An initiation wouldn't be too much," Amanda pleaded.

"We're game to follow the rules," Jess promised.

Viv had reclined, adopting a blasé posture and an evasive frown.

"Yeah," Conner said. "I'd be dope as fuck at whatever you guys have going on. I'm a badass getaway driver and Campbell knows how to pick locks."

Campbell coughed, surprised. "Only the lock on my door when one of my sisters locks me out of my own room. But I know a dude who sells fireworks." He sounded relieved to have something to offer. "The illegal ones from China that can blow out walls and set stuff on fire. I've never used them myself."

Graham stroked his jawline, encouraging them, *Convince me.*

"Once I used a wire hanger to unlock my car," Trent offered eagerly.

Rachel huffed. "Forget that. I can lift a wallet."

Harry snorted.

"She can," Jess said. "She lifted three wallets off guys at the Harvest Festival. Ghost hands."

"I brought the wallets to lost and found," Rachel said with a toss of her hair. "I don't need the money or anything."

Amanda, not to be outdone, claimed, "I'm the stealthiest. We TP'd a hundred houses in middle school and never got caught." She flushed, possibly remembering she'd hit our houses. "And I mean, that's kid stuff . . . Conner and I broke into one of his dad's developments and trashed a house."

"Amanda," Conner said, standing suddenly, knocking an empty bottle over on the floor.

"Relax. We busted the bathroom mirrors and Con broke the counters in the model home."

My pulse raced. Our initiates were trying to convince us of their worth.

"And we all know you've got street cred," she continued, leveling a finger around at the four of us. "IV. You guys are seriously twisted."

We traded dramatic stares. Took our time. Deliberated. Harry was all hands in his hair. Graham had retrieved his spectacles and was polishing them on his shirt, looking deep in thought. I worried the gold necklace at my throat. At last, I whispered, "Okay. But we need a few days before telling you how this will work."

"Thank you," Amanda murmured with so much reverence I nearly laughed myself to the floor. Viv drew me over to sit with her on the blankets. The mosaic of green cider empties expanded on the table. I participated halfheartedly in a debate about pledging to a sorority next year. Harry and I caught each other's eyes as he went for the fridge. He motioned to a bottle, then to me. I shook my head and was about to mouth that we should go when Conner blocked Harry's path from the fridge.

"Hey, sport." I strained to hear Conner over the other conversations. "You and me calling a truce. That shit is *something*. It's cool though, I guess. I don't mind that you're poorer than dirt." Conner cuffed Harry's neck. "Or that if this were medieval times, I'd basically own you and your family. Feudalism was boss."

Harry removed his car keys from his pocket, angled one, and popped the lid off his cider. He took a sip and licked the bubbles from his upper lip. Conner's hand stayed on him. "Sure, Con. I'll try to forget that you're an arrogant, privileged waste of space." He took another sip. "And that if this were medieval times, the rest of the serfs and I would jump you and probably leave you disemboweled in your father's field. But I'll make you a deal."

Conner's face pinched between amusement and scorn. "Yeah?"

"Yeah. Don't put your hands on me again."

"What're you offering?"

"I'll keep mine off you." He left Conner staring after him. Harry winked at me as he perched on the table by Graham and Campbell.

. . .

A little while later, Graham tapped me on the forehead. "Walk?"

Graham and I emerged into a black-and-white world. The '90s hip-hop faded behind us. He was a timeless portrait, hair lifting in the breeze, shirtsleeves hiked up past his elbows, one black suspender swinging at his thigh, the other hooked on his shoulder,

"Not anachronistic," I whispered.

His head dipped. "Come again?" There was a trace of his dimple.

"Not anachronistic, exactly," I told him. "You look timeless, like you could always exist and you always have. Like a vampire."

He tipped his head back and barked a laugh. "You're yammed."

"Am not." I rubbed my stomach. "Delirious with hunger, maybe."

He unbunched the jacket in his hand and offered it. I waved it off.

"We can sneak into Viv's kitchen," he said.

"Nah. I'm fine." The barn's door was a tiny caramel rectangle behind us. "What are we going to tell them? I mean, all that in there, it was brilliant."

His mouth pursed and then he shook his head. "No idea—yet."

The trees along one side of the pool bowed in the wind. Viv's house was lightless. Graham settled on a poolside lounger and I sat next to him. He tried to pluck my hand from my thigh. I wouldn't budge it. Holding hands right then wouldn't have felt friendly and innocent.

"You're pissed," he said.

My thoughts staggered backward and I remembered our dance and what he'd said about Viv and the kiss and my secret. "I'm not."

"You're angry that I kissed Viv, which is selfish."

I faced him. "Excuse me?"

Clouds blew across the sky, muddying the light. "You hate that I was both of your first kisses," he said, his voice having lost some of its chilliness.

"You were not her first kiss," I said, loud and clearly. "She was confused or kidding or—I don't know what she was— but you were not her first kiss."

He smirked. "You think I don't know about her theater camp trysts?"

I shot up, flushed and surprised. "Why tell me that you were both of our first kisses then? Just to bring mine up?" I turned away from him. I marched past the pool. The stone path was wet and slippery as I rounded the corner of the house.

Ninth grade, right before Thanksgiving, Harry and Viv were out of town. Graham and I ended up at a classmate's house party. We were standing too close to a game of truth or dare. At Graham's turn, he said "dare" with his typical bravado. The junior dared him to kiss me. Graham asked if it was okay, whispered and in front of the other players in the circle. I nodded, dumbstruck. I'd never kissed anyone before; he hadn't either. It was gentle. His braces nipped my lips. Kids watched, joking, critiquing our form.

I made it to the front porch swing as Graham emerged from the other direction.

"Izzie," he said.

"Go away."

"I'm redacting everything. I put my foot in my mouth. I shouldn't have brought our kiss up. I shouldn't have kissed Viv at all. It was the night, the rock, our ceremony, the way you both looked. You were in your *underwear*. I wanted to kiss someone." He fisted his hair. "The opportunity presented itself."

It had. I crossed my arms, blinking at him.

"Why do you mind?" he asked.

Graham and I had crossed an invisible line freshman year and I worried at the time that we wouldn't be able to return to the side where we were best friends. My worry was for no good reason. "You kissing Viv could have ruined everything."

"But you and Harry dating couldn't?" He held his arms up, agitated. "I regret kissing you that way. On a dare. I'd do it over." He was breathing like an asthmatic.

I couldn't settle on what I wanted from him. To apologize more for kissing Vivian. To never kiss anyone again. Jealousy contracted my stomach. Graham belonged to me. He was my oldest friend. I wanted to keep him from kissing other girls, but I didn't want to kiss him myself.

I took his hand, warm and familiar, soft scar on his palm

from the blood moon ritual. I thought about the tattoo scabbing over on my ribs, identical to his. I cupped his palm and pressed my lips to the scar. I tasted salt and cider. "There. Do-over complete," I said. "I'm sorry."

His expression was shadowed. He wasn't talking. I couldn't even hear his breath.

Nervous, I offered, "You could still make an epic connection with Jess. Let's go back and try."

He held his arm taut, resisting me for a moment. Then a plaintive sigh, and his arm slackened, and he shuffled after me.

When we were under the trellis, a few yards away from the bumping music, I heard him whisper behind me. His voice ghosted into the night and I pretended not to notice.

I wonder, what if I'd stopped. Faced him. And listened.

Retrieved from the cellular phone of Vivian Marlo
Transcript and notes prepared by Badge #821891
Shared Media Folder Titled: IV, Sun., Oct. 13, 2:06 a.m.

Video start.

V. Marlo levels a finger at the camera. "I am not drunk." She laughs. "Okay, maybe just a teensy little bit. The head drama instructor at the Lessing Summer Theater Academy is this ancient hag who once upon a time starred in an off-Broadway production of *The Fantastics*." She twirls a finger in the air. "Stuff of legends, I know. She's a million years old, a cigarette dangling from her mouth, and wine stains on her coat. Most of my fellow thespians consider themselves too advanced to humor her. But once she heard me say that acting is the best kind of lying, lies even the liar believes, and she pulled me aside where she breathed her rancid old-person breath into my face and said, 'People are all lies, Ms. Marlo, lies piled on lies, on top of lies, and they almost always believe their own hype. To be a truly great actor,' she wheezed past her cigarette, 'is to forget the truth.'"

She stares at the lens for a long time. When she speaks again, she's whispering. "The old crow was right. Last night at homecoming, I forgot the truth. Those girls." She slowly shakes her head. "Jess always acts way over the world, so when she thinks you're interesting, it's major. Rachel is the best sidekick ever. She's all *uh-huh* and *absolutely* and *amirite* to everything. She said her dad could show my headshot to one of his clients who represents models. And Amanda, she was the best. All reminiscing, like *Remember when you played Lucy in* Dracula, *now I can say you were the be-all end-all.*"

She smiles slyly. "And I almost bought it. Those slippery bitches. I grinned, said thank you, danced, and shared their flask of raspberry vodka. I loved the way they sat in one another's laps, fell over hugging, and acted grossed out by the boys but were all flirty anyway. By the end of the night, when Amanda air-kissed me good-bye after her little performance confessing to breaking and entering, I saw it in her eyes. Amanda thinks she played me. She thinks I'm dumb enough to ever trust her again."

She hugs herself. "I'd hold a grudge against that girl after a hundred years of her kissing my ass. Some things you never forgive."

Video stop.

21

Our story has to be a tragedy. Epic. Shakespearean. Greek," Viv proclaimed, arms thrown wide as she balanced along the edge of the stage. "It'll have betrayal. Intrigue. Murder. Maybe an exiled queen. And heroes." She went up on her toes to pivot and reverse, her black dress lifting and swirling. "I just love a tragic hero."

I was on my stomach, idly kicking my socked heels together. "Tragic hero. Murder. Intrigue," I recited, adding each to my notes.

"People like their heroes to be partly bad," Graham said.

I typed *antihero*.

Harry's calculus text thudded on the stage as he said, "Not really."

I highlighted *antihero*; hit backspace. On second thought, I added it again, with a question mark.

Graham considered Harry with an intense stare. "We'll agree to disagree on the subject of heroics." He chomped down on a fistful of chocolate-covered peanuts, ruminating over his next thought. "The Order's story has got to be a spectacle of blood and guts. Like the apocalypse of an ancient civilization who worshipped our idol."

"But if this ancient civilization ended, who passed their story on?" Harry asked, propping his elbows on his knees. "History's written by winners, and winners say sucky things about losers. They don't pass on their legends and stories."

"Maybe they weren't completely obliterated, then. There were a few survivors of a fallen kingdom and they kept the story alive," Graham said. "Satisfied?"

Harry scratched the back of his head. "It's too complicated. Amanda, Conner—they begged us to join. They bragged about their crappy behavior. We're allowing them in. No convincing needed."

"Do you think that'll be enough for them to do whatever we say?" Viv asked. "Like, if Amanda goes, *Why do we have to do blah-blah rebellion* and we say, *Because*, it'll be enough?"

"We'll say, *Because the rebellion punks this or that jerk*," Harry said. "And yeah, I think it'll be enough."

"But if it's not?" Graham asked. "If they're punking us and if we don't prove to them how serious we are, then what?"

"So keep it simple," I said. "Have a story about the Order, how we discovered it, and why they should follow its rules. Just use what's right in front of us."

"Chocolate-covered peanuts," Viv said, sinking into our circle.

"No." I side-eyed her. "The meteorite, the drawings, the birds, and Goldilocks."

"I mean, communism." She opened and closed an outstretched hand.

Graham slid the bag of chocolate in her direction. She caught it, ignoring an escapee peanut that dropped off the stage. Viv had reserved the auditorium to practice her blocking and lines, but when I stopped by to say good-bye after Monday's classes, she was on her back, kicking the red velvet curtain and swiping through pictures on her cell. "I can't concentrate on *Antigone* when there's a better performance to plan," she'd whined. And there we all were, on the stage, an appropriate place to reinvent the Order of IV.

"Hmmm. Use what's right in front of us," Graham murmured to himself. To us he said, "But we have to start out with a demonstration of conviction. Blood. Guts. Something so they know how serious the Order is. Too bad we already cut our hands."

"I am not doing another blood offering," Viv said, thumbing her freshly healed palm. "One scar is character; two's deformity."

Graham kept brainstorming. Viv struck down each of his ideas. I clicked over to my web browser; it was already open to a missing persons database. I scanned the photos that were new in the last week. I couldn't imagine a scenario where her family failed to notice that Goldilocks was missing for five years. Where was this girl's version of Graham, Harry, and Viv?

All those eyes of the missing inhabited my computer screen. I gave each a perfunctory glance. *Don't let them in.*

Nothing familiar about any of the girls, except the sense that they could be in the back row of any of my classes. Regular girls. Biting their nails, twisting their earring studs, and singing off-key.

Viv reclined on her back beside me. The gold buttons on her black dress were the shape of scarab beetles, marching up her front. "All we need is for Amanda and Conner to play along. The rest are lemmings," she stated matter-of-factly to the stage lights. "I wish I knew how they all became friends. How Conner and Amanda became king and queen."

I smiled at the Viv classicism.

If she vanished, what would I do? There were hands in my stomach turning it inside out. What if there was someone out there who'd been able to help her, and instead they pulled indifference and their comforters over their heads to go back to sleep? Threw out her shoe. Washed away her blood. Rage brought tears to my eyes. Screw indifference. What would I do to her killer? Goldilocks had one, a fact I kept glossing over. It was difficult to grasp. The adults weren't interested in holding anyone accountable for her death, and even if I didn't like it, their thinking influenced mine. I had to remind myself there was someone to blame above all the rest. Someone who deserved punishment far more than Denton, Carver, and our neighbors did.

I closed the browser. A mere few weeks before, leaving my friends for college seemed like a tragedy. How privileged, flimsy, and naive of me.

• • •

On Wednesday afternoon, Viv delivered instructions to Amanda and Conner. With their four friends, they were to arrive at the barn without cell phones, dressed in white, at midnight on Saturday. All would be revealed. Viv warned them that if a hint of this arrangement was whispered to anyone outside the six who were invited, the invitation would be revoked.

As instructed, they came, ghosts slipping through the orchard. Graham, Viv, Harry, and I were in our places, backs facing north, east, south, and west. We'd cleared the furniture from the center of the barn to make room for the formation of white candles we surrounded.

The muffled laughter outside grew louder. Viv clutched the idol to her breasts, the cut of her black dress low, a lace choker at her thin neck. We were in dark-colored Victorian-era costumes that she'd pieced together from the wardrobes in her attic. My lace collar was high and tight, curling like flower petals under my chin. Viv's black fingerless gloves accentuated her red talons. Graham stood tall in a vest under a long, unbuttoned jacket. There was a vampiric quality to his stiff posture, pale skin, and ruddy mouth; only the needle-points of sweat gathering at his brow gave him away. Harry had left his jacket behind in the attic, his shirtsleeves were rolled up, and a watch chain ran from a buttonhole to the pocket of his vest.

"We have to shock them into submission," Viv had told me when she presented the costumes. "It has to be a production. We have to commit."

The initiates filtered into the barn, wide-eyed, whispering, wearing white. The girls wore slightly old-fashioned dresses, either by coincidence or Viv's direction.

Graham took charge. "Jess and Trent, stand between Viv and Harry. Amanda and Conner, go between Harry and Izzie. Rachel, you're here, and Campbell, you're between me and Izzie." They filled the gaps of our circle around the burning candles.

Their eyes had the glassy strain of holding back laughter. Only Campbell met my gaze with curiosity. If one of them burst, we'd lose the rest. Forget the ridicule; if they laughed, left, there'd be no reason for them not to out us as IV.

Viv lifted the idol above her head. The initiates struggled to smooth their expressions. "Before we can welcome you into our ranks and share our secrets, there are a series of initiation rites. The first will be administered tonight." The conviction in her voice was a hypnotic lullaby. "If you complete the initial rite, we'll tell you about the Order."

Breathy echoes of "the Order" traveled the circle.

"The first rite is a show of good faith," Harry said. "Because these traditions are built on the secrets of the land we're standing on, we require each of you to share a secret with us." Somehow his staring uncomfortably at the wall worked, making him seem captivated by an unseen presence.

Graham's arms were crossed high on his chest and his voice was commanding, kingly. "You'll wait outside for your turn and then one by one you'll take a sip of our truth-telling serum and offer us a secret. We will either accept or deny

your bid to join us. We swear on the Order that we'll keep
your confidence so long as you keep ours."

"Objections?" I asked. I expected there to be, which was
why I was about to follow up the question with a threat: If
they chose to leave without sharing a secret and told anyone
about the Order, Harry would reveal their friends' secrets on
the school news blog.

They played the roles of devoted initiates. They filed out.
Amanda remained, beaming, hands nervously ticking over
her pin-straight hair.

Graham indicated the clearing in the formation of candles where he'd placed an old, dusty blue bottle brimming
with a homemade concoction of animal blood and a pine-
flavored liquor that Stepdad Number Four left behind.

Amanda was given the idol. She made her way amid the
candles, her hem fanning the flames, distorting her shadow
on the wall. Her free hand grappled with the heavy bottle.

"Take a sip of the truth serum," Graham said. He believed
that if we told the initiates it worked, it would. Power of
suggestion.

I widened my eyes at Harry as Amanda took two long
drags.

She coughed with the second; a fine spray of red dots
left on her white collar when she was done. "Blah," she spat.
"Tastes like blood and dirt." She placed the bottle at her feet
and let the idol hang at her side.

"Put her against your heart," Viv instructed.

Amanda hugged the statue, cheeks flushing.

"The Mistress of Rebellion and Secrets will burn you if you lie," I said, a growl to my voice. "Begin."

Her eyes narrowed. "How can I be sure you aren't going to blab what I tell you?"

"You know we're IV," I said. "You know what we did to the police chief's and the mayor's houses. That's leverage." I could practically hear Graham thinking sarcastically, *And mutual assured destruction never fails*.

One of Amanda's thin blond eyebrows lifted. "Okay. Just as long as you know how screwed you'd be." She drew back her shoulders. "What do I get if I have the best secret?"

Harry grunted his inquiry.

"If my secret is better, do I get to stop being an initiate first?" she clarified.

I opened my mouth to say no when Viv said, "I promise that if your secret is best, you'll have a better role in the Order once you're all not initiates anymore. More power than your friends."

Amanda's thin lips spread into a superior grin. "That'll do." She hardly paused a beat. "When Con and I went out we used to meet up at night in his dad's model homes. But then he got wasted while we were at a USB party and was all over another girl, right in front of Jess and Campbell. Like they wouldn't tell me. Then Con's older brother, Bowden, was home from school and I was angry with Con, so I went with Bowden to one of the models. Bowden and I were, you know, and I heard someone coming up the stairs. Over Bowden's shoulder the door opened a crack. I figured it was

Con, following us, jealous. I got all moany to rub it in while he watched. Make sure he knew his brother was better. When we finished I went to the window to see how pissed Con looked getting into his car. It wasn't Con."

"Who was it?" I asked, caught up in the scandalous story.

Amanda's smugness faltered and her voice strained as she answered, "Sebastian."

"Conner's dad?" Harry exclaimed.

"Gross," I said. Viv's fingers never stopped toying with her choker. Her features conveyed the same expression of aloof all-powerfulness as the idol in Amanda's arms.

"Gross if he wasn't so hot," Amanda aimed at me. "He's even hotter than Bowden." A tilt of her head. "Come on, you've noticed."

My mind scurried to recall Sebastian Welsh. Blond. Tan. Suit. Cocky smile like Conner's. Fancy car. Mom and Dad didn't socialize with him. He'd been over a few times when they designed one of his developments. "I guess," I said doubtfully.

"He's like, only forty," she said.

"Only," I muttered.

"The best secret, amirite?"

None of us spoke. She left, a swing to her hips, shaking her hands out at her side like she was shaking off a character.

"Was that for real?" I asked.

The boys made indistinct sounds. Viv arranged the beads at her collar. "Amanda would not lie."

Then came Jess: nervous flutter of hands. Rogue red

lipstick on her overly whitened front teeth. "My dad has a drinking problem," she confessed in a bored tone, eyeing Graham. "He's been to rehab four times. I think he'll probably have to go back soon. I think he likes it there. It's our dirty family secret."

Next, Trent: refusal to look us in the eyes. A burp loud as a truck horn after the truth serum. But there was something in his manner that made him seem like he wanted to impress us.

"Amanda said she and Conner messed stuff up in his dad's houses, but they got that idea from me. Con and me, we used to do all kinds of shit in his dad's first block. It was that shitty street with the small houses that backs up against the freeway? Little dumps. His dad used to put furniture in them to show people what their crap would look like. I jacked a Plasma from one. We sold it at the gas station for a dime bag. Skank weed, too. Ripped off bad, but we were like thirteen."

"You guys get caught?" Harry wondered.

"You shitting me? No way. Con's dad blamed the real estate agent and that dude blamed the guy who mowed the lawn. Can I put her down now?" He clipped a candle retreating from the idol.

Rachel: pink, puffy face upturned, ready to confess to the loft. There was sweat beading on her forehead, the hundred tiny flames making her glisten. "Can I take another sip?" She indicated the serum at her feet.

"You may," Graham said.

Her arm shook lifting the bottle as she took a drag longer

than her first two. After setting the bottle down, she bit her lip purple. "I'm totally into this, really. Uhhhh, lemme think." She hit her palm to her damp forehead, until finally she made a little surprised yelp. "I know: I almost got a DUI freshman year. I didn't even have my license. But my dad plays golf with a prosecutor and he made it go away. Didn't even get community service."

Rachel left in a relieved and sweaty flurry.

I broke the stunned silence. "We shouldn't know that." It was occurring to me that secrets weren't only dangerous for those who kept them—it was dangerous to know them.

"We're exactly the ones who should know about a corrupt prosecutor," Graham said, and went to continue, but the sliding door opened and in came Campbell.

Campbell made his way uneasily along the narrow passage in the candles. In place, he looked over his shoulder at Graham. "Wait. I can't face you all at once. What about . . ." He started to turn. "Is this okay?" He adjusted to face me. I inclined my head with a quick smile, finding it a bit harder to appear the unforgiving Order member with Campbell. He lifted the Mistress and studied her face. "My sisters would either love this thing or be majorly creeped out. Hard to tell."

"The truth serum," Graham reminded him politely.

"Whoops." Campbell cradled the Mistress as he took a sip. "Blah. Oh, crap. That really sucks balls, guys."

Viv and Harry exchanged a faint smile.

"Your secret?" Graham's stare prodded.

"Oh yeah," he said conversationally as he returned the

bottle to the floor. "I've got this secret thing all figured out. I was a little freaked because I can't usually keep things to myself. My older sister looks at me and knows what's up and my younger sister is a huge snoop. So this isn't a secret from them, but a secret from all of them." He jerked a thumb toward the door.

"Your friends," I said.

He bobbed his head. "I moved here the summer before high school. We used to live in Chicago. I was really skinny, wore glasses—no offense, man," he said aside to Graham. "Didn't know what music was good, geeked out over the wrong stuff, and didn't have a lot of friends. I was beat up on. Bad. During the first summer here, I worked out, got contacts, and my older sister took me to concerts and helped me pick out new clothes. Being from Chicago and moving to this tiny place helped. Everyone was impressed. They thought I knew rappers because I was from Chicago and, well, black." He pointed to his face. "They thought I was this big stoner guy and I let them all think it, telling them stories about stuff that never happened. I just slipped right in with Trent and Conner. Easy."

"Do you think they'd like you if they knew?" Viv asked.

His shoulders shrugged up to his ears. "Sure. Definitely. They're my friends."

"What about your old friends in Chicago?" she pressed.

He coughed, stalling. Her question had shaken him. "Um, I don't really know. I haven't texted or called them, and if we were friends on social media or something, my friends now would see what I used to be like."

She opened her mouth and I knew she was going to say, *If you think your friends now wouldn't care, why hide what you used to be like?*

"Thanks, Campbell," I said, sending him from the barn.

Next, Conner. He tried to appear hard to impress while standing at the center of our circle. He swished the truth serum around his mouth, tipped his head back, and gargled before he swallowed. He checked the bottom of the idol like he was looking for a "Made in China" sticker. He rapped a knuckle on her head.

"Stop it," Harry said. "Tell us your secret or get out."

Conner's perpetually bored smile turned cruel. Then he rolled his shoulders back, and while staring into the idol's face said, "I've cheated on every girl that's ever gone out with me."

"*Who* has ever gone out with you." Harry didn't miss a beat. "They're girls, not 'its' or objects or animals."

Conner glanced up from the idol, one bushy brow hitched, mocking Harry. "Whatever you say, Chief. Was that juicy enough? You all hard? I pass?"

"No," Graham said, "you don't."

"Why the fuck not?"

"It has to be a secret you mind people knowing," Graham said. "You'd write *serial cheater* on a T-shirt and parade it around school."

Conner snorted. "Not the parading part." He balanced

the idol on his open palm as he thought. "I ran away once."

"More," Graham demanded.

"After my mom died. I put protein bars, a picture of us in a macaroni heart frame she saved, and this dumb frog stuffed animal in my backpack. It was two days until my dad and brother noticed I was gone."

"Where did you go?" I whispered.

"The tunnel didn't used to be shut off," he said, stifling a yawn.

"The Ghost Tunnel?"

"Yeah."

"How old were you?" I said.

He scowled. "Why are you so nosey?"

I shook my head and stammered, "Sorry."

"Happy?" He set the idol by his feet and left.

Viv licked her thumb and forefinger and pinched the flame of a candle at her feet.

"It worked," Harry said, a heaviness to his words.

I knelt, feeling out of breath before I even started blowing out the flames.

Another wick sizzled between Viv's fingers. She was smiling, almost like she was baring her teeth.

It *had* worked. We were going to wield them as weapons against Seven Hills. Use them. They'd injured my friends. Didn't that make them my enemies? Conner and Amanda especially. Shouldn't I have wanted to use my enemies?

Another candle died between Viv's wetted fingers.

"You're going to burn yourself," I said.

Viv lowered her head and blew.

I couldn't look our initiates in their eager eyes as we met them outside of the barn, as Viv passed around glass jars with candles burning brightly within, and Harry and Graham led them into the trees toward the meteorite. Toward our stage. For Goldilocks, I promised myself. For her revenge. For us.

2 2

Graham took a winding route though the orchard. The boughs were thick and golden with leaves. Without their apples, the trees seemed taller. The initiates held their glass jar candles, one after the other, a light-touched tunnel burning through the dark.

I brought up the caboose with Viv. Her warm arm intermittently pressed against my skin.

Amanda and her friends slowed through the borderlands of the orchard. They stopped with the trees. The rock loomed ahead. For the six who hadn't played on the meteorite as children, its landmark meant wilderness. It was death and mystery and nothing good.

Graham, standing on top, silhouetted against the bonfire, waited. Jess pushed to the front and crawled up first. Brave girl.

Halfway up the rock, my hands went slippery. The meteorite was like a conduit for mysterious appearances. I hesitated putting my toe in the last groove. Here we were, tempting it again. Only this time we were using it as a prop in a play. Even Goldilocks had become a prop. I winced. *Stop*. This was all for her. All for revenge.

The initiates gathered together. Graham and Harry flanked an old-fashioned leather trunk they had delivered earlier, when we built up the bonfire.

My eyes picked at its lock. Its rusted iron key was tucked in Graham's pocket, yet I hoped it wouldn't open. Let the key snap. Let the trunk's resident stay hidden. Alive.

Graham flung his arms in the air and the chatter fell silent. He breathed loudly through his nose. "Thousands of years ago this meteorite fell to Earth. It came slowly and defied gravity. Left no crater." The initiates toed curiously at the rock. This wasn't what they'd expected. Odd. Kids in Seven Hills tended to forget that our town was home to mysteries.

Harry cleared his throat and began. "There are written legends found all over the world with a single common thread. They include a rock, large as a house, falling from the sky and landing softly at the base of seven hills." The bonfire exhaled a whorl of embers. "Visions of this meteorite are in the histories of civilizations separated by thousands of years and thousands of miles. Told by shamans, diviners, and priestesses."

Viv floated to the boys, spindly and ethereal as a spider. "These civilizations sent their explorers and hunters out in search of the meteorite. Some of those who looked believed the rock was a source of magic. Others believed it was a hungry spirit that needed to be fed sacrifices." She withdrew a collection of hat pins from a satin pouch. Each were burnished to a piercing shine, capped with black stones, her great-grandmother's once upon a time.

I was sure I could hear the stampeding heart of our captive sensing the instruments of its death near. "Living in these hills was a strange pack of animals." I recited my lines without giving them thought, too distracted by listening for the beat of wings. "The animals were carnivorous. They fed on the people who came. This went on for thousands of years, tribes arriving to find the seven hills and the rock, the hoofed beasts driving them away. This idol belonged to a group of believers who worshipped her in a land far away from here," I said, brushing the Mistress in Harry's arms. "Her name translates to the Mistress of Rebellion and Secrets. Her Order of followers had a prophecy."

Viv pressed her finger to the points of the pins as she spoke dreamily. "It foretold her falling to Earth on a star. Her believers only needed to find the star and then she'd bestow on them the ability to tell the future. When they learned of this rock and our seven hills, they knew it must be the place. When they arrived, the fanged animals met them. But they were different from the tribes that came before. They were skilled warriors. And they killed the entire pack and put their corpses on the meteorite to swear a blood oath to their goddess."

"Just as we'll swear a blood oath tonight," Graham's voice boomed. A collective shiver coursed through the initiates.

Harry took over from there. I was caught in staring at Graham, his cookie-stealing expression amplified, pulling a heist on the whole world. "The Order of believers soon realized that their Mistress had fallen to Earth *as* the star, not *on* the star," Harry said. "And every hundred years they buried two birds, animals they believed were from the sky like the star, as a blood sacrifice. This went on for four hundred years."

"But then the settlers came," Graham said.

"Seven Hills was founded right where my house is," Viv told the group, her eyes skittering across the timeless dark beyond us. "It was lawless, and the strong took advantage of the weak. The Order of IV put aside their ceremonial robes, buried their idol, and retreated into the hills, where they became a mountain rebel force."

"A guerrilla army." Graham grinned menacingly. "Their idol and their history were buried to be recovered in a safer time. They had passed down stories of the fanged creatures that had lived in the hills, and so the Order left paw prints in blood and animal carcasses on doorsteps. They frightened away the worst people from Seven Hills. Whenever injustice was here, they marked the guilty with blood. They kept order."

"You remember when the scientists came to study this rock—our meteorite—and its drawings?" I asked. I knew they did. The scientists and their findings inspired months of lessons in our classrooms. For a while it was our town's claim to fame and curious tourists would trickle up on the Marlos' property until they posted all the *Private Property* and *Trespassers Will Be Prosecuted* signs.

"One of the anthropologists was younger and she used to talk to us. Her expertise was in folklore and legend. She excavated the birds that were buried in sets, wings pointed north, south, east, and west," I said. The initiates drew forward. "Everyone knows about the birds. But what she never shared with the other scientists was that she also uncovered this idol. The birds, the meteorite, the drawings, and the idol were all parts of an urban legend. She'd thought the Order of IV was just a story, until her discovery confirmed its existence."

"She told Graham, Izzie, and Viv the story we've told you," Harry said. "She made them promise to keep the idol safe until it was time to revive the Order of IV in Seven Hills."

"She told us we'd know when the moment was right," I said. "And we did. We started out small with the school dress code and Bedford. But the Order isn't small." I went to stand in the exact spot I'd found Goldilocks in. "A girl not much older than us was killed in Seven Hills. She was left right where I'm standing, five years ago. Someone tried to make her look connected to the rock. The police didn't care. The mayor didn't care. Our neighbors didn't care even though some of them heard suspicious noises the night she died. No one helped. All of them think they've gotten away with it. They think she didn't matter because she was young, because they called her a runaway." I raised my chin in defiance. "The Order of IV has come back to Seven Hills. It's time the adults know we're watching them. They're not in charge anymore. It's time we make them pay for the girl's unsolved murder." There were four sets of glassy eyes on me—the girls and Campbell nodding with conviction, ready to march off to avenge her. There was a skeptical slant to Trent and Conner's heads.

"Seven Hills is ours," I said. "It can be yours too." I met Conner's stare. "We're its keepers. We decide who's wrong and right. Who gets punished. You can too." I paused, let it sink in, felt victory surge through me when Conner swallowed. He wanted it.

"To join us, you'll have to complete initiation rites," Harry said. "After these rites, you'll belong to the Order of IV." Empty promise. They'd never belong in the way we did.

Viv explained the procedures for the rites. An acolyte's role to play was a rite; these rites together added up to the larger rebellion. Initiates would be given a sequence of them. Instructions would be delivered in secret, one at a time. The initiate needed to memorize it and then destroy the paper trail.

Graham crouched to open the trunk as Viv handed a hat pin to each initiate, touching the lance to their shoulder like a queen knighting subjects.

"Each of us will drive a pin into the same heart and swear an oath to the Order of IV," Viv said unfalteringly.

Graham's legs straightened and he turned, revealing the dove. It was frozen in terror, a dim rattle coming from its throat.

Jess cursed under her breath. There was a nervous flutter of laughter, a *This is not for real* feeling. But they all came forward. The dove's head twitched back and forth; its yellow talons curled in on themselves.

I broke into a cold sweat approaching it. I needed to be certain my pin hit its mark, not too low in the liver or too high in the crop. No suffering, only instant death. I'd studied anatomy charts. I'd examined the downy white bird this morning, mustering a clinical indifference that made me cruel. Necessary so the initiates drove their pins into a corpse.

The flutter of the dove's tiny heart thrummed under my fingertips. It knew. Goldilocks likely hadn't been given an instant, painless death. Not a skewer through the heart. *You won't suffer.* I set the pin's point in the spot between its ribs.

Graham whispered, barely moving his lips, "It'll be over soon." Whether it was meant for me or the dove, I didn't know. I applied pressure, steadily slid the needle in, and felt the last throb of the bird's fragile body.

"I pledge my blood, secrets, and rites to the Mistress of Rebellion and Secrets. Seven Hills will be judged by her." A cry swelled in my throat; I choked it down.

The hat pin stayed piercing the dove's heart, a compass to those following. I felt for the flask tucked inside Graham's vest and brushed past the others. The wind beat the trees, and I tried to hear only the creaking branches. *Let them all break apart. Let all of Seven Hills hear the wind's reckoning.* Their oaths rose above the wind, spiraling into the sky, threatening menace.

I drank steadily.

Out of the corner of my eye there were blood-striped

hands. With each delivered pin, another initiate descended on the crate of cider. The first sip freed them of guilt, enchanted the rock, welcomed them to dance, sing, and howl as if it were all a play.

Viv and Amanda channeled Lady Macbeth.

"Out damned spot," Viv crowed.

"Who would have thought the bird had so much blood in him," Amanda answered with a depraved giggle.

I turned my back to the sacrifice. To the green goblin bottles working their magic. To the last oath given.

"Hey," Harry whispered. His eyes were careful on mine.

I offered him the flask. "It tastes like lighter fluid."

Harry smiled crookedly. "That's okay."

We stood in silence. My limbs seemed to be melting away, along with the sensation of the dove's heartbeat in my fingers. I took another sip.

Graham came between us with his arms slung around our shoulders. "Why aren't you two celebrating?" He took the flask from my hand and drank, his arm tightening around me. He hissed with an open mouth. "Stepdad Number Three had crap taste in libations."

I couldn't tear my eyes away from the stars turning as neon as the stickers in my closet.

"We have six more to help us," Graham murmured into my ear. "The bird had to be done. It convinced them we're serious."

Graham's head was bent watching me, Harry's at a sharper angle beyond his. They looked slightly scared and

I thought it was because they were waiting to hear if we'd crossed a line killing the bird.

Maybe, I thought—optimistic drunk that I was—we hadn't crossed the line but kicked it so it stayed out in front of us. It still existed. A limit. A threshold for escalating mischief.

I took the flask back, raised it, and said, "For Goldilocks."

2 3

The following morning Harry and I buried the dove in a grave under an apple tree. The fabric of my dress was a stiff shell from spilled cider, smoke of the bonfire, and sleeping on the barn floor. I navigated over the irregularities of the orchard with tenuous steps, searching for just the right spot.

I withdrew each hat pin from the bird's breast. Harry made a strange sound over my shoulder. I thought he was trying to keep from crying, but when I looked, his eyes sparked with anger.

Shovel braced on his shoulders, arms hooked over it, Harry walked in front of me on the way back to the barn. I had trouble finding words. We had our army. At a cost. I took comfort in sketching the next rebellion in my mind.

Viv knocked on my front door at midday. Cheery sun splashed on the porch, a lip gloss smile behind her chai, its twin with my name in barista's scrawl. Her scarlet rain boots shrieked in the foyer and up the stairs.

In my bedroom, "Graham thinks it's going to rain" was the first thing out of her mouth. "It'll rain and everything we're planning—the blood, the fire, will be ruined."

She practically smelled of sunshine. "He's paranoid," I said. She chewed a lock of hair, unconvinced. "Vivy, the universe wouldn't let it rain this week of all weeks. The universe wants us to have our rebellions."

Her gray eyes cleared and she nodded adamantly. "Yeah. The Order of IV needs it to be dry. The Mistress of Rebellion and Secrets won't let it rain."

She threw herself onto my bed, piling the lavender throw pillows under her back. I removed the lid to my chai and took a big gulp. "Yum. So. How's revenge going?" She furrowed her brows at me. "On Amanda. I can help, if you want."

Her top lip twitched. "I haven't decided on the how or when yet."

"Ideas?"

She tipped her head, meaning anything.

"We could bribe someone in yearbook to delete her name under senior portraits. Oh." I hopped up from the desk and sat on the bed. "We could get them to change her senior quote. Make it a really stupid one."

A jaded smile. "Haunting. I'm sure Amanda will need years of therapy after that."

"The whole initiates thing, us bossing them around, making them our pawns, isn't that sort of like revenge?"

Viv's smile spasmed. "That's ordinary comeuppance for her being a brat—that's Amanda's whole group's punishment."

"You sound like Graham," I said, meaning it lightly.

She crossed her arms at her chest, one hand toying with her hair as she frowned. "I sound like me. If I were Graham, you'd be going along with everything I said."

Taken aback, I abandoned my chai on the bedside table. "I understand why you're angry with Amanda."

"Not angry, Izzie." She swung her legs over the side of the bed. "Hate. I hate Amanda Schultz." She stomped a boot. "I'm used to it. You and Graham. Brain twins. Partners in adventure and crime. You act like I wasn't always your audience. You guys had your wild adventures and I was the one who carried bandages in her pockets for when you got hurt. Or a water bottle because we'd randomly have to disappear into the hills. Do you know I always had a granola bar in my purse in case you made me miss dinner—what eleven-year-old thinks that far ahead?

"All those stupid stunts. You never, ever told Graham they weren't good ideas." She was rigid, her knees reddening to match her boots. "But I can tell that you don't really think I should go after Amanda. I see you," she said emphatically. "I know you like Harry. I know part of you likes Graham. I know that finding Goldilocks messed you up. I know you look through pictures of missing girls. I know you have a sketch pad in your desk full of drawings of her. I know you think I'm a drama queen. But don't you know that I'm that way because I've been competing with you and Graham? I want to take up as much space as you two do. I want you to notice me as much as you notice each other."

Viv's chest heaved. Her words upended what I thought of myself as a friend. How hadn't I shown Viv what she meant to me? I stepped up on the mattress.

"You aren't going to jump, are you?" she asked, hurt giving way to annoyance.

I reached for the large, rectangular basket on top of my bookshelf. "I don't think the bed is high enough to end it." I kneeled and dumped the basket's contents onto the comforter. A few cootie catchers tumbled onto the floor. "Most are from middle school. I didn't organize them chronologically. You made them, and how could I throw away our maybe-futures?"

She picked through the shapes, like white paper flowers of all sizes. "You kept all of them. You are a cootie catcher hoarder."

"Guilty."

She tucked her fingers in the folds of a catcher with different kinds of dogs we wanted to have on the outer flaps. "Remember the one with super powers, or the Halloween one with the grisly deaths, or the one we used to tell the first Broadway role I'd land?"

"Christine in *Phantom of the Opera*," I said.

I scooped up about ten cootie catchers and let them fall into the basket. Viv studied the flaps of each before placing them away.

"Viv?"

She looked up.

"You are my drama queen." There was a funny quiver

to the words, but I meant them. Without judgment. To me, friendship meant seeing a person. Seeing their flaws. Loving them more for them.

She smiled drowsily, like she hadn't slept well.

"Forget brain twin. You want to be my heart twin?" I asked.

Her red rain boot nudged my knee. "Shut up, sappy."

I grew serious. "I am sorry. You take up space. No one else has a whole shelf dedicated to them in here."

She toed one boot off the side of the bed, then the other, and squirmed back onto the pillows.

"So, I said you like Graham. Want to talk about it?"

"No." I stared at the cootie catchers interrupting the violet pintuck comforter. There was one, somewhere in the pile, that we'd written Harry's and Graham's names as potential senior prom dates. "I like Harry." It came out meek. "He's the one I want to kiss and go on dates with. Graham is, I don't know, maybe without Harry. But Harry . . . is." I swept my arms encompassingly. That was wrong. I tapped my hand over my heart.

"I know," Viv said. "But liking them both, in different ways, it wouldn't make you bad. Not like my mom and your dad." My eyes felt cornered by hers. She smiled. I couldn't help returning it. "Okay. Harry." She sprawled forward, a new lightness to her voice. "You went to homecoming together, but he didn't make a move—granted, the afterparty hijacked the night."

"I'm going to his house later," I said, nerves strumming my throat.

"Is it like, an official date? Or a hangout?"

"The difference?"

"An official date means he'll probably kiss you. A hangout makes it ambiguous, and if he kisses you on a hangout, it doesn't mean as much as if on a date."

"Says who?"

She smirked. "Says every magazine's dating advice." Viv was the only person I knew who subscribed to magazines that arrived in the mail.

"Then it must be gospel," I said with an eye roll. "What if I kiss him?"

"Yes," she said exuberantly. "Go for it. It took him five years to ask you out and I'm not waiting five more to find out how he is. But wear a pretty bra."

She deflected the pillow I tossed at her. "I'm just talking about kissing him."

"If only you were more scandalous. I want to live vicariously through you." She sighed wistfully. "Do you think he's done it before? Sex?"

"Uh. No." My head wobbled in indecision. "I actually don't know. Maybe."

"There was that mysterious girl bagger last year."

"True." I bit my lip. "I want to know what it's like."

"Sex?"

I nodded.

"Me too. I mean, I think it's different, depending."

"On what?"

Viv's brows angled together as she said, "Mechanics. Position. Formulas. Aerodynamics," imitating Graham.

"Formulas?"

She nodded sagely. "Formulas that equal one sum. It's supposed to feel really good. Especially for the girl, or I guess girls if there are two involved, but somehow I think it would automatically feel good if two girls were having sex since they have the same equipment."

"Sound reasoning."

"Graham hasn't done it," she continued. "Not with a human girl. He would have told us. Tried to make us jealous." We sat lost in thought, until Viv added, "We're all going to school separate tomorrow so we can deliver the rites before classes. Easier to be clandestine if we're not rolling as a pack. We can each take one or two initiates theirs."

"We have to decide what order the larger rebellions will come and on what nights," I said. "Plus, we have to break them down and assign each initiate their rite."

She nodded, saying, "We'll finish tonight."

In Harry's front yard, I paused by his mom's flower bed. All her pretty violet and orange flowers were mangled, their stems bent, buds brown and dry. The soil was upturned like someone had ridden a bike through it.

"What happened to your mom's flowers?" I asked as I ducked under Harry's arm holding the front door for me.

He craned to see. "Maybe moles."

"Mutant moles," I said.

His dad shouted hello from the kitchen table. Simon

was sprawled out on the living room floor surrounded by flash cards with Italian vocabulary words on them. "*Buon pomeriggio*, Isadora," he called as Harry led the way down the hall toward his bedroom.

"His accent kind of sounds—"

"German. I know," Harry said.

"Isn't it weird that Simon's the only little kid we know? Eight-year-olds who learn Italian and build robots and act like tiny adults are our normal."

"Normal Simon is not. He isn't the worst, though." Harry's tousled hair stirred and resettled as he collapsed onto the carpet. "Remember when he'd tell jokes without punch lines? He's getting funnier at least."

I sunk to the ground in a gap between the records laid out over the floor. "I used to want a brother so bad when I was little," I admitted.

"And then you met Simon and thought, forget it," Harry said with a chuckle.

"Nah. Then I found Graham in kindergarten and it was better than getting a brother. It was like getting a twin." I felt guilty for bringing Graham up, which led to feeling weird for feeling guilty. "What were you listening to?"

Harry grinned and lifted up on his knees for a stack of records on his dresser. "I've been searching for the perfect song."

"And you think it might be hiding on one of these?" I tapped a black disk on its paper sleeve. He had hundreds, on shelves, in piles, on the floor—almost every surface covered in vinyl.

"Not anymore. I listened to them and it isn't here," he said.

I could imagine that all the light in his eyes came from listening to music, a fleck of gold added with each note. "How will you know it when you hear it?"

"Ummm." He drummed his knees. "It'll sound sort of familiar. But also really different."

"The same and different," I said. "Like the worlds you used to imagine in space."

"Exactly like those."

"You want to hear my perfect song?"

"I might not have the record."

I pulled my cell from my pocket. "Is it blasphemous to play music on a phone surrounded by vinyl?"

He reached over and brushed a strand of hair stuck to my cheek. I felt his fingertips after they were gone. "I'll give you a pass on the blasphemy." He held up the inciting finger. "One time only."

I was nervous and selected the wrong song. "Errr, definitely not that one." I found the intended. Its beat quickened and segued into the initial chorus. The bedframe bit into the back of my neck and I stretched my legs out, absorbing the music.

Halfway through, Harry's hand closed softly around my ankle. He leaned forward, peering at the cell between us like he could see the notes streaming out.

"Never heard this band before," he murmured.

Goose bumps spread up my leg from Harry's sustained touch. "They were on a soundtrack—best thing about the movie. But this one, it's my favorite of theirs. You know how you can play a song so much it loses its effect?"

"Absolutely."

"This one never does. His voice sounds about to crack because he's sad but trying to get over it, and I always wonder if maybe this is the time it will crack. This is the time it'll be too much for him. Just listen to it five hundred times and you'll get it."

"I understand," he said. "It's like you." He exhaled, puffing out his cheeks. "You don't lose your effect. On me."

Harry crawled forward. His hand slid up my ankle. My perfect song began playing again, on repeat. Harry was up to my knees, smile scared but measuring as the distance between us closed. *I'll keep my eyes open*, I thought. I wouldn't miss any part of kissing Harry.

"Thanks for playing your perfect song for me," he said, and I felt the words on my lips as much as heard them.

The doorbell chimed, trailed by Simon's holler of "Harry" from down the hall.

Harry's face hovered an inch from mine, his palms warm on my thighs.

Footfalls thumped louder. Harry sat back as the door slammed open.

"Har." Graham was out of breath. "Oh, hey." He focused on me. A stride into the room, he halted, appraising the scene. "Jesus. Are you listening to every record ever recorded?" I fumbled for my cell to stop the perfect song, like it would reveal too much.

"What's up?" Harry said. There was a faint crease on his forehead as he watched Graham clear space to sit. Graham's fingers hiked up his sleeves. He looked from my pink, blotchy neck to Harry's flushed cheeks. I pulled a pillow off the bed and hugged it.

"Here it is." He slapped a notebook on the ground. His handwriting ran across the page, coming up diagonal at the end of each line like it did when he wrote fast and frantic. "I've been working all day."

"On . . . ," Harry said, hands hooked around his knees rather than touching me. I wanted him to touch me again.

"Goldilocks. Her killer."

The inebriated warmth of being close to Harry vanished. I threw the pillow aside and curled over the notebook with a jitter of dread and anticipation. "What are these?"

Graham had fifty or so bullet points on the first page.

"They're the facts. Basics we know for sure, like someone who knew about the meteorite and the manner in which the birds were buried staged Goldilocks's body, and she sustained two injuries, a large contusion to her front that might not have been fatal, and a bruise around her neck that suggested strangulation and would have been."

I flipped the page.

"Those are the reasonable conclusions I can draw from the facts. For example, the person who knew about the meteorite and birds and staged Goldilocks is her killer, and the initial injury to her torso happened when they hit her with a car." He paused only to take a quick breath. "She dragged herself away, tried to escape; they went after and finished her with their hands. Since it was nighttime, they were likely driving to their home in our neighborhood, or they were a guest leaving a house in our neighborhood."

On to the next page.

"Questions I have for witnesses, informed by the reasonable conclusions and facts. Like, did you ever go to the window during the course of that night and see a car on the road? If so, did you recognize it? Were there any signs of prowlers or did anything go missing from your yard or home during the days leading up to the date in question? Were you aware of your neighbors having guests? Do you have a criminal record?" There were eraser smudges and dried water blots. It reminded me of the notes Graham left in the books we passed back and forth.

"There's one more," he said, brushing my hand aside to turn the page. "My theories. We're operating under the assumption that the first injury was an accident, the second only to cover it up. What if the first wasn't an accident, though?" I sat back on my heels to stare at Graham, as he spoke with untroubled curiosity. "What if it was to shut Goldilocks up, what if she saw something she wasn't supposed to? What if she was running from her killer? Or what if her killer wasn't rational and it was a kill for fun? What if we're dealing with a predator? He tried to run her over and when that didn't work, he went after her on foot."

The night Graham conjured played in my head. Girl pursued. Run down with a car. She crawled toward a front porch, tearing the skin on her knees. Footsteps at her back, heavier, louder. A fistful of her hair and he'd stopped her. His hands fitted around her neck. Her lungs convulsed. Dead.

The bottom of the image dropped out as I had a premonition of Graham at our neighbors' houses, demanding answers.

Graham saw a challenge where there was danger. It was jumping without looking all over again, except the bandages in Viv's purse wouldn't be enough.

"You can't do this," I said.

He'd been nodding down at the notebook, as if affirming the rightness of his course. He met my eyes. "Yes, I can. I'm going to knock on doors and demand answers tomorrow after school."

"No," I said. "This is different from hiding behind IV. Different from targeting Carver and Denton, even the whole city. You'd be announcing to whoever killed her that you're looking for them." I snatched up the notebook, clapped it shut, and thrust it to his chest. "What about the unlikelihood of solving a cold case? You blabbed all these stats about the cops never doing it and the charges not sticking even if they do."

"I'm not talking about getting the police to solve it. *I'm* going to solve it. The Order can deal with the killer."

"Are you stupid? We're the Order." I shoved the notebook at his chest again, harder. He gaped at me, fumbled to accept the book, and climbed to his feet.

"Funny," he said, going for the door. "I thought you'd call me brave."

I closed my eyes for the barest second.

There was a muffled conversation once Graham reached the living room. A minute later, the front door shook Harry's bedroom window.

He moved to sit beside me. The mattress gave at my back. "It's okay. Graham will be focused on the rebellions by the time we go over there tonight."

In my head I turned over the methodical way Graham had broken down the night of the crime and the killing itself. "I really shouldn't have said he was stupid. All those notes were genius."

"Going after a killer is dumb. Dumb and crazy," Harry said, turning toward his records.

Two minutes before, I'd been dead set against Graham looking for Goldilocks's killer. Letting his plan sink in emboldened me. Yes, Graham saw a challenge instead of danger. But so did I. I used to jump without looking right alongside him. I didn't used to care about bandages any more than he did.

There was our escalating threshold for mischief. Perhaps there was also one for danger. I ran my finger along the ridge of the scar on my shoulder. Graham was just continuing what I'd started at twelve years old when I went looking in the tunnel.

"Do you think he could really hunt down who killed her?" I asked Harry. Before he answered, I thought, if anyone could solve a cold case, it would be Graham.

Harry returned a record to its sleeve. "Identifying the bad

people in the world isn't the same as busting them. Graham finds out who this guy is, then what? You heard him—we're going after bad guys and we'd have the worst one."

I sunk lower against the bed. Knowing would be dangerous. I ached to know, nonetheless.

24

We gathered at Graham's that evening. He met Harry and me at the front door, took the pizza box from my hands, and smiled easily. But his gray eyes were as elusive as shadows. Viv was already there, lying on the sofa, her boots hooked over the sofa back, her hair tapering to the carpet.

"It's about time," she grumbled, hoisting herself up, teetering with a red face to take the pizza from Graham.

She led the way into the attic, the box ajar, a piece hanging from between her teeth.

Graham's mother had a collection of artifacts that would have made a museum drool. In addition to her own acquisitions, Stepdads Two, Three, and Four were academics, and because their marriages with Graham's mom had dissolved as spontaneously as they germinated, had left trunks and crates in the Averbach house.

I haven't said much about Graham's mother. This is mostly because she's a puzzle to me. She was as majestically beautiful as the crowned crane on its dusty mount in her attic. She was the kind of college professor who taught students rarely and traveled on research sabbatical often. From the invitations sent by foreign governments, I had the impression that she was a big deal in her field of nearly extinct civilizations.

In her absence, Graham was curator of the attic museum, with special collections like wood carvings from Papua New Guinea, rare butterflies of the Amazon, and rudimentary agrarian tools from the Jordan River Basin. We weren't searching the clutter for anything as humdrum as pinned insects.

Stepdad Number Three was a professor of evolutionary biology. Graham was sure he'd left one of his skeletons behind. It was ideal—untraceable to us. I remembered the skeleton as being kept in Graham's study during Stepdad Number Three's reign. I had dared Graham to stick his fingers in the eye sockets. He had dared me to kiss it.

Viv drew a smiley face in the snowy layer on a nearby wooden crate. "It's romantic up here. All the old things."

"I'm not going to kiss you again, Vivian, no matter how much you hit on me," Graham said with an impish wink.

Viv pursed her lips at him. "If I want another kiss, I'll take it. Open the window. It smells like cheese and dust." Graham took a circuitous route around boxes toward the lone windowpane leaking sunset into the rafters. Its bronze chain allowed a few-inch gap to siphon fresh air inside. Graham whipped a white sheet off of a shrouded table like a magician snatching away a cloth.

"Massage table?" Viv called.

"Hospital gurney," I guessed.

Graham hopped up on its center and swung his legs. "A Civil War–era autopsy table."

Viv dropped the leather chest she was holding and yelped as it thudded to her feet, popped open, and freed a rush of jingling coins. Harry fumbled on the floor, trying to stop their rattling and ricocheting with Viv.

Graham leaped off the table. Rather than help he took a lock of my hair between his fingers and tugged. From the floor, I shoved his kneecaps. He was angry, immature, annoying. I wanted to get him alone. To tell him. It was dangerous for Graham to hunt for Goldilocks's killer, but in the hours since he stormed from Harry's bedroom, I'd come up with a solution.

Rather than hunt for Goldilocks's killer, we would force her killer to reveal himself.

Amid the upheaval of boxes and crates, we finished segmenting the rebellions for our initiates.

"I found him—errrr—her?" Harry called from a dark corner of the attic. He lifted the skull from the box.

"Don't touch it," Viv said.

"We've got to wipe it free of prints anyway," Graham said.

Viv muttered, "Because it's gross."

The skeleton had wires protruding from its bones, but his or her pieces were loose, an anatomical puzzle.

The outside light had dimmed by then and a single, dangling bulb from a rafter illuminated the macabre discovery.

Viv nudged the skull with a finger. A minute later she was cradling it in her hand and peering into its eye sockets. "Do you think there's another skull up here?" she asked. "Because this would be the greatest prop for my *Hamlet* audition next semester."

"Ophelia didn't have a scene with a skull," Graham told her.

She raised her chin, preparing to be challenged. "I want to audition for Hamlet. A girl Hamlet."

"That's brilliant, Vivy," Harry said.

Graham nodded approvingly. "We'll find you another skull before then."

We turned back to appraise the bones in the box.

"What if the initiates—if Amanda—open their first rite and say screw this?" Viv whispered. "They tell everyone everything and we spend the next eight months as pariahs. Doing community service to atone for vandalism."

"We were outcasts up until a week ago," I reminded her.

"Ouch," Harry said teasingly, hands pressed over his heart.

"Kings and queens without a court," Graham said.

Harry chuckled. "Worry about what's more probable. Someone smuggled in their cell last night and we're two minutes away from a video of Graham with the dead bird in his bloody hands going viral."

He was met with horrified stares. "I'm joking."

"It's worth the risk," I said. "For Goldilocks."

"For revenge," Viv murmured.

Graham unfolded a piece of paper from his pocket. Harry read its title over his arm. "'Standards of Data

Selection from Human Skeletal Remains: Estimating Sex from the Human Skull.'"

"It's a work sheet I found on an archaeology blog," Graham said. "See, they break the steps down. You pick which characteristics of the skull match which in these diagrams. Each has a point value and you total the four diagram point values up, and whichever range the sum falls into tells you if the skull's biologically male or female." His finger traced the back of the skull and then he referenced the paper. Three more times he studied features of the skull and consulted the work sheet. His lips moved as he tallied up the values in his head.

"She's a girl," he proclaimed.

A girl. Like me. Like Goldilocks. Exactly what we needed.

All our rebellions with the initiates would be displays Seven Hills couldn't look away from. Nightmare-inducing. Perhaps that Goldilocks had been tucked away on our rock, high on its altar so that even the neighbors who stood in the orchard couldn't see, made her easy to ignore.

Several minutes later in the living room, Graham paced, hair on end, worked up by his fingers. "All six initiates take part in each of our rebellions."

"What if the initiates won't follow through?" Viv said.

"They will," Graham said.

"They just stabbed a dove in the heart," I reminded them.

"How can we be sure, though?" Viv pressed.

Graham took a deep, considering breath. "One: peer pressure—Amanda and Conner are in. Two: We've explained that rebellion and subversion is the mission of the Order. And three: We've promised them they'll benefit from playing along, because they'll graduate from initiate to member and be able to use the Order's mischief against whoever they want. Only one out of three of these incentives needs to stick for them to go carry out the rebellions."

"People do way worse for less," Harry said quietly on the sofa, a socked foot balanced on his knee, wireless headphones around his neck putting out a wisp of music.

I recognized the incentives Graham described from a book he'd read and shared the year before about how ordinary, usually kind people were convinced to do crazy things or radicalized to belong to murderous cults. I didn't comment, not about to draw parallels.

Harry's finger brushed occasionally, accidentally, against the side of my leg.

Viv dropped the cold pizza crust she'd been gnawing on and said, "Oh my god, brilliant idea. We could get them to do anything. I could make Amanda do embarrassing stuff. Like, why not toss in a few rites that are funny? Stuff the initiates can do at school." Her shoulders bounced, but her mouth pinching told me it wasn't as spontaneous as she was pretending.

I wondered, *Was this the revenge Viv wanted on Amanda?*

Harry's finger grazed my leg. On purpose. "What do you think?" I asked, turning slightly to him. Brown eyes stirring with thoughts. Bowing pink lips. His finger traveling down my outer thigh. The song playing faintly was familiar.

I listened, my shoulder pressing his. My perfect song.

"I'm good with funny or embarrassing rites." He looked to Viv. "But no going overboard. We have to agree to send only a couple to *any given person*." He meant Amanda. "And they can't distract her or him from the important rites. No unnecessary risks."

"I am the king of necessary risk," Graham said from the corner of his mouth.

"We should pick initiates to send them to so they won't get embarrassing rites on the same day from more than one of us," I suggested.

I watched Viv casually pick lint from her skirt, lips pursed at the alpaca throw that had shed on her. With an unconcerned smile she said, "Sure. I call Amanda. Oh, I have a good idea for a way to start them off. Can I have Campbell for the first one at least?"

"You guys care who you get?" I asked the boys.

Graham said, "Harry's earned the right to embarrass Conner. I'll take Rachel. You want Jess or Trent, Iz?"

"Trent, if I'm picking the person I want to embarrass. I can do Jess too, though."

I wanted to define the rules more. The when and how. But Viv was chewing on the inside of her cheek, lost in thought. If this was what Viv wanted, how she planned to get her revenge on Amanda, I didn't want to tie her hands up with rules. I trusted Viv's judgment; she wouldn't endanger the Order, but she could be ruthlessly calculating. And so I clapped and said, "That's that."

. . .

It was a few past ten when Harry and I reached my front door.

My key in the deadbolt, hand on the knob, I stopped and turned to him. "I had fun today. With the music. With you."

He laid his hand over mine. "The beach," Harry said. "Let's go."

I smiled. "Right now?"

He tipped his head and laughed softly. "After school this week. Just us."

My hand stretched under his, enjoying the cover of his warm fingers. "Definitely."

I waved at Harry when he turned one last time, a few houses up the street, before he jogged the rest of the way home. Then I stole into the shadows between lampposts.

Graham was framed by the front window under a reading lamp, a book propped on his chest, close to his face. No spectacles or contacts.

He squinted at me as he opened the door. "Forget your cell?"

My finger jumped involuntarily to my lips. "Shhhh." Paranoid, I looked to the sidewalk. Why? Harry and Viv would be home. No one else would think me at Graham's suspicious.

I spun him around, gently pushed him inside, and shut the door with nary a click at my back. "Close the drapes. You can see in from the street," I whispered.

An eyebrow shot up as he asked, "What are we doing that you don't want people to see? May I make a suggestion?"

"No," I snapped. I shook my head, frustrated, and went to pull the drapes closed myself.

"You're weirding me out," he said with too much amusement for it to be true.

"What if Viv or Harry really did leave a cell and they see me in here when they come back for it?"

"What if?"

"No, Graham. It has to be a secret. I mean, I guess there are a million possible reasons why I'm here and not necessarily the reason I'm really here for." I paused. "The reason I'm really here for . . . ," I repeated to myself; shook my head to clear it.

He smiled crookedly. "You seem nervous, Izzie."

"I don't think you made eye contact with me the whole night. Not once." I leveled a finger at him. "And I know I shouldn't have called you stupid, but you don't believe I think you're stupid. Not for a second. Never would you doubt the giant brain sloshing around in your skull. So just stop being a jerk to me already. Don't ignore me again."

Hands shoved into his pockets, he shrugged. "Okay."

He was all eyes now. The knob was cold at my back and I'd started to replay Viv saying, *It's okay to like both of them.* It wasn't. I didn't. I'd never. "Jesus. Blink or something."

His face reddened and he kept his voice low, though it warbled, "Stop bossing me around and tell me what you want me to keep secret."

"Harry and I went to homecoming together and then you walked in on what was our second date today. We were about to kiss and you ruined it. I just want to make sure you know because I haven't said it aloud to you." I barely had breath left to squeeze the important part out. "I like Harry."

His expression was unreadable. "You're babbling."

"I like Harry," I said more emphatically.

His jaw tensed. "Not twenty seconds ago you referenced the enormous brain sloshing around in my skull. You said I wasn't stupid. You plus Harry. I've gleaned it already."

"Giant. I called it a giant brain. Enormous—that's just cocky."

"I am sorry that I interrupted you guys when you were about to hook up."

"Kiss," I said, "and don't apologize."

His fisted hands rubbed at his eyes. "What is the secret, Izzie?"

The grandfather clock in the hallway ticked five times. I felt each down to my bones.

"Want to find a killer with me?"

Retrieved from the cellular phone of Isadora Anne Pend-leton
Transcript and notes prepared by Badge #821891
Shared Media Folder Titled: IV, Mon., Oct. 21, 12:05 a.m.

Video start.
I. Pendleton sits in her mostly dark bedroom. "It finally happened," she whispers. "I got home from Graham's about an hour ago. I thought my parents would be sleeping because they go to bed superearly. Wrong. I was going to the kitchen for water when I saw my dad at the dining room table. In the dark. Just sitting."

She pauses.

"He said he was sorry for startling me and I asked if everything was okay, even though I knew it must not be. Then he started to cry. I froze at the other end of the table. Waiting. I got all antsy, like I wanted to scream at him to just say it already. He goes, 'We don't want you to be worried. Your grandma needed your mom to stay with her a while is all. Nothing specifically wrong with her health. Mom'll just be gone for the week.' And I'm like, 'In Denver?' He nods and I go, 'Did you bring her to the airport?'

"He says, 'No, she took a taxi. You just missed her.'" She exhales loudly. "We've flown to see Grandma a billion times, and there are so few flights out of Santa Barbara and they're always during the day. By the time Mom gets to the airport, it'll be one a.m. It's a teeny-tiny airport. They don't have red-eyes. No. If something else wasn't wrong she would have slept here and left early in the morning. She must have found out about Dad. I can't think how. Maybe he finally told?"

Her expression wavers between a frown and a smile. "She knows about Dad and Ina and she left. I don't mean she left me—technically, yeah, but she'll be back. Obviously. I just mean she didn't hang around to argue. To let him weasel his way out of trouble. She ran. I guess I'm kind of surprised and proud of her.

"When I got up to my room a little while ago, I called Viv to tell her what I thought had happened. She said her parents were asleep in their room together. She'd gone in and said good night to them when she got home and they were totally normal. She doesn't think my mom found out about Dad and Ina, because if Mom knew, wouldn't Viv's dad have heard too? Wouldn't he be angry and have left? I don't know what to think. I guess I'm just relieved it's not up to us to tell or not tell anymore."

Video stop.

25

The dark hours of Monday morning saw the delivery of the initiates' first rites. I kept low as I stole up Trent's driveway. I was in luck; he'd left his car window cracked open, and I slipped the envelope through the gap. Trent would find both an embarrassing rite and the rite all of the initiates would receive, which added up to our larger rebellion.

I delivered Jess's rite to her locker at school, my footsteps the only sound echoing through the campus. It fell to Viv, Harry, and Graham to deliver the rest of the instructions clandestinely.

I considered giving Jess two rites, like I gave Trent. But the night to come, revenge for Goldilocks, Mom gone, the embarrassment I planned for Trent, and mine and Graham's emerging plan took up too much space in my head. And honestly, the more I'd gotten to know Jess, the less I wanted to embarrass her. She was quick-witted, world-weary, and interesting.

There was a vague nagging that deadlines for college applications were coming. Later, I told myself. After, I promised. Once Mom got back I'd write my personal statement and ask her to read it.

The crowd in Cup of Jo was thin; it was early. Chai latte in hand, I went to sit across the street in the gazebo at the center of the knoll. I gave a finger to the founder's plaque affixed to the right of the short staircase. From the gazebo's axis all of the town square stores were visible; likewise, all of the stores had a clear shot to the gazebo. I spat a mouthful of chai on the ground. It smelled normal but there was a mysterious bitter taste on my tongue. Bullshit. The nasty taste came from the recording I'd left in our shared folder the night before. Chances were, it was the roses I had delivered to Ina's clinic from my dad that got them caught. The flowers arrived on a day Ina didn't work; a curious nurse or doctor must have flipped open the card, and they told someone in a gossipy whisper. It took over a week to reach my mom.

Seeing Dad as a zombie in the dark got me thinking about how hard Viv would take it. I was afraid; I couldn't admit to her that I'd set my dad up. So I faked shock and called her, then I recorded myself talking about it. I was a liar. Lying about the truth in which I tried to tell the truth. It was complicated.

I watched the line curl around the corner at Holy Bagels. Tons of middle school kids standing beside their bikes and trying to look older by acting busy on their cells. If I shouted, they'd all look my way. I stood up on the bench that ran the perimeter inside the gazebo and inspected the rafters of the roof. The gazebo was a better stage than our rock.

I texted Graham. Do you still have that spy cam?

Graham's reply dinged. Think so. Inspecting train tracks.

Where?

Ghost Tunnel to knoll.

How?

Walking them. Will be late for class.

I lobbed the chai into the wastepaper basket and went to stroll around the square, on the lookout for security cameras. A girl was taking out the recycling in the alleyway between Holy Bagels and Cup of Jo. She'd worked the counter for at least a few months at Holy Bagels.

The recycling lid slammed shut and she was wiping her hands on her jeans when I reached her. "Hey," I said.

She whirled around, mouth open in surprise.

"Could I ask you something?" She checked over her shoulder to the back door of the bagel shop. "I'll be quick," I added.

She crossed her arms and gave a beleaguered sigh. "What's up?"

"I was studying in the gazebo yesterday and left my bag while I went into Cup of Jo. I didn't notice until I got home, but my cell was missing from inside. Do you know if the bagel shop or anyone has cameras up? I could watch their tapes to see who took my phone."

"Don't you remember crap-ageddon?" She laughed at my confused face. "A few months ago. Someone let their dog crap all over the knoll. Kids kept stepping in it. They stationed a cop after the third week or something. Like a cop literally sat in the gazebo all day to keep the crapper away."

"Oh yeah. So no cameras."

"No. Sucks. Sorry." Her thumb jerked over her shoulder. "I gotta go."

"Thanks. Bye," I called, walking backward up the alley.

Perfection that the first funny rite happened when Viv and I were in the same third-period classroom, along with Trent, Jess, Conner, and Campbell. Of course, perfection happened by Viv's design. It began as rustling. A sharp intake of breath. A pop that made me jump in my seat. A smell. I've never had a pet, but there is something all-at-once recognizable about the repulsive scent of canned cat food. I was convinced that if Harry's boy from another planet, *a catless planet*, had been in that room he would have named the smell instantly like I did.

"Oh my god," I heard Jess say.

I swiveled around. Mr. Novak muttered something about keeping the chatter down, barely taking his eyes off the whiteboard.

Campbell, at the desk behind me, was fixing the newly opened can of cat food with a doomed stare. A top layer of gelatinous goo reflected the fluorescent light. A mauve processed meat jelly peeked from under it. A can opener lay abandoned. Viv stood at her desk for a better view.

"Oh shit," Jess said, up on her knees, staring over Campbell's knit beanie.

"Duuuuude. That is rough," Trent said. He extended a fist

across the row for a bump; Campbell left him hanging.

A gag burped up from Campbell's throat. He withdrew a spoon from his pocket. I covered my mouth with a hand. The spoon cut into the jelly meat. I wanted to look away. The spoon disappeared inside his mouth; it came out clean, except for a few streaks. His eyes went red and teared. There was a gurgle from his stomach. His hand shook putting the soiled spoon into his pocket. He took two audibly deep inhales and exhales.

Trent and I exchanged a look of revulsion. "You're a champion, man," he told Campbell.

"I'm going to puke," Campbell said weakly. Trent grabbed the can, held it far from his body, and speed walked to the trash at the back of class. When he returned to his seat, Campbell had his forehead planted on the desk.

The rite had been unmissable. Every kid in that classroom had watched in confusion and disgust. Presently I think our whole plan hinged on Campbell and his courage without us realizing it. If he had refused, chucked the can in the trash, told his friends, it would have been too easy for the rest to bow out also. Campbell had done the disgusting without complaint. He was a champion. The rest of our initiates would carry on.

For the rest of third period I couldn't shake the feeling that Campbell had deserved the cat food rite less than any of his friends. And I wondered, had Campbell's secret, that he was once a kid a lot like us but had shed that old identity for a shinier, popular one, made Viv angry with him?

Word of one more rite reached me by the start of lunch. Rachel stood up in the middle of the history class she and Graham shared. She told Mr. Rooney, their teacher, that his curriculum made her want to puke because it glorified the colonizer and ignored the slaughter of indigenous nations who were already here before *here* became the United States. She ended declaring that America, the land of the free and the home of the brave, in fact was a country built on stolen land and the corpses of indigenous peoples and slaves. She was ordered out of the class for the rest of the period.

Even if I hadn't known that Graham had chosen Rachel, it was undeniably his work.

Viv insisted we eat lunch in the courtyard's amphitheater, on the top cement riser. We had good seats for when Trent stripped down to his boxers and humped the flagpole. Students crowded around. Whooped and hooted. Trent continued for longer than I'd told him to in the embarrassing rite's instructions. There was a furious whistle, signaling the arrival of campus security. They hauled Trent off the flagpole. He held his clothing against his chest, a victor's grin causing a few kids to ask if Trent was on antipsychotics.

It was better than I'd imagined.

Viv lazily tossed a grape into her mouth, chewed, and then waved to the sky. "Behold, we are the masters of the universe."

Harry snorted.

Her words bounced around in me for the entire afternoon.

•　•　•

Our initiates met us at the western corner of the apple orchard, two rows of trees in, along the dirt lane. It was half-past midnight. Concealed by the trees, we distributed black beanies with two holes cut for eyes and mouths. Graham gave out cans of red spray paint and I recapped the plan.

"Everyone knows which houses they're hitting? Good," I said.

"Don't deviate," Graham warned.

"Keep your masks and gloves on at all times," Harry added.

"At one a.m. exactly, Jess, Amanda, Rachel, and Campbell will run home using the green belts," I said. "Conner and Trent will stay to finish breaking the windows with us because we all live on this street." Each of us had been assigned the houses nearest to our own to help with a fast getaway.

"Won't it be suspicious when none of your houses are hit?" Jess asked.

Graham said, "Who says we're not hitting our own houses?"

"You guys think you can re-create the drawing?" I pressed.

"It's not exactly a Picasso," Amanda said snidely.

"Good. Then you shouldn't have a problem making sure it looks like a bird," I retorted.

"Everyone set their cell alarms so they vibrate at one," Harry said. "Masks on. Gloves on, and—"

Graham cut him off. "Move out."

Our formation broke apart as we hit the sidewalk, each of us splinters aimed at our targets. I flew uphill in the direction of my house. The neighborhood would be transformed into a nightmare landscape within minutes. All the oblivious, selfish families on our street would wake up to red, red, red. We would make them feel a fraction of the fear Goldilocks must have felt. They deserved it.

Four of our neighbors had kept secrets about Goldilocks's death. Three of them had heard cries for help or the car crash. Two of them had destroyed evidence of the crime. None of them had come forward after her body was found, when they must have realized they'd witnessed a sliver of her murder. What they knew might have helped find her killer; it might have forced the police to investigate the residents of Driftwood. Who knew how many others might be guarding their own secrets? This was why we planned to hit every house on the block. By that logic, we were condemning our own parents. All but Graham's mom had been home.

The Swintons, Holloways, Kirkpatricks, and Yus would receive indictments spelled out in letters cut from Viv's magazines. Graham, Viv, Harry, and I had a note for each of them in our pockets, and we'd deliver them at the end of the night's rebellion. We'd make sure they understood that the blood covering Driftwood was their punishment.

Graham would jog to Carver's and Denton's houses using the green beltways we took for the blood rebellion. Once he'd left our demand in their mailboxes, he'd sprint back in time to hit Kirkpatrick's house and await the final stage of the rebellion in chorus with the rest of us.

It hadn't been enough to make Carver's and Denton's

front yards bleed. Where was Goldilocks's pound of flesh? The Order demanded a sacrifice. The police chief's and mayor's authorities would be restitution. Our notes to them read *Resign and it will stop*. Perhaps the Order would be satisfied then. I hissed into my mask. Perhaps not.

Night sounds were muted, the gentle purr of the ocean like background static. Nothing, and then a rush of footsteps to my right that made me veer onto a nearby lawn. A figure in black charged by me. Conner turned halfway and tipped a hand to his masked forehead in salute. Harry was close behind.

He came to a stop. "Did he push you?"

"No. I was just startled."

"Because if he just gives me another reason . . . ," Harry said.

I laid my hand on his shoulder. "No time to think about him right now."

Harry stayed trotting by my side until we reached Mrs. Holloway's. I waved him off when he hung at the mouth of her driveway, reluctant to leave. He had his own houses to hit, though.

With the can of spray paint I made an X that spanned the length and width of her front door and a smaller X at the center of her front window. I painted a large IV on the welcome mat.

Next I moved on to the bird—two humps, the splayed wings, and a fringe of feathers under them. Same position as the birds' and Goldilocks's makeshift wings. It was nearly ten feet wide, slashing red across her driveway. *There, Mrs. Holloway, try ignoring that like you did her cries for help.* I improvised, sketching the outline of a dead body like at a crime scene on her flagstone path. Pausing a second, I gazed at the street around me. Faceless figures clad in black. The hiss of spray paint. One house after another was painted in garish red, morbid drawings.

The following two houses went faster. By the time I sketched the bird in my own driveway, my strokes were fluid and smooth; I imagined the can to be a knife, the cement cut open and bleeding. A buzzing in my pocket. It was one o'clock. The initiates who didn't live close had their head start to get home before we woke the neighborhood.

I jogged soundlessly back to Mrs. Holloway's. There were fifteen minutes until the louder phase of the rebellion began. Fifteen minutes to locate a rock, big enough to break a window, small enough to throw.

The neighborhood felt empty with almost half of us gone. Conner was up the street near his house; Trent down at the bottom by his; and four of us were stationed at the houses we needed to deliver letters to. Conner and Trent were told to pick any house close to theirs.

I found the perfect river rock and secured the letter with a rubber band around it. Viv already wiped the fingerprints from the glossy paper using art gum and a technique she learned on the Internet.

In a crouch, I tried to remain invisible behind a rosemary plant. The second buzz would come soon. I struggled to control my breathing. I'd need to be ready to flee.

There was the shattering of glass from down the street. *Shit.* I went to stand like I might see it; sank back down. Was it Viv? Graham? Trent? A second crash from far up the street. *Too early.* The heel of my sneaker caught the sidewalk and I fell, tailbone on the curb, spine finding the street. Shouts came from up the street. A porch light flickered on in my peripheral vision. I fumbled with my phone—six minutes early. The others wouldn't wait. It was now or never.

As I threw myself to my feet and ran for the Holloway's lawn, there were two loud, ringing clatters. I wound up and released the rock, hitting the high left corner of the window. At first only fissures spread, then came a tinkle like falling rain. The glass dropped out in segments. The rock hadn't made it inside. I lunged forward across the grass, diving into a shrub. Searched the ground. Found it. Hurled the brick through the gap in the glass. I was running for my house when I saw the shard of glass sticking out from my palm.

My hand seized up as I groped for the doorknob. Someone's security alarm wailed. More yelling from up and down the street. In the foyer I heard the floor above me creak. I ripped the mask from my face and stuffed it and the spray paint under the couch cushion as Dad came down the stairs.

I stood at the window, peering out, my gloved hands tucked under my arms, the glass digging deeper. "Daddy, what's happening?" I asked. "Someone's shouting." It was nauseating playing innocent and scared.

He blinked sleep from his eyes, becoming gradually more

alert standing next to me. Mom would have noticed that I wasn't in pajamas. She would have heard the ragged pant of my breath as I choked down pain.

Dad told me to stay inside, he was going to check it out, make sure no one was hurt. Where had he been five years before when someone out there actually did need help?

The door slammed behind him.

My hands shook as I held them over my bathroom sink a minute later. A shard of glass stood from my left hand. An iceberg that pierced through the black fuzzy glove and my skin. The glove sponged blood on the white porcelain as I rested my hand, palm toward the ceiling.

My good hand trembled, knocking the cell from the ridge of vanity into the sink. I wouldn't ask anyone to risk leaving their house. And showing up at the emergency room with glass in my hand wasn't an option. There. I counted three distinct sirens.

Finally my finger steadied enough for me to video call him. Two rings and Graham's spectacle-clad face appeared.

"Holy shit," Graham answered. "Who threw seven minutes and forty seconds early? No. Don't tell me. I know. Had to have been Conner."

"Graham," I croaked.

"I actually had to dive into a juniper bush to hide from the Horowitzes. With the bloody spiders, Izzie. Cobwebs in my face until they went back inside to call the police. You look pale."

Shakily I held the phone so he had a view of the glass.

"Fuck."

"It hurts."

"I don't know if I can leave the house without it looking suspicious." I saw a flash of his ceiling, then his face again, peeking through his bedroom blinds. "I'll figure something out, okay?"

"No," I said. "No. My dad's awake. Just stay on with me." I tried to shove the pain away. Think. Stop feeling. "Should I pull the glass out or remove the glove first?"

"Does moving the glove move the glass?"

I propped the phone so it was standing against the water faucet. Delicately I pinched the fabric near the glass and pulled up. I cried out.

"Affirmative. Shit," he said. "How deep do you think it is?"

"Deep."

"Bend your fingers."

"Can't." With my good hand, I reached under the sink. "There are lots of towels."

"At least you won't bleed to death."

"How comforting."

"Be careful not to break off the tip when you pull it out."

I gave my head a shake; even the small reverberation stoked the pain.

"Okay," Graham said, maddeningly calm. "Do it fast. Pull the glass. Rip the glove off. Stop the bleeding. It'll be easy. One, two—"

"Three," I whispered, wrenching the glass. The wound spurted blood. I panted at the pain shooting up my fingers.

I dragged the glove off and dropped it with a wet *thump* in the sink.

"Let me see." Graham's voice came from down a tunnel. I couldn't keep the phone steady as I held him up. "Put pressure on it. Izzie. You hear me? Put pressure on it. Now."

With a bath towel and my hand clutched to my chest, I curled up against the bathtub. I tried to focus on slow breaths in and out. Graham sat near my shoulder on the tub's ledge; he appeared to be perspiring.

"Distract me," I whispered.

"Tell me"—a pause as he stalled to figure out what to say—"Pendleton, would you smile or frown in your mug shot?"

My laugh turned into a blubbery cry.

"It's your left hand, right?"

I grunted.

"You're going to have near identical scars on both hands. The stories you'll be able to tell. All that character. I just may copy you."

We said good night, and I fell asleep on the cold tile floor. Five years after the girl with the glass in the Ghost Tunnel, there I was, another piece of glass, another scar, all in the name of Goldilocks.

Retrieved from the cellular phone of Vivian Marlo
Transcript and notes prepared by Badge #821891
Shared Media Folder Titled: IV, Wed., Oct. 23, 2:07 a.m.

Video start.
V. Marlo is in her bedroom. Sirens can be heard in the background.

"I, Vivian Marlo, belong in a Greek tragedy. I have a fatal flaw." She takes a deep breath. "Once upon a time, despite everything Amanda Schultz had done to me for eons, I was willing to let it go and be her friend." Her eyes close for a beat.

"In the sixth grade Izzie and Graham pretended they had chicken pox. They were home from school recuperating"—she makes air quotes—"for a week. I put the sugar water on myself too, but when the mosquitoes started landing, I jumped into the pool.

"Don't get me started on what a nightmare PE was. I had no one to block me in the locker room while I changed into my sports bra. Humiliating. I told my mom I was achy, and she wrote a note excusing me from participating."

She cups her chin with her hand. "Amanda was a sickly worm in sixth grade. A mental patient. She lost it over her parents' divorce. I mean, hello, parents get divorced—not mine, obvi, but it happens—and not everyone goes bald. She always sat out PE. At first we didn't even look at each other even though we were a foot away. But then Emerson Talbott got her PE shirt hooked on her braces and she couldn't get loose. Hysterical. Laughing led to talking.

"Amanda and I had tons in common and it was super-nice to talk about clothes and boys with another girl who cared. And don't you dare roll your eyes, Izzie, 'cause you know you're not into that stuff. Amanda said I could come to her birthday mani-pedi party and we were making all these plans.

"But then I was in the bathroom on Friday at lunch—in a stall—and I heard Amanda tell a bunch of other girls, *I can't believe her mom's only going to have one boob.* And one of them asked if it would grow back." Her eyes tear up. "And Amanda said, 'You should ask her.' Then they all laughed and talked about how desperate I was for Amanda to like me. She told them I'd begged her to be invited over her house and to her mani-pedi birthday.

"I told Amanda my biggest secret like a brainless loud-mouth and she blabbed it. She laughed about it." She wipes away the mascara under her eye. "Remembering makes me want to shove a hat pin in *her* heart. It makes me sick that I trusted her and that I was such a desperate moron thinking she'd be my friend.

"But my god. Tonight, when I thought everything was going to hell and that maybe we'd get caught, I realized exactly what I need to do."

Video stop.

Retrieved from the cellular phone of Harrison Rocha
Transcript and notes prepared by Badge #82827
Shared Media Folder Titled: IV, Wed., Oct. 23, 5:04 a.m.

Video start.

H. Rocha's face is shadowed. "I slept like crap." His voice froggy. "I just convinced Simon to go back to his own room." He sniffles. "I'm a horrible big brother. I didn't think about how scared Simon would be when he heard the sirens. Or how he'd look out his window and see blood. And that it would remind him of Dad's attack and visiting the hospital." He shakes his head slowly. "There are other kids on this street. Littler than Simon. They didn't deserve to be punished.

"I can hear Graham—I can hear you, bro—in my head saying *collateral damage*. Telling me it's not worse than anything kids see in comics. I'm pissed about Goldilocks too. That girl—she should be alive. Someone should pay. I'm not saying that assholes who hear a girl crying for help and don't do shit don't deserve it. They do. Worse." He groans. "The Order, its power, it's a high. I feel it. But it's also like this shadow I keep seeing out of the corner of my eye. I turn my head and it's gone. It's there. Dark. Waiting." Another shake of the head. "I'm rambling. Just tired is all.

"I should be figuring out an embarrassing rite to give Conner. The others all gave out a funny one already, but everything I come up with is too sadistic. Or dangerous. The problem is, I don't want to embarrass Conner. I want to take him apart."

Video stop.

26

I didn't wake up until half past six in the morning. My legs straightened and kicked the vanity cabinet, my head pinned between the toilet and tub.

Gingerly I peeled the crusty towel from my hand. Dried blood marbled my skin. Afraid to twitch my fingers for the pain it could bring, my hand stayed an arthritic claw. The wound was a black divot. Deep. Hadn't even scabbed. Likely needed stiches. I dabbed a damp washcloth around it to remove some of the blood. I placed a large square bandage over it, like the one I'd had on the opposite hand a couple weeks before. I flipped the lid off the aspirin bottle using my teeth and swallowed three.

An hour later, I sat on the porch waiting for Harry to pick me up. While I did, I thought about what Dad had shared at breakfast.

A neighbor at the base of our street arrived home late last night from Santa Barbara. His high beams streaked across houses as he turned into his driveway. There was red on the front of his neighbor's house. It was nearing Halloween—decorations, he figured. Then a sensor triggered his porch light. Red on oak. His front door was marked with an X. *All* of the front doors on our street were. He heard a crash a couple houses away. Spied a masked figure. He ran after him, but fell over a shallow retaining wall dividing his neighbor's property from his own.

His wife woke at his shouting and parted her curtains to see what the matter was. It snowballed from there, neighbors calling neighbors, people in their robes and slippers on front lawns. Dogs barking. Those with broken windows dialed 9-1-1. Officers with flashlights searched backyards. A manufactured dawn lit the street for half the night.

Dad came inside after half an hour of the bedlam, assuming I'd gone back to bed. He was shaken up enough to set our alarm for the first time in years. He wondered aloud at breakfast, *Why were the doors marked? Was it a threat?*

Harry's sedan puttered up to the sidewalk, coming from downhill rather than his house.

I dropped into the front seat. "Hey."

He fixed my injured hand with an intense stare. "Graham called this morning. He said it's bad. ER bad. I'll take you if you want. I don't care about getting caught."

"I do." I held it up. "It's nothing. See." Flexed my fingers. Swallowed the urge to scream.

"It isn't nothing. You got hurt because someone didn't follow our instructions."

"I didn't throw the rock with the letter hard enough. I

had to pick through the glass in the yard. Totally my fault."

"This never would have happened if *Conner* hadn't gone early." *Conner,* he said, like the name tore at him.

"The first window break came from down the street—Trent. Not Conner," I said. "And it wasn't his fault. His neighbor came home and it was probably a now-or-never situation. If Trent had just run rather than follow through, the neighbor might have called the cops and one of us could have been caught as we waited outside for seven more minutes."

Harry's huff was so derisive and unlike him that I did a double take.

I could see the effort it took him to smooth out his scowl. "Where'd you just come from?"

He stifled a yawn. "I've been up since five. Interviewing and taking pictures. Sorry for the bad mood, I'm just tired."

"Interviewing?"

He looked at me sideways. "I'm a reporter for the Seven Hills news blog and last night my entire street was vandalized. It would be suspicious if I didn't write about it."

Harry honked as he pulled into Viv's driveway.

"Lemme see your damaged goods," Viv demanded, climbing into the car a minute later.

She grabbed my wrist and I winced at the ferocity of her inspection. "At least it's not so big you can't wear a bandage." She tugged my sleeve down over it. "Keep it covered. The cops are looking for vandals who busted windows. Even a bandage is suspicious."

As we drove, I stared at a couple of adults bent over a bird illustration. Harry pointed at a group of middle school–aged kids snapping pictures of a giant *IV* painted on the siding of a gray house. "There've been kids out the whole morning taking pictures and selfies with the graffiti."

Graham was particularly keyed up, his blue eyes extra piercing as he greeted us with, "IV is trending. *Trending*. Across platforms. Whole streets are not usually vandalized with iconography that doesn't appear to be gang related. We're an anomaly and it's gotten people's attention." He rucked up his sleeves rather than wearing his usual neat roll.

The red paint ended abruptly as we turned from Driftwood.

Viv pressed her nose against the car window. "Stuff looks the same."

"Did you expect citywide looting and fires in the streets?" Graham asked. "That Seven Hills would revert to tribal law or that bands of cannibals would be hunting for breakfast?"

I glanced at Harry to share in a laugh. He stared straight ahead, the muscle in his cheek flexing and releasing.

Viv may have been disappointed with the scene out the car window. I was not. There were the subtle signs of a population unnerved. Cup of Jo was closed, an event so rare and unexpected that a throng of confused patrons had formed under its awning, peering through its windows, rapping knuckles on the door. The owner of Cup of Jo, Lottie Cooper, lived on our street. Her house had been defaced with the others.

Holy Bagels was the only game in town for caffeine today,

and in line, Graham overheard that Lottie had packed her three kids in the family minivan and driven to her parents' house in Portland. The abrupt departure was attributed to the eerie graffiti and broken windows. We'd scared a single mother out of town. I flexed my wounded hand, named the pain a souvenir from the night, like the tattoos had been, and smirked.

"Satisfied?" Graham asked Viv as we returned to the car.

She indicated her to-go cup of coffee. "That I won't have chai or espresso for the foreseeable future? No, I most certainly am not."

"I am," Graham said. "People are going to unwind without their fancy espresso beverages. First triple shot mochas, then what, running water goes? We've got hysteria in the making." He shook his fists in the air, happily crazed.

In the school courtyard, Jess's upraised arm beckoned us to the flagpole. Our six initiates had deer-in-headlight expressions. A thrilled energy manifested in ragged surges of conversation. They snapped their lips closed almost as soon as the words escaped. They couldn't believe what they'd pulled off.

"We're famous," Rachel crowed, indicating the feed on her cell. "Everyone I know has posted pictures."

A scolding finger in the air, Graham said, "IV is famous. Not you."

"My dad was on the phone with the security company the whole morning," Conner gloated. In his excitement, he forgot to look superior. "He was so pissed. Kicked a door right off its hinges. Hurt his foot and everything. He's having a camera installed up on the gate. He's hiring a rent-a-cop to sit on his new development at night."

"Overreact much?" Viv said.

Amanda batted Conner's shoulder. "Conner gets his temper from his dad."

"My mom caught my little sister with her chalk trying to color in the bird's wings in the driveway," Trent said, eyes growing large. "She lost it."

Conner channeled his pleasure into destruction, kicking at the branches of a rose bush in the planter surrounding the flagpole. "I got rocks off into three houses before I made it home."

"You were only supposed to hit one," Harry said.

Conner kicked harder.

Trent shook his head. "Not me, man. I barely got one off before this dude came bum-rushing me."

"About that," Graham said.

Trent fake punched Graham's shoulder. "C'mon, man. I know what you're gonna say. It was either throw it or give up and go home. I had to go early."

"I know. You made the smart call." Graham swallowed like the words tasted foul. "None of us would have known that someone was about. He might have alerted the police while we were still outside, waiting, like sitting ducks."

"Unbelievable," Harry muttered.

"Dude, what is your problem?" Trent asked.

Harry's usually calm veneer shattered. "Izzie got hurt because you couldn't follow simple directions. Because you're

a dumbass who doesn't consider anyone else but yourself."
He stepped forward, holding himself tall. "What if someone
had come outside and caught one of us because you threw
when we weren't ready?"

"Step off him, man," Conner said, arms thrown out like
he might shove Harry.

"No one got caught," I said. "This"—I waved my palm—
"is nothing. It doesn't even hurt."

"Oh, hold up." Conner tucked his square chin into his
neck. "I know what's going on. You're crashing the custard
truck with her." A finger ran connecting Harry to me.

"Oh my god, you're repulsive, Conner," Viv announced.

Harry let out a ragged sigh of frustration. "I can't be
around him without wanting to hit him," he said while looking at me, though everyone heard. Conner made kissing
sounds and a flush crept up Harry's neck. He hiked his backpack high and thrust himself into the sea of our classmates
like he was throwing himself from a cliff.

"Jesus, Conner," Jess said. "We're all getting along, remember?"

Hands in his pockets and staring at his shoes, Campbell
muttered, "It didn't feel like it while I was eating cat food."

My cheeks warmed. Viv's rite for him had been brutal.
I opened my mouth to assure Campbell there'd be nothing
like that again. But I couldn't promise anything. Not without talking to my friends first and trying to add rules where
none existed. Not without forcing the issue with Viv, who I
assumed wanted the secret rites to get revenge on Amanda.

Amanda had been oddly quiet, mouth twisting as her eyes ping-ponged around. She committed to a smile and damage control. "So, guys. What's next? Because we all really, *really* want to do more. It's next-level shit."

The courtyard was increasingly crowded.

"The next *get-together*," Graham's cautious whisper came, "is Thursday night—early Friday morning, really."

"Thursday. *Thursday*," Amanda said, like the promise of a new rebellion tasted delicious.

It was easy to track our initiates in the throng of students after the bell rang. They were all wearing at least one article of white clothing. It could have been coincidence. Or compulsion, the Order worming its way into their brains.

"Jesus. Harry's got it bad," Viv was saying.

I asked with my eyes.

"The protective boyfriend routine. Made him way hotter," she answered.

"I think it was more about hating Conner than sticking up for me."

She brushed her cheek to mine. "You're cute and naive. Later, gator."

The aspirin wore off too fast. I wore my hoodie until third period, when being in class with Viv, Jess, Conner, and Trent emboldened me. So what if someone saw a Band-Aid on my palm? The police probably weren't even looking for a girl as their suspect, let alone a girl who was a solid student, seemingly docile, a wolf in sheep's clothing.

Harry's coverage hit the news blog that period. Our peers

weren't usually abuzz over our student news organization, but given the strange events and the silence from the adult-run newspaper in Seven Hills, I got the impression kids had been hitting refresh on the blog's homepage all morning.

Harry was clever. Through the guise of sharing facts, he gently directed the reader in the direction we wanted. A graphic inset in the text was made up of thirty-six smaller pictures, the driveways of every house on Driftwood painted with a red bird, wings splayed. All those pictures, little tiles in one big square, took your breath away.

Harry quoted an anonymous source who lived on the street:

"That bird symbol means something to people who live on this block. It makes us think of dark times. It's identical to the way those bird skeletons were found, wings wide open, by the archeologists on the Marlo property years back. That poor dead girl found in the same area was also staged with her arms wide open, rocks and her T-shirt cut to look like wings. Poor thing. The authorities never even could give her a name. Doesn't take a genius to see someone wants to dredge her murder up."

Apparently Harry had spent the first two periods of the day collecting comments from the student body. There were those who called IV a vigilante, others a badass, and a few who wondered what they'd pull next. Harry's finishing lines cut to the quick: *This journalist, for one, sees a clear connection between the actions taken by IV and the unsolved case of Jane Doe's death. Someone is angry and it appears to be over a cra-*

venly negligent investigation and the unsolved death of a young woman in Seven Hills.

At lunchtime there was a current of what-the-hell running through the student body. For the first time ever, I overheard snippets of conversation, kids asking details of the unsolved murder and guessing at how IV was connected.

We met to eat in the courtyard again.

Harry said, "I've been assigned a follow-up piece." He reached up from the ampitheater riser below me and touched my wrist. "Your hand still okay?"

I waved off his concern. "Tell us about the follow-up."

Harry glanced over his shoulder at the kids eating on the riser below him. Their backs were to us, but still. Curiosity was at a fever pitch. "The perp—IV—broke Lorin Yu's living-room window. Lorin found the brick that did it, and get this: there was a letter rubber banded to it. Lorin took a picture of it. Sent it to friends and one of those friends brought it to Ms. Hendricks. The cops took the original from the Yus and told them to keep quiet about it—ongoing investigation. Hendricks called the police for a quote. They denied the letter exists. She's suspicious. I'm interviewing Lorin about the letter and trying find out if anyone else received them. She wants me to start with the houses that have broken windows. She says that given the content of the letter, it's significant that some houses have worse damage than others."

"Fascinating," Graham said.

Viv, picture of nonchalance as she tamed the wisps of

hair blown into her eyes, said, "Why would the cops want to keep the mysterious letter a secret?"

No one expected for any of the letters' recipients to do anything but throw the letters away. Hide their crimes. But why had the cops done it?

"What did the letter say?" I asked. It was the obvious next question if the kids nearby could overhear us.

Graham held up his cell. He typed out a message. It traveled around the circle.

The cops are keeping the wraps on the letters for the same reason they denied the significance of the bloody animal prints. As long as they can avoid acknowledging a connection to past events, they don't have to talk about one specific past event that if brought up could make them look bad. Potentially. If people in Seven Hills give two more shits now than they did five years ago.

"The letter's pretty messed up," Harry said without skipping a beat. "I'm printing the whole thing on the blog tomorrow, but the gist is 'For your crime of indifference. You heard someone crying for help. You went back to sleep. You found her shoe on your lawn the next day. You threw it away.'" Harry had recited the note verbatim. All the other notes took the same form, but each explicitly stated what the recipient was guilty of.

"When are you interviewing Lorin?" I asked.

"Tonight. After her lacrosse practice."

I was deep in thought and almost didn't notice the accessories a few upperclassmen were wearing. My eyes stuck to a junior boy with a bandana around his bicep. His T-shirt revealed a strip of tan midriff, the armband torn from its hem. *IV* written in black marker stared back at me, like a joke my eyes were playing. I scanned the throngs and circles of students. Five more armbands among them, one headband, and another few where *IV* was simply written on the fronts or sleeves of T-shirts. I socked Graham's shoulder.

"Use your words and say excuse me," he chided, nosing up from his book.

"Look," I said, and pointed.

After a lot of sighing and fussiness over marking his spot, he said, "And what am I looking at, darling?"

I jabbed my finger at the air with subdued violence.

"What's up?" Harry asked, removing an earphone.

"You guys aren't letting me nap," Viv complained, propping up on her elbow from where she reclined, one eye squinting into the light.

Word of the city's official response to the vandalism on Driftwood Street soon came as breathless babble from Amanda. Our city had outlawed the display of the symbol *IV*.

Some of our peers had already adopted our moniker to sign their own mischief over the last weeks. These kids and others saw the symbol as a finger to authority. When they heard it was outlawed, some of them started penning it on T-shirts and backpacks. The protest got official when student gov became involved with their armbands. They considered banning the symbol a civil liberties violation. And then there were those classmates who just wanted to be a part of it because it seemed major. Not so different from kids who wanted in or were afraid of missing out.

Whatever you want to call them, they turned us into spectators that day.

Amanda and the others joined us on the top risers. One by one they sat alongside us. Companionable even, with Amanda passing out cupcakes from a large, pink pastry box after informing us it was her half birthday.

The members of the Order of IV had been thrown off the stage and into the audience. I felt like I was watching a play I'd spent the fall writing, and the version being performed was spinning off-kilter. Out of my control.

Retrieved from the cellular phone of Harrison Rocha
Transcript and notes prepared by Badge #821891
Shared Media Folder Titled: IV, Wed., Oct. 23, 1:35 p.m.

Video start.

H. Rocha stares at the lens. "I have to vent about Conner, the wizard of assholery. Fifth period. That's where I'm supposed to be right now. But I'm here." The phone pans to show school tennis courts. "I was going to explode in class. I had to get out. I thought he was giving all that Rags and Riches stuff a rest. Except no. Why would he? He's a lying, sadistic . . . He's inhuman. He texted me: 'You think your dad needs extra cash? Mine wants to pay the gardener to clean up the graffiti from last night on the house, but I could tell him your dad'll do it for a twenty spot or something.'

"No way is my dad cleaning up the graffiti he put on his house. Not after everything. I'd break both Conner's arms before. Is he insane?" Harry drags his hand over his face.

"I can't do this for much longer. The others—I don't mind them. They're not friends but they're not enemies. Campbell's okay; even Trent's standable. But Conner. I just. I just can't keep on. I tried. I've been trying so hard to let it go. Think about next year. But truth is, next year, best-case scenario is I get financial aid and go off to school and my parents still live in that house. Dad will still work here.

There will be other Conner Welshes looking down at him like he's nobody. They don't know. My dad listens to me. We build stuff together. We laugh. He taught me to surf . . . before. He's worth ten of them. No. A hundred."

Video stop.

27

Graham had the skeleton from the attic laid out on his mother's expansive desk in her study. We'd been at his house all afternoon. Harry was working at Hilltop Market and Viv was at school for rehearsal. *Antigone* was set to open in three weeks.

Graham stroked his chin, appraising the bones like he was considering reanimating them. From the swivel chair I drew the skeleton, with one modification: her torso and limbs remained bones, but her face was fleshed out and belonged to Goldilocks. The ends of her hair curled at her collarbone. "Won't your mom find her in here?" I asked.

"Mom's gone until Friday. I'll bring the old girl to my room before then." He touched its left foot affectionately.

He'd set me up for a so-you'll-finally-have-a-girl-in-your-room joke. I shaded in Goldilocks's hair. "You're getting a little touchy-feely with the skeleton. Should I have Jess ask you out for her super-secret rite?"

"Izzie."

I fluttered my eyelashes. "Yes, darling?"

"Please, do not."

"I'd just be giving her an excuse," I muttered. "I can tell. She's into you."

"I'm thinking I'll have Trent draw a penis in marker on his forehead. Wear it to class," Graham said.

I looked up from the fringe of bangs I'd given Goldilocks. "You can't. Trent's my initiate for secret rites."

"I thought after the first round we'd reselect initiates?"

My head wobbled. By my design the rules had gone unsaid.

"Then I'll have Rachel do it, if I'm stuck with her."

"Be nice," I said. "She's so . . ."

"Grating. Obnoxious. Exhausting."

I tried to scold him with my eyes. "Lonely seeming."

"Okay. You've won her clemency." I smiled at him. "I found my spy cam," he added.

I tucked the pencil into the spiral of the sketch pad. "Good. I figured out the rest of my plan."

Graham slouched against the deep jade grass cloth, leg bent, foot against the wall. "Tell me again why your plan is so much safer than mine?"

"Because your plan involves solving Goldilocks's murder by asking lots of nosy questions. Mine doesn't involve alerting the killer that we're looking for him. It just forces him out of hiding."

His mouth scrunched up. "See, that's the part you were vague about the other night."

I glared at him.

"You were. *Graham, rather than solving the murder*"—he spoke in a breathy voice that dipped up and down, his smile wicked—"*we'll just force the killer to identify himself by setting a trap that can't be traced back to us.*"

"Come over here so I can flick you in the nose."

The cleft in his chin darkened. "Tell me, Pendleton, what incentive would prompt someone who'd gotten away with a killing to reveal themselves as a killer?"

"We convince them they haven't gotten away with it."

He tilted his head, stumped. "But they have. The physical evidence is gone. The police never investigated to begin with. They are the Webster's definition of gotten away with murder."

"You're forgetting something."

"I am?"

"Someone. Someones even."

"I give up."

I grinned. "The blonde who cut me. The other girls in the Ghost Tunnel. The killer may know Goldilocks was sleeping in the tunnel. He might even know she wasn't alone. He might not. Doesn't matter because we know both for sure. We mention this to our most gossipy neighbor. Swinton, I say. We tell her that a bunch of high school kids were at a party in the Ghost Tunnel the other night and a woman showed up, ragged clothes, late twenties. She was talking about the girl who was killed five years ago. Claimed to be her friend, even that she was with her here, camping in the tunnel. She's tried to get over it. Forget what she saw. But she can't. She knows it's someone who lives here, on our street, and she can prove it."

"Under what pretext do we spill all that to Swinton, an elderly woman you and I haven't spoken to since we sold her wrapping paper in grade school?"

My posture went straight and my pitch high. "Hi, Mrs. Swinton. You know me, Izzie, from up the street. I write for my school news blog; yeah, it's on the Internet, and I'm covering the recent acts of vandalism on Driftwood and Landmark and their connection to the murder of Jane Doe five years ago. You remember her, yeah? I got a lead from some kids at a party last week and"—I fell out of character—"simple as that."

Graham's nostrils flared. "And Viv thinks she's the actress."

"Swinton gets wind of that and she'll tell people. They stood on Viv's lawn and admitted to hearing the girl's murder and not doing crap about it." My fist pounded the sketch pad. "They gossiped about criminal negligence. They'll gossip about this. If the killer lives on this street, even just in town, they'll hear."

"And then?"

"They'll go up to the tunnel to see for themselves who it is. To kill her. To buy her silence. To scare her. Who knows. They won't be able to resist."

"But they'd risk revealing themselves to a possible witness."

"If he or she doesn't go, they risk someone else or the cops going up there to find a witness who may know who they are."

"You want to leave the spy cam by the tunnel. To catch whoever it is on film."

"Abso-freaking-lutely."

"Best-case scenario is we capture someone on camera we *think* is responsible for the killing. It won't be evidence enough to convince the police."

"Who needs the police?"

Graham mimed tipping a hat.

"That's why I don't want us to tell Harry or Viv. Setting the trap isn't dangerous, but the information we'll have afterward, what we do with it, will be."

"We're never going to tell them?"

"It'll be dangerous," I said emphatically.

An understanding passed between us. Graham and I had always toyed with danger. We would protect Harry and Viv from this.

"I have a working theory of who," he admitted, staring at the floor.

"Tell me."

"It isn't ready."

I kicked off the desk and the swivel chair rolled in front of him. "When?"

"I'm going to Trent's tonight. Video games." His hand passed nonchalantly through his bronze hair.

"Are you being coerced?"

"No, it's . . . complicated. I'll have a better handle on my theory afterward. Your plan may very well confirm it."

Forty-five minutes later I balanced unsteadily on the step of Graham's laced fingers. We picked a pine nearest to the mouth of the Ghost Tunnel. He boosted me to the lowest branch. I shimmied up, cursing under my breath when the bark bit into the wound. The bough was thin and I flexed my thighs around it to stay put. Stared at the blood seeping through the bandage on my palm.

On the second toss of the camera, I caught it. I'd dug up my old iPod armband, the one I used to run with when Viv and I decided it'd be cool to be girls who jogged. Really, that lasted a week. The tiny camera fit into the clear plastic pocket. The armband stretched taut around the tree bough and fastened in place.

"Can you spot it from there?" I called to Graham, who went to stand at the maw of the tunnel.

"Not at all." He checked the camera feed on his phone. "Tilt the lens to the left. Your left."

I hung sharply to the side of the bough and fiddled with the lens through the plastic. My clenched thighs began to shake. "Good?"

"More to the left. No. Wait. Up a little. Good, good, good. Freeze."

I held my hand in the air. "You sure?"

"Perfect."

He jogged through the pine needles as I squirmed to sit.

"How do we know it won't die?"

"The camera accesses my cell plan. I have service here so it won't black out. I'll be able to watch from my phone. The battery life is supposed to be at least a week as long as I'm deleting old footage, so it doesn't need to store a lot."

He extended his arm. "Catch you."

I jumped down beside him, wincing at the jolt to my ankles. Picking the dead ants and bark from my injured hand. "Let's go see about hijacking that train car," I said.

Graham dropped me of at my house before driving to Trent's. I went inside to change into my most believable student-journalist ensemble. A cardigan and pearl studs would make me appear above suspicion to Ms. Swinton. The kind of outfit I wore for lunch with my grandmother.

It went according to plan. Ms. Swinton invited me inside. She apologized for having to entertain me in the dining room, since the window hadn't been fixed yet and the living room was cordoned off with thick sheets of plastic.

She served me chamomile tea and we sat on either side of the oval table. I chatted about the school news blog and the bullshit article I was writing on the spree of vandalism. I rounded it out with, "My friend was at this party in the rail-road tunnel—you know the one, right? Up in the hills behind my house? Well, there was a woman there saying she saw the car that hit Jane Doe five years ago and that she's not leaving until she figures out who was driving it. My friend thought she was maybe camping up there? Isn't that all just bonkers?"

I spoke fast and blinked too much from nerves—how often did honest people blink?— and was it suspicious I was hiding my hurt hand in my lap?

I left my tea untouched; the dredges settled at the bottom of its pool. Practically fell down her porch steps I was so eager to get away from the seed I'd planted, like it was a magic bean a moment away from sprouting to crush me.

The air was full, leeching moisture into my hair. Maybe Graham wasn't paranoid for worrying over rain. Viv would be home from play practice and I needed to talk to her about the secret rites for the initiates. None had been delivered, as far as I knew, since that first day with Campbell eating cat food, Trent doing a pole dance, and Rachel's speech in her and Graham's history class. We had been busy with the rebellions and we'd agreed not to let these smaller rites overshadow what mattered. But I'd seen the hurt in Campbell's eyes over the cat food, and I worried about the storm gathering for Amanda. Not worried for Amanda, per se, but the possible fallout.

Through the glass door of the barn, Viv sat cross-legged, palms on the floor. The lights off. A candle flickered on the book that lay open in front of her.

I tapped the glass. Her face snapped up. Shiny with tears.

"Hey," I said, closing the door behind me. "You reading something sad?"

"Hi. No."

I hung at the outskirts of the candle's glow, which fell softly around her. She pulled a tissue from a skirt pocket and blew into it. I went to sit across from her and waited until she was ready.

"I failed." Her voice was low, holding back. She took a steadying breath. "You've got to understand that Amanda, Jess, and Rachel—they're not all equally friends. Anyone can see it." Viv's hands trembled. "Amanda only ever asks Jess to do stuff. Jess brings Rachel or Rachel just shows. Amanda does sneaky shit. Every time Rachel talks, Amanda winces and holds her ears like Rachel's too loud. Or she'll tell Rachel not to be rude or obnoxious right before they go into stores to shop, as if Rachel doesn't know how to behave.

"Amanda always has stories about how wasted Rachel got once, or how she's so sloppy and desperate. Rachel denies it, but Jess says, why would Amanda lie?" Viv huffed nasally in disbelief. "Because she's evil. I bet that's why Rachel actually started drinking too much. She became the lie. There are holes in their little triangle. I tried to stick my fingers through them." Viv gave a scathing bark of laughter. "As if destroying Amanda could be as easy as getting her to fight with her friends."

"Why make them fight? If Amanda and Rachel already have issues."

"I wanted them to have their *last* fight. The fight that would end the group. Their fights were never so major that Jess had to pick a side. So . . ."

"So?"

"I started repeating what the other said. Not when Jess was around. Stealthy, like, *Oh, Rachel, Amanda said you keep a flask in your backpack. Can I have a sip if you do?* Or, *Hey, Amanda, I don't want to get her in any trouble, but Rachel was reminding a bunch of kids about when you lost your hair.*"

Viv let out a long sigh, deflating. "It didn't work. Rachel got sulky. Amanda didn't care. She'd shrug or laugh or say, *Whatever, she's probably drunk.* I failed. I had this unicorn of an opportunity to destroy Amanda, and I barely made her frown. Once Amanda lost Jess, the boys would have gone too. They like her way more than Amanda. Then Amanda would be alone, like a lame animal forgotten by her herd. No one to protect her. Then IV could have cut her down."

I looked away as she wiped her runny nose on her shoulder.

"Maybe it's okay, Viv? This year's going to be over like that." I snapped. "You'll never see Amanda again. The Order did what it was supposed to—it gave us all these one-of-a-kind memories." I grabbed both her hands and held them tightly. "We'll be friends forever."

Her eyes flitted from our joined hands to my smile. "Hold on to this feeling, Izzie—the 'we're going to be in each other's weddings, live next door and have a thousand cats, and celebrate holidays together' rush."

I crinkled my brow. I liked but didn't understand where she was going. She pried her hands free. "I failed at my first plan. I have another. More diabolical." She was fraying the hem of her dress. I watched for a minute or two, until she looked up, determined, and said, "You promise you won't stop loving me?"

I pulled on a thread she'd been working to free; it began to unravel the hemline. "I promise."

"I recorded them telling us their secrets," she whispered as one blast of dishonest air. Her eyes ticked to the armoire. "My cell was on top. At first I was doing it to keep us safe. Like if one of them betrayed us, we'd post their secret on the news blog. And maybe, maybe, a little of it was because I thought Amanda might say something I could use against her."

Viv had called trying to incite a fight between the girls for her first plan. But recording the secrets had come before the rebellions and rites. Mere days after homecoming. How hard had Viv really tried to make their group explode knowing the ace she kept in her back pocket?

"But then Amanda's confession," she said. "Sex with Conner's brother, right after Conner broke up with her, and while his dad creeped through the crack in the door. It's . . ."

"Gross. Awful," I said.

"Yes. Disastrous, too, if it got out."

"But Viv. That would be—"

"Slut shaming. I know. I would never make a girl feel bad for having sex with whomever she wants. Really, I wouldn't normally. But this is Amanda." Her shaking hands appealed to me. "This girl has tried to ruin my life."

"Viv—this—it's beneath you."

She wagged her head. "Maybe I'll be doing her a favor? The secret is just as much Bowden and Sebastian Welsh's. Everyone will know."

"Bowden lives at school. I guess it might get his dad in trouble, which he deserves. But when celebrity sex tapes come out, the guys get high fives and the girls get called names. That's what you're counting on. If people weren't going to say nasty things about Amanda, it wouldn't be worth doing. You've already thought it through."

She dropped her head, nodding. "I have."

"So why haven't you done it yet?"

She peeked at me, avoiding facing me head on. "If I post the video, even though I'll do it anonymously, she'll squeal about the Order because she'll know it came from me. Maybe she'll tell people all about the Order. Maybe only the parts she didn't have a role in. But we've been signing all the rebellions—we go down for one, we go down for them all. Even the stuff we didn't do, like the beach curfew signs and Harper's car."

My mind raced. The Order wouldn't just end. We'd be in trouble. Police trouble. Destruction of private property. Trespassing. Worse. My mind had wandered these avenues at night. The secrets we had on the initiates wouldn't protect us if they were under duress—questioned by the police, cornered by a suspicious parent. I had settled on a solution: insurance.

"She doesn't have a death wish, figuratively speaking," I said. "She won't tell on us if it means taking herself down with us. We need proof that she's involved, more than just us claiming it's so. We can hang that over her head. She'd have to keep her mouth shut." I stopped to collect my thoughts.

"I'm not saying you should share her secret. It's wrong. But I was already thinking about getting more leverage. We're committing crimes. We aren't safe unless Amanda and all of them believe their fates are tied to ours."

I scooted closer. "But promise me you'll think about it more, Viv. Sharing a video of a girl talking about sex only to embarrass her and get kids to call her slutty makes you a certain kind of girl. That's not who you want to be."

Her lashes brushed her cheeks for the barest second as she tipped forward, ashamed. I could see my eyes reflected in hers, the candle flame dancing in our breaths. There was nothing between us. She'd laid all her secrets bare.

I went home soon after, angry at everyone in the world but Viv. Graham, Harry, and I should have anticipated how far she'd consider going to hurt Amanda. We should have sensed how hurt and reeling she was. I believed Viv would decide on her own not to shame Amanda.

I knew Viv—didn't I? Even at that late hour in October I experienced certainty in my bones. I knew her better than anyone, which I understand now is saying nothing at all.

Retrieved from deleted data of Graham H. Averbach III's cellular phone
Transcript and notes prepared by Badge #821891
Shared Media Folder Titled: IV, Wed., Oct. 23, 11:52 p.m.

Video start.
G. Averbach sits inside. Shelves of books at his back. "I'll likely delete this once I'm done. Some things have to be said. You can't hold them in."

He removes his glasses and pinches the bridge of his nose. "I just lied to you, Izzie. I texted you driving home from Trent's. I said my theory was bunk. A lapse in judgment. Too embarrassing to share." He points to his own face. "Liar.

"My theory panned out. They usually do. You'd call me arrogant right about now. Yeah. I am. But that doesn't mean I'm not usually right."

He raised a glass, ice tinkling as he swirled it. "I'm going to pretend I'm talking right to you. Get it out. Delete it. Move on. Here is what I know, Izzie. Have you ever noticed Conner's bruises? For the last year I've been noting a correlation between days he has physical injuries and days he goes after Harry. He had a split lip the last time he hassled him about his lunch tray. He walked with a limp the last time he shoulder-checked Harry in the halls. Yesterday, Conner had bruises across the knuckles of one hand and his lower lip was swollen, and despite our truce, he baited Harry. They almost went at each other. I suspect that Sebastian Welsh hits his son. I think Conner's older brother used to go after him too. Conner didn't used to be a bad kid. Played fair. Was kind of quiet. I theorize that's before the abuse started. And now, feeling maligned and like the victim brings Conner's mean streak out, and *wham*, he goes for Harry.

"Sebastian Welsh." He says the name slowly. "Abusive dick does not always a murderer make, I know. But then there was Conner's secret. He ran away from home after his mom died. Camped up in the tunnel. And I got to thinking, didn't his mom pass away in middle school? Wasn't it at the end of sixth grade?"

He sips his drink. "I loosened Trent up with my flask and got him talking about it. Really, he likes the sound of his own voice as much as I do. So Conner's mom died one month before your Goldilocks, Izzie. Trent seemed to remember it was a few weeks after Conner's mom's death that Conner told him he was running away from home. Trent was a good friend, kept his mouth shut as long as he could, but when Sebastian Welsh finally noticed his younger son was gone, he bullied Trent into spilling. Sebastian went up the hill to find Conner. Trent wasn't allowed to see him for weeks, had the naive idea that Conner was sick or something, needed to stay in bed. When Trent finally got to go over, Conner had some stories about a group of girls who babied him up there in the tunnel. Kept him for two days like their pet, fed him, dried his eyes when he cried about his mommy. Trent thought Conner was full of shit.

"That's what I know." He slid his glasses back on. "Here's what I suspect. Sebastian Welsh marched into that tunnel. He laid into twelve-year-old Conner with his fists. Goldilocks and her ilk saw. A couple days later, Goldilocks left at night, told the others she was going to the gas station because they'd try to stop her if they knew the truth. She was going to check on that poor little kid with the daddy who beat on him. Knows where he lives from spending all that time with him. She cuts through our neighborhood, maybe even makes it to Conner's house to see if he's okay. Sebastian Welsh chases her down in his German luxury vehicle. Hits her. Maybe he means to. Maybe he's just trying to scare her and he goes too far. Regardless, she's got to die when the car doesn't finish her off. She knows who he is. The rest, we all know."

He stares at the middle distance. A minute later he refocuses. "You don't know how bad I want to tell you, Iz. Here's your murderer. Your ultimate villain. But the other night, at my house, when you showed up all breathless and scheming, even without a plan fully formed, I saw it in your eyes. You'll want to hurt this man who killed a girl. The Order has made it possible.

"I'm afraid you will hurt him. I'm afraid you'll go too far or I'll go too far because I'll know it's what you want." He shook his head. "I'm frightened you'll get hurt or do something you can't take back."

He drags a hand over his mouth.

"You used to say there wasn't a line with all our dares. I pushed you. You pushed me. You think I don't look when I jump. Maybe not. But I always look where you're going to land. And this is the line."

Video stop.

28

Look at that fascist," Graham spat. One of the security golf cart squad deserted his vehicle to chase down a kid in a IV armband. During the first half of Wednesday's lunch, we'd seen six other kids asked to shed apparel bearing the mark. Graham snapped a picture on his cell of the security goon hooking the kid by the neck of the T-shirt. "They're just stoking the flames."

"Two kids were pulled out of first period and sent to the office," I said, snapping the lid back onto my untouched salad. A pressure built deep in my stomach. Anticipation. Hunger. Not for food.

"Armbands?" Harry asked.

"No. *IV* in Wite-Out on their backpacks." My eye snagged on Viv's nails decorated with *IV*s. The school admin didn't catch subtle clues. Her eyelashes made a slow drop, then snapped open as she shifted into a less comfortable position. I imagined she had stayed up late the night before, guilty and sad.

"The squad burst into my second-period class and hauled Henry up from the seat like he was a criminal. Henry, from the *Brass Bandits*," Graham said. "The kid's never even gotten a warning for being late."

"Was he wearing a *IV*?" I asked.

"Headband—commando style. I swear, that kid has spirit."

Harry's brow became a ledge. "He come back?"

"I saw him by the band room in between third and fourth. Get this." Graham slapped his own knee. "They *questioned* him."

I dropped the laces of my sneaker I was in the middle of retying. "About what?"

"What do you think?" He held up his hand, thumb folded in. "Full-on interrogation. Henry tried to explain it was a civil liberties issue; he wasn't actually associated with IV, just you can't outlaw wearing a Roman numeral and not expect people to cry foul."

"Poor Henry," Viv said.

"Poor all of them. They're dragging everyone they catch with a *IV* in for questioning," Graham said.

"I heard they set up an interrogation room in one of the deserted portables near the tennis courts," Viv said, fighting off a yawn.

"What?" Harry said sharply.

"Yeah. No joke." She gave a weary smile.

"Is that allowed? Questioning students without their parents?" I wondered.

"If the police aren't there and they're asking about

activities on campus. Actually"—Graham scratched his head and threw up his hand—"I don't have a fucking clue. They'll probably drag you in soon." Wave to Harry. He elaborated, "Harry's been writing about IV's *activities*. Harry's been interviewing people. He's quoted anonymous sources. He's one of the few people in the position to make an educated guess about IV's identity. Of course, putting this all together would require the school admin to use reason. Not their anthem."

Viv blinked at him. "Anthem?"

"It's slang."

"I know," she said. "I'm just surprised you do."

Harry removed his headphones from his backpack. He stared down at his knuckles as they blanched and flexed around the plastic. His hands, the angry focus sharpening his eyes, the shift in his jaw, all made me think Harry was imagining strangling someone. "Let them question me," he said, voice dead calm. "I've got some questions, too, like how come they didn't question anyone when my dad was attacked on campus?"

He yanked the headphones on. Tapped his phone to play his music. Graham and Viv went back and forth showing each other pictures of Driftwood and Landmark online. Popping up in their feeds were kids at school posting selfies: showing four fingers; donning *IV* on their T-shirts; video clips of snickered *IV's gonna get you, Seven Hills* on a loop. The drone of Harry's music was the distant clashing of pots and pans. Angry. Not what he usually listened to. The pressure in my stomach pulsed, taking up a little more volume. I had a bad feeling. Nothing like a hunch or premonition. No. A real hunch lay too far beyond my fingertips. A ghost had slipped in one ear and out the other. The echo of its whisper. Important. *There are things happening around you. Don't close your eyes.*

"We should sear *IV* into one of the hills," Viv was saying.

"Yes. Like a brand on the whole town," Graham responded.

Who knows why the authorities bothered outlawing *IV*. It was useless. Graffiti, trespassing, broken windows, and blood splashed on houses were in themselves acts against the law. Telling lawbreakers that they were guilty of one more minor offense, what did it matter? The adults in charge couldn't fully comprehend that even if they outlawed the symbol from Seven Hills, it existed a hundredfold in everyone's cells, laptops, and tablets. A space they couldn't patrol. Seven Hills couldn't strike IV from social media feeds and from our thoughts—I brushed my fingers along my T-shirt where my tattoo was—or our bodies.

Harry's phone buzzed where it sat on his backpack between us. My gaze cut down to read Amanda's name on the screen. My stomach turned. I found her down in the courtyard. Hand hooked on the flagpole, hanging, other hand cupping her cell. The phone quit buzzing. Amanda slid her cell into the back pocket of her jeans.

If she wanted to talk to us, why not mosey up like she had the lunch before? Unless it was not the four of us or a public conversation she wanted. I shook my head at myself. I was Isadora Anne Pendleton, creator of the Order of IV, an army of underlings at my beck and call. That fierce girl didn't get jealous.

"Lemme see." I brushed Viv's ankle. She crawled over, pressing her side to mine, scrolling through picture after picture on her cell, tiny little rebellions that we had inspired.

The day went gray. Graham and I hadn't had a moment for just the two of us, so I'd texted him asking about the camera footage of the tunnel. He promised to run through what had recorded and to text me if he found anything of interest.

On our way home from school, Graham's elbows were on Harry's dash as he scrutinized the clouds crowding the sky. Viv had stayed behind on campus for rehearsal.

"I walked around the square late last night and bagel girl was right," Graham said, "no cameras pointed on the knoll."

"You might not have seen them," Harry said.

"I hope you didn't look like you were casing the knoll," I said.

Graham pushed his glasses higher on the bridge of his noise. "I'd see the cameras. And no, I didn't arouse suspicion. But I want to walk around once more. Drop me off."

"We can go around together," Harry offered.

"No," Graham said, hastily gathering up the ever-growing library of books spilling from his bag, dropping a few of the titles, cursing under his breath. "I want to inspect the tracks again and plot our course for tomorrow night." As he exited without a good-bye or wave, *Ritual Madness* was braced at his chest.

"Beach?" Harry asked.

"Definitely."

Harry and I walked along the beach to a spot unblemished by driftwood. He dropped to his knees and scooped out two craters side by side in the sand. We sat in them. I tucked my hands into my sleeves and ignored the throb in the injured one. It was on the verge of cold. The wind threw our hair forward and then off to the right in abrupt gusts. Harry's arm went around my shoulders, shielding me. "I should have brought my portable record player," he said, close to my ear.

I wormed my cell from my pocket and balanced it on the top of my sneaker. "What do you want to listen to?"

He didn't say anything at first. I swiped through playlists for a long time. I didn't have anything right. I'd never wanted romantic songs before. "You," he said. I turned to him, confused. "I want to hear what you think about everything."

We lay back on the sand and I told him about how I used to want to be a professional singer, but that I'd always had a horrible singing voice, and I described my grandmother, my mom's mom, who traveled all over the world and how I didn't understand how my mom had stayed put for so long. I asked him if he remembered the day we walked home from the barn and he'd said he could tell I was upset and that he'd listen when I was ready to talk. He remembered. I explained about Ina and my dad and my mom leaving, but that Viv refused to believe it was because she'd found out. Her mom and dad weren't fighting.

There were grains of sand caught in his eyebrows. When

I rubbed my lips together I felt grit on them, too. The stormy sky cracked open, fragments of clouds blew away, and sun seeped everywhere. It turned Harry's irises amber. I sat up to shrug off my hoodie and looked back at Harry. Arms folded behind his head, a hollow under his chin that my thumb would fit in, his eyes downcast and watching me through fans of brown lashes.

I focused on his lips. I was pretty sure he wanted to kiss me, too.

It felt like we were stealing the last bit of the year's sunshine. Like we were existing as our own little planet, in a tropical solar system Harry invented. And weren't we, a little? We'd invented a secret order and rebellions and history. Were there any stars we couldn't touch?

I knelt over him. He was fighting a smile as I bent to touch my lips to his. He tasted like sand and salt wind. A seagull screeched across the sky. "Isadora," he whispered. My grown-up, sophisticated name. I kissed him again. No longer self-conscious about my weight on top of him or my breasts pressed to his ribs or my knees on either side of his hips.

It was later, almost five o'clock, and we'd ignored the chirping of both our phones two or three times, when we were brushing the sand off each other. His hands racing down my jeans was almost as exciting as our mouths linked. The sea had calmed as it darkened. Harry took my hand and we started up the gentle slope of dunes.

As we walked over a red *IV* and two grooves in the asphalt where one of the curfew signs had been in the parking lot, Harry asked, "Are you afraid for tomorrow night?"

I squeezed his fingers. "No way. We're pros by now."

"We could get busted. It's been all trespassing and vandalism so far. The train car, the fire, the gazebo—I don't know
what they'll call it, but it's serious. Unlawful destruction,
maybe."

I rocked my shoulder into his. "How is unlawful destruction different from lawful destruction?" Fear didn't exist in
that moment. The swelling thing in my gut had deflated.
Harry was someone I'd never had before. I was used to having
three best friends. But Harry, he was a one and only.

"Still not afraid," I said. "You?"

"I should be, because—consequences." He emphasized
that one word and I knew all he meant by it. Each of us had
plans that would be messed up by getting into trouble with
the police and school. It seemed so far beyond worth-the-risk
that the consequences became dull annoyances, flies to swat
at or ignore.

He stopped and faced me. Light shone from his eyes—
the sky was gray again and I was convinced that the sun had
come from him. "Are we—going out? Dating? Hanging out?
What do you call it?"

"According to Viv, people mostly say going out. We
should call it whatever we want, though. I've never had a
boyfriend," I added, unnecessarily since surely Harry knew.
"Why didn't we hang out with your last girlfriend?"

"Because." He swayed his head side to side. "Because,
you."

"Me. That was like a year ago."

He looked to the sky, counting. "Ten months."

"You liked me ten months ago?"

"I loved you ten months ago."

"Oh," I said, and shrugged. "I've loved you since I met you. All three of you."

Harry laughed. I didn't understand why. "C'mon," he said. "I want to buy my girlfriend a pizza before the barn."

Graham laid his map out on the table. His finger traced a double line he said represented the railroad tracks. The map included the knoll and the foothills that ran from behind the stores on its east side. They rambled slowly to the Ghost Tunnel, before shooting up in altitude, forming a ridge as good as a wall around our town. The gazebo was indicated with a red circle. A rectangle with wheels marked where the town's railway station used to be, where the knoll was now.

"I checked the railway car and you were right, Har," Graham said. "The air compression brakes aren't on."

"The air used to control them comes from the locomotive," Harry said to Viv and me. He added, "That's the way train brakes have worked since the 1800s, according to the Internet."

"The tracks follow this course." Graham indicated the double line. "It runs a mile downslope and a mile of flat ground before it hits the knoll."

"If it's moving too fast, it could derail. Go off the tracks," Harry warned.

"The area's deserted. No houses," Graham said, zigzagging his finger over the blank space he meant.

"Does it cross the road?" I asked.

"A couple times—but that late at night, no one's going to be driving on a road that only goes to a lookout point," Graham said.

Viv pursed her lips at him. "Night is when people visit lookout points, Graham Cracker."

"At four a.m.?"

"People have been known to make out even at four a.m.," she said, toeing my foot under the table. I looked up from the pen I'd been using on my fingers. On the inside of each knuckle I'd written a letter, all ten spelling "Goldilocks."

She considered me with grave eyes as Graham wrung the back of his neck and said, "If we wait any later, people could be awake, commuting to work."

Harry had his elbows on the map, studying it. "You said it's a mile of flat ground leading to the knoll where the tracks stop?"

"I tried to calculate speed but the grade of the hill is different in so many spots and it grew too complicated to solve," Graham said.

"Physics," I muttered, trying to poke my recollection. "There's a formula for finding the velocity of an object on an inclined plane. But we'd need its rate of acceleration and something else. Forget it, I think a mile's plenty of space."

"So four a.m. in the Ghost Tunnel. We hit the gazebo on the knoll at, what, three thirty?" Viv said. "Cover it in blood."

She wriggled her fingers in my direction and cackled like a witch.

She was being silly. Involved in planning. But our plan as it was left me racking my brain for more. "I want to frighten them," I said, my fist smacking the table and jolting their water glasses. Harry slid back into his seat and regarded me with concern.

"We're talking blood and fire on a grand scale," Graham said. "What's not scary about that?"

"This rebellion needs to be an obvious escalation. It needs to send the message that we're not fooling around. We told Denton and Carver to resign. They didn't do it. Everybody knows IV is angry over Goldilocks. She's dead. I saw her dead body. Blood that looks like paint isn't enough. It's not the same as showing people a body."

The wind whistled through the gap in the sliding door.

"The bones are for the final Goldilocks rebellion," Graham said gently. "Not this one."

I pushed away from the table and stood too quickly. Stars firing off before my eyes, I blinked at the bandage on my palm. Its corner had caught on the table. The scab was a black divot, like a wormhole on my hand that led anywhere. I said, "Not bone. Flesh and blood."

"Like the dove," Viv stated.

Driving pins into the dove's heart made the initiates more malleable. Doing something that forbidden changes you. It brings all the other taboo acts out of the middle distance. No longer on the horizon. They're possible. Close. Just say yes.

I wanted to leave a symbol like the dove for Seven Hills. But not to make them conspirators like our initiates. Sure, our neighbors worried they'd get hit again with spray paint. Maybe they even slept with the lights on, bats rested against the bedframes to be ready for the vandal. But it wasn't the same kind of fear Goldilocks had experienced right before she died. Real fear didn't live in Seven Hills. I wanted to crook my finger. Welcome it. Not to actually hurt people. Never, I told myself. Fear was enough.

"All those books you've been carrying around"—I pointed at Graham—"ritual sacrifice and guerilla movements and insurgencies . . . You've been reading about secret groups."

He thumbed the dimple in his chin. "I have. Mostly because it's an academic interest."

"We've started a secret society, Graham." I spread my arms, spun. "You had us recruit initiates. We're calling ourselves an order. You haven't been reading to help us?"

"Curiosity, Izzie. You understand that. These aren't the kind of groups you want to model us after."

I shook my head, ponytail swinging defiantly. "Isn't there one thing—one thing you can think of to use? C'mon, Graham. Don't chicken out on me now." It was unfair appealing to his ego. It did always work, though.

Elbows on the table, he tented his hands under his chin. For a long time we stared at each other, unblinking. We were the monster the other had created—all our pushing and daring. We scooped up the line, tossed it far afield. Finally he sighed. I'd won. "There was a group in South America. They hung dogs from the lampposts while everyone slept."

I swallowed. Viv covered her face. "Not dogs," she said weakly.

"It was in Peru," Harry said. "The Shining Path and the dogs represented the dogs of capitalism. They were a Marxist group."

"And it worked," Graham said. "People were terrified."

"What about an animal that's already dead?" I asked. "Like roadkill?"

"We just go driving around looking for corpses?" Graham said.

Viv rested her head on her folded arms. "I can't believe we're discussing this. I am not here."

"I just . . ." I held my head. "Denton and Carver haven't resigned. They didn't take our note seriously. A girl is dead. A girl is dead." My voice cracked. I felt apart from my three friends sitting calmly, watching me. I was closer in spirit to the night through the sliding door. I wanted to break something. Leave its pieces all over Seven Hills.

Harry walked over and put his arm around me. "We know, Izzie. We'll make the rebellion horrifying. Maybe we can—"

I held my hand up, silencing him. "Let's just get back to going over the plan, okay? Please?" I softened my face. I needed to focus. I wanted to think and plan, and if they didn't have the stomach for what needed to be done, so what, I did.

His hand ran down my arm, fingers catching on mine, as he nodded.

· · ·

The interior lights were all out except the foyer lantern when I got home. Dad was asleep. I still hadn't thought to return my mom's calls; five had registered on my cell as missed since the morning after she left. I wasn't angry with her; I just didn't want to think about anything other than the Order.

Not entirely true. I wanted to bring Harry inside. I thought about kissing him more. Keeping him in my room with me the whole night so I didn't have to be alone. But more powerful than that desire was the pull of my fingers, itching to flick through photos of dead girls on my laptop. My anger needed more fuel. More fire for tomorrow's rebellion. For what I believed needed to be sacrificed.

29

The next morning I woke up with the sun. I got dressed hastily, hit the button on the coffee maker in the kitchen, and waited for it to brew as I ate a Greek yogurt. With one thermos of brimming-hot coffee in my cup holder, I drove up the hill to Conner's house. I could have walked, but I sensed that out on the street, Graham or Harry or Viv would see me, stop me, want to tag along. And then I couldn't ask Conner for a favor. Give him a secret rite I didn't want anyone else to know about. Break our rules; well, rules we hadn't been explicit about. And misuse the secret rites in exactly the way I worried someone else might.

The four of us had agreed that the night's rebellion was too sensitive to commit to paper. Instead, we'd tell our initiates where and when to meet us and what to bring.

It was a little after seven as I parked behind the other vehicles in the Welshes's driveway: an SUV, a four-door sedan, a two-seater, and a boat. They were displayed, sparkling clean, with not so much as a frond from the palm trees on them. Even the sleek, modern design of the house made me feel like I was on the set of a music video.

I listened at the front door. Somewhere in the house there was the thump of bass. My finger fell away from the doorbell without pressing it. What if Sebastian Welsh opened the door? He was the most disturbing thing about Amanda's secret.

The door was opening inward when I realized I should have texted Conner that I was coming or, better, to meet me out front. A woman in a plain gray dress and white apron stared at me.

"Hi. I'm here for Conner," I said.

I hugged myself on the way to Conner's room. The thumping bass grew louder as we got closer. It was noticeably colder inside the house than outside, all the polished concrete floors creating an atmosphere of refrigeration. Or a crypt. I could vaguely remember Conner's eighth or ninth birthday and a party he invited the whole class to. I hadn't been inside his house since then.

Conner's room was immaculate. All polished chrome and black lacquer and a TV that took up most of the wall. Every surface dusted. No clutter of magazines or books or clothes. He looked up, startled, half stood, knocked his breakfast onto the carpet, and hit mute on the music playing.

"You must have a serious case of OCD," I said in way of a greeting.

He descended on the fallen bagel, blotting up jam from his rug with a paper towel. "My dad gets on my case if my room's messy," he said.

I snorted. "I'm not sure my dad's been inside my room since middle school."

I closed the door behind me and hovered between the bed and the TV.

"Lucky."

"Not really."

"You're dad's a decent guy. He helped me change a tire once on the side of the road."

"So." I rocked up on my heels. "I bet you're wondering why I'm here."

He was done cleaning up the bagel and returned to the foot of his bed. "Nah. Remember?" A suggestive lift of his eyebrow. "I had you pegged for the freaky one from the start. Knew you'd want some of this."

"Shut up," I said. "It's Order business."

"Oh." He straightened up, attentive.

I took a calming breath. "I have a secret rite for you and Trent today. In addition to the instructions you're going to be given at school."

"I'm in."

"You don't know what the secret rite is yet."

"This IV thing has been more fun than I used to have"— he lowered his voice to a whisper, eyes flicking to the closed door—"busting up my dad's model homes."

"You know how there are always goats along highway eighty-nine eating grass? Along that deserted span after the Oak Hurst exit?"

"Yeah. It's near a goat farm or something."

"I need you and Trent to go after school and get one of them. But not a baby, okay?"

"A kid—that's what the babies are called," he said unexpectedly.

I nodded. "Swear you won't get a kid."

"Sure."

"So you and Trent will do it?"

He shrugged. "Yeah. Trent's got a pickup."

"Don't let anyone see you take the goat, though, okay?"

"No, really?" He rolled his eyes.

"And you'll bring it with you tonight?"

"If that's the rite. Yup."

"Okay. And don't mention it to anyone—not your friends. Not even mine."

He smirked. "Not your boyfriend?"

"I don't want him to feel culpable about the goat. Bad for it."

"You don't care if I do?"

"No. I don't, Conner. You're an irredeemable asshole."

"You didn't think I was an asshole when I forfeited my title of Tetherball Champion of Seven Hills Elementary to let you win after your grandpa died." He smirked. "How could I forget? I got teased so bad for a month because the boys thought a girl beat me."

"A lot's happened since then, Conner."

He inclined his head. I gave him an awkward nod

good-bye. Halfway out the door, I added, "Oh. Here." I set the thermos on his dresser. "I brought coffee in case I had to bribe you to steal the goat."

"As people do."

My smile was genuine, because in that moment I hated Conner a little less than usual.

We met our initiates in the turnout on Old Creek Road at three a.m. It was a quiet side street; head north and you'd hit the Ghost Tunnel; head south and you'd end up at the beach. Eucalyptus trees with great swaths of peeling bark framed the turnout.

I stepped out into the chilly night scented by the trees; almost like peppermint balm. Amanda, Jess, and Rachel sat on the tailgate of Trent's truck. Campbell paced, hands gripping his beanie, muttering to himself.

Conner kicked haphazardly at the gravel of the shoulder, sending rock sprays against one of their parked cars.

Graham spoke to them first. "Did you see any other cars on the road? You remembered to take Lagoon here rather than Main Street with the traffic cam, right?"

Rachel dabbed the corners of her eyes with a sleeve. Amanda's face spasmed. Conner spun around like he was waiting for someone to come out of the trees. "Trent," he called, "hurry up pissing."

"God," Amanda muttered, "shut up already."

The four of us traded uneasy glances.

"What's up?" I asked.

"Trent killed it," Conner said, gesturing wildly at the truck bed.

A cold nausea swept through me, my skin turning clammy, my ears ringing. I was the only one out of my friends who understood. I was going to have to explain why I wanted the goat and what fate I'd had in mind for it.

"Uh, killed what?" Viv asked. Silence. "Jess?"

Jess rapped a fist on the truck. "Better look for yourselves."

"You gave them one job. One job. And they screwed it up," Amanda said empathically. "This is so not on me."

"Or me," Rachel echoed.

Graham, Harry, and Viv walked tentatively for the truck bed. Harry glanced uneasily back at me when I didn't move in tandem. Their harsh intakes of breath came as they made sense of the motionless lump.

"What is a dead goat doing in the truck?" Harry asked.

Trent came from the trees fidgeting with his zipper, apparently having just relieved himself. He took in the scene. Raised both hands like he was surrendering to the police. "It was an accident. I drove the truck into their pasture because I thought it'd be easier getting a goat with the truck right inside the gate. And it was. But then I backed up."

"And?" Graham said.

"I ran over one."

"And rather than bringing you a live goat like you asked for, they showed up with this dead one, and then told us the whole story," Amanda said. She was angry not over the goat's death, but because she thought our rebellion required a live animal. My fault. I'd unleashed Conner and Trent on the goats in the first place. I had intended to kill one. To take another life.

Harry sputtered, practically writhing with anger. I took his hand and squeezed. "It's the goat we needed for tonight, Har." I spoke softly, imploring. "You know, to hang in the gazebo. Like they did with the dogs?" Confusion, understanding, and disappointment registered on Harry's face in quick succession, marring his beautiful features.

Graham went from covering his open mouth to nodding. "Oh yeah, thanks for procuring it for us." He slapped Conner hard on the back, keeping his gray quizzical eyes on mine. He wondered why I hadn't told him. I wouldn't have an answer for him. "You saved us the trouble of killing him or having you kill him—but on purpose."

Viv was tellingly silent.

"Wait," Trent said, "we were going to kill the goat?"

I busied myself with the supplies in Viv's trunk as I said, "Yes."

"See," Trent went on, "I didn't ruin anything."

"Let's stop wasting time," I said. "Did everyone leave their cells at home?"

"We're going to need more than nods, people," Graham said. "Us getting away with this requires that all cells are home. This isn't graffiti tonight. There will be a full-blown investigation."

They gathered by the trunk, surveying the supplies. I'd confirmed three times that we had everything. Accelerant in a red plastic tank. My Polaroid camera. Coil of rope. Ten water bottles full of blood. One can of red spray paint. Flashlights. And a lighter.

I pushed the goat and my deception out of my head. Now was the time to be calculating. Alert. "Gloves on," I said.

Harry withdrew a black beanie from his back pocket. "Masks on at all times. We don't think there are cameras, but we don't know for sure."

"I'm sure," Graham said testily. "Keep them on in case there are witnesses, though."

"You." Harry pointed to Conner. "Carry the goat. Izzie, do you have . . ." His voice trailed off as he noticed the rope coil. I wanted to pull him aside to defend myself. Seven Hills deserved this. They needed to see actual death. Flesh and bone and blood. Harry rolled the beanie down, cutting off his expression from me, turning. The moment gone.

Water bottles of blood were distributed. I wore the rope over my shoulder. Graham took the spray paint. The accelerant, flashlights, and fire starters stayed behind for the tunnel.

Graham checked the time on his wristwatch. "Three ten. Let's move."

We jogged down Old Creek Road, its mild slope snatching our bodies forward. My muscles got looser, my gait light as a gazelle's—no, a predator's. Stealthy in the night. Prey hooked over the neck in front of me. I paused at the bottom of the slope, listened. Only the savage song of the sea.

The others brushed past me, intent on the knoll. I grinned

at the sound of their stampeding footfalls. I felt powerful. They were there for the Order I invented.

Harry slowed to a stop a few yards from me. The square cut of his shoulders, tilt of his head, earnest eyes—obviously him. I shouldn't have kept the goat from any of them or the camera up at the tunnel from Harry, or that Graham had been fast-forwarding through hours and hours of footage, scanning for a suspect. How could I admit all that to Harry? He was our moral compass. Never pushing. Never urging you over the line.

"I'm sorry," I whispered. "Asking Conner and Trent to bring the goat—it wasn't a compliment. I told them to do it because I was too cowardly to do it myself. I would have seen all those goats in their field, kept driving."

He came closer. "Isadora," he said and took my hand. "Don't ever apologize for doing what you believe needs to be done." Those words, they still rattle my heart in my chest.

We reached the knoll. The lanterns along the square swung in the wind, shifting shadows. The others were phantoms stealing up the pathways that crisscrossed the grass. Halloween decorations were out: bales of hay; an old-timey wooden wagon overflowing with pumpkins and gourds; stuffed scarecrows on pikes in the dirt; the gazebo festooned in shimmery spiderwebs.

They converged onto the gazebo. Leaped up its twin staircases. Climbed its banister that ran above the spindles. They tipped their water bottles against the posts at the roof and the blood seeped down. Harry and I stopped at the plaque affixed to the gazebo. SEVEN HILLS: FOUNDED IN 1898. Viscous red coated it from top to bottom.

Conner dumped the goat on the blood-splattered deck of the gazebo. Harry crouched opposite me and together we wrapped the rope around its neck. Its dull, alien stare bore into me; those rectangular pupils, lifeless, knowing. I'd sent death seeking it.

The rope slid through my hand as I pulled tight, burning my palm, biting through the bandage. I gripped it again, hauled it up. Harry threw one end of the rope over a rafter in the pagoda roof. He caught it as it fell on the other side. Hand over hand, he began to hoist it up.

"Wait," I said. I grasped the rope between his fists. "Together." We pulled. The goat dangled at the end of the line, one foot above the deck, two, three, we stopped when its hind hooves were at eye level. Harry anchored the rope around a spindle.

Viv darted from the gazebo to the wood wagon, stepped up its wheel, and rained blood onto the pumpkins. She'd wrapped herself up in the gauzy fake spiderwebs from the eaves. Wore them like a cloak. Queen of the night creatures. The others were blurs of mischief and blood. Jess gave some of the scarecrows slit throats. Campbell squirted others haphazardly. Amanda, short black jumper blowing up in the wind, painted the pyramid of hay bales.

There were shambling footsteps on the roof above us that shook the gazebo. Harry and I jogged down the stairs and onto the grass. Graham stood over the finial of the roof, drizzling the blood from its center, rivulets running over shingles, water falling over its edge. He'd set the goat swinging. Back and forth like the pendulum of a clock. Counting down to when our sleepy town would wake.

I whistled for Graham's attention. Made a sign like I was spraying something in the air. He tossed down the spray paint.

On the side of the wagon I wrote: *One of you killed a girl.* Across the wooden steps of the gazebo: *IV is coming for you.*

Graham swung down from the roof; his sneakers balanced on the banister, set the goat swinging harder. The clock sped forward. Nearly four a.m.

We gathered the initiates up and moved as a herd to the cars. Everyone piled into Viv's SUV. I shared the front passenger seat with Harry as Viv drove up the hill, the cobwebs batting frantically in the wind off her shoulders. The windows were rolled down so we could listen for sirens. I stared into the rush of air, barely able to breathe, heart pounding against my ribs. *Almost there. Almost done.* With the car parked in the turnoff—on the asphalt, not the dirt, no chance for tire prints—we switched out the supplies in the trunk and I pulled on my backpack.

Then: the spongy give of the pine needles under my sneakers, bolts of our flashlights swinging, the sloshing of the accelerant in its tank, my backpack jumping with each step, our breath drowning out the ocean as we reached the tunnel. We passed the tree where our camera was concealed, Graham and my little spy that hadn't yielded any leads yet.

The red *IV*s on its walls had darkened with moisture. I bounded over the charred remains of a bonfire. Gasps and whoops echoed around me as others followed.

We came up on the train car fast. Its wood and metal walls were corroded and timeworn.

"Will it even make the descent?" I asked.

Graham patted the rust-mottled exterior. "Sure she will."

"Why do boys always call cars and boats and stuff 'she?'" I said.

"Harry named his car Einstein after he bought him," Viv piped up.

"I can't believe you remember that," Harry said, pleased.

Graham was crouched at one of the train car's four sets of wheels. "I know, I know, Harry is so much nicer and less pervy than Graham. Can we focus? Guys," he snapped at Trent, Conner, and Campbell, who were standing back looking dazed and overwhelmed. "Remove the blocks from in front of the wheels—the direction we're taking *him*. Not the ones behind the wheels. Can't risk it rolling the wrong way."

Viv and I knelt for one of the wooden blocks, crammed our fingers under its edges and lifted. They were heavy and solid, pinning the train car in place.

Nine of us would push the train car. Graham would position himself outside the car, on the metal risers so he could reach the puddle of accelerant, and jump. The fire would catch inside the car. The rush of the wind as it moved would keep the flames from spreading too quickly. When the car reached its destination by the knoll, likely in a matter of minutes, it would ignite. Ideally. We hoped. There were a million things that could go wrong or end in serious injury, but none of those consequences occurred to me. What did: a girl was killed, someone got away with it, we had the right to punish Seven Hills, Graham was used to jumping.

But first, leverage. "Amanda," I said, "C'mere." She trotted over, rosy cheeked.

"This is cool as fuck," she gushed.

I thrust the red plastic tank into her arms. "Time for souvenirs," I said. The ten of us filed inside the car. I fought to keep the memories at bay. The piece of glass that scarred my shoulder was probably still in there, discarded on the floor, a part of me that would soon go up in flames.

"Amanda, Jess, all you guys there."

Viv, Graham, and Harry hovered in the rows of seats behind me. I took my Polaroid camera from my backpack. "Hold the tank above your head, Amanda. Yeah, yeah, you look so cute." I peered through the viewfinder, made out their forms in the light of the flashlights. "Say 'arson,'" I called.

"Arson," they giggled in unison. My camera flashed. Their crime was caught on film.

I slipped the photo into the pocket of my backpack. "You take one of us?" I asked Jess.

She obliged and Graham, Viv, Harry, and I posed by the door, arms linked. I took the camera from her quickly. "Here, I'll keep it safe with the other pic."

Once everyone had exited the car, Graham made a pool

of gasoline at the far end, and a thin stream that ran from it to the door.

"Everyone but Graham at the rear," Harry called outside in the tunnel, ignoring the dirty jokes Trent made loping over.

I jumped from the bottom riser. Turned to look up at Graham. "You sure?" I asked under my breath.

He braced against the railing and leaned over me. I tilted my head to meet his eyes. "Have I ever wussed out on a dare?"

"This isn't a dare, so it wouldn't ruin your perfect record."

"Just get this thing rolling and stand back once it is." He winked at me. "Don't be a hero."

Eighteen gloved hands set against the train car. We heaved. Dug our toes into the ground. Levered our weight. The train car gave an inch. Another. A few more. It lurched forward. Rolled at a walking pace. I tried to push through the initiates who'd stopped dead in front of me, shoved Rachel to the side when she didn't respond to "Excuse me."

Harry kept parallel with the front of the train car. No longer walking, jogging. My breath got louder in my ears as I gained on him. Viv yelled something I didn't catch over the roar of the rolling car.

My thighs burned closing the distance. "Why isn't he jumping?" I shouted. "Harry, why isn't he jumping?"

Gravity was dragging the car down the gentle slope, faster. Faster.

Harry's head bobbed as he accelerated. "It won't light," he yelled.

"It doesn't matter. Tell him to jump. Graham. Jump!"

I pushed myself harder. Ten feet behind Harry. Five feet. "He won't," Harry wheezed.

For a split second, I was neck and neck with the front of the train car, the metal steps, the metal grate of the deck where Graham was supposed to be standing, and he wasn't there.

30

The black, empty rectangle of the train car door seared into my eyes. Graham was inside a tinderbox. With the lighter and accelerant. The mouth of the tunnel was fifty yards and closing. I was slowing down, legs not cooperating.

Over a dip in the tunnel and up a small summit, the train car's speed eased just a little. A flash of black shot from its front. With his arms outstretched, Harry ran at it—at Graham—like he could stop him from colliding with the ground.

I came up on both of them in a heap in the dirt, near enough to the tunnel's mouth that they were bathed in the light of the three-quarter moon.

The night whisked the car away. Gone. Its rumbling receding as I hit my knees by Graham. On his back, legs hooked over Harry's midsection, eyes winced closed. Harry's frame was juddering. Laughter coursed through Graham too.

My arms went slack at my sides and I crumpled into

them. "I'm going to vomit up my heart," I managed to say.

Viv was there then, tears striping her mascara, falling into me, elbows gouging my ribs. "I'm going to kill you, Teddy Graham. Kill you. Murder you. Leave you hanging with the goat," she blathered.

Finally, when it was apparent to everyone that Graham wasn't hurt and that our train car had either reached our mark or derailed somewhere along the way, we escaped home.

The morning staff of Holy Bagels arrived at work at five a.m. Their ovens would be preheated and laden with bagel dough, including cinnamon raisin, my favorite, by five thirty. They never got that far. Fire trucks arrived on the scene fifteen minutes after the 9-1-1 call. Meanwhile Viv and I sat in my bedroom, dressed for school, in the dark.

"And when he wasn't jumping off the train, I thought, oh my god, we've killed Graham," Viv said, barely a whisper, our heads sharing a pillow propped against the bedframe.

"It was too risky having him set the car on fire while *inside* the car. Should have done it another way."

"Like he would have listened." Her pinkie hooked mine. "He was dying to be the hero."

"And then Harry kept alongside the train, like he was going to try to jump on it or run it down."

"He wanted to play the hero too," she said. "But it was you I worried would actually leap on to a moving train for Graham."

I laughed softly, remembering what the two boys had said about heroics and how they'd differed in opinion—Graham swearing that most liked their heroes to be a little bad and Harry disagreeing. I liked them both ways and in the same story.

"Do you hear that?" she asked, bouncing off my bed and rushing to the open window. All of Seven Hills likely heard the wailing sirens.

Fifteen minutes later, whirring helicopter propellers passed over Driftwood. We raced downstairs. I smelled a pot of fresh coffee. Dad must have been up already, but we didn't see him as we slipped out. At the car, I said, "Will it look suspicious if we go down there?"

Viv slapped the top of my car. "Sirens and a helicopter— there'll be a crowd. If anyone asks, we're getting bagels and working on a project before class starts."

The sky's dark cloak was fading to gray. Still, it was night enough that the fog absorbed the fire, leaving downtown smudged with luminance.

I pulled to a stop by a group of middle school–aged kids with their bikes on the sidewalk. They were slack-jawed and barely noticed us joining them. Across the street, the knoll was chaos. Four fire trucks idled, lights revolving on the storefronts. Black uniforms and badges gathered below the gazebo, staring up at the goat that was still swinging. Marking time until something else. The night before, I'd worn a mask. I'd been a different person. Standing before the fire, dawn riding up the horizon, I could see the act against the goat clearly for what it was. A vicious mistake. It was not merely dead but strung up like a prop.

The train car had made it to the knoll. A mile hadn't been enough room for it to slow, though, let alone stop. It appeared to have skidded off the tracks, flipped onto its side, and crashed into the trunk of a eucalyptus tree. It was reduced to a smoldering skeleton, only the metal frame and wheels surviving.

The fire had spread to the tree trunk, the dry, peeling bark combustible fuel. The branches and clumps of leaves were still burning. The smell harsh and medicinal. Some branches laid dismembered, burned off by the flames, smoldering on the ground, runs of fire striking out from the eucalyptus to the bales of hay. Pure luck that it hadn't spread to the gazebo or the wagon and ruined our spray-painted messages. I nauseated myself. No, it was pure luck the train car hadn't plummeted into a storefront or killed someone. We'd set it loose thoughtlessly. Damned the collateral damage.

"It's a train," one of the middle schoolers said dumbstruck to his buddy. "*A train.*"

The kids took selfies with the fiery destruction in the background until the fire hoses started spewing water. Wind shifted and a cloud of mist came our way. Viv and I climbed back into my car.

We weren't the only civilians out there. A crowd had amassed under the awning of Holy Bagels, smaller clumps dotting the perimeter of the square. Almost everyone had their cell phones out.

I'll never forget Graham's expression when he and Harry arrived at the knoll. He pulled up, swung out from behind the wheel, and just stood in the road. A commander stepping back to admire the carnage of the battlefield. It was absolute ego—ego like he'd had ego muffins and ego smoothie and ego spiked coffee for breakfast before styling his hair with ego and yanking ego on his feet rather than shoes. It was a light-year past bullshit.

Kids trickled in late to first period long after the bell rang.

In third period Jess whispered into my ear, "The goat's still up. Active crime scene." My hands went slick with guilt.

In fourth period an announcement came. The principal assured the student body there was nothing to fear. Urged anyone with information on the criminal identifying as IV to come forward. Said it was a miracle no one was injured. "Or really good planning," Trent muttered under his breath. I shot him a withering scowl.

At lunch Graham was zipped to his chin in a fleece, alternating between glaring at the hovering clouds and the additional school security officers who were patrolling the courtyard.

"My parents are going, is your dad?" Harry asked. He nudged my foot with his. I looked from the rubber toe of his sneaker to his eyes. "Is your dad going tonight?"

Mayor Carver had called an emergency town meeting. A discussion of the city's heightened security measures. Check points. Increased patrols. In sixth period, word spread that the

Seven Hills police department was canvassing. They'd search the knoll. Whether they knew the train car came from the Ghost Tunnel wasn't clear; there were multiple tracks that converged from the hills onto the run that lead into town. If they did scour the tunnel, they'd find weeks-old remnants of a massive party. And that, for some reason unknown to everyone but the ten of us, the police chief had left town. Denton had resigned. An interim officer needed to be named.

He'd left Seven Hills. I was hollow at the triumph, save for one thought: too late.

Denton should have left town eight years ago, seven, six, so he wouldn't have been the one called when I found Goldilocks. *Nah, hon, nothing like you, just a runaway asking for it.* Without Denton there may have been an investigation. Without Denton the Order might not have had its wicked shape. It just would have been pranks, fun, and little rebellions, with nothing to do with blood, revenge, and dead girls. And there'd be no blood on my hands—not the dove's or the goat's. No. How had Denton suffered? How had he paid? The Order shouldn't have sent him away—*not yet*. I spent the rest of sixth period in the restroom, sick with remorse over all the revenge on him I'd forfeited.

In the midst of all this there was chatter about the goat. Who. Why. How. The theory I heard floated most was sacrifice. IV took its life in the name of an unseen and blood-hungry vigilante force. With the gossip, the theories of who IV was changed from vigilante hero to crazed disciple of a cult. IV was tormenting the town to pay fealty to a pagan god who craved anarchy. And then hours passed and kids felt this was bordering on way too superstitious and that IV was obviously just a teenager who was as sick of being bossed around at school and home by grown-ups as they were. IV was saying *fuck you* to everything adult. IV was pissed that a fellow teenager had been killed in town and wasn't it super messed up that no one had done anything about finding her killer?

The four of us postponed our final rebellion for the following Wednesday. The plan was to meet with the initiates at Viv's on Saturday. We needed to talk about staying under police radar. We needed to stay calm. Invisible. I needed to remind them, gently, of the Polaroid I had tying them to the train car and fire.

We'd come so far—sacrificed, rebelled, and planned. I wouldn't allow anything to derail us before our finale. And already I'd stopped considering it a finale, an end. My breath stuttered at the thought of no more rebellions. No more revenge. How could I return to being weird, helpless, inconsequential Izzie? I wouldn't. I refused. I had invented the Order. I had aimed it at Seven Hills. I had vowed revenge for Goldilocks. And though I wasn't certain what shape we'd take next, rebellion had dug its claws into my heart and wouldn't let go.

31

We gathered together on Saturday night. The barn was removed enough from the street that we didn't worry about any of the patrols hearing us. We wouldn't dance on the rock or light a fire. I've never felt so thirsty for a party. I was giddy with restless mischief; guilty and wonderstruck at our nerve.

I stood on a chair in the middle of the barn. Nine faces turned up to me. I raised both Polaroids for everyone to see. "These are going to be buried in a chest where the idol was found. Even though we can't take credit for being IV, we'll all know there's proof of it, of what we've done, somewhere secret." I felt a foreign and threatening smile spread my lips. Let the proof of their guilt stick in our initiates' heads. Let its threat linger. Let them remember that only the four of us would know where the damning evidence was buried. I raised the bottle. "To doing wicked things for just ends. To the Order of IV."

Bottles clinked.

Harry offered me his hand. Linked together I felt more

grounded, less like the barn was topsy-turvy with bodies. I ached for our next rebellion. The momentum had us, as if we were bolting downhill. My bones, blood, and heart wanted to wield the Order again. Again, again, again.

Harry and I drifted to where Graham was opening a cider—he'd had a few already.

"Want one?" he asked, turning from the fridge. Behind his glasses there was a wet, shimmery glaze to his stare.

"No, thanks," I said. Harry shook his head.

"My mom got home tonight. Asked me why we'd received a letter in the mail about the city outlawing any use of a Roman numeral four. She was baffled." He popped the cap of the cider and let it ping on the floor.

"What'd you tell her?" Harry asked.

"About Driftwood Street, the knoll, the blood rebellion, the goat, the train car—all of it."

"She couldn't tell it was you though, right?" I said. "You didn't give it away by acting proud or smug?"

His thumb traced the rim of his cider bottle. "If she suspects, she didn't say."

I struggled to read his expression, not used to working so hard to understand him. "Do you think she might?"

He blinked at me. "You know my mother wouldn't get involved. Too much of a scientist. She sees things in context. Nothing we could do would surprise her because in context, our actions seem insignificant. A drop of mischief in a broken world."

I narrowed my eyes. Graham didn't usually sound jaded.

Where was his victor's bluster? "Is that the nihilism or fatalism talking?"

Viv's voice rose above the chatter before he could respond. "Don't be loud outside—my parents might be home." She was chasing Jess and Amanda, who'd escaped out the door. "Iz—Harry? Can you help me?"

Harry pressed his lips to my temple and went after her.

Graham took down half the bottle in his next sip, eyes stuck to me. Heat crept up my neck. He knew that I knew he'd seen. First person to see Harry kiss me.

"Maybe you shouldn't get wasted. If your mom's home, I mean."

He tapped me on the nose. I swatted his hand. "Izzie. My mother wouldn't mind if I started selling hallucinogens out of *her bedroom* as long as I kept getting good grades." He spoke with a bitter swagger. I wanted him to turn it off. To act like himself.

"It's hot in here. Let's race to the rock," I said.

He smiled like he thought I was joking. "We're in the middle of a party."

I jabbed a finger into his shoulder. "Two weeks ago you'd have paid me to give you an excuse to leave."

Graham set the cider on the top of the fridge and rubbed his hands together. "If you think I'm letting you win, you're going to be disappointed." He vaulted over dislodged throw pillows and sent Rachel's cider flying as he dashed between her and Conner. A shouted "Watch it!" came after he was already through the door.

All the initiates disappeared for me. I sprinted after him.

His path through the trees was marked only by nearly bare branches shuddering. When had all the leaves fallen?

I don't remember who won, only that we arrived at the rock seconds apart. We lay on top of it and talked about nothing important. On our way back, our pace synchronized from so many years of marching off to find adventure. And I realized what an idiot I'd been to have ever worried about Graham moving on from his friend Izzie. We'd been permanent before the Order. How hadn't I seen that?

Viv was leaving the barn as we rounded its corner up the path. She sighed—a long, suffering sound. "I'm tired," she said, brushing past us. "Make them keep it down."

I watched her vanish from the party. I almost went after her—twirled her under my arm, swore to her we'd find a way together to take down Amanda.

But Graham said "Look," pointing to the sky. "Those are nimbus clouds. I can't remember if they predict rain or not." He pulled his cell out and was looking it up as I spotted Harry and Amanda under the trellis halfway to the barn.

"Uh-oh," Graham murmured. "They produce precipitation. I guess it could rain with the skeleton. It wouldn't necessarily ruin it. But not ideal conditions. See?"

He followed my gaze.

Amanda had her hand on Harry's shoulder. I wondered, what could they be talking about? Had I ever seen them have a conversation? I remembered Harry's phone buzzing and Amanda's name flashing.

The party broke up early. Graham stayed in the barn.

Harry walked me home. I shoved away the desire to ask Harry what Amanda wanted. I wouldn't stoop so low as to feel threatened by her. I trusted Harry. It was six houses between Viv's and mine. Two police cruisers passed us in the short distance. The initiates were going to provide us the subterfuge that drew them away for the final rebellion.

Seven Hills was besieged by an invisible threat. It wasn't real. We weren't going to hurt anyone. Not really. Fear inflicts its own special damage.

Sunday raced by, unmemorable.

On Monday morning Harry posted on the school blog a chronology of all the crimes and pranks the party known as IV was accused of. Just part of his ongoing coverage, except it was the first of his articles that alleged the Seven Hills police department had a history of choosing not to investigate certain crimes like Jane Doe's murder and the brutal attack that left Harry's father permanently limping. My chest constricted as I read it. Harry had been adamant that we not use the Order for his father, but perhaps now, now that he'd seen what we could do, perhaps our next business would be to avenge Harry's father?

Harry's title and not the article's content incited controversy on campus. "One Man's Freedom Fighter . . ." The rest of the quote, "Is Another Man's Terrorist," was common enough that the dot-dot-dot was lost on few. A schoolwide argument ensued. One side, the minority, argued that IV was a terrorist in the sense that they were terrorizing Seven

Hills. The majority argued that IV was fighting for justice, given their concern over a sexist school dress code and an unavenged dead girl.

A few of the AP teachers decided to go with the fervor and organized a formal debate after classes. I didn't attend.

In third period, Trent, bushy eyebrows dancing suggestively, said, "So Rocha and Schultz. Fucking random, huh?" For a moment of blankness I had no idea who he meant.

"Harry and Amanda," I said like I was sounding their names out.

"Yeah. Hit it hard behind the barn," he said, and gave his hips a pop.

My head swayed slowly. "Wait. What?"

"Saturday. At Viv's house. Hey." He leaned over in a confidential manner. "Is your girl, like, with the other dude? Graham."

"No," I said.

"Not that I like her or anything." He swung away. "I might need a date for the next dance is all, and Viv's scary intense but hot."

I put Trent out of my mind. Amanda too. I knew Harry. He wouldn't do what Trent said. Not ever. Especially not now. By lunchtime I'd heard four more times how random the pairing of Amanda and Harry was. No one questioned the rumor's authenticity, only parroted it to me.

The four of us ate on the highest ledge of the amphitheater. Walking to join them, I'd experienced appetite-erasing dread. Then I arrived and Harry was Harry. Earphones around his neck, sweet smile my way after he tossed me his last chocolate cookie, and dreamy, heavy lids as he settled back to listen to music. I didn't care if the rumor reached me five hundred times, I'd never believe it.

Amanda picked a lousy day to join us. Short dress showed off her goose-pimpled legs. A fuzzy beanie the colors of funfetti frosting with flecks of silver thread reminded me of the holographic tape in the orchard. Made me miss summer, when there was fruit on the trees. She squatted on her backpack, knees kissing, a perfect triangle of crotch in the gap below for anyone who looked.

She talked to Viv, who responded periodically as she glanced up from scrolling on her phone. Amanda was really trying with an eager smile, the patient silences where she picked at her nail polish until Viv's focus landed back on her. I wondered why she didn't huff off. Viv was done playing with her. Keeping her enemy close hadn't paid off.

At last Amanda slung her backpack over one shoulder and gave an awkward wave.

"Maybe I'll see you after school?" she said, staring expectantly at Harry.

Harry, headphones on, looked around our circle of blank stares, and shrugged.

I spent that afternoon driving an hour to a craft store to buy black feathers. With Viv in my room, door locked, we used wire and glue guns to make wings. An old sketch of

Goldilocks and her T-shirt wings stayed propped up against the bedframe until we finished.

I texted Harry sometime before dinner.

He showed up a little after. Texted that he was in front, asked me to come out.

He was at the sidewalk, sitting on the waist-high brick wall near our mailbox. His back was to me, the curve of spine showed through his hoodie

"Do you want to come inside?" I called, pulling my sweater closer, walking to meet him. It was dark already, a little past seven.

"Is your dad home?" he said without turning.

"In his office."

"Can we stay here?"

I perched on the wall next to him. We were side by side, basically facing each other but his eyes didn't go to mine.

"Everything okay?" I asked. He was chewing the side of his thumbnail so ferociously that it was bleeding. "What's wrong?"

His hand dropped into his lap. "Are you testing me with Amanda or something?"

"Or something," I repeated in the strange tone he'd used. "Huh?"

"I've been racking my brain to figure out what's going on." He was speaking softly. "Have you been giving her secret rites and telling her to hit on me? Seeing if I'd go for her even though you and I are going out?"

"Because that sounds exactly like something I'd do," I said, more confused than furious.

"It doesn't." He gave his head a shake. "That's what's thrown me. You're usually honest. No filter. I love that. I thought you were—uh—not like this. Not sneaky."

I stood. "And I thought you didn't have your head up your ass."

"Wait. Don't walk away." His voice shifted behind me, as though he'd started to follow. "I know you wouldn't ordinarily do this. It's your dad and mom, right? You're freaked out and thinking that all guys do . . . you know."

I stopped, rigid and facing the house. "No. I am not testing you, Harry."

"Izzie. Amanda told people that she and I—that we had sex Saturday behind the barn." I turned slowly. His eyes bugged out. "Sunday she texted me inviting me over. It was ten at night. After school, after the debate, she asked me. She was all, 'When are we going to hook up?' It was an accident that I even talked to her at the debate. I went to cover it for the blog. She called me over. She'd never really spoken to me before all this—ever. And I realized, you gave that secret rite to Conner for the goat. You could be delivering secret rites to her, telling her to come on to me. What am I supposed to think?"

"You're not supposed to think that I'm testing you to see if you'll cheat or flirt."

"Isadora—"

I pointed savagely up the street. "Go home, Harry."

"Wait—"

"No!" I shouted over my shoulder.

"I don't know what's going on."

I crossed the threshold and turned to slam the door. It was too dark to make out his expression, but I hoped he could see how heartbroken I was.

32

I'd felt trapped in a poisonous fog since Harry's accusation against me the afternoon before. I had stared listlessly out the window at pumpkins, hay bales, and police patrols as Viv drove us to school.

There was a dense crowd gathered around the flagpole when we arrived. My attention went to Harry's feathery brown hair in the crowd, drawn to him by a magnetic and annoying force. He was standing next to Graham, their shoulders touching. Trent and Conner were beside them, Campbell and Jess a yard behind them.

Viv made a small gasp.

A rabbit was hanging from the flagpole.

"The biology bunny," Jess said darkly, when she noticed us standing beside her and Campbell. I remembered the white-and-black rabbit from freshman year; Ms. Stevenson kept its cage in the classroom.

Now there was a noose around its furry neck. The bunny

was limp, hind legs extended, ears lank. An empty-of-life sack of fur. There wasn't a lot of chatter, just a stunned sense of horror keeping everyone trapped, watching.

"I don't understand," Viv said. I braced a hand against someone's shoulder, realized it was Campbell. The biology bunny was swinging like a kite tail in the wind.

"What happened?" I whispered. His grim eyes flicked to Conner and Trent.

He shook his head and muttered, "I think."

I was seized by a conviction that the bunny was my fault. If Conner and Trent had stolen the rabbit, killed it, and strung it up, I'd inspired them with the goat. I'd led them to believe that the Order of IV demanded bloody sacrifices. We had sown the seeds as soon as we'd asked them to drive pins through a dove's heart.

Graham's angry but restrained voice rumbled from in front of us. Conner held his eye, a defiant tilt to his jaw; Trent was staring at his trembling open hands.

"I'm done," I heard Campbell say, more to himself than anyone. "I am done."

I held my finger to my lips.

He bent down to whisper into my ear. "What does this have to do with the murdered girl, Izzie? How is that rabbit helping her? What about the goat? The bird?"

He drew back, and his sad expression became harder.

The top of a ladder bobbed to my left. Security was on its way over.

Viv clutched my arm. "Look what's written on it," she whispered. I caught a flash of red. The bunny pirouetted on its leash. I kept losing sight of whatever side bore the mark. Security stomped up the ladder. A razor sawed through the rope. The bunny thumped against the top rung. Security shoved the bunny into a black garbage bag. An upside down *IV* was visible for a fleeting second, then gone.

Campbell hurried away. I opened my mouth to call his name, but Jess was already gliding past me. "I'll talk to him," she said, giving me a meaningful look. "Don't worry."

But I did. Campbell had said so much to me in that last glance of his. He looked at me like he didn't just consider me a monster. He thought me the maker of monsters.

Conner and Trent going off book, the sense that I was somewhat culpable, Harry's and my fight, the increased patrols, and the school administration's promise to find and prosecute whoever had been responsible for the death of the bunny made the day feel like it was closing in on me.

"They're not satisfied with sitting in the wings," Viv explained at lunch. "Who wants to be an understudy when you can have a starring role? Jess and Amanda say Trent and Conner are sorry. They thought we'd be happy."

Harry choked on a sip of water. "Happy?" he coughed.

"After we use them tomorrow night, we're going to need to put the fear of the gods in them," Graham said. "We need them to back off the Order. Convince them it's a necessity because of increased police activity."

"How are we going to do that?" Viv asked.

When I'd thought about the end of our rebellions for Goldilocks before, disengaging the initiates had seemed easy. But the Order had its claws hooked in them all, except for Campbell, who was eager to be done.

We four went our separate ways after lunch. A text came in silently to my cell in between sixth and seventh periods. It was from Harry, asking if I'd meet him in the parking lot after school. I didn't respond, but when I was halfway to Viv's car I veered to where I could see Harry waiting under a palm tree. I couldn't ignore him.

His smile was sweet and shy. "Will you go with me to the beach?"

I tugged open the passenger door of his car and climbed in.

He took my hand as he steered with the other, but it was a loose, friendly grip. Out on the sand he cleared away the driftwood. I was biting back tears. Were we about to break up? Had we already ended things the afternoon before? Had we ruined our friendship?

After we sat and watched the whitecaps of the waves for a while, Harry spoke. "We shouldn't have started, not with everything that's going on. It was too soon."

"Yeah," I said. "It took us five years. Way too soon."

Harry's stern expression faltered. "Graham." He nodded and drove his sneaker into the sand. "Graham would be better for you. He's liked you forever. Don't play like you don't know. You have to. You and Graham."

"Graham. Do you realize what a paternalistic jackass you

sound like? It's not your job to tell me who would be good. Girls aren't just hungry for boyfriends, like any boy will do."

"I know that. Maybe—listen to me, Izzie." He freed his shoes. "Maybe someday when we're out of here and older, you and me—we'll talk on the phone and we'll meet up and it will be the right time and it'll work."

"It was working now."

"Graham and you."

I laughed meanly. "That's what you keep saying."

"I just—don't you think you like him a little? You guys have all this stuff in common."

It was beyond insane. "*We* have stuff in common."

"I know we do."

I held my hands up. "I'm not going to talk you into being my boyfriend, Harry. I shouldn't have to convince you. But you can't talk me into being with Graham, so stop trying."

I threw myself up from the sand and drove my feet into the white puffs like they were snowbanks. I never looked back. If I had, I'd have seen him pull out his cell phone to record the video.

I walked home, checking over my shoulder the whole way that Harry wasn't about to pull up and offer me a lift. I held myself against the crisp autumn edge of the day. The tang of rotting leaves settled in the back of my mouth. Their rust-colored, slippery skins made my sneakers shoot out, tipping my balance.

What Harry said about Graham snapped over my eyes like lenses. I peered back at the last month through them.

Saw the altered reality—reality itself. Graham was methodical, even in his missteps. Didn't say anything by accident. Bringing up our kiss, kissing Viv; confessing to having been in love with Viv and me hadn't been accidents at all. They were hints aimed at my head. He'd been talking about liking Jess for years, and then once he actually had a shot with her his interest dried up. He wouldn't say anything explicit, except she wasn't what he really wanted. All this struck me with a force that sent me careening to Viv's, where I sat on her bed, talking and crying as her skilled hands braided ribbons into my hair.

How to say what unfolded in our final rebellion the following night?

The original four met at the barn.

I threw every inch of my focus into the rebellion. When the sight of Harry threatened to make me cry, I thought about how the Order would keep going. We'd pick up a new mission. Turn back time to tell secrets, though surely we didn't have any left, and dance under the moon. Eventually I would stop remembering how Harry's hands had skated under my shirt to press against my back as we kissed. I would forget the taste of Harry's skin as I kissed his neck. I would be able to listen to my perfect song without it slashing open my chest. Wouldn't I? We'd return to loving each other as friends forever.

Our rebellion didn't feel as final as I understand it is presently. Our initiates were safely one town over, on the bluffs of a beach, each armed with a prepaid burner phone Graham

398 • ALEXANDRA SIROWY

and Harry bought with cash at gas stations along the inland highway. Jess had been successful in convincing Campbell not to walk away from the Order, though I am not sure how. The initiates would wait for midnight to call in their sightings. At their designated times, two minutes apart starting at the stroke of twelve, they'd call the police to report seeing a woman roaming the streets of Seven Hills, all in white, a bloody *IV* painted on her front and back. They would draw the police from one location to another. Each fake location would be gradually farther from the knoll and its clock tower. When our initiates were done with the lure, they'd dump the phones into the ocean and take one car back to Seven Hills. If they were stopped, they'd tell the police they were coming from a party at USB.

The skeleton rode in Viv's trunk, her wings already wired on. At midnight the texts began dinging, confirming that the calls were being made. We headed to the knoll. Halfway there, the sirens began to sing. Mist was wafting off the ocean, the moon's light netted in it, giving the town a fairy-tale glitter.

Viv and I held hands at the foot of the clock tower. We wore our beanies with eyeholes and had removed Viv's front and back license plates. Her black SUV was common enough; there were at least five just on our street.

Any minute a police officer who recognized the reported sightings as subterfuge could drive by. Danger was as intoxicating as Graham's truth serum and I found myself twirling under Viv's arm, collapsing against her side as she kissed my forehead and hummed.

Graham had reconstructed the skeleton, fastening her wires together. A rope looped around her spine. Harry wound the opposite end around his wrist and used the stones protruding from the facade of the two-story clock tower to climb twenty feet to the clocks hands. He threaded the rope over the hands and ran the slack toward the ground. Graham caught it and pulled. Viv joined him, gradually raising the skeleton as Harry scaled down.

I stepped off the curb, just to take the whole scene in. My three friends dizzyingly beautiful, like three bolts of light. And though my heart felt raw and pummeled, there was so much love inside me for them that I was convinced the Order of IV had served its purpose. We were bound together. We would grow old loving each other.

In the barn we relived what we'd pulled off and toasted the Order with ciders. The Mistress of Rebellion and Secrets lay in Viv's lap. Harry slipped out without saying good-bye as Graham spouted facts about the history of fermented beverages. I pressed my cheek to Viv's feverish one. Graham walked me home.

We sat on the porch swing. My feet didn't touch the ground and their swinging made me feel carefree, like when we were little. He took my hand. We looked at each other. His flinty stare threw me back to being a little kid whose heart was in her throat and whose pockets were full of cookies, racing into the hills behind her house, her mother's voice a distant reprimand.

400 • ALEXANDRA SIROWY

Graham was my oldest friend. He loved me and wanted me.

My fingers walked up his arm and pinched his earlobe. I smiled drowsily at him, attention shifting to his mouth. So familiar, it wasn't any stretch to imagine my lips on his. Graham kissed me. His nose brushed my cheek. I tasted the cider and something spicier on his tongue. A sweet, little groan escaped from him. A noise I'd never heard him make before.

I thought I knew what was coming next.

Graham yanked himself away, slid to the far end of the swing with the look of someone restraining himself. "I delivered a secret rite to Amanda instructing her to get Harry to ask her out. I made it clear that if she succeeded, she'd bypass any additional rites and be made a full member before her friends," he said as one long blast.

I dragged the back of my hand across my mouth. The clove taste lingered. "Smart. It's what she was asking for before she told us that horrendous secret of hers, but instead Viv promised her a better role in the Order, after initiation."

"Har wouldn't bite. She came on to him. Nothing. She made up that preposterous rumor about sex behind the barn. He told me, completely horrified, that she was sexting him as some kind of booty call. He didn't want any part of her." We blinked at each other for a long time. "Don't you want to know why I'd try to break you and Harry up?"

I stared at the scars on my knees. "This one's from when we learned to roller blade." I pointed to another. "This one's a burn, when we lit matches to see who'd drop one first."

"We kneeled facing each other and I dropped mine first," he said. "I burned you."

"And then you started to blubber like a baby."

"I was scared I had hurt you."

I just kept staring at that scar, considering all the years Graham had been my steadfast friend. "The Graham I know would never try to hurt me."

"You've been mine since we were five," he whispered. "You don't need to say it. You're yours. You're Viv's and Harry's, too. I know. But I didn't want to share you. I wanted you to pick me. I went crazy when you didn't."

"Pick you? Did I miss you asking me out? Am I not remembering you asking me to a dance or telling me you liked me or being honest about your feelings? All you've done is talk about hot Jess and check out other girls."

"Are you shitting me?" The disbelief in his eyes needled me. "That's how you see years of me throwing myself at you?"

"Throwing yourself at me?"

"Holding you. Holding your hand. Hugging you. Letting you sit in my lap and ride on my back. Staring at you. I've never had a real girlfriend, Izzie, because I was waiting for you. And we kissed freshman year." His words shook. They tore at me. "You had to have known how much it meant to me, and then you never wanted to talk about it. I tried a hundred times after. You hugged yourself and acted like it was nothing but a trauma to kiss me."

"That doesn't excuse you hurting me, Graham. You hurting Harry."

"I'm not trying to say it does. My scheming was inexcusable. Unforgivable. But let's not pretend that you haven't always known that all you had to do was say yes. This wasn't an unrequited crush. You wanted me there, running after you. The question was out there, always. Even now, even after I'm sick to death of standing in line behind Harry." His face hardened to stone. "Are you through with me?"

I regarded his figure all in black. The meaning of everything that had passed between us over the last months had been laid bare. Only Graham's nervous fingers rolling up his shirtsleeves betrayed his composure.

"No," I said. "Angry and sad, yes. Harry's through with me, though."

"Never." He caught my chin as I turned away. "I'm not going to kiss you again," he said as my eyes warned him off. "I just want you to pay attention. Harry is not through with you. He'll get himself sorted out and he'll be groveling for your forgiveness."

I removed Graham's hand, probably holding on to it longer than I should have wanted to. "Maybe he really is done with me and I'll fall madly in love with you in ten years. But you'll already have fallen for Viv and it will be a real catastrophe."

He winced ever so slightly, but he said, "Is it a deal?"

What else to say about me and Graham?

Graham and I had been connected since we were five years old. In a parallel universe without Harry, Graham and I started dating in ninth grade. We had our first kiss before the truth or dare party, it was every bit the whispered secret it should have been. We went to prom and snuggled on the rock as Graham talked about the stars and I wondered about what else fills space. It was all romantic and built on friendship and our adventures. We graduated college and spent a few years traveling, returning for Viv's opening nights and movie premieres. Maybe we got married, maybe we decided we didn't believe in it, but we did have a sly-smiling, cookie-stealing kid who we loved.

My world doubled on the porch, and alongside Graham I saw the parallel life unfold. Harry was a lot like our meteorite. He wasn't only the flash of a meteor; he was the cosmic debris that made it into your atmosphere. He left his mark. He spun Graham and me off course.

I both hate him and love him for that.

3 3

It doesn't say anything good that the Seven Hills police department missed the skeleton dangling like an angel of death from the clock tower.

A little after dawn, on Halloween morning, an assistant arrived to the real estate office at the first floor of the tower. She told the 9-1-1 dispatcher that a monster was hanging from the clock. A line of police cars raced over, officers brandishing guns. The opening crew at Holy Bagels who'd been at the center of the previous week's disaster came running. One of them snapped a bunch of pictures while the police waited for the interim chief and Mayor Carver to arrive.

The police weren't forthcoming with details. Meetings were behind closed doors. Mayor Carver announced by lunch that in light of new evidence recovered, unrelated to IV, the police department had reopened the case of Jane Doe's death. She stated that it was possible that upon reexamination, new leads might come to light. Graham said the police were saving face. They couldn't appear to be caving to the pressure of a vigilante, a criminal, an arsonist, a vandal. As for IV, the police vowed to continue looking for the parties responsible.

The initiates had ideas for new rebellions. *Can anyone get a real cadaver? What if we set the school on fire?* They were sledding downslope, ice hard and shiny under them. Destined for collision.

"We've got to convince them to lay low for a few months," Graham said.

"Or maybe that the Order's got to end. Period," Viv said. When she focused on my look of dismay, she added, "Not for real. It won't end for us."

Harry ruminated silently.

We needed to dismantle the Order in a way that prevented the initiates from picking it up and keeping it going themselves. Not just behead the snake; make sure it didn't sprout a new head—or six. We'd tell them IV needed a hiatus until the police pressure had eased.

Our next move was hazier. Either we'd stall and eventually the initiates would lose interest—senior year was bound to distract—or we'd stall and they wouldn't lose interest, in which case we'd reinvent the Order again. Its reincarnation would be benign: parties and bonfires.

For the four of us, the Order could return to what it had been at the start. Our little universe. We were afraid of letting another day go by without telling the initiates the Order was going into hibernation. If we waited, how long until Trent and Conner acted out again? What if they got caught?

The Order and its initiates, who were full-pledged

members at that point, would meet for a bonfire. That night. We'd break the news. If needed, I'd use the Polaroid picture to force them into submission.

Harry showed up on my doorstep. He knocked and retreated to the lawn where he waited.

"What's up?" I said from the doorway.

"Can you come and sit out here?" he asked.

I wanted to slam the door. I went out and sat on the bottom step with him.

"I know you're angry. Really pissed. But would you do something for me if I asked?" When I didn't answer, he kept going. "I have been your friend—one of your best—for more than five years. Hopefully I'll be your friend forever and the four of us can be buried in the same plot." I laughed despite myself. "Seriously. Will you promise me something? The why will be obvious to you in a day or two. And you can chew me out and I can start delivering the first of a million apologies I owe you."

"Okay, what." I toed the lawn and avoided looking at him.

"I want you to stay home tonight."

"No," I said, firm and fast.

"I want you to stay home for the rest of the night and I'll see you at school tomorrow."

I narrowed my eyes at him. "Why?"

"It's important to me."

"So what, Harry? Being there is important to me. It's important to Graham and Viv. Why should what you want matter more to me than what I want?"

"It shouldn't. But I'm asking you for a favor."

"You don't deserve one. You broke up with me using bogus reasons. You insulted me. You called me sneaky. You hurt me, Harry. More than anyone ever has. Do me a favor and spare me your requests."

"Please."

"Why?"

"I can't tell you."

"You're ridiculous. You are insane asking me this. I invented the Order. You know what it means to me."

"I do. Doesn't that tell you that I have a really good reason if I get what the Order means to you and I'm still asking?"

I watched an ant cross the length of a flagstone.

"Don't call Graham or Viv. Shut your cell off. Tell your dad not to answer the home line. Stay in your room all night. We'll explain to Graham and Viv tomorrow that I asked you to flake. Okay?"

"I'll think about it." Liar. I would not give up this slice of the Order for Harry, not after he'd torn my heart out and left it to be picked at by the seagulls. I wanted him to leave and I couldn't figure out a quicker way of accomplishing that without appeasing him.

Harry took the lawn in a few strides before one last look back. His eyes bright and burning with the electricity of thoughts, beliefs, and dreams. "I love you, Isadora Anne Pendleton. I think your perfect song is mine too."

The air went out of my lungs watching his caramel figure take off in a sprint. I only whispered "I love you too" when he was too far to hear.

I called Graham from my room. "Have you watched the footage today?"

A long pause and then a loud exhale. "I haven't. Hold on, let me pull it up and I'll e-mail it to you."

I flipped open my laptop and waited.

"There. Sent. I'd go through it but I've got to prepare the truth serum for tonight." We said good-bye. Thirty seconds later, I rang him back.

"Graham. The camera's aimed at the ground, not the tunnel. How long has it been like this?"

"It is? Shit. Your armband must have loosened."

"You said you watched it yesterday though, right?"

"Uh, yeah, I was going to, but I didn't."

I glared at the cell. "It could have been like this for forty-eight hours? What if we missed him?"

"We didn't. C'mon. The plan wasn't going to work. At first I thought, maybe. But the more thought I give to it, the less likely the whole thing seems. No one's going to incriminate themselves like that."

"I'll see you at the rock."

"Don't hang up angry. If you believe it'll work, we'll walk up there in the morning before school, okay? We'll fix it first thing tomorrow."

"Yeah. Okay."

"See you in a couple hours."

"Yeah." I hung up.

I paced like a caged animal for about five minutes. I yanked my hair, kicked at worn pajama pants on the floor, and decided it was stupid to wait for Graham to help me fix the camera.

I'd do it myself. A twenty-minute hike up, a fifteen-minute hike to the rock. I wore red—a dress as Viv made me promise—slipped on leggings underneath, and boots, a fleece coat she never had to see over it.

Equipped with a flashlight, I entered the open space through the gate in our backyard. The rock formations and trees melting and wavering in the orange sunset. It would be dark soon. I took the trail worn into the grass that ran behind the Driftwood properties. Where the pines dotted the hills, the grasses couldn't grow because of the acidity of the needles they shed. I used the flashlight under the broken canopy and kicked the pinecones from my path. Once, Viv and I had collected a basketful. We were going to paint them gold until pincher bugs began escaping their crevices and headed for her bedroom carpet.

In passing, I rested my hand on the tree with a constellation of hollows in its straight trunk that made it easy to climb. Graham and I dared to its top. Neither of us got higher than ten feet. There was still the frayed rope on its lowest branch from our rope swing.

A few scant sunbeams filtered in through the trees. Specks of dirt and pollen hovered in and out of the light. Then, as if a giant had shuttered the sky, the bolts of light were gone. The sun had tucked under the Pacific. Near to the tunnel I began to wonder: What if the exact moment I visited the camera was the exact moment Goldilocks's killer checked the tunnel for a witness?

I sniffed and swung my arms harder. I was not afraid. How unlikely—near impossible—that would be. A tiny quivering voice in me answered, *As unlikely as a meteorite not leaving a crater*. There was the tree ahead. I spotted a knot about four feet up its trunk to step on. I flipped the flashlight off, tossed it to the ground, hiked up my dress, and grunted and shimmied my way up. The branch really wasn't so high, eight or ten feet from the ground. I was unfastening the Velcro of the armband when a distant crunch froze me.

I tried to peer to the ground by looking over my shoulder without losing balance. Crunches like footsteps came from the direction of the turnout where we'd parked the SUV the other night. My breathing picked up, lungs suddenly desperate for air, hands soggy gripping the bough. *Let it be Graham*. Of course it had to be him; he'd got off the phone with me, realized what a jerk he'd been, how important fixing the camera's angle was. I opened my mouth to call out his name, but the strobe of a flashlight and a brown sleeve attached to it locked my jaw shut.

I knew that jacket. The evening wasn't so dim that I couldn't recognize my father.

Dad grimaced as he walked. His pace slowed approaching the mouth of the tunnel. He disappeared into its shadow. Emerged after an amount of time I measured only by how deeply my fingernails dug into bark. He stood undecided, shifted his flashlight back and forth. I could no longer make out his face.

He trudged the way he came. When my nails were pulling away from their skin, I dropped from the branch. Nothing caught me, not my feet or my hands. I rolled forward onto my shoulder, needles stuck in my hair and jacket as I staggered up.

Panic came in waves. Rolled up from my gut to my chest to my head. The tree trunks doubled, tripled, the sparse wood transmuted to a forest. I careened down. Running. White sheets fell over my thoughts. Not blankness. Shapes moved under them. Rippled them. Things I couldn't let myself think yet.

I clipped a trunk, spun out, hit the ground. Stayed on all fours. I was angry at a jacket; I tore mine off. Left it in the dirt. Up again. I'd lost my flashlight, or maybe left it by the tree. I ran from memory. I could see the rock, or rather the golden eye of the bonfire saw me.

There were figures milling around on the meteorite. Mine. It wasn't a scary place. It wasn't responsible for Goldilocks's death at all. Our games and dares and questions didn't draw her in. Not us kids. The grown-ups did it. I shook my head into the night. Clamped my mind shut. I wasn't ready to think. To acknowledge.

I crossed the field for the rock. Caught my breath. There: this is how lungs work. Breathe in. Out. I picked pine needles from my hair. Let each one fall to the ground. Reordered my features until they belonged to an ordinary girl who knew nothing.

"Where'd you come from?" Graham asked as he noticed me prowling around the rock.

Harry turned. His features fell. I didn't imagine that. Both boys wore red like I did.

Viv was amid the initiates. They'd come, all in white like we'd instructed. Viv swung her hips between Rachel's and Jess's, dancing to music I couldn't hear, the red tulle of her skirt flaring out. I smiled at her. Felt warmth in my chest; felt alive again. Why had I experienced such ugly panic minutes before? I'd washed the reason from my thoughts. It no longer existed. There was Viv. Celebrating. Happy. As radiant as she was onstage.

I went to her. Took her hand. Twirled her under my arm. "You're late," she said, pretending to pout, eyes like gemstones, a tiny red rose tucked behind each ear.

"I'm here now," I said, words tinny and strange.

She offered me a flower. "For you." Viv slipped it behind my ear. She opened her arms and wrapped me in them, pressed her cheek to mine, and whispered, "No matter what happens, I am so grateful that you are my best friend."

Graham cleared his throat. Called out for everyone to gather around, make a circle. For the life of me, I couldn't remember my lines. There was a script. But my mind was wiped. Viv would jump in; she was good about memorizing every line in a performance. The initiates' faces were out of focus, like pencil drawings I'd taken my finger to. I felt like I was standing unnaturally still. Like glass. No. Not glass. A stronger substance, surely. Iron. Space rock.

Graham pointed our dagger to the sky, nicked his palm with it, took a drag of a new batch of his truth serum, and passed both items on.

My eyes landed on Harry. His lines were sharply drawn. He was beautiful. Staring back at me. I mouthed "I love you" because I could. Because it was true. Because vaguely I remembered him saying so to me the day before in my front yard, and even before that, at the beach, and standing on the rock, front heated by the fire, I got that he had not meant it in the same way we loved the others.

There was a trace of a smile on Harry's lips and his glowing eyes were on mine until the second Conner stepped in front of him.

It was so unexpected that no one believed it was happening. One boy throwing himself at another. The boys slammed to the rock, one of them on his back and the other on top. The boy on top throwing fists. Conner delivering three or four punches before they started to roll. I let out a scream that was echoed by others. The edge of the rock was close. They thought they had more room. Harry was trying to regain a little ground.

But Conner and Harry flew from the rock. They fell, embracing. They were on their own, together, plummeting to Earth like the meteorite had tens of thousands of years ago.

The difference: Harry was flesh, blood, and spine when he hit.

Conner's weight was on top of him.

Graham ran for the edge of the rock. He jumped. I scrambled down its side, found Graham shoving Conner's body off Harry. One of them was crying, big, shuddering sobs. I thought it was Harry; he was the hurt one. His eyelids were half closed, crescents of irises and pupils stared up at space.

Conner cried, "No, no, no man. You okay? I had to do it. I was supposed to do it."

"Har?" I leaned over him. "Harry?"

Nothing. His eyelids began to make a slow drop.

I stopped being a human girl. I was a crouched animal at Harry's side, terror all I tasted. There was more shouting from the rock. Viv's voice shot through the racket. "An ambulance is coming," she yelled.

"Get your mom!" Graham screamed.

I must have turned to see Viv go, skirt tangling around her ankles as she ran, or else I've played the night over and over and I've invented memories so that I can see it from every angle.

Graham was on his phone, dialing 9-1-1.

"They're coming," I said up to him. But he stood over us. Conner's outstretched arm reached for Harry. Graham was there, heaving him back, shoving him hard. "Don't touch him," he bellowed, knocking his glasses from his face, leaving them in the dirt.

Back on the phone, a precise, clinical voice that had panic slowly bleeding into it. "Tell me what I can do for him. No— listen—he's fallen onto his back, twelve feet up. Tell me what to do. I know you've sent an ambulance, but what can I do now? Now. Tell me."

I held one of Harry's hands between mine. It was burning up but strangely limp, like the dove in the moment after I drove the pin through its heart. Harry's lids had finished their drop. I leaned over, put my ear near his parted lips, and caught the barest whisper of breath. I moved my mouth to his ear.

"Harry, the ambulance is coming. Viv went to get Ina. Harry, please, just keep breathing." My ear went to his mouth again. I waited. I held my breath. I can't explain it except to say that it was the roar of the ocean trapped in a seashell coming from Harry. My ear pressed to his mouth, capturing the last sound he'd ever make. I kissed the corner of his lips.

I whispered to him, "Harrison Rocha, I have loved you since you showed up to save us from boredom and our bad tempers and the incomplete lives we had before you. Graham and Vivy and I love you, Harry."

34

Modern medicine pulls off all kinds of miracles, and even after the paramedics had set his neck in a brace, shined lights in his undilating eyes, and administered three bursts from paddles on his chest without results, I held out hope. How could I not? He was Harry. We'd been sent on a course to find each other. We had invisible forces on our side. We were the Order of IV.

They loaded him in an ambulance as the police arrived. I took three running strides to chase it. Arms closed around me—a police officer—and I tried to throw them off. I was shoved between Graham and Viv. Ordered to stop fighting.

"If I'd stopped him," Graham kept saying, rubbing hard at his forehead. "If I'd stopped them in time."

The ambulance had taken too long to arrive. Fifteen minutes of waiting for it to spot Campbell and Jess, who went to flag it down at the mouth of the access road. Viv had returned from her house in that time; Ina wasn't home but at work.

The police took their time processing the scene. Photographing. Shouting urgently when they found the dagger tipped in blood. The *IV* drawn on the rock. The truth serum they sniffed warily. The Mistress of Rebellion and Secrets on her throne of rocks.

The police drove us to the hospital in the back of a cruiser, and two officers came into the emergency room with us. Sat by the door, silently watching. In the waiting room, Graham sat doubled over, tears spotting the tops of his shoes, his glasses abandoned by the rock. Viv spoke urgently to the woman across the receiving desk. She raised her voice when answers weren't given. She could really project—I think about that a lot, what a set of lungs she had, how she could make herself heard, how I was counting on spending my whole life hearing her talk and act and laugh and sing.

"He's Harry," I said. "He's going to be okay. Isn't he, Graham? Isn't Harry going to be all right? They'll fix him. Induce a coma. Stop a brain bleed. Give him medicine. Maybe he has internal bleeding?" I couldn't say enough. If I kept listing off possibilities, hope hadn't run out.

Harry was dead on arrival. Dead before the paramedics got to him. No way to save him. Broken neck. Severed spinal cord. Brain-dead instantly. More than his broken body, the thought of Harry's mind being gone was unfathomable. How if a song had been playing, he wouldn't have been able to say if it was his perfect one or not.

Harry's parents arrived, bracing each other, quickly ushered back to Harry. Beyond the nurses' station, in a white anonymous room they'd probably never forget. Simon was there too. Simon didn't have a big brother any longer. When the officers watching us went to get coffee, Graham whispered to Viv and me what Harry set in motion.

"I was supposed to drag Conner off once he got a few good hits in. It was Harry's idea. *Let him split my lip or break a couple ribs*, he said. Begged me. *Pull him off once he's done damage for the cops to see.* He'd slipped the secret rite in Conner's locker the day before."

"Why?" I wanted to know.

"Harry's dad," Graham said. "It was Conner; Conner's older brother, Bowden; and his brother's friends, partying on the bleachers by the soccer field. His dad saw their faces. Took the beating. Didn't tell anyone. I guess he didn't want to get into it with Sebastian Welsh. Harry's mom loves their house. Loves this town. Harry's dad was groggy and medicated after one of the last surgeries, muttered something to Harry. Harry put it together."

"Harry—"

"He did it so one of the fucks who hurt his father would be held accountable for something," Graham said.

Graham, Viv, and I didn't need to promise not to breathe a word of this to anyone. There was nothing in this world or the next that would make us implicate Harry in provoking Conner. We would keep his last secret no matter what.

Soon, we were taken to the police station. The questioning began friendly enough. All of us together. Our parents, except for my mother, standing around.

An officer said, "Tell us about the events leading up to

your friend's death. Tell us about the events of October and September." The Seven Hills PD was not so dim after all, given that they suspected us immediately of a larger conspiracy—of being IV.

I said, "October happened because September happened because August happened."

Graham sounded like he had a bad cold telling them the only official answer we'd give them. Ten kids around a bonfire. Peaceful. Shooting the shit. Conner Welsh, a boy who'd always been a bully, rushed Harry. Fists flew, a deranged Conner knocked Harry off balance, the two boys fell twelve feet from the meteorite. Harry's head smacked a rock, neck crimped, Conner on top of him.

Our version was obviously a lie. What about the dagger? Why were you four in red? Why the others in white? What was the wooden doll by the fire, on a throne? A break in our questioning. Then the others started talking. Not all of them. Jess, Amanda, and Campbell denied knowing anything about IV. They denied that we were involved. They told a story almost identical to ours. Conner had snapped. Gone after Harry. The boys had fallen. Whether they lied to the police out of self-preservation or loyalty to us and the Order, I never found out.

It was Conner, Trent, and Rachel who bleated the truth to the police—the truth as they knew it. Not a party, but a ritual ceremony. A secret order born from the history of our town. They divulged all of what they knew about the Order of IV. They spilled our rites and rebellions on the linoleum floor of the police station. Conner swore he'd received a secret order to go after Harry on the rock. A note in his locker. No proof, though; he'd thrown it away. He'd figured Harry had sent it himself. He wanted a fight with Conner but was too chicken-shit to throw the first punch.

The police weren't treating us like criminals yet. They hadn't found Harry's IV tattoo. They didn't know if the *IV* in blood on the rock had been a bit of rebellious pretend, as harmless as the kids' armbands and emblems at school. We hadn't been cautioned or arrested. Their official opinion of us was too colored by what good students we were; what nice Seven Hills families we came from.

Mom flew home from Denver on the red-eye. She arrived with the sun the morning after Harry died. Harry. He would never see the sun again.

The authorities had separated Viv, Graham, and me by then. They had one shiny new piece of evidence that we were IV, or that at least Harry was. The doctors at the hospital emergency room reported the IV tattoo on his rib cage. Then, at midnight, the video of Amanda sharing her secret posted on the school news blog from an anonymous user.

In the restroom of the police station, Viv said that logging onto Harry's news blog account had been easy. Two days before she'd borrowed his laptop at lunch. We were all sitting there, without a clue. Harry's username and password auto-populated as soon as Viv loaded the blog. She uploaded the video clip of Amanda from her e-mail, saved it as a draft, selected that it would post anonymously, and set it to publish at midnight on the night we had planned to tell the initiates that the Order of IV was dissolving for a time.

She cried that she'd only uploaded the video to make herself feel like she had the upper hand over Amanda. Only set it for publication so she felt closer to revenge. She wasn't going to go through with it. She would have told Harry to delete it in time. At least that's what she swore to me as I shook my head silently at her in the bathroom stall.

"You had Conner and Trent kill a goat. You weren't satisfied until there was death on display for the whole town to see," Viv said. "Why are you acting like you don't understand? I needed to hurt Amanda. She deserved it just like the rest of them did."

I dropped to my knees in the bathroom, and threw up into the toilet.

So there. The police had a video, shot in the Marlos' barn, showing all four of us surrounding a sea of candles and Amanda holding the same strange wooden doll they'd found us with up on the rock.

They went after us. Tried to play us against one another. Swore to me that Viv and Graham had confessed to being IV. That they were cooperating. Lines straight out of true crime television. I remained silent. Arms folded on a table. Head resting on them. Tears falling intermittently. Not one word slipped from my lips from the time they split us up to the time a lawyer my parents hired came in to say I was going home. Eight hours. Never for a fleeting second did I worry that Graham and Viv were in rooms somewhere betraying

Harry's secret. If we told about IV, even just confirmed what the police suspected, Conner might not be held completely responsible for Harry. Harry might be made to share the blame.

None of us would ever hold Harry accountable.

When we arrived home, in my bedroom, I told Mom everything about the Order of IV, Dad's affair with Ina, and how Dad fell into our trap at the Ghost Tunnel. I shared every detail but one: Harry's rite to Conner. After I finished, she stared out at the waves like she was waiting for answers to wash ashore.

She confronted Dad in their office but with the door open. A little over five years ago, he and Ina had gone to dinner up the coast; it was her first time eating out after surgery. Dad met her behind her clinic; they went in her car. They both drank at dinner. Champagne. Ina had medication and painkillers in her bloodstream. Still, she wanted to drive. Wanted to feel in charge, alive, normal. So she was the one driving up Driftwood when Goldilocks came flying out of the orchard. She was the one who mistakenly hit the gas rather than the brakes. They got out of the car. Ina assessed her injuries. She didn't feel a pulse.

Dad didn't share the conversation they had. What transpired, though, is clear. They decided that their lives, all they had to lose, was more important than the helpless girl who lay before them. She was dead—whether they believed this or not, I'll never know. Ina drove home to hide the car with its dented front bumper in the garage. Dad ran up the street to our house to get his car. They needed to move the body. Dump it far away from Seven Hills. But when he got back, the girl was gone. He idled slowly down Driftwood, killed the engine when he heard a cry.

Goldilocks was strong. Determined. She'd dragged herself a ways before collapsing in front of Mr. Kirkpatrick's house. Blood bubbled from her mouth. She convulsed. Dad believed she was dying. How could he call 9-1-1? There was evidence all over Ina's car. I heard my mom begin to cry. He had thought about himself, his family, Ina, the Marlos. He didn't consider what he'd be doing to Goldilocks's family. At that point I heard Mom, voice shaking with fury, "Don't ever say you did this for us again."

Dad wrapped his hands around Goldilocks's thin neck. Closed his eyes. Squeezed. He had realized the folly of loading her up, driving her when he could be stopped by a traffic cop on the highway, where a camera could catch him, where campers on the beach might spy him. He threw her in the back of the car, drove to the Marlos' house, carried her through the orchard, placed her on the rock, and made her look like some cult fetishist's kill. No one would ever look at Viv's family. No one would ever look at anyone on Driftwood.

"Izzie found her. Our baby found her dead body," Mom said.

"Ina was supposed to find her. Ina was supposed to go up there in a day or two, after she'd taken the car out of town to be repaired. The girls were supposed to be at the beach that day."

I hadn't remembered that. But yes, originally Graham, Viv, and I were going to throw the watermelon out to sea, to see if it could float.

The days that came after were confusing and numb. My senses were off—vision poor and ears ringing, like I'd survived an explosion. I'd catch the gentle roar of Harry's last breath every now and then. Whip around, expect to see him. It hurt too much to be with Graham and Viv. The three of us in the barn was too nightmarishly diminished.

Despite our refusals to confess, the authorities' investigation moved forward. Graham's fingerprints were found on the skeleton. The butcher who sold us the blood recognized Harry's picture on the news and called the police. A home surveillance camera caught what was clearly the bottom half of Viv's face. I burned the damning Polaroids. Conner, Rachel, and Trent fingered us for the four who'd started it all. Jess and Campbell continued to deny that there was any such secret group. Amanda's lawyer wouldn't allow her to comment.

There were many police interviews, though after that first night I don't remember much from my time with Seven Hills's illustrious officers. When I wasn't considering the irony that the cops were working so diligently to solve our case when they hadn't done anything for Goldilocks, I sat thinking about Harry. Wondering what he'd do in the situation and, unable to guess, I drifted off with my eyes open. They weren't sure what to make of me. The police strongly suspected us of grand collusion. They treated us as idiot kids and then as evasive masterminds. The reality lay somewhere in the middle.

A secret society, an idol, iconography, blood rituals, sacrifices, bonfires, pranks, arson, damage of private property, and all that blood. It was a lot to attribute to a bunch of kids who'd never been in trouble before.

There are parts of my time spent with the police that stick with me. The bitter, burnt coffee they poured in Styrofoam cups. I stopped drinking chai and took my coffee with honey the way Harry had liked it. How exhausted I was despite spending most of my time asleep at home or asleep at the police station or drinking coffee. I was delirious, had trouble with basic questions like, *You hungry for lunch or can we keep going?* I never shared our secrets; I never said a thing about the Order. It was all I had left of us. My eyelids were in a perpetual slow drop like Harry's were in my memory. Unlike his, mine wouldn't just close for good. I went to sleep, I woke up, I remembered that my universe was short.

Dad moved out during that time. Mom said it was best we not tell anyone about what he and Ina did. I kept his secret, not because I agreed, or because I thought I wouldn't survive losing him, but for Viv. I would never take Viv's mom away from her.

Mom sat quietly alone a lot, but there was a hopefulness to her sadness, like she could see the end of it up ahead. Not me. Food lost its flavor, all but the metallic taste of coffee. Music lost its relevance; they were never lyrics for me, but a kind of secret language meant for people whose lives involved happiness, or even sadness that could be quantified. Contained in a three-minute song.

The videos we'd been taking came close to being our undoing. The police got permission to confiscate our cell phones. Graham had the wherewithal to delete the videos from the shared folder before they came for his, but a tech officer was able to find them on the cloud. I thought about Graham's obsession with watching the clouds for rain—he'd been so close.

The police printed up transcripts of each video and confronted us with them. They expected a prisoner's dilemma scenario where the three of us raced to confess in hopes of garnering good favor and leniency before the other two could. We kept silent. No comment. Heartbroken tears over Harry in the interview room.

Things were looking bad even still.

The threat was nebulous. Different days, different shapes. Our parents were scared we'd be charged with something serious—conspiracy, manslaughter, arson. What did we care? The last laugh Viv and I had was over whether or not they'd send us to the same prison. Maybe we could convince them that we were mentally unfit and end up sharing a padded room forever?

Then Graham left the country. His mother took a position teaching in Beirut; they were gone within twenty-four hours of him telling Viv and me.

"I don't deserve to know anyone—to know anything," Graham told me, "but I especially don't deserve to know you. To love you. Not when Harry can't." Good-bye.

Graham was in Beirut when we learned we weren't going

to be charged with any crimes. Seven Hills had received too much negative attention. For weeks, reports of suspected teenage vigilantes going by the alias of IV had tantalized high schools everywhere. After Harry's death, accounts of Conner's harassment were shared by other students. A lot of people had witnessed Conner's cruelty against Harry.

The story of Goldilocks's death was everywhere. National news organizations alleged a coverup and corruption in Seven Hills. Charging a bunch of kids who'd drawn attention to the murder wasn't going to help make Seven Hills PD look innocent. They dropped it; they dropped us. Instead they pursued Conner for Harry's death.

Viv and I will be called to testify by the prosecution. It will be the first time in nine months that we're in the same room. Viv was accepted to UCLA's performing arts department. I heard that she decided that school would be a waste and instead is auditioning for work in Los Angeles.

The last time we spoke was a week before Christmas of senior year.

"Maybe someday the sadness won't feel like it's chewing us up? Maybe someday I can use it, like some actors use traumatic experiences?" she sighed wistfully over the phone.

Something in my chest tightened until it snapped. "I love you, Vivian," I said, feeling all at once hollow. It was not difficult hanging up on her, and each time the old urge to call her again sent me reaching for my cell, Vivian wondering if someday she'd be able to use Harry's death in her acting was in my head. I thought of how she'd revealed Amanda's secret so that others would call her slut or whore or find a way to shame her.

I had enough credits to graduate a semester early. I took the necessary finals, told them to mail me my diploma, and was done with Seven Hills High School before the year ended.

Graham and his mom are in Amsterdam now. Graham writes letters, although they are short and too generic to be from him to me. No lectures on what he's learning. Impersonal notes about the weather. There was once a haunted *I miss him most when I'm breathing.*

For a full week after I read that, I obsessed over using my graduation checks from my grandparents and buying a ticket to Graham. In the end, I couldn't do it. Graham loved me, wanted me. I hadn't wanted him enough in return. And losing Harry made every thought of Graham feel stolen and wrong.

I was accepted to the University of Southern California in the history department. Imagine, me and Viv in the same city. I deferred a year. I'm still in Seven Hills. I live with my mom; Dad is in San Diego. I see Ina at the farmers market. She tells me to come over, to have tea or take a swim with her. She reminds me that the barn is still mine if I want it. I nod and pretend like I might come. Like I don't hate her. Like I don't imagine the reckonings she and my father deserve. I wonder who would be alive if Dad and Ina never met.

For a while I blamed the Mistress. Calm, immortal apathy rolled off her after she'd been returned to me by the police, once the investigation into IV was closed. We'd pledged our blood and swore an oath to her—in pretend, I kept needing to remind myself. I couldn't find a place to keep her, so she sat on my desk. Mistress of Death and Sacrifice. *Lay your lovers and friends at my feet so I may devour them*. I'd catch her out of the corner of my eye, maw dripping with Harry's blood. I'd turn to see that cruel, cold, unchanging smile gleaming at me. So I burned her on a pyre of sticks. Watched the jaundiced smoke spiral into the night. I hummed that eerie little snippet Viv liked from her play about witches.

And then I turned on our meteorite. Not ours. Never again. Another universe's. It had drawn Goldilocks in. Planted a writhing little whisper inside our heads, *Wonder, ask, search, imagine*. I climbed on top and took an ax to its crown. Ax blade collided with stone, sparking, sending violent jolts through me. Three swipes and I was done. Breathless. Muscles crimped in my neck until I cried. Pathetic.

I needed a softer surface to scrub our history from. Make it like it never happened. I raced home, ax deserted in the sleeping orchard. I pushed through the clutter of a kitchen drawer. Selected a box cutter and ran for my bathroom. There, *IV* was inked on the left side of my ribs, under my arm. The tattoo seemed to pulse in the mirror. Alive. I held the tip of the blade to the V. It pricked my skin. But those tattoos bound us together. Wherever we were. The blade clattered into the sink. The tattoo remains untouched.

I spend most days driving to record stores, where I hunt through albums. I buy what Harry's collection is missing and then rush home to listen. I won't stop until I find Harry's perfect song. Once or twice a week I go over and build robots or practice Italian with Simon. It comforts me to think that in a way he has an older sibling. Someday, when I feel music as well as hear it, I will likely be happy to have Simon, a little more family.

There is so much to rage against.

I will never know Goldilocks's real name. Never be able to tell her family that I tried to make things right for her. I'll be sorry for the rest of my life for the actions of my father and Ina, and for what they took from Goldilocks.

I wonder how things got so out of hand. We invented a secret society. We invented its history, rituals, and rites. We never wanted to say good-bye. We were sick of being told what to do, what was important, what to care about. In this we were not alone. All those *IV*s scrawled on backpacks, armbands, T-shirts, and bathroom walls were proof. To see a broken world through young eyes and to not rebel would have been madness.

Was there a better means to an end than revenge? Would it have been so hard just to say, *We care about what happened to the girl on the rock?* Goldilocks had no voice; we felt like ours was too quiet. The Order of IV got people's attention in the only way it could; in a language of blood, bones, and fire. Did we give it its power or did it bestow invisible power on us?

In the end, we weren't so different from those cult members that Graham and I had read about. We pushed one another, none more than I. Our fiendish grins fed fiendish deeds. There had to have been another path.

Harry had that name buried inside him. *Conner, Conner, Conner.* He'd shoved it down deep like a sleeping monster, until it awoke, snapped its jaw in rage, and destroyed him. I am angry with Harry. I wish he had told me what he knew. I wish we'd been able to hold Conner accountable together. Harry made a sacrifice I don't believe he should have.

I wonder at what point the secret rite for Conner wormed its way into Harry's head. Was it the night we strung up the goat? Did my secret rite prove to Harry that Conner would follow through with ugly tasks? It was easy deciding a goat would be sacrificed. No pause. I needed an animal. I would have killed it with my own hands. Sweet Harry told me never to apologize for doing what I believed needed to be done. Did I blow that dark thought into his head?

I am furious with myself. Not with Izzie, Icky, at the mercy of her parents fighting, so afraid she'll lose the three people who know and accept her. I'm angry with Izzie who had power to aim: Princess of the Night; Inventor of the Order; Master of Mischief, Rebellions, and Blood; and Acolyte of Revenge. I've spent months locking that girl up inside of me. I shoved her down into a place that looks a lot like the Ghost Tunnel. She's hunched by a fire. There are other girls crouched around it too. Lost girls, surviving. I am more like them now than I used to be. Warming my hands, gripping a shard of glass if ever I need to fight again, and I'm worried I'll let her loose someday. I'm worried I'll let the anger blind me. The world probably needs someone like the girl inside of me, avenging all the nameless girls. Fighting for those who are thrown violently by the world, just as Harry was thrown violently from the rock.

I want to believe there's a way to change the world without burning it.

I still think about the invisible forces that make people collide. I will always believe that the strongest things we do not see are friendship and love, their evidence as tangible as they are not. When I forget this lesson, I need only to think three names.

Harry. Graham. Vivy.

However much you think I loved them, I loved them more.

And because they are not here to share my final secrets with, I'll share them with the universe and hope that wherever my three soul mates are, they'll sense the invisible forces swirling around them.

I have never written a love letter. I have never written a hate letter.

I find that this is both.

These words are for my three best friends. One who is certain never to see any of us again, and the others, who may be able to come together someday, when it hurts less, when we've forgiven, who might read this if I ever work up the nerve to send it.

While I never go to the barn, my feet take me to the rock often. I sit up top, right where Goldilocks rested, by the three indents my ax left. Or right at the edge that fell out from under Harry. I think about space and time and Harry's planets, where there's probably a boy a lot like him going on living—the same and different—and that makes me miss him a little less.

I've also solved the riddle of the meteorite, which is probably the first thing I'll tell Graham when I see him again. The meteorite had an impact radius. It was just delayed a hundred thousand years.

When I lie up there, under a watchful moon, I pretend that I'm Graham and I think back about the Order of IV in the way he probably does. I linger over the ideas that moved us to fight. Their power. What we risked for them.

My pretend moves on to Viv. She considers the Order a Greek tragedy, us its imperfect heroes, fatally flawed, in the performance of our lives. She closes her eyes to conjure up the costumes, rituals, and pageantry.

At last, I think about what Harry would care most about. The just purpose of the Order. How lucky we all were to have one another. How the four of us were as much family as blood can make you. How you protect your family.

And then lastly, I try to figure out what I believe. What was the Order? A pageant? Experiment? Rebellion? Mistake? What does it matter?

All that counts is this:

The four of us met.

Loved one another.

Danced under a blood moon.

Shared our secrets, though too few and too late.

And for a time, together, our friendship was a universe.

Retrieved from the cellular phone of Harrison Rocha

Transcript and notes prepared by Badge #821891

Shared Media Folder Titled: IV, Tues., Oct. 29, 2:56 p.m.

Video start.

H. Rocha stares at the camera. Rocky bluffs rise up behind him. The sound of the ocean is loud. The camera is unsteady, shaking.

"You're going to think that I called us off because I was trying to protect you, Izzie." He passes a shaking hand through his hair. "You're going to be pissed and you'll probably call me paternalistic again." A soft laugh. "I'm not trying to protect you. I'm trying to keep you from protecting me. I've got to figure out how to keep you away because I know you, Isadora. You'll be there, getting right in the middle, stopping him. And I can't have him stopped until he's done his damage.

"If Graham's holding you back, he won't be able to pull Conner off me, once Conner's gotten his hits in. I don't know how else to do this. How to handle Conner. I've tried everything. Pretending his words don't hurt. Striking back at him—keying that car of his. Ignoring him. Bearing it." His eyes unfocus. He gives his head a jolt. "I'm afraid." He's barely audible over the waves. "No one wants to get their ass handed to them. But I guess we live in the kind of fucked-up world where guys like Conner win.

"I won't let him, though. I'm doing this so he gets held

accountable. For something. I'm doing this so that one of the guys who jumped my dad gets in trouble." He stares at the camera. Birds call from beyond the lens. "I'm doing this because it's the right thing to do. And people don't do that enough."

Video stop.